BRIGHT BLADE

BRIGHT BLADE

THE BYRHTNOTH CHRONICLES: BOOK 3

CHRISTINE HANCOCK

First published in Great Britain in 2019 by
Madder Press
www.byrhtnoth.com

Cover Design by Cathy Helms (www.avalongraphics.org)
Cover Image © Jacek Wojnarowski

ISBN 978 19160528 57

British Library Cataloguing in Publication Data.
A catalogue record for this book is available from the British Library.

Dedication

For Andrew and John
The best sons a warrior could have.

PART I: Lent 948 AD

Chapter 1

I sat in the sun sharpening my sword and thinking about the man I would kill. Not that I knew when and where the deed would be done, only that I would do it, and I hoped it would be soon. Holding up the weapon, I squinted down the length of the gleaming blade. It was straight and true. I plucked a hair from my head and dropped it onto the edge. The two halves fell to the ground. It would do, for now.

I had never possessed a sword like this: new forged and entirely my own. Lord Athelstan had sent it and my wife had presented it to me on our wedding day, as part of that ceremony. It was a reward for my service for him the previous year.

We had married at Christmas, now it was close to Easter. My wife had named the sword Wolf's Claw. I remembered the night when the garnets of the hilt had glinted in the firelight like eyes. She had explored the barely healed scars on my body inflicted by the wolf I had fought in Northumbria. She had her own scars. I could not blame the wolf for fighting for his life, but I did blame the man who had marked her. I thrust the sword back into the sheath as if it was his bloody flesh. The blade was eager to taste blood, Egbert's blood.

The birds in the tree overhead ceased their constant twittering and their wings beat as they scattered. It was a beautiful day, one of those days when you know winter has finally departed, so why did I feel unsettled?

Wulfstan emerged from the hall, blinking in the bright light. He held a piece of parchment, and before I could make an escape, he spotted me. He made his awkward way down the steps and limped towards me.

"Lord Byrhtnoth, there has been a messenger from Lord Athelstan. There is to be a meeting of the Witan at Easter. The Ealdorman wants you to accompany him." He handed me the letter, and I scanned the contents, brief and to the point. I had no option except to obey.

"I'll have to go. If only to ask him for leave to continue my search."

"Is that the search for your father, or the search for Egbert?"

I gave him a sharp look. He knew me better than anyone. We had been friends since childhood, but no longer. Perhaps we would never regain the closeness we had shared. "Does it matter?" I asked, handing back the letter.

"Have you had news of his whereabouts? Not your father. That man."

"Nothing. Perhaps I can learn something at the Witan." I picked up the cloth and rubbed at a speck of mud on the sword hilt.

"Do you intend to kill Elfhere as well?"

Was I so easy to read? "I don't know. Saewynn says he tried to help her. Egbert was in his service; Elfhere should know where he is. I'll decide what to do when I return from Winchester."

"If you are away for Easter, it will reduce the food we need here. The winter stores are getting low."

I nodded and held up the sword to admire the hilt. Every time I inspected it I discovered a new aspect of the pattern. I ran a finger over the worn pommel. "I wonder who the original owner was?"

"There was no one there to ask," remarked Wulfstan.

"What do you mean? Sit down." I made room for him on the log. "Does your leg pain you?"

" I'm glad winter is over. It's worse when it's cold."

"You found this." I touched the hilt. "It was part of the hoard you discovered last year when we were at Rendlesham?"

"Yes. It was Leola who led us to the place." My dog raised her head, beat her thin tail once and returned to her doze in the patch of sun nearby. "May I?" I handed him the sword. "It's heavier now. The original blade had nearly rusted away." He lifted the sword, and it shook in his hand. "It nearly killed me. It would have if Saewynn hadn't been there. She pulled me out."

"My wife rescued you?"

"I was determined to retrieve it and ignored the warning signs. There was a storm, and the rain loosened the soil. I was buried alive." He gave me back the sword.

"Then it should be yours. You fought for it." I tried to give it to him.

"What do I need a sword for? Anyway, I didn't do it for myself."

"Then, who?"

Wulfstan shifted, moving his leg into a more comfortable position. He avoided my curious glance, staring into the distance, "I did it for you."

"Me? Why?"

Wulfstan shrugged. "I don't know. It just felt like the right thing to do. I knew how much your father's sword meant to you, then it was stolen as soon as you won it. You have done so much for me: saved my life, found a future for me. I could never repay you. Until, beneath the earth, I touched that sword, and I knew that this was something within my power, to give you a sword."

"You did it. For me?" I leaned the sword against the trunk of the tree. "I wonder if that sword is cursed."

"What do you mean, cursed? The treasure I found helped Saewynn obtain her freedom, and now you have a sword. The blade is new, forged for you. How can it be cursed?"

11

I shook my head, trying to capture the thought. "Perhaps she would have been safer if she hadn't been freed."

"But she's all right now. She's happy." Wulfstan frowned "Isn't she?"

"Yes, of course. But Saewynn suffered so much; she still suffers. Her hand..."

"I know. I've been thinking about that."

"There's nothing to be done. We must learn to live with it." I stared at the sword, avoiding his eyes. "It destroyed our friendship."

"Perhaps I should have left it in the mound." Wulfstan toyed with the letter. "I'm sorry about what happened. I knew that she could never be mine. It was always you that she loved."

"I wish you'd told me that earlier. It would have saved us all a lot of pain."

"You had to work it out yourself. Anyway, you never take my advice." Wulfstan struggled to his feet, his face burning. "I'm sorry, my lord, I must get back to work."

"This ends now." I grabbed the sword and stood up.

"What?" Fear crossed his face. "I shouldn't have spoken. I'll leave. You'll never see me again."

"Don't be stupid." I drew the edge of the sword across my palm, then took Wulfstan's and cut that. I dropped the sword to the ground and grasped his hand in mine. I stared into his face as our blood mingled.

"We have been friends for a long time. Now we are one. We are brothers, and I swear that no one, no cursed sword, no woman will ever come between us. Do you so swear?"

"How can you even ask? I swear."

"Good." I wrapped my arm around his back and pulled him close. He did the same, and we stood together as one. Never had I felt such relief.

Finally, we parted. No one except Leola had noticed the conversation. Roused by the smell of blood she danced around us before attempting to push her long dark nose between us.

"No dogs either," I laughed and bent to pat her. "What do we do now? We've made a bit of a mess."

"You always have to make the big gesture," he replied with a smile. "If that sword really is cursed, we'll probably both die from loss of blood."

"No, we have purified it by our sacrifice."

"Come on. Let's get cleaned up. I wonder if we'll need stitches."

"I don't think so." I studied my hand. "The blood has already stopped."

Chapter 2

Saewynn sat beside the river and stared into the water.

"Is something wrong?"

She hadn't realised anyone was near and reached for the cloth that always covered her hair in public. When she realised it was Byrhtnoth, she let it drop, although she hid her crippled hand beneath it. She hated anyone to see it, even him.

He settled on the grass beside her.

"No. Nothing wrong." Her voice didn't even convince herself.

"Has someone upset you?" She shook her head, then the sight of blood on his clothes drove all her thoughts away.

"You're hurt. What happened?" Saewynn asked, looking at him properly for the first time.

"Just an accident. I was cleaning my sword and misjudged the edge. It was sharp."

"Let me see."

He showed her his hand. "It didn't bleed much. The cut has already closed."

"You must let Wulfstan examine it."

"It's all right, he was there when it happened." He sounded pleased.

"I suppose you were showing off as usual." She turned away, angry that she had let a minor injury upset her.

"I don't show off." He flexed his hand and frowned. "What have you been doing?" He pointed to the wilted flowers scattered around her. Saewynn swept up a handful of the yellow petals and threw them into the water. She watched in silence as they swirled in eddies at the edge of the river before the current caught them and they floated away, downstream. He put an arm around her shoulders. "Tell me," he said softly.

"It's not important," she said, attempting to shrug off his arm.

"If you are upset, it is important." He stroked her hair. It had grown, although it still hardly reached her shoulders. She was glad that as a married woman, she was forced to cover it.

"Some children from the village picked flowers for me. I wanted to make garlands, crowns for their heads. I failed... they left." She had thought it would be easy. It was impossible with only one hand, and that her left. "I'm useless."

"No, you're not. It's not the end of the world if you can't make daisy chains."

"Primrose, the flowers are primroses."

"There you are. You know more than me about flowers. Shall I make you a crown?" He picked up one of the flowers; the stalk was mangled, and the petals drooped. "How do you do it?"

"It's too late, the flowers are dead."

"I'll find you some more. They go well in your hair." He found another flower and tucked it behind her ear. She brushed it away.

"I'm a married woman now, I don't wear flowers in my hair."

"You can wear them in the chamber." He leaned close to tell her what he would do with the flowers.

"Stop it." She blushed and pushed him away. "Someone might hear."

"I don't think they care." He pointed across the river where a duck was introducing her ducklings to the water. She watched as they lingered on the brink, before casting themselves into the

16

water, bobbing on the ripples until their mother rounded them up. They swam off in a decorous line.

"There's been a message from Lord Athelstan. I have orders to attend the Easter Witan in Winchester. Why don't you come with me? I can show off my beautiful new wife."

"I don't think so." Her body trembled beneath his sheltering arm. She had tried to hide her fear of strangers, but sometimes it caught her unawares, especially now.

"Are you still scared? You have me to protect you now." He hugged her tighter.

"You won't always be here." What if Egbert came while he was away?

"I won't be gone long. If you are afraid, I'll leave men here to protect you. When I return, we will resume our search for my father. I had already planned to leave after Easter. You will enjoy the voyage. It will be like old times to feel the spray on our faces. I need you to navigate. That's something you do well. I wonder if Lord Athelstan will lend us a ship? I'll ask him."

She longed to go with him, it was the only time she felt happy, free of all care. "I cannot," she whispered.

"This is more than some silly game with flowers." He turned her to face him, taking her hands in his. "What's wrong? Are you ill? You were sick the other day. I thought it was something you had eaten. I'm sure that smoked fish was off."

"I have felt unwell recently, it's nothing to worry about... I didn't know how to tell you."

"What is it?"

"I am to have a baby. You are to be a father."

He frowned as if he hadn't understood.

"How?"

"How do you think?" She struggled to escape. "I knew you wouldn't like it."

"What makes you think that?"

17

"It's not something we've ever spoken about. I didn't know... I thought you only wanted me for..." Tears filled her eyes. "I'm sorry."

"Don't be sorry, my love." He gently wiped away her tears. "This is wonderful news. It's just that I hadn't expected... I hadn't thought."

"You shouldn't be surprised, it's not as if we haven't..."

"Several times." Her eyes met his, and she blushed, remembering what they had done in the darkness of their bed. "Many times. Now I come to think about it, I don't know why I was so surprised." He pulled her into his arms and hugged her tight then drew away. "Sorry, I don't want to hurt you, it."

"You won't hurt me or... our son."

"Our son." He laid a hand gently on her flat stomach. I can't feel anything."

"It's too early."

He slid his hand up to cup one of her breasts. It was larger, fuller than it had been. "I noticed this. I thought you'd been eating too much."

She pushed him away. She didn't know how to react. Wasn't it wrong to feel like that when he touched her? Didn't it stop now she was with child?

"I understand, you don't want me to..."

"It's not that. I want you more than ever." Then the words flooded out, the words that she had tried to suppress. "I wish it hadn't happened so soon. I don't want to be a woman stuck at home while her man leaves to fight and win glory. I want to be at your side; why do you think I wanted to learn to fight? Now I cannot fight," she clutched her ruined right hand to her chest, "and I cannot cook, or weave, or any of the things that a wife is expected to do. How can I care for a child?"

"I didn't understand." He gathered her to him and held her until her tears were exhausted. "I can't avoid going to Winchester," he said, "but when I get back, I will stay here with you. I

18

promise. We can search for my father next year. When is the baby expected?"

Saewynn wiped her eyes on her sleeve. "Hild says after harvest, Winterfylleth perhaps. A honeymoon baby. It's supposed to be good luck."

"A quiet summer then. It's about time I learned more about my lands. Wulfstan talks about crops and grazing, and I hide my ignorance. I should be administering justice to my people. Sometimes I see someone in the village and do not know who they are. I have other properties. We can visit them. You will be allowed to travel?"

"Yes, I can travel; for a while anyway. Won't you be bored?"

"Not with you." He grinned. "I have been searching for my father, whether I knew it or not, all my life. I can wait for another year. But what about your family? Didn't... someone say that my father knows the truth about that."

"It was Elfhere," she said, pleased that she had managed to suppress a shudder. "I don't know, it doesn't seem to be important anymore." She had almost forgotten about the piece of parchment she had carried since she was a child. Wulfstan had been excited when she had asked him to read it. "This is my home now. I have you, and soon we will have a child. That is all the family I want."

"Not even if your mother was related to Mercian royalty? Perhaps you're right." He kissed her on the forehead, and then the lips. "You're my queen and that's all that matters."

Chapter 3

I stood outside the hall and waited for the horses. The blacksmith was busy. The sun had brought out the villagers and their tools, neglected all winter, needed repairs, or an edge sharpened. Cenwulf was there as his seax needed attention. I frowned. He knew we were leaving this morning; he shouldn't have left it until the last moment. He had joined my band during the winter, a local lad craving excitement. I was still uncertain as to whether he would be of much use. He was talking to a woman holding a bent cooking pot. She must be waiting for the blacksmith.

There were raised voices amongst the waiting men. We hadn't even left, and already arguments were breaking out. As I searched the crowd to find the culprits, the noise died down, perhaps Godric had sorted it out. There was a burst of laughter, and a man walked away from the group. He exchanged a greeting with one of the watching women and continued to the forge where he spoke to Cenwulf.

What was his name? Thurstan, that was it, one of the men who had followed Elfhere and joined my troop with the others. He did as he was asked without complaint, never causing any problems. He was of average height with nondescript brown hair and a neatly trimmed beard, older than the others, not one of the men I had trained with from childhood. He must have joined Elfhere when he was in the north. Who was he and where had he come from? I needed to get to know him better; this trip would be a good opportunity. He might even be able to tell me more about Egbert. As he disappeared into the mass of men and horses, I realised he would make a good spy, always present and never noticed. I wondered if there was more to him than I suspected.

"They'll be here shortly." Saewynn joined me "Thunor was playing up. You should ride him more often, then we wouldn't have all this fuss."

"I was trying to remember when I was last in Winchester. I haven't been back since we left to track down those raiders." I recalled the early departure, the excitement of our first proper expedition as a fighting troop. I glanced towards the new men; they must be feeling the same. It made me feel old. "It was that same day I met you, hiding beside that stream." I smiled down at my wife. "I wouldn't have noticed you if I hadn't slipped and fallen into the water."

"Two years ago, thereabouts," she said.

"A lifetime." I wanted to put my arm around her, but this was a formal occasion. We had said our goodbyes the night before, in the privacy of our bed, lying awake far into the night, talking. Not the words of love that usually kept us enthralled, although there were many of those, more about the future: plans for the child and what would come after. There had been no time before. We had married so quickly, and the honeymoon was barely over. I exchanged a glance with her; we knew each other better than ever now. Except... she hadn't mentioned Egbert, and neither had I. Time enough when the man was dead.

"It's not for long. You won't notice we've been gone. I'll leave Leola here with you." I bent down and scratched her soft dark ears, especially the one that fell forward over her topaz eyes. When I told her I must leave her for a while, she stepped from my heel to Saewynn and licked her hand. They would look after

22

each other. "It's a pity Wulfstan needs to go to Winchester as well. I don't like to leave you here without either of us. I've left plenty of men. You should be safe."

"Stop worrying. Here are the horses."

Edward led Thunor. Saewynn was right, he was restless, and sweat marred the black sheen of his coat. "So that's where you went to early this morning," I whispered to Saewynn.

"I wanted him to be smart, at least for the start of the journey. No one else can get close enough to do it properly."

"I know, thank you. You should be careful though. What if something had upset him? You might have been injured, or even worse."

"He wouldn't hurt me."

I watched the horse's rolling eyes and searched for an excuse to delay my departure. My sister crossed the yard with Inga from the village and they seemed to be arguing. I had meant to talk to her before I left.

"Edith," I called. Her head snapped around as if she had been caught doing something wrong. Inga moved her child from one arm to the other and strolled towards the forge. Did she have her eye on the new man?

"Yes brother, what can I do for you? Has Hild packed enough food for the journey?"

I had seen her handing bundles to Godric and giving him last minute instructions. "That's all under control. I wondered if there was anything that you need from Winchester. Or Lunden; we are meeting Lord Athelstan there."

"Give my regards to the Ealdorman." She thought for a moment. "We need some fine linen. I haven't found anyone in the village to weave cloth fine enough. We need it for shifts and the like, and the child of course, when..." She glanced at Saewynn and her face reddened in embarrassment. "Only if you can find it at a decent price, mind." She glared at me.

"Is that what you were arguing with Inga about? She's been helping with the weaving, hasn't she? I've noticed the baby's basket close to the looms."

"No. Yes. The girl's fit for nothing except the coarsest work." Edith was flustered.

Thunor was still restless. Wulfstan sat on Sleipnir, just behind him, a grin on his face. I turned back to Edith. "Well, it's good of you to take an interest in her and her baby, although I wouldn't have thought..." I glanced at Saewynn, who was frowning. I changed tack. "I suppose it's not surprising, there are a lot of babies around the village. I saw Inga's just before we left for the north last year." It was newly born then, and I gave her a coin for the child. "Ugliest baby I'd ever seen, hair almost white, like thistledown. It's dark now." There was silence.

"Babies change a lot when they grow - as you will find out. If you don't get on that horse now, you'll still be standing there when this one is born." Saewynn touched her hand to her stomach then stepped forward to grab Thunor's bridle from Edward. She stroked Thunor's long face to calm him and beckoned Wulfstan and Sleipnir forward. Saewynn gave me a nudge, and I was forced to mount.

The animal quivered beneath me. I would need to hold on tight when we set off. My axe was hanging from the saddle. Did I need it now I had a sword? Anything might happen on the road. I adjusted my sword belt so it was comfortable and patted my shield.

"Cenwulf! Are you coming or not?" I shouted towards the forge.

The blacksmith handed him his seax with a grin. Inga leaned forward and gave him a quick kiss as he fumbled the weapon into its sheath. He ran for his horse and I shook my head. Perhaps Saewynn should have a talk with Inga. Her attention was already focused in that direction. She would deal with it.

People were gathering to see us off. Before I left, I had something to say. I held up a hand for quiet.

"We travel to Winchester, to attend the king's witan. My Lord Athelstan, Ealdorman of East Anglia has requested my presence." Someone cheered. "I will not be away for long. It may be that there will be fighting this summer in Northumbria. I hope to remain here this year. Whatever is planned I will be back in a few days. Meanwhile, my wife will rule this village in my place." I sensed the rise of her head and felt her eyes on me. "You will obey her in all things and protect her during my absence." She had an expression of shock, and perhaps pride, on her face and tears in her eyes. I bent from the saddle and touched her cheek. I swallowed, and whispered, "let him go."

She released the horse and stepped back briskly. Thunor stood a moment, not realising he was free to move and I had time to say a quick farewell before he leapt forward. Wulfstan followed, and I heard Godric issue orders. We swept through the village, scattering people and stock and headed for the road south.

Part II: Easter

Chapter 4

Lord Athelstan looked up as we entered the hall; we had missed the start of the evening meal. My mouth watered at the sight of the display of meat.

"We thought you weren't coming."

"We rode as fast as we were able, my lord." We had lingered too long in Lunden.

"You're here now. You know the Ealdorman of Essex?" I nodded to the thickset man sitting next to him.

"Of course. Your daughters are well, Lord Elfgar?" A servant brought me a cup of ale. I took a sip and remained standing before the table.

"They are. Ethelflaed has not remarried, she wishes to enter a nunnery, but is busy supervising the upbringing of the young athelings. Lord Athelstan has been telling me about young Edgar's exploits, he's a bit of a handful." I nodded in agreement. "Elfflaed has yet to find a man worthy of her exacting standards." Lord Elfgar gave a wry smile.

"Yes, my lord." I had once thought myself in love with his younger daughter, although I was well down her list of suitable partners, even lower in her father's estimation. I was glad it had come to nothing, although I could have done with the wealth she would have brought me. "Perhaps she should enter a nunnery. Christ might be the best husband for her."

"If she doesn't make up her mind soon, it's where she'll end up. I'm not getting any younger, and I want her settled before I go."

"You've got many years left," Lord Athelstan told him. "Sit down, Byrhtnoth, and we'll get down to business. You spent several months at Bebbanburg last year, after the truce."

"Why did you go?" Lord Elfgar leaned forward. "Surely there was no need of hostages?"

"That was what he was told. It was a ruse to keep an eye on Lord Osulf," said Athelstan.

"You mean I wasn't in any danger?" Why hadn't they told me? "I needn't have left in a hurry when we heard his son had escaped." I had a sudden thought. "Did he escape?" I asked Lord Athelstan, "or did you send him back?"

"He escaped, although he wasn't closely guarded."

"Unlike me."

"You got away, didn't you?"

"Only when I was forced to." I remembered the steep rock face, the dark sea pounding below. "Why didn't you explain what I was supposed to do?"

"There was no time. You went rushing off on some adventure. By the time you got back, I was on the way home. At least it helped you act the part."

"What was it like?" Elfgar interrupted before I lost my temper. He pushed a dish of roast pork in my direction.

"Bebbanburg? Big and cold."

"Did Lord Osulf treat you well?"

I chewed a slice of the meat and swallowed. "He was friendly, once he was back on his own lands."

"The King's lands," Athelstan pointed out. "He's the Steward, not Lord, of Bebbanburg, not anymore."

I imagined Osulf's views on that but nodded agreement. I picked up another slice of pork. "I became friendly with his younger son, Uhtred. We trained together a few times. He was injured during a wolf hunt, just before I left."

"Badly?" asked Elfgar.

"Serious enough. A nasty bite in the shoulder. I don't know if he'll fight again. But he's still young and his mother wants him to go into the church."

"Lord Athelstan tells me you rescued him."

"I did."

"You managed to get out then?"

"Only for the wolf hunt. The rest of the time I was allowed to come and go, so long as I didn't leave the fortress."

"You know the defences. Any weaknesses?" asked Athelstan.

I took a bite of meat while I thought about it. "None that I noticed, and I spent a lot of time walking the walls. Are you thinking of attacking?"

"Information is always useful." He took a sip of wine.

"What did you think of Lord Osulf?" asked Elfgar "If it came to war, whom would he back? He fought with King Athelstan, years ago. He is thought to favour us although he supported Erik last year. Will he do the same this year?"

I thought about things he had said, or not said; the visits by neighbours and messengers from across the north. "I think he would support..." I remembered the riches we had taken north. "He supports himself alone," I said with confidence. "He will follow his own road, and that would be the one that benefits him the most."

Lord Elfgar exchanged a glance with his companion, who gave a brief nod.

"Would you agree that, given incentive, he would avoid war?"

"He was away from home a long time last summer. He won't want to do the same this year. Not with his elder son growing hungry for power. Then there are the Scots across the border. With Osulf away again they might be tempted to invade."

A new king had come to the throne of Scotland a few years before. He would be eager to test his boundaries. It was the old king, Constantine, who I had been told knew something about my father's fate. I hoped he was still alive. Pushing away the thought, I concentrated on the conversation.

"That's what we assumed," said Lord Athelstan. "Thank you. You must be tired from the road. Get some sleep. "

Godric had found a space close to the hearth. I dumped my things nearby and asked him where Wulfstan was.

"He's gone to find Abbot Dunstan. He might spend the night at the Minster. Do you want him? I can fetch him if you need something."

"It's nothing. I wanted to discuss something, but it's not urgent." I sat on my bed and watched the bustle. Late arrivals were still sitting at the boards, taking a final opportunity to eat. There would be no food tomorrow as it was a fasting day. Even the thought made me feel hungry.

Wulfstan had mentioned he had business with the abbot but hadn't said what. Had he decided to go back to the monastery? I picked at the scab on the palm of my hand. Had I been too eager to patch up our friendship? A clerk clutching a bundle of letters knocked on the door to Lord Athelstan's chamber. Was it about the coming war, if there were to be war?

An attractive servant girl was collecting dirty plates from the table. She gave me a friendly nod, and I smiled back. She moved towards me but I shook my head. She shrugged and continued on her way. I lay down and pulled my cloak over my body, staring at the wall, missing Saewynn. What was she doing? Was she all right? I would be back soon, although I knew I would miss her terribly if I were away for longer.

Chapter 5

That Good Friday it appeared that the whole of Winchester was packed into the Minster. I followed Ealdorman Athelstan as his men pushed a path through the crowd.

"They've added more pictures to the walls since we were here before." I pointed out a brightly coloured one to Godric.

"Someone told me King Alfred's tomb is covered in gold. Keep your eye on your purse, there are some shifty men around."

"We won't get anywhere near that. We'll visit when it's quieter. Has the king arrived yet?" I asked.

"You're taller. Can you see anything?"

I surveyed the seething crowd. "The royal party will be at the front, close to the altar. Lord Athelstan is heading that way. Keep close." I pushed someone out of the way before we got left behind. "Excuse me." The man took in my height and scuttled away, deciding not to complain.

The crowd thinned as we got closer. Guards turned away those not welcome. The chanting grew louder and I caught a glimpse of the Bishop and the monks. It was dim, a dark cloth covering the altar, and the candles were unlit. The only illumination came from the small windows high up in the walls. King Eadred was kneeling, his head bowed. He wore a rough grey gown, similar to those worn by the monks. It exaggerated his thin frame. Beside him knelt his mother, also soberly dressed. She gave the king a worried glance before returning her gaze to the altar.

Athelstan gave a sign that we were to wait while he joined the King. I backed away to let another group approach the altar and stepped on the foot of someone behind me. I turned and my apology died in my throat.

"Hello, Byrhtnoth. I see your feet are as big as ever." My hand leapt towards my sword before I remembered I had left it at the entrance.

"Elfhere. You haven't changed." Godric and the others had moved away. I scanned the crowd behind Elfhere for the man I had promised to kill.

"He's not there. He left."

I checked again and relaxed slightly.

"Why?" I stared at him. The last time we had met, I had come within an inch of killing him.

"We need to talk. Shall we find somewhere quieter?" I saw Godric pushing people out of the way to reach me. "I'm not going to kill you," said Elfhere in a quiet voice. "Although you should be more careful. I could have put a knife between your ribs just now."

"I don't expect to be attacked in church," I replied. "There's space over there." I pointed to a pillar that obscured the view of the altar. Elfhere nodded and walked away. I stared at his retreating back proving that he trusted me not to attack.

"What did he want?" Godric finally reached me.

"To talk. I don't trust him, even if Egbert's no longer around. Wait here and keep watch."

"Yes, my lord. If he tries anything, he won't get out alive."

I followed Elfhere slowly to where he leaned against the pillar. "What is all this about?"

He stared down at the floor. "You'll think I'm mad." He shuffled his feet, raising a small cloud of dust, "I want to apologise."

"Apologise?" I crossed my arms and frowned. "Why?"

He looked up, before quickly dropping his eyes. He picked at a piece of loose skin beside a fingernail.

"What we did... what Egbert did," he said in a rush, "it wasn't right. I tried to stop him. He ignored me. I hadn't realised how much he had undermined my authority. It had happened so slowly. That time we visited your village, remember?"

"Yes." Did he think I could ever forget that night, the blood, the violence? Edith had never been the same. Was it the shame of what had happened to her that had stopped her returning to her monastery?

"It was supposed to be a bit of fun, Egbert said, disturb the feast, break a few things and leave. I drank too much, went too far. I'm sorry." He raised his hand to his face, to the scar that disfigured it. "I deserved what you did to me."

"Why didn't it stop you?" I should have killed him, not given him reason for revenge.

"I was angry. Egbert stoked my rage. He said you should be punished. He can be very persuasive."

"That day in the forest, I believed you were to blame for...what he did." The memory came flooding back. I clenched my fist and slammed it into the pillar, just above Elfhere's head. He flinched, and I shook my hand in pain. "That was a stupid thing to do," I muttered. Faces turned in our direction. Godric frowned. I shook my head.

"You've recovered from the axe blow?" I asked, controlling my anger.

"It was painful, a broken collar bone. You should have seen the bruising. It has mended." He gave an exaggerated shrug to demonstrate.

"How did you get rid of him?"

"He must have decided I'd provided enough entertainment." His twisted lips curled in disgust. "One day he disappeared. His belongings had gone, along with some valuables from my father's hall. His horse was missing from the stables. No one knows where he went."

Like he had gone after Wulfstan was injured, all those years ago. "I don't suppose he left my sword?"

"No chance. His pleasure was doubled, knowing how much you wanted it. You won't see it again."

"I don't know. Egbert will be unable to resist taunting me again. Then I'll kill him."

"If I get any news, I'll let you know," he said with a smirk.

"The service is over. I'd better go." The building was emptying rapidly. "You have apologised. Did you expect forgiveness?"

"No, I didn't. I know you."

"You would be right." I searched the thinning crowd for Lord Athelstan. Wulfstan had appeared and was talking animatedly with Godric. They looked in our direction.

"I know we will never be friends."

I frowned. It had been a long time since we had been friends.

"Can we, perhaps, not be enemies?" Elfhere asked.

"That will depend on you. I expect I'll see you at the Witan." I had a thought. "Was this your father's idea? Some political arrangement?"

"Certainly not." His reaction belied his words. "Things change. I hope I've grown wiser. We both serve the king; we're on the same side. We shouldn't be fighting." So, the king was involved.

"I've got to go." I walked away.

"One thing."

I paused. "What now?"

"The girl. Did she survive?"

I stood still. What should I say? Tell him she had died? Would it make him feel more guilt? I decided on the truth.

"She survived. She was damaged. She has scars."

"I'm sorry. I will offer wergild for her injuries."

"There is no need."

"I see. She has gone into a nunnery. I will donate the money to the church."

36

"That is not necessary. She has married, she is cared for."

"Who would marry a girl like that? I suppose you paid someone to take her."

"In a way." I looked into his eyes. "She is my wife."

"Your wife? Why? I thought..."

"You wouldn't understand. Goodbye, Elfhere."

Chapter 6

We watched our old instructor finish with a group of boys in the practice yard. They were so young. I supposed we had been that small once.

"Byrhtnoth, Wulfstan, just in time for a drink. Let me get rid of this lot first." Oswald gathered up the boys, commenting on how they had performed and offering advice on further training. "I told them you would come back another time and give a demonstration. Have a knock about with some of the better ones." He led us to his hut. "Make sure you wash properly, before the meal," he shouted after them. The recollection of his instruction almost caused me to follow them.

"How are you, Oswald?" said Wulfstan. "You're looking well."

"A few aches and pains, I'm not getting any younger. Ale all right for you?"

"It'll be fine. Knowing you, it will be the best in the place." I took a sip and nodded. "You haven't changed." He was greyer and moved slower but he still terrified us.

"You have. How much taller are you going to grow?" he asked me.

"Not too much, we hope. We've threatened to cut his feet off when his head reaches the roof," said Wulfstan, laughing.

"What's this latest batch of boys like?" I said, changing the subject.

"Same as ever, some good, some not. Usually I can tell how they'll turn out as soon as they arrive. Never had anyone as good as you though. What have you been up to? I heard you went north after the truce. What happened?"

"I ended up at Bebbanburg. Boring most of the time, Hunted some wolves."

"He saved the life of Lord Osulf's son," added Wulfstan. "The younger son; the older one tried to kill him."

"It was nothing. The wolf caused more damage than Eadwulf's sword."

"You made a friend then, I assume Osulf was pleased his son survived, but also made an enemy," said Oswald shrewdly. "More ale?"

I asked him if he knew the area. He must have fought up there a few times with King Athelstan. For the first time I wondered if he knew anything about my father. Was that the reason I had been sent to him for training?

"Pity Athelstan died when he did. He was a proper king, not like this weakling we've got now. Don't suppose he'll last long."

"Then it will be one of Edmund's boys. They're both young yet. I've met Edgar, what's the other like?"

I was on my third cup of ale before I broached the question I wanted to ask. "Do you remember, just after we arrived, you discovered one of us was a girl? You sent her away."

Wulfstan gave me a puzzled look, but Oswald nodded.

"I regretted that. She was a good fighter, better than most. Strange you should mention her. She works here now. We needed someone to do the washing and other woman's jobs. You heard my wife passed away?"

"Yes, I was sorry to hear it. You must miss her." I said.

"More than I expected, considering we fought all the time."

"I remember the flying pots," said Wulfstan.

"I didn't expect to miss those." Oswald reached for the jug, but I got to it first.

"That's strange, I'd heard the girl died. Must be over a year ago." I poured the last of the ale into his cup.

"You must be thinking about someone else." Oswald took a sip and rested his cup on the table. "Elfhere brought her here when he heard I needed help."

"Elfhere?" I exchanged a glance with Wulfstan.

"Yes, it surprised me too. She brought a child with her; perhaps it was his. She works hard, helps with the training when needed. Do you know her?"

"I met her a couple of times. I'm glad she found somewhere safe. It's time we were going or we'll miss our meal. Expect it will be fish again, better than nothing."

"Will you be back? The boys will be disappointed not to meet you."

"I have to attend the Witan with Lord Athelstan. I'll try and get away later."

*

The smell of sweating bodies closely packed together overwhelmed the incense that lingered from the earlier services in the minster. We had waited impatiently for the arrival of the king. Eadred had arrived late and now sat slumped in his chair, occasionally sipping from a gold cup. An attentive servant had already refilled it once with wine. Abbott Dunstan sat next to him amid the piles of rolls heaped on the table. There were no seats for the rest of us, stools were brought only for the most elderly. We had already stood through the lengthy prayers of Bishop Elfheah. He hadn't changed much from when I had met him several years before. Beside him, Oda, Archbishop of Canterbury, nodded and then added his own prayers. Other churchmen were gathered around them, some with eyes closed in concentration. Perhaps they were asleep.

The Ealdormen stood nearby. Lord Athelstan of East Anglia was closest to the King. His eyes were fixed on Dunstan and the

King. Every now and then he exchanged a few words with his eldest son, Ethelwald, who stood behind him. I had met him once. He was as crafty as his father and fitted in well at court.

Further from the King stood Elfhere with his father, the Ealdorman of Mercia. I nodded briefly before my eyes moved on, identifying the other great men in the nave of the old building.

A bell chimed, drawing my attention to the King. Silence fell as he stood up. He was dressed in purple, and the jewels in his crown sent coloured reflections across the walls as he turned his head to inspect the assembly. His face was pale and his body shrunken beneath the magnificence. He said a few words, impossible to hear. He coughed, took a sip of wine and started again.

"Thank you for attending today. It is a long time since we last met. I have fresh news from the north that must be discussed." Murmurs travelled through the crowd. "Last year we took an army north to deal with the unrest in Northumbria. Erik Haraldsson and others submitted to me. A truce was declared. We thought it would last forever and England would be at peace." His gaze roamed around the roomful of grim faces. Everyone knew what was coming. "We have received news from the north. Wulfstan, the Archbishop of York has ignored our summons to attend here today." The King scanned the ranks of churchmen as if the errant bishop had somehow arrived and was hiding at the back. "This disobedient cleric has acclaimed the evil imposter, Erik, once more king of York and overlord of our beloved land of Northumbria."

Shouts broke the silence as the crowd pretested.

"It cannot be allowed." King Eadred slammed his fist on the table, causing the cup to jump. Wine spilt across the surface like blood. Dunstan swept some documents out of the way, and a servant rushed forward to mop up the liquid. "It will not be allowed," screamed the king.

The room erupted. I watched men's faces. Some were genuinely enraged; others were already considering how this would benefit them. Lord Athelstan's face was still. He knew that everyone must have his say before the decision was announced.

It was an illuminating lesson in character. Most were in favour of war, though framed their words differently, offering praise to a man they wished to impress or opposing someone for the sake of enmity. I was too insignificant to be asked my opinion and still had a lot to learn.

First, I needed to decide where I stood. My first duty was to my King. He would make the final decision, advised by the Witan. I knew I stood no chance of advancement, not after my behaviour when his older brother, King Edmund, had died. I was lucky to still be alive. After the King, I served Lord Athelstan. Everyone said that he controlled the King. I watched as he exchanged words with Abbot Dunstan; they worked well together. Any chance of a future lay with them. Who would be king after Eadred? Surely he did not have a long life ahead of him and he had no sons, Edmund had left two, neither old enough to become king, not yet. I knew Edgar, the younger, he was a good lad, but barring accidents, the elder, Eadwig, would reign.

The noise diminished; everyone who wanted to had spoken. What was the decision? I had promised Saewynn I would not go, although my heart beat faster at the thought of war. The King rose. Excitement had added colour to his cheeks, or was it anger? Revenge had influenced his decision. He had lost patience with Northumbria, and he demanded it should be destroyed.

Those who lived close to the Northumbrian border were in favour of action. I remembered the devastation that the army had caused the previous year, and that was in a land considered friendly. They had suffered then, and would be happy to attack their neighbours and take land for themselves. Those in the south worried about the loss of trade; the north produced many products desired by Wessex. Others knew the consequences: hungry northerners trekking south. How would the Scots react? Would they flood south to fill the empty gap? No one thought about the ordinary people who would die.

The king had made up his mind, and it would be war. We would leave as soon as the fyrd was called and an army assembled to strike Northumbria before they even knew we were coming. Would the ships be sent north, like last year? I glanced in the direction of Lord Athelstan. His face was inscrutable.

The army was to be divided. Wessex would head straight north. Mercia would gather at Chester and attack from the west. There was a discussion about the Welsh - they were quiet at the moment. Talk moved on to the sea. Lord Athelstan nodded. Our ships would sweep up the East Coast, transport men and horses north of the Humber and attack York from the East. I thought about how it should be organised. The King moved on to plans for the West coast.

"Lord Elfgar, you still have responsibilities in Devon?"

"Yes, my lord, I was Ealdorman there for many years, since becoming Ealdorman of Essex..."

"Devon has become somewhat neglected." What had this to do with the war in Northumbria?

"They guard the coast against pirates. It has been quiet recently." Lord Edgar's face flushed.

"I have had reports that the ships in Exeter are in a poor state, not fit for battle."

"I apologise, my lord," said Elfgar. "I will send someone to deal with it."

The King picked up his cup and took a sip of wine. He stared at Lord Elfgar over the rim. "The ships are needed. You will go yourself. Leave immediately, prepare the ships and take them north. We must discourage the Irish from joining their friends in Northumbria, and keep an eye on the Welsh. We will decide a landing place in the north later."

"My lord, I know nothing of ships. The man who arranged those things died, and has not been replaced," blustered Elfgar. I felt sorry for him, but it was his own fault for letting things slip.

"You will have to spend some of your store of gold and find someone who knows what to do." He scanned the room, men avoiding his eyes. It would be a thankless task. I was glad I would be sailing with Leif and the others. The king's glance slid over me and on. I relaxed but it returned.

"Thegn Byrhtnoth. We have not seen you at court for a long time. Ealdorman Athelstan tells me you did well last year. Burning the enemy's ships stopped the battle and enabled the truce to be struck." He sneered. "Some would say that it was not the success we thought at the time." Several men laughed. Those standing close to me stepped back, leaving me exposed.

"I did as I was commanded to do."

"Good. I command you now to go with Lord Elfgar to Devon. You know about ships so you shouldn't find it difficult to sort things out."

"But..."

"You have other plans?"

"Of course not." I glanced towards Lord Athelstan. He gave a small shrug and continued his conversation with his son.

"I think that's all the business for today." Dunstan nodded his agreement. The Witan was over.

Chapter 7

"Leave him alone. He's too young to hit that hard." The sharp words sunk into my angry brain. My attention slid back to the boy I was fighting. He was stretched out on the ground, panting. He still held his wooden sword and a determined look, with only a trace of fear.

"Sorry lad." I reached out a hand and pulled him upright. "My temper is foul this morning That was a good stroke; now you know how to block it. Go and cool down."

The other boys crowded around him, giving me a generous berth. I had fought them all, and yet anger still simmered in my breast. It was not their fault; I must control myself.

"That will do for now. Practice some of those moves between you. You're coming along well; soon you will be fighting in the shield wall with the men." Several of them grinned, and they divided into their accustomed training pairs.

I walked over to the fence where a woman clutched a basket of wet washing.

"They are all too small for me," I muttered.

"I imagine most of your opponents are." She shaded her eyes from the bright spring sunshine. "You need a decent adversary, to release some of that anger."

"What makes you think I'm angry?"

"I know men. I'll give you a bout."

"I don't know..."

"You think women can't fight?"

"It's not that," I said. "My wife fights... used to fight. She doesn't anymore."

"Your wife?" She frowned. "I suppose you stopped her doing such things when you married."

"No." My anger simmered. "She was injured. She cannot hold a sword." I lifted the wooden practice weapon.

"I'm sorry." Her hand touched mine before withdrawing. "Was it an accident?"

"Someone did it deliberately." She gasped, and I lifted my eyes to hers. "His name was Egbert. I think you know him?"

"I do." She spat and we watched the liquid sink into the ground. "Do you want that fight now?"

"Yes," I said and she put down the basket of washing. "Don't you need to change?" I pointed to her skirts.

"I can manage." She reached between her legs, pulled through a bunch of material and tucked it into her belt, cinching it tight. She climbed over the fence and landed beside me. "Throw me a weapon." One of the boys selected a sword and tossed it to her with a grin. She plucked it from the air and swung it towards my head. I stumbled backwards, narrowly avoiding the wooden blade.

"Nearly got you." Her teeth were bared in a grin. I noticed a gap where one was missing. "It always distracts the men."

"What?" I blocked another blow and prepared to attack.

"My legs."

As she had planned, my eyes dropped to the length of naked thigh, and I caught a heavy blow to my sword arm. I backed away and heard laughter from the boys. She grabbed one of the small practice shields and we faced each other in the centre of the space. I aimed a blow which she diverted with the shield. Her sword snaked toward me, and I caught it with mine. The

48

hilts locked and I twisted my wrist to disengage. She followed my action and I pushed, expecting to force her backwards. Her bare toes dug into the ground and she maintained her position. I pushed harder, she held her ground. I jumped back, pretending I had intended that move. Her eyes narrowed and she attacked. I worked hard to prevent a blow from reaching me.

The shouting increased. Were they cheering for me, or for her? I attempted a wide swing at her head. The woman ducked, as I expected, and I continued the action, aiming a slice at her undefended legs. She jumped like a bird taking flight and, before regaining her feet, landed a blow on my shoulder, shuffling backwards as I punched forward with my shield. She caught it with hers, and her sword flashed towards my stomach. I heaved on the shields and the sword missed by a finger's breadth. Another push and she overbalanced. As she fell backwards, I approached for the killing blow. Instead of remaining flat on the ground, she sustained the momentum. Legs tucked in like a practised acrobat, she rolled back like a child's ball, bouncing back onto her feet.

"Come on, you big oaf. Can't even catch a woman?" I had fought enough men to know not to react to insults.

"If you want to fight, why run?" I walked away to the centre of the ground. I saluted the boys. A sudden intake of breath warned me she was close. I spun and caught her sword with mine. The wooden swords grated together. Being taller I brought more strength. She wavered then her shield hit me in the ribs. I jerked away, and our swords parted.

We circled, each searching for an opening, neither landing a blow. It was dawning on me that if this had been a real fight, she would be difficult to kill. She was untutored, so her blows, although clumsy, were unpredictable.

"Get on with it," shouted one of the boys. The cheering was changing to boos.

"What do we do now?" I asked her.

"What do you suggest?" She swung her sword arm around and around in circles, faster and faster. Was she going to throw it? She was giving me plenty of warning. The sword left her hand but she seemed to have misjudged the timing; the wooden sword sailed up into the air. My eyes followed the motion, and that was when she struck. She hurled herself forward, one leg outstretched. I managed to move just enough so that her stiff foot hit my leg, instead of her intended target. The pain knocked me back.

As she struggled to rise, I dropped my sword and shield and pulled her to me, wrapping my arms tight around her. I lifted her off her feet. She struggled. I squeezed harder. She kicked with her feet, and her arms, trapped by mine, scrabbled at my body. I stared into her eyes. Her struggles ceased, and I saw fear blossom, I stopped squeezing.

"Do you surrender?" I asked

"No."

What did I do now? If I continued, I would crush her ribs; perhaps kill her. If I let her go, she would have won. She read my thoughts and her lips twitched. "Do you?"

Cold metal pricked my neck. It moved and I saw my own knife. She had stolen it; that struggling had had a purpose. I stared into her eyes silver as the blade, the sharp grey of death. They were unreadable now. What did she intend? Years before I had failed this girl. Was this her revenge? I had been stupid, walked to my death with eyes wide open. I didn't fear death, only regretted that I would never see my child.

"I surrender." I opened my arms. As she dropped to the ground, the knife touched my face and blood fell. I took a step back and bowed to her, scanning the ground for my dropped sword. She had gone, receiving the acclaim of the boys. Others had joined them, to watch the fight and my defeat.

One of the boys handed her the cap which had fallen unnoticed from her head during the fight. She bundled up her unruly brown hair and replaced it. She smoothed down her skirts and offered me her hand.

"Thank you, I haven't had such a good fight for ages. Let's have a drink. I found some mead that Oswald had hidden away."

Someone opened the gate, and I followed her out, wiping the smear of blood from my chin.

Chapter 8

I recognised the building as soon as we entered. I would have known it just by the smell: wet clothes and burnt wood, a hint of soap and herbs, and dirty feet. The large barrel, used for both washing linen and small boys, still stood in the centre of the room. Steam rose from the cauldron beside it, although the fire beneath was out. Damp washcloths hung from ropes strung across beneath the ceiling

"This way." She drew back a curtain that hung across one end and rummaged in a chest. She drew out a stoppered flask in triumph. One cup stood on a small table. She searched unsuccessfully for another. "Sit down." She pointed to the bed, there was nowhere else. She poured some mead into the cup and handed it to me then raised the flask in salute and tipped some of the contents into her mouth.

"That's better." She wiped her mouth on her sleeve and sat down beside me. "I heard you were asking about me. What do you want?"

"I was told you were dead." I took a sip of the mead. She was right, it was good. I took a bigger mouthful and savoured the taste as it slid down my throat.

"Obviously I'm not," she took a sidewise glance, "although I came close, just now."

"Not as close as me." I touched the cut and winced.

"It's just a scratch. If I wanted to kill you, I wouldn't have missed."

"I'm glad of that. I did wonder."

"Why should I want to kill you?"

Should I tell her, perhaps she had forgotten? Too late now. "Years ago, I caught you stealing, the king's meat, if I remember rightly. I promised to help you, find you a job. I forgot. I have felt guilty ever since."

"It was the day your friend won the riding competition," she said. "We arranged to meet after the feast."

I nodded. "Someone arrived to take me back to the village. I forgot everything else."

"I'm not surprised. You were very drunk."

"How did you know?" I looked at my cup and put it back on the table. "Mead. I try not to drink too much nowadays."

"I saw you meet the man. He was acting suspiciously. I wondered if you needed help, but I was... busy."

"Busy?"

"Yes. Nice young man, met him at the feast. Forget his name now, he supported me for a few months."

"You didn't need my help then after all?" Curiously, I was disappointed.

"No, although I appreciated the thought. Who told you I was dead?"

"Elfhere."

"Elfhere? He found me this job here."

"That's what I don't understand. Elfhere tried to kill me. We fought." I remembered that hot, horrific night. "He said he and his men had... bought you before they went to war. He said they refused to pay you afterwards. He gloated about it. I'm sorry, it's what he said."

"Don't apologise, it happened. I wanted to kill all of them, but by the time they finished, I was in no fit state to do anything." She took another swig of the flask.

"He said you drowned yourself in the river."

She snorted, spaying mead across the room. "I'd never do that." She mopped ineffectually at the table with a corner of her sleeve.

"He said you had a child."

"I did, he died."

"I'm sorry."

"It doesn't matter." She dashed a hand across her face and swallowed more mead. "It was for the best. Why did he tell you that?"

"To make me feel bad, guilty. Elfhere said you blamed me, that I had ruined your life."

"You didn't do that." She patted my hand. "You did all you could, more than most." She paused a moment. "Was Egbert there?"

"He must have been, although I didn't recognise him at the time," I remembered the bite marks on Inga's shoulder. The same that he had inflicted on Saewynn. My hand balled into a fist.

"That's it. It was all Egbert's fault. He had Elfhere under his thumb. I heard he disappeared," said the woman.

"I know. I met Elfhere the other day. He apologised. Is that why he found you work here; to clear his conscience?"

"It might be. I thought he wanted something in exchange, although he never asked."

"At least you've found a home here. You're happy." I noticed the twist of her lips. "Aren't you happy?"

"I suppose so. I don't mind the hard work, and I love working with the boys, although it's nice to have a proper fight sometimes." She grinned. "It's Oswald."

"Does he beat you for stealing his mead?"

"He wouldn't dare. I don't mind taking over his wife's duties in the washhouse, but he expects me to replace her in his bed."

"Do you want me to talk to him?"

"No. Oswald offered to marry me. I don't want that. I've had enough of men unless I can choose them for myself." She gave me a glance and cocked an eyebrow.

"Sorry, I'm a happily married man."

"I'm glad to hear that." The curtain was pulled aside.

"Hello, Wulfstan. Is it time for the feast?"

"Not quite, it's time we were getting back." He frowned at the girl.

"I'll be right there. You remember..." What was her name? "I'm sorry. I don't think I ever asked your name."

"I don't think you did. My friends call me Aelf."

"Am I a friend?"

"Of course. I let you win the fight, didn't I?" I was glad she hadn't told the truth.

"You won't remember, Wulfstan, we first met her here, in this very room."

Puzzled, Wulfstan examined the small space.

"Out there." She pointed towards the curtain "I was the girl who was thrown out by Oswald, for not being a boy. Not that it was my fault."

"Of course, I thought I recognised you. You've grown a bit."

"Haven't we all?" I said

"Especially you," said Wulfstan, and we laughed.

"Is something wrong?" I asked Wulfstan. His smile had quickly turned back to a frown.

"I'm afraid it's bad news."

"Not Saewynn? Is she all right?" I started to stand.

"Nothing like that. Could I have some ... what is it? Mead, at this time of day?"

"Here," Aelf filled the cup and handed it to him, "Looks like you need it."

He nodded and took a large swallow, coughing at the strength. "I've just met Egbert."

"Egbert? Where?" Alarmed, I searched for a weapon. Why had I left my sword back in the lodgings?

"Not here. It was down in the Minster. I was waiting for the Abbot of Glastonbury; he was busy with the Easter services. I was sitting there in a draughty corridor, and there he was. There was nothing I could do. He was with the Archbishop of Canterbury. Of course, he recognised me immediately, didn't bat an eyelid. Apparently, Oda is some kind of relative. They were in the middle of a discussion about the relics of various saints."

"I didn't know Egbert was interested in that sort of thing," I said with a frown. He had never struck me as being particularly religious.

"They had just come from a meeting with the king. Egbert had that gloating expression he gets when he is planning something."

"I overheard someone talking about the forthcoming campaign," said Aelf. "They mentioned the richness of some of the monasteries in the north. They have some strange saints up there that the Archbishop might hope to add to his collection."

"And the King," replied Wulfstan. "His grandfather, Alfred, and his brother, Athelstan, were both mad to collect such relics."

"You must know about such things. Didn't you go into a monastery after..."

"After I was crippled?"

"I didn't mean that." Aelf stood up. "Does anyone want more mead? Not that there's much left." She weighed the flask in her hand.

"I don't think we should have any more," I said, "we need to keep our wits about us if Egbert is in Winchester."

"He asked about Saewynn," said Wulfstan. "I'm, sorry, I had to tell him you were married."

"What did he say?" I didn't want that man knowing anything about me or my family. "You didn't mention the child?"

"Of course not, I'm not that stupid." I only grunted. "He seemed surprised, then offered his congratulations. He smiled."

"I trust him least when he's smiling." What could I do? Was Saewynn in danger? "Why did the king send me off to sort out Lord Elfgar's ships? You said Egbert had been meeting with King Eadred?"

Wulfstan understood what I was thinking. "You think he had something to do with the decision?"

"I wouldn't put it past him. You can't get much further away from the fens and home, than Devon." I made a decision. "I can't disobey the king, and Lord Athelstan didn't protest, so I can't escape my duty. I'm sending all the men home with you. That should be enough to protect Saewynn."

"What about you?" said Wulfstan.

"I can look after myself. If Egbert thinks I am an easier target, I might get a chance to kill him after all." Perhaps things would work out better than I had thought.

"At least take someone you can trust with you. I know you will be travelling with Lord Elfgar, but you need someone to watch your back."

"All right, I'll take Thurstan with me, perhaps one of the boys, Cenwulf to look after my kit. Edward will be jealous, but he's got to learn he's not indispensable."

I found myself staring at Aelf. She was a woman, and she could fight.

"You said you were having problems. If you're not happy here, why not join us? Saewynn is pregnant," I told her. "She needs protection, and I think she'd enjoy another woman to talk about fighting with. I've been trying to get her to use her left hand more, perhaps you can help."

"It's a big decision. I've never lived anywhere except Winchester."

"Think about it. Wulfstan will stay here for a few days. Have you managed to see Abbott Dunstan yet?" I asked him.

"No, I didn't wait. I came straight to find you."

"If you want to take up my offer, get in touch with Wulfstan,"
I said. "You can ride back with him. Protect him. Do you have
a weapon?"

"Only this." She produced my knife.

"Oh, yes, can I have it back?" For a moment, I thought she
would keep it. "Wulfstan will find you something better, a seax
perhaps?"

"I'll think about it." She handed back my knife with reluctance.
"I'll come and see you anyway, Wulfstan. I saw your battle with
Egbert many years ago." She managed not to look at his twisted
leg.

"You were there?"

"Yes, I had plenty of time to hang around. I'd just had my first
decent meal for years." She gave me a wink. "I'll tell you about
it later," she told Wulfstan.

As we walked back to the king's hall, I spoke quietly to
Wulfstan. "Don't tell Saewynn that you met Egbert. It will only
worry her. She tries to hide it, but she's more upset about what
happened to her than it appears. Sometimes she stiffens when a
strange man comes too close to her. And now with the child, it
all happened too soon, we should have been on our way to search
for my father by now."

"Don't worry, I'll keep her safe."

"I know you will." I laid a hand on his shoulder.

"Saewynn said your father might know something about her
parents. I still haven't worked out what the connection is. I'll ask
Abbot Dunstan about it."

"Is that why you were waiting to see him at the Minster?"

"That, and a few other matters."

"Good, don't hang around in Winchester too long. Remember,
you could be in danger from Egbert as well."

"I think I'll get your warrior woman to look after me, she looks
as if she can protect me."

"Good idea."

59

Chapter 9

"What do you mean, the king commanded it?" Saewynn stood in the yard, hands on hips. "Byrhtnoth swore he would come straight back after the meeting."

"I'm sorry, there was nothing to be done." Wulfstan barely had time to dismount before Saewynn came rushing out to meet them. "Lord Athelstan complained, but King Eadred insisted: Byrhtnoth was needed in the wont Caldormun Ellgar was responsible for the ships there. An expert was needed, and Byrhtnoth was it. Serve him right for his success with Lord Athelstan's ships last year." Saewynn glared at him. "It was a joke," he explained.

"I hate him."

"Byrhtnoth?"

"Yes." She put a hand to the nearly invisible swelling of her stomach. Now the sickness had declined, she wanted her husband back, to reassure her everything was all right. "Of course not. The King. He hasn't forgiven Byrhtnoth for attacking him; I doubt he ever will." How many times had she told her husband that nobody thought him responsible for the death of King Edmund? He still blamed himself.

"He had to go with Ealdorman Elfgar? Did the King arrange that specially? He must know they dislike each other."

"I don't suppose he had any idea. He was arranging people like gaming pieces on a board. Picking who would be best for a job, regardless of the convenience to them. It will be fine. Elfgar only disliked Byrhtnoth when he thought he was after his daughter."

"Elfflaed." Saewynn knew her former mistress well. "Was she at court?" It was bad enough her husband going away, but with that woman? She knew how Elfflaed manipulated men, how beautiful she was, much more attractive than her. Saewynn pulled her veil to hide the scar that ran down the side of her face.

"I didn't see her. Her sister was away visiting the late king's son. Not Edgar, the other one. Elfflaed would have been with her. She might even have a husband by now. Don't worry, Byrhtnoth will be far too busy to look at other women." Godric coughed behind him. "Cheer up, I've got a present for you, two in fact. Let's go inside, it's been a long ride, and my leg aches."

*

"Abbott Dunstan made it himself. I sent him measurements."

"So, that was what you were up to. Did Byrhtnoth know what you were doing?"

"No," said Wulfstan uncomfortably. "I wasn't sure he would approve, or if it would work. Does it fit?" He leaned forward eagerly.

"What do I do with it?" Saewynn prodded the object. It was a glove, made of soft leather. The fingers contained metal rods, with joints that enabled them to bend. Lying on the table among the remains of the meal, it looked like a severed hand.

"You wear it, like any other glove. The metal will help to straighten your fingers. It can be adjusted to different positions. I'm sorry, I doubt it will bring back the use of your hand, but it might help to make it appear..." He searched for the right word.

"Ordinary?" That was what she wanted most. For people not to stare, or worse, offer sympathy. She looked around the hall to see if anyone was watching.

"Shall we go into the chamber to test it," asked Wulfstan.

"Yes," she whispered eagerly.

*

"If we bend the fingers of the glove, you should be able to slip your hand in." Wulfstan made some adjustments.

"It won't work. I can't get my fingers straight."

"Haven't you been stretching them like I told you to?" Wulfstan took her twisted fist and uncurled the knotted fingers. They reverted to the original position when he let go.

"I'm sorry, it didn't make any difference."

"It doesn't matter. You need something to hold them in position. This device will do that, God willing." He held up the glove. "Use your left hand to straighten the fingers of the glove and push them onto your hand." He watched as she struggled.

"I can't do it." She pushed the glove away with tears in her eyes.

"Yes, you can. It will need practice. I know you can do it. If you managed to persuade Byrhtnoth to let you train as a warrior, you can do anything."

She gave him a watery smile and tried again. Eventually, she got her fingers into the right place, although her thumb was still bent into her palm. "Will that do? I can manage with just the fingers."

"It won't stay on without the thumb to anchor it. Don't you want to hold things?"

"Is that possible?" Her eyes opened wide.

"You'll never know if you don't try."

"Hold it still." With a grimace, she pulled back her thumb and forced it into the final opening of the glove.

"Does it hurt?" asked Wulfstan.

"Not much." She stared at her right hand. It was no longer clenched tight. It lay on the table as if waiting to hold something. Wulfstan smoothed the soft leather over her skin.

"It fits, that was my first worry. Can we get the fingers straighter? Tell me if it hurts, and I'll stop at once."

"Carry on," she said, her excitement growing.

63

Wulfstan inspected the device carefully. "You still have movement in your wrist, that makes it easier. We'll leave the thumb for now." He took hold of her little finger and pulled it straight. He checked her expression, and she nodded. He did the same to the next finger. In the silence, she heard the click of moving metal and felt the ache as shrunken muscles extended.

"Can I do it myself?"

"Take it slowly, don't force anything." He let go of her hand, and she pulled the next finger into place. She took a deep breath and pushed the last, the index finger. It joined the others, straight, except the very last joint that remained bent.

"That will do for now. How does it feel?"

"Strange, as if another hand is holding mine."

"Try pushing back, one finger. It shouldn't be difficult, it wants to return to where it was." She watched, fascinated as her middle finger shook and bent.

"It won't go back."

"Straighten it again with your other hand." She did, and then lifted her hand as if she had never seen it before. This was more than she had ever expected.

"It's wonderful. It's better than normal." She reached forward to touch Wulfstan's hand, then stroked it. "I can feel, not as good as before, but enough to know something is there."

"The leather is thin on the fingertips. Abbot Dunstan didn't know how long it would last, so he sent more to repair it." He placed a bag on the table. "There are replacements for some of the metal pieces and tools to make adjustments. I'll find out how it all works. And there is this..." He pulled out a second glove, soft and limp. He pulled it over her left hand. "Now they match."

The leather was pale, not the same shade as her own skin, but close enough, at a distance, to pass as natural. She held her hands out in front of her. It was almost impossible to believe; she was whole again.

There was a soft knock on the door, and Hild peered in.

64

"Sorry to interrupt, my lady, where do you want to put ..." She noticed Saewynn's hands. "What's happened? Are you healed? It's a miracle."

"It is," Saewynn grinned, "although not the way you think. It's a glove, see." Hild rushed forward, reached for her hand, then paused.

"It's not magic, is it?"

"It can't be, Abbot Dunstan made it. Wulfstan brought it back for me. It's made of metal. I don't know how it works."

"Gently," added Wulfstan as Hild reached out a finger. "We don't know how strong it will be."

"He's a clever man that Dunstan." The voice came from the door. At first, Saewynn thought it was a man, although something about the figure's stance was wrong.

"I told you to wait outside," said Hild." I'm sorry, my lady. I came to ask where you wanted to put this... woman."

"You must be Saewynn, Wulfstan told me all about you." The woman strode forward and held out a hand. Saewynn took it apprehensively with her right hand, and the woman grasped it gently. Saewynn's hand closed around it and the woman beamed at Wulfstan. "It works."

"Saewynn, this is Aelf. Byrhtnoth sent her; she has joined the troop."

"Have you known my husband for long?" Saewynn tried to maintain her dignity while disentangling their fingers.

"It needs a bit of practice." Aelf sat down beside her and helped straighten the glove. Saewynn gave up and studied this strange person. "I met him and Wulfstan, and the others a long time ago, when they first arrived in Winchester. I was forbidden to train with the boys. Oswald, bastard, wouldn't allow it. Byrhtnoth gave me his old tunic and some food. He was kind."

"Yes, he is," said Saewynn quietly.

"I met him again when Wolfie here had his triumph with his horse." Wolfie? Wulfstan spread his hands and shrugged. "That caused problems with Egbert. I met him later." A flash of hate crossed her face. "I'm told he hurt you as well." Saewynn hated it when people talked about what had happened to her. Aelf patted her shoulder.

"Your husband said you wanted to become a warrior."

"I was a warrior. I was good, but..." Saewynn looked down at her hand. Could she use it again?

"Byrhtnoth learned to use his left hand, he uses both. Have you thought about that?"

"You've seen him fight?" Wulfstan hadn't mentioned there had been fighting.

"I don't know about seeing him. I fought him, just a friendly bout."

"Don't tell anyone," Wulfstan leaned forward, "but she beat him."

"You beat Byrhtnoth?" Saewynn stared at the woman open-mouthed.

"I did cheat a bit, distracted him with a flash of leg."

Her husband had seen this woman's legs? Had she shown him more? She experienced a stab of jealousy.

"Nothing else happened." Aelf put an arm around Saewynn's shoulders. "Not that I've have objected if it had." She winked at Wulfstan before noticing Hild's scandalised expression. "All right, I'll go. I'll find a place in the hall until you know what to do with me." She stood up and looked down at Saewynn. "Perhaps we can practice some time, see what you can do."

Saewynn's hand went to her belly. "Oh, I don't..."

"I fought up to the day my son was born, no problem."

"You have a child?" asked Saewynn eagerly.

"Not anymore." Aelf swung on her heel and made for the door.

In the hall, Godric asked a question, Aelf replied, and laughter followed.

"I must get on." Hild rushed out.

"Godric had better watch out," said Saewynn. "He'll get no meat tonight if he upsets Hild."

"Are they...?" asked Wulfstan.

66

"She's been trying to get him to say something before... before the men leave for the summer." At least Hild's man had come home from Winchester, unlike Byrhtnoth.

"He won't get far with Aelf. She doesn't like men."

"She gets on well with them, though. Does she have a husband? What happened to the child?" Did it die of disease or accident? Would this woman be a danger to her own child?

"I don't know, there's no husband. I expect she'll tell you everything eventually."

"Why did Byrhtnoth send her?" Saewynn stared at Wulfstan. Was there more between her husband and Aelf than he was saying?

"She was working with the boys. She was taken on to wash clothes but spent most of the time training. She had a few problems with Oswald. You've heard about our old trainer?" Saewynn nodded. "His wife died, and he turned his attentions to Aelf. She wanted to get away. She'd never left Winchester before. I think she's a bit shy."

"She doesn't show it."

"It's just an act. Byrhtnoth thought she'd be useful here, to help Godric with the training, and protect you."

"Do I need protection?"

"Of course not," said Wulfstan hastily. "But when most of the men are called away, we need someone to protect the village. He thought you would enjoy another woman to talk to, about weapons and things. Do you want to take that off now?"

Saewynn had been flexing her hand as she talked. "A little longer." It was painful, but she wanted to keep it on forever.

"You mustn't overdo it. It might cause damage."

"More damage than there was already?"

"I'm sorry, I should have done more."

"You did more than enough." She patted his arm with her new hand. "And now you've brought this." She frowned. "It must have cost a fortune. How did you pay for it? Did Byrhtnoth give you the money?"

67

"He doesn't know anything about it."

"But...?"

"I didn't know if it would work, if it was even possible. It caught Dunstan's interest. He enjoys making things, and this was a challenge. He'll be pleased to know it works. I'll write to him straight away." He reached for the bag that contained his writing things.

"Not now, it's growing dark. The meal will be ready soon if Hild has finished with Godric." Saewynn leaned back and held out her hand. "Take it off. I'll try again tomorrow."

*

Saewynn lay in bed, nursing her aching hand. Would it make any difference? Would she be able to use it, or did it just improve her appearance? Did it matter? She turned over and plumped up the pillow. The bed was too big without him there. She missed him so much. He had said he didn't mind about her hand, now she hoped he would be pleased. She pulled the wolfskin over her head. It was heavy, and with the days getting warmer, it would soon be too hot to sleep beneath its soft shelter.

It had been a welcome arrival during the coldest part of the winter. It was the skin of the wolf that Byrhtnoth had killed in Northumbria. Everyone admired it, a thick, deep black, with not a single white hair. He had been evasive when the messenger had announced that it had been sent by the Lady of Bebbanburg. Why not from the Lord? Perhaps Lord Osulf's wife had been especially grateful that Byrhtnoth had saved the life of her son. There could be no other reason, could there?

The wolf must have been large, the pelt had covered Byrhtnoth's long body. Did it still hold his scent? She buried her face in the thick fur and inhaled. Was it fading? She pushed it away and thought about the new arrival. She was not sure about Aelf. What was her real name? No one would give a child a name like that. She had spread her mattress in the hall with the men, close to the door to the chamber, claiming her place as bodyguard. Saewynn remembered Edith's reaction when they had been introduced. "Not another one," she had muttered, glancing in her direction.

Saewynn turned onto her back and stared into the darkness. Would she have become like that, if it hadn't been for the attack? One of the men, ready to fight at his side? She had thought that was what she had wanted. Was that what Byrhtnoth wanted, a woman to fight at his side? Was Aelf her replacement, a companion while Saewynn stayed at home to bear his sons? She consoled herself with the thought that if that were so, he would have taken Aelf with him, not sent her back to his home.

Why wasn't Byrhtnoth there to explain?

Chapter 10

The ships were kept at Exeter. As soon as we arrived, Elfgar told me he had other business to attend to. It was true. Men had gathered as soon as they heard he was there.

"I thought I was done with this place," he told me "I can't be expected to deal with events here, as well as in Essex." He had been complaining all the way from Winchester.

"Is there no reeve to deal with such things?" I asked.

"He died. I haven't had time to find anyone new."

"You spend a lot of time with the King. Why hasn't he appointed a new Ealdorman to Devon? There must be plenty of suitable candidates."

Lord Elfgar shrugged. "It takes time, he has to find just the right man." And the longer the position was vacant, the longer he would collect the revenue. Why was Elfgar so eager to obtain more land if he was unable to manage it properly? It was none of my business.

"Find the ships, inspect them. Let me know what needs to be done."

"Yes, my lord." I collected Thurstan and the other men, wishing I had brought Wulfstan with me, to make lists, calculate expenses. I would have to manage without him. Elfgar might provide a clerk, although now he had arrived, most of them would be run off their feet.

We walked down the hill to the quay. Beneath us, the river lay quiet beneath a veil of morning mist. The sun would soon burn that off, it was becoming warmer with every passing day. How far was it to the sea? The river disappeared out of sight around a bend. Did the tides reach this far? So much to discover. First, we had to learn the condition of the ships.

We passed a pair of merchant ships, perhaps the first of the season to cross the channel. Sailors swarmed over them, unloading barrels: wine from Frankia, or oil from the south. A fleet of fishing boats arrived, crammed with piles of shimmering fish. Men hurried from the buildings along the quay with stacks of baskets. It was quieter at the far end.

"Is that them?" asked Thurstan. We studied the abandoned ships.

There were four, perhaps five, it was difficult to tell. They lay low in the water and no masts or oars were to be seen. A long low building stood nearby, similar to the ones I had seen at Wudebrige, where masts were stored. This one appeared abandoned.

Thurstan asked if we should go on board.

"I don't know if we can risk it." I pushed the bow post of the nearest. The boat rocked gently. "At least they're not stuck in the mud." The motion released an ominous smell of rotting wood.

"What happened to the crews?" said Thurstan.

"Good question, we need to find out. No point in getting ships ready to sail, if there's no one to sail them." I saw a man watching from beside the building and beckoned him forward. He was old, with a bushy white beard and narrowed eyes surrounded with wrinkles. His gait rolled like a deck in heavy seas. A sailor. If he couldn't tell us about the ships, no one could.

"Do you wish to buy one, my lord?"

"Are they for sale? Don't they belong to the King?"

"They did. Haven't been to sea for years, so reckon they belong to us now." He gave a belligerent stare.

"Haven't they been required? You've had no attacks along this coast? No pirates?"

"Not close. Anyhow, the crews have gone."

"Where?"

"Other ships, other work. They leave fast when they're not paid."

"Why weren't they paid?" Was someone diverting the king's money? Lord Elfgar? It might explain why he was reluctant to involve himself with the ships.

"Who knows?" The old man shrugged. "We pay enough taxes, and get no benefit. The crews were paid to start with, then received nothing but promises."

"I see." I stared at the ships. "What condition are they in? Are they safe to board?"

"Safe enough, though no one's been near lately."

"Cenwulf, you're lighter than me, check if the hulls are sound. Be careful, leave if you don't feel safe."

"Don't worry, I will." He clambered aboard the first ship, moving carefully to the far end. "No problem with this one. There's water in the bottom, no more than you'd expect from natural rainfall."

"Why didn't they cover them, or drag them ashore and upturn them?"

"If you hadn't been paid, would you bother?" said Thurstan.

"Where does that smell come from?" I asked Cenwulf.

"I'll check the next one." After leaning over to scan the state of it, he clambered over. "Some of the benches at the far end have rotted, the water's deeper there, I can't see any holes." He shuffled about in the belly of the ship and moved to the next. "This is the same. Someone's removed some of the covers from the oar holes. Perhaps they wanted it to sink. "The fourth ship suddenly dropped beneath his feet. I moved closer, ready to rescue him, but he heaved himself over into the final ship.

"This one's sound." He stamped along the centre, splashing water like a child through a puddle and climbed out onto the quay.

"We have four ships, repairable," I said. "We might be able to salvage the fifth or scavenge it to repair the others. I don't suppose they left any oars?"

"They went with the rowers," said the old man.

"What about masts?"

"I don't know. There may be a couple in the shed. The sails disappeared long ago."

"Can new ones be found?" I asked.

"There's always weaving women in port towns."

I walked from one ship to another, inspecting the empty hulls. Could it be done?

"You've spent a lot of time with ships," I said to the old man. "You must know what repairs are needed. How long will it take to repair these ships and get them to sea?"

"Depends how much time you have, and how much money you have to spend."

"We have to meet up with the army, when?"

"Pentecost, my lord," said Thurstan. I was pleased to see he was paying attention to what was going on. Cenwulf was watching the fishermen further along the quay.

"Good, we've got seven weeks to rebuild the ships, train crews and get up to Chester to meet the army."

"You must be mad." The old man frowned. "You can't do it in that time. And what about the cost?"

"That shouldn't be a problem. The King has instructed the richest man in England to get it done. I'll go and speak to Lord Elfgar. While I'm away, bail out the ships." I reached into my purse and pulled out all the money I had and handed it to Thurstan. "Find someone to help. You," I pointed to the old man. He had brightened when he had seen the money. "I'm sure you can locate a few men from the original crews. I'll be back later."

I started up the hill to the hall, hoping I hadn't made a big mistake.

Chapter 11

The hall was full and Lord Elfgar was hidden by a swarming mass of people. Not a good moment to ask for money. I didn't want to be there, but since I was, I was determined to make the best of it. Angrily I pushed my way through the crowd, pushing people out of the way without apology

I reached the table and Lord Elfgar looked up. I placed my hands on the board and raised my voice. "Why did we come here?"

"To sort out the ships." He leaned back and called for wine. "What have you found?"

"It's not good. The ships need repairs and the crews, if they can be found, have not been paid for a long time."

"But can it be done?"

"I think so, although it will be expensive." I glanced at the coins piled on the table beside him. A guard stared back at me with a stony face. "There are two alternatives. You can pay for men and repairs. The more generous, the quicker it will be done. It will cost a lot.

"And the second?"

"You go back to Winchester and explain to King Eadred that he cannot have his ships. It's up to you." I crossed my arms and waited. I didn't care what he decided. If he refused to pay the money, of which he had plenty, he would get the blame, and I could go home. It didn't take him long to work out which would benefit him the most.

"How much do you need?"

"Lend me one of your clerks, and I'll bring you a list by the end of the day."

He spun a coin between his fingers as he thought. He put it down with regret and called a young monk who was assisting one of the senior clerks.

"Get this counted and bagged up, then go with Thegn Byrhtnoth." He eyed me. "I assume you'll need some to get started?"

"It would be a great help, my lord," I said It was more than I had expected.

"Make sure you account for every penny," He warned the monk who gave me a worried look and nodded. He sat down at the bench and counted the coins, scribbling figures on a spare piece of parchment.

"I'll meet you outside," I told him. "Thank you, Lord Elfgar, I'll let you get back to your other business."

The crowds were building up behind me, complaints increasing. Elfgar noticed and frowned. "Good luck." He waved me away, took a sip from his glass of wine and leaned forward. "What do you want?"

*

I asked the monk his name.

"Edmund, my lord." He had found a heavy chest for the money. I hadn't thought about how we would take care of it. I praised his initiative.

"Do you want a hand with that? My name is Byrhtnoth."

"I know, my lord. If you take the other handle, I think we can manage it between us. Do we need a guard?"

"Don't worry, this will discourage any thieves." I drew my sword a couple of fingers width from the scabbard, before pushing it back. He gave a relieved nod. We walked back to the river at a brisk pace.

By the time we arrived, the first of the ships had been emptied of water and was being separated from the others. A small group had gathered to watch.

"We've found a few of the original crews," reported Thurstan.

I looked them over; most had the broad shoulders of expert rowers. "Has Thurstan told you what we intend?" I asked. Some shook their heads, and one of them stepped forward.

"Are you preparing to take them to sea?"

"Yes, we head north, to take Northumbria back from Erik Haraldsson. We will pay double the previous rate, and there may be opportunities for plunder." I didn't approve of what the king planned, but it might encourage some of the men. Several of them exchanged glances. "I assume you can fight, as well as row." Some nodded enthusiastically. "We'll talk about that later. Who crewed this ship?" I pointed to the one being moved. Two men raised their hands.

"Give your names to the monk, then help my men move it. That one is beyond repair." I pointed towards the ship that was slowly filling with water. "Anyone who belongs to it, join one of the other crews for now." A middle-aged man stepped forward.

"I'm Petroc. I was captain of that ship. May I take a look? I wouldn't want to give up on her if she can be saved."

"If you wish. I know what it's like to lose a ship." He gave me a searching look before turning to a boy, his son judging by the resemblance.

"Run home and fetch my tools and while you're there, put out word that the ships will sail again, and there's good money to be earned."

We watched the boy run back towards the town. "You must know the area well, the river and the sea hereabouts."

"Born and bred just up the coast. I've sailed from here many times."

"Good. You can show me around. First, which way is the sea?"

79

*

When the first ship was ready, we took her out to sea. It was good to take the helm and feel the wind in my hair and blow away the riverside stink. The ship performed well, and it gave me hope that we might achieve our goal.

We were approaching the river entrance when the captain shouted a warning. A strange ship, a ship of war, was nosing its way into the haven. The men dipped their oars, and I steered the ship towards the intruder.

As we got closer, I recognised the vessel and waved. The other ship changed course and slid towards us through the flat water. The sail dropped and was tidied away. It slowed to a stop, and a rope tossed to us. I surrendered the steering oar and jumped across the narrow gap.

"Leif! It's good to see you." I enveloped my friend in a hug. "What are you doing here?"

"Lord Athelstan sent me. He heard rumours of the state of the western fleet. He thought you might need help. Is this it?" He gestured towards the ship beside us. The ship was watertight, but not pretty. It had a full set of oars and men to use them, but that was all.

"We are working on the others. The problem is the masts, there are none to be had along this coast. We tried to commandeer a couple from some merchant ships. It nearly caused a riot." At least it had given the men some fighting practice. "Even if we had masts, we have little in the way of sails to hang from them. I don't suppose you have a spare with you?" I scanned the ship without much hope

"Afraid not. Can't you afford masts?"

"We've got the money, once Lord Elfgar realised he would have to make excuses to the king if we weren't ready in time."

"There are plenty of masts in Hantune. Perhaps I could go and fetch some for you. For the right price, of course." He grinned.

"It's getting late, follow us back. We can discuss it over a meal." I climbed back onto my ship and gave the instructions to head for port.

When we returned to the quay, Petroc insisted on showing us his ship

"Will it be ready in time?" I asked as Leif, and I stood watching the activity. It still didn't look safe to me.

"Everything's sound. Just a coating of tar and she can join the others." Petroc stroked the smooth boards.

"Good. If Leif can find us some masts, we might finish on time." The rest of the ships were anchored in the river, ready to be fitted out. "This one was in the worst state," I told Leif. "Petroc has worked night and day to repair it. What do you think?"

"I'd need to take a closer look. May I come on board?"

Petroc gave permission, and soon they were involved in a complicated discussion of strakes and scarfs and trenails.

The old man, who we had learned was Petroc's father, lingered nearby. "What about you? Is she ready?" I asked him.

He stared gloomily at the vessel. "I never thought I'd see her sail again. She was beautiful when she was new. Almost sank beneath me once, but I prayed to St Petroc, and we survived. That's why I named my son after him."

"Here's the tar." His grandson, also called Petroc, was known as Young Petroc. He struggled with the heavy bucket, and I took it from him, handing it across the gap to his father. He went to stand beside the old man and watched as his father added the protection to the boards. Leif grabbed a brush and helped.

"Can I come?" said the boy

"Come where?" His father paused and frowned up at him.

"To sea. On the ship with you."

"Certainly not." The old man put a protective arm around the boy. "The sea is dangerous, and when they reach their destination, there will be fighting, it's no place for a boy."

Young Petroc's face dropped. I knew how hard he had worked with his father to repair the ship.

"When the painting is done, we will take her out to test her. You can sail with us then." I glanced at the old man who nodded reluctantly. "Your grandfather can come too. If the ship sails well, perhaps we can take her out beyond the sandbank."

"Can I?" the boy pleaded.

"I don't see why not," said Petroc.

"You will be needed here after we leave," I told him. "You will be the man of the house. You must take care of your mother and sisters, and your grandfather."

"I suppose so." The boy ran his eyes over the ship. "You'll need more tar, I'll fetch it." With a brief wave, he ran back along the quay.

Chapter 12

We had taken over a corner of the empty mast shed. I was on the spot to deal with any problems, and it saved having to return to Elfgar's hall every night. The large door stood open, and Brother Edmund sat at his desk, angled towards the last rays of daylight. He scribbled a few more words, laid down his pen and stretched his aching back.

"Good evening, my lord. Everything is up to date. Would you like to check the figures?"

"Not at the moment. I've got good news. This is Leif, I sailed with him last year. He can fetch as many masts as we need from Hantune."

"Oh, dear." The monk frowned down at the black marks on the parchment. "I'm not sure we can afford them now. All the money's gone."

"How? There was plenty this morning. Has it been stolen?" The locked chest still stood beside the monk's chair.

"You know that promise you made to the women? Double pay if they delivered the new sails by a certain day?" I remembered. It had seemed like a good idea at the time.

"Which day did I say?" I guessed the answer from his smug expression.

"Today." He pointed to the bundles of cloth, heaped in the shadows. "They need weatherproofing, we've got the stuff for that, and the ropes will be ready when they're ready to raise, but..."

"We've got no masts." I took a deep breath. "How much do we have left?"

"Not enough." Brother Edmund kicked the chest. It slid along the floor with an empty clatter. I sat down on the pile of rags that served as my bed and put my head in my hands. Why had I been so stupid? There was only one thing for it.

"You said the accounts are up to date?"

"Down to the last sceat."

"Good. Gather everything together. We feast with Lord Elfgar tonight. Leif, come with us. You can discuss the amount you need for the masts with Edmund on the way. Don't forget to add enough for your expenses."

"I won't," he said with a grin.

There was a commotion as Petroc's wife appeared with the evening meal. It smelled like fish soup. Her daughter followed with a basket full of freshly baked bread.

"I saw the new ship arrive. Thought you would be feeding the crew, so I made extra."

"Well done. I'm off to the hall, with the captain and Brother Edmund. We'll eat there."

"In that case, there'll be plenty for everyone else." She smiled.

"Will you be back tonight?" Thurstan and the men gathered around the food.

"I don't know. If I'm not, you know what needs doing." Thurstan nodded, his mouth stuffed with bread.

"You're not going like that? Comb your hair at least." Petroc's wife pointed a dripping ladle at my head. I had been out all day on the water, and my hair was knotted and damp with spray.

"I'll comb it on the way," I said, halfway through the door.

"It might be an idea to change into something smarter," whispered Edmund as he lifted the empty chest. I considered the

84

idea and dismissed it. The savoury smell of the soup had reminded me of how hungry I was.

"No time, and it's not as though it's a formal feast." It would be more lavish than fish soup though. "Come on, we don't want to be late. Leif, tell your crew to join my men." The building was filling rapidly. Should I take a sample of one of the sails to show to Elfgar? No, the pieces had been sewn together and were too bulky to carry up the hill. "Let's go."

*

"The town is busy," commented Leif.

I had been concentrating on how to persuade Lord Elfgar to give us more money. I looked around. Leif was right. There were people everywhere and the closer we got to the hall, the more there were. I raised a hand to a merchant I recognised. He started to respond, then frowned and hurried on, his rich garments glowing in the light of torches. I grabbed Edmund's arm.

"What's the occasion?"

"I'm not sure. I heard the men have arrived to sail with you." With the pressure to prepare the ships, I had almost forgotten what it was for. Would they need to be trained? I hoped they were used to serving on ships. If they were here, departure must be close and we couldn't sail without masts. Elfgar would have to provide more money.

I watched the merchant disappear into the hall. A steady stream of other men followed, some with wives dressed in all their finery. I retreated to the side of the door. A guard pointed a spear in my direction. Brother Edmund opened his mouth. "Don't you dare," I told him.

"No, my lord. I'll take this to the clerk's office. I must report to the Bishop." He bustled away. Leif leaned against the wall with an amused smile.

"If we hurry, there may be some fish soup left."

I walked away and took in the view over the town and river. I found my comb and pulled it through my hair, it stuck fast.

"Let me." Leif pulled me away from the crowds. He cleared the tangles and tamed the wildness. I stood patiently as he brushed down my clothes. A scattering of wood shavings landed on the ground and dust drifted in the still air. "Take my cloak, it will hide that black mark on your tunic. What is it?" I didn't remember, tar? "Keep it hidden." He straightened my clothes and gave a cautious sniff. "When was the last time you washed?"

"I've been busy."

"Never mind, just don't get too close to anybody. Give your hands a good wash as you go in. You have every right to be there. Good luck." He pushed me towards the door.

"What about you?"

"It'll keep till tomorrow. And that fish soup smelt wonderful."

*

"I apologise for my rough clothing, my lord. I came to discuss the ships, I didn't realise there was a feast tonight."

"Didn't you receive my message?" asked Elfgar.

"I was out all day on the water. The first ship sails well and the rest are near to completion."

"Never mind. Take a seat." An attractive woman was sitting next to him. She moved along the bench and smiled at me. As I sat down, the smile turned to a frown, and she widened the gap between us. "I suppose you want more money," said Elfgar.

"A ship has arrived. I know the captain. He says there are masts available in Hantune; they will be expensive."

"We'll talk about it tomorrow. Brother Edmund has the details?"

"He has taken them to the head clerk." A servant poured wine into my cup, and I took a sip. It was good quality.

"Have some of this fish, it was fresh out of the sea this morning." Lord Elfgar pushed the dish in my direction.

"Thank you, I'll have some pork." To my certain knowledge, the fish had been hanging around on the quay for at least two days. I cut off a piece of the meat and chewed slowly. "Have you received any orders about what we are to do with the ships?"

"Yes, I was going to tell you tomorrow. You will be ready in time?"

"I think so, as long as we get the masts."

"All right, get on with it, you know I'll find the money. There's no point in preparing the ships if we can't sail them. Have you been told the destination?"

"Someone said something about Chester. Why there?"

"That's where the Mercian army is assembling." He looked around and lowered his voice. "They will travel towards York, burning Northumbria as they go. You are to take as many men as you can carry and transport them ready to attack from the north. Avoid the area of Northumbria north of the wall. We don't want to upset Osulf of Bebbanburg."

"He knows that, does he?" I asked.

"He has been paid enough."

I remembered the chest of silver that had travelled north with us last autumn after the truce and nodded. Had this year's campaign been planned all along? King Eadred had suggested it was because of Erik Haraldsson's refusal to surrender the throne of York. Had he known that Erik would not honour his oath?

"Lord Athelstan's ships will raid the east coast and transport men to the heart of the kingdom, my apologies, we mustn't call it a kingdom. Eadred rules over it now, or so he likes to think. The king's army will approach from the south. With York surrounded and the countryside devastated, Archbishop Wulfstan will have to abandon his support of Erik. If Bloodaxe decides to fight, we should have enough men to defeat him, once and for all."

Again, I would miss the fighting. "What do you want me to do with the ships when we've delivered the men?" Perhaps we were to keep watch for any attacks from Ireland.

"Do?" Elfgar looked at me in surprise "Don't worry about the ships. You… we… will accompany the men."

"You're coming as well?" I had assumed he would remain here in Exeter, or return to Winchester.

"Try and keep me away. I've got to recoup the money I've spent repairing these ships. Should make a decent profit out of it. You didn't think I'd let you grab all the plunder. Don't worry," Elfgar patted my arm, "There'll be plenty left for you. If you're lucky, you'll be a rich man after this adventure." He grinned and dug me in the ribs. I barely noticed. Yes, I wanted to be rich, but did I want to achieve it by destroying other men's homes and livelihoods?

"I need to get back," I told him. I had overheard some of the comments from my neighbour on the bench. "There's still a lot to do before we sail."

As I walked slowly back to the harbour, I thought about what we were to do. It didn't sound a very honourable way to fight. Then I brightened, perhaps Erik Bloodaxe would be forced into battle. I looked forward to meeting him in the shield wall. Maybe I would win glory at last. It would be something to tell Saewynn about when I returned. I hoped she, and the baby were well. Leif had seen her, perhaps he would have more news. I quickened my steps.

Chapter 13

"Edward, you're back as well. Did you enjoy the trip?" It seemed everyone had returned except Byrhtnoth.

"Yes, I'd forgotten how busy Winchester is. I saw the King and all the Ealdormen. I wish Byrhtnoth hadn't sent me back, I wanted to go to Exeter to see the ships. What will he do without me to look after him? That new boy won't know how to get the rust off his byrnie properly."

"He sent you back, so you could continue your training," said Wulfstan. "You want to become a proper warrior, don't you?"

"Of course, it's just that it's so boring here. Nothing ever happens."

"And thank God for that," muttered Wulfstan under his breath.

"Oh, I nearly forgot, someone sent you a message, my lady. I can't get used to calling you that."

"It doesn't matter," she smiled, "we're old friends, you're allowed to call me Saewynn. Who is the message from?" She could think of nobody in Winchester who would send her a message.

"Someone you met last year, in the north." She had met many people during the negotiations. Perhaps it was one of the women she had met over the campfires. "He seemed disappointed to hear you were married. Did my lord Byrhtnoth know you had a special friend in the camp? Oh dear, I shouldn't have said that."

"Just give me the message, Edward, I haven't got all day." Saewynn wasn't sure she wanted to hear from anyone she might have met up there. Was it that tall Irishman? Byrhtnoth had told her he had become friends with him on the journey to Bebbanburg. She wouldn't call him a friend. And hadn't he gone back to Ireland?

"He said he was happy to hear you were expecting a child." Saewynn frowned, had Byrhtnoth been telling all his friends the news? She supposed that's what men did. "He wished you well and said he would come to visit, perhaps after the birth."

"That was kind of him," said Saewynn, struggling to think of who would this strange man was. "Can you remember his name?"

"Yes, of course," said Edward, "it was Egferth."

"Egferth." She glanced at Wulfstan, who was staring horrified at Edward. Egbert had been at Winchester and Wulfstan had known. Panic flooded through her body. Egbert was coming. She had to escape. She picked up her skirts and ran.

*

Wulfstan found her in the stables, her arms around the neck of Byrhtnoth's horse.

"Why did he send Thunor back?"

"What? Oh, Byrhtnoth will be sailing with the ships. He can't take the horse with him."

"You knew, didn't you? You knew Egbert was in Winchester. Why isn't he dead? Byrhtnoth said he would kill him. Why didn't he? Was there a fight?" She turned a tearstained face towards him. Is he injured? No, you would have brought him home. He can't be... I would have known."

"Byrhtnoth is fine, he's probably reached Exeter by now."

Wulfstan stepped forward, and Saewynn backed away, hiding behind the bulk of the horse's shoulder.

"Go away. Don't come near me. I thought I was safe. You betrayed me."

"I haven't betrayed you." Wulfstan pulled up a stool, and stretched out his leg with a sigh of relief. "It was impossible to get near him. Egbert was with the Archbishop, they had been in a meeting with the King. I knew you would worry if we told you that he had been seen. I didn't realise you were still so anxious."

"I thought I was over it." Saewynn gripped her damaged right hand in the other, to stop her body shaking. "With Byrhtnoth here, I wasn't afraid anymore - I knew he would protect me. Now he's gone, and I don't know what to do. I was so honoured that he left me in charge. I thought I could cope, but I can't. What use am I? I can't even hold a knife to protect myself, much less others, and now with the child... Sometimes, I wish it hadn't happened. We shouldn't have married, I'm no help to him at all."

"And you think I am? I was in despair after my leg was injured, I still am at times, but Byrhtnoth stood by me."

"But you're useful, you look after the village, organise the crops and the animals."

"So are you. You are learning to run the hall, supervise the women, most of them, you'll never take over the kitchen from Hild." He smiled. "More significantly, you are carrying his child, the most important job of all. I know you would prefer to be out there fighting, but for now, you can't. That's why Byrhtnoth sent most of the men back here, to keep you safe. Even Thunor's here to protect you."

The horse pricked his ears at the mention of his name, and Saewynn stroked the smooth black coat.

"If you worry about defending yourself, and the child, there's no need. That's why he sent Aelf from Winchester to help. Like you, she can fight, and she's not a man. You can trust her."

"Can I? Go away, I want to be alone."

*

The next day, Saewynn followed the sounds of shouting to the training area. It appeared every man in the village had gathered

91

to watch the fighting woman in action. She sent the idle servants back to their duties and joined Godric by the fence.

"Is she any good?" she asked.

"See for yourself," he said, not taking his eyes from the combat. Aelf was fighting one of the boys who had been training for a few years and was nearly ready to join the men. Aelf might have been another man. She was dressed as she had been when she arrived. She had discarded her heavy tunic and wore a dirty linen shirt, held in place with a broad leather belt. Her shoulder length hair was tied tightly back. There was not an ounce of fat on her slender frame, and her corded muscle bunched when she swung the heavy wooden sword as if it was a feather. Saewynn noticed the long slender legs, there were muscles hidden beneath the well-worn trousers and leg bindings. Any man might be distracted by them, she thought, before becoming engrossed in the fight.

Finally, the boy was disarmed. Aelf helped him to his feet, explaining what he had done wrong and correcting the angle of his shield. By the time she had clapped him on the back and dismissed him, he was smiling.

"She's a good teacher," she admitted to Godric.

"But how long would she last in a fight with a real man?"

"Why don't you have a go?" Saewynn wondered if he had heard about Aelf's fight with Byrhtnoth.

Godric was dubious. "I wouldn't want to hurt her."

"Aelf!" Saewynn shouted across the ring. "Someone thinks you need a real man." She pointed at Godric.

"Oh?" Aelf surveyed the cheering audience. "Are there any here?" Ignoring the remarks that were hurled in her direction, she walked across to Saewynn. "Good morning, my lady. Is this the best you've got?"

"Apart from my husband," said Saewynn, "and he's not here." She pushed Godric onto the hard-packed ground of the training ring. He paused, then walked forward to pick up the abandoned sword. He raised it to the crowd, and someone shouted suggestions as to what he should do with it. Saewynn apologised to Aelf for the language.

"I've heard a lot worse." She ran on light feet towards Godric. His back was towards her, and a powerful swing of Aelf's sword across his rump sent him sprawling in the dust.

"That's cheating."

"Does your enemy always wait until you are ready?" A flurry of blows sent him shuffling back across the ground. Aelf scooped up the shield and threw it at Godric. He ducked, and the audience scattered as the shield skated along the ground. By the time he had picked it up, she was on him. He crouched beneath the storm of blows. Aelf retreated to the centre of the ring and beckoned him forward. He followed, and when he was in range, she jumped high into the air, swung her leg and kicked him hard in the stomach. Gasping, he folded, and Aelf tapped him on the top of the head with the flat of her sword. If she had been in earnest, he would have been dead. As it was, he sprawled motionless in the dust. He hadn't landed a blow.

She acknowledged the cheers with a wave of the hand, before strolling back to Saewynn.

"Satisfied?"

"Very." Now she understood why Byrhtnoth had lost his fight. How humiliated he must have been. "Ale?" She held up a jug.

"Just a sip," Aelf took it and tipped some down her throat. She wasn't even out of breath. "I don't want it to slow me down." They watched as friends dragged Godric upright and propped him against the fence. "I'll take him some of this." She raised the jug.

Saewynn nodded. "I've got things to do. Enjoy the morning. Find me later. We need to talk."

"I will." Without another word, she carried the jug across to Godric and held his head while he drunk. Soon they were chatting like old friends.

*

Saewynn leaned against the paddock fence. The grass was growing fast. Most of the horses had been sent to the meadows but the riding horses were kept here, close to the village. Thunor's coat shone in the spring sunshine. He had been led home from Winchester; even Edward was afraid to ride him. Byrhtnoth would want him in peak condition if he returned before the men went north. She frowned, the horse needed proper exercise, and she was the one person he allowed on his back apart from Byrhtnoth, and he only tolerated him.

"He's a beautiful animal."

"He is. Do you know much about horses?" Saewynn asked Aelf.

"Nothing. I'd never been on one until a few days ago," Aelf rubbed her backside and grimaced. "I know power when I see it, though."

"The experience didn't stop you fighting. How do you manage to jump so high and kick like that?"

"Practice. Aim a little lower, and you don't even need to hit the man over the head."

"I know. I did it to Byrhtnoth once." Aelf's eyebrows rose. "Accidentally, and it was a long time ago."

"No long-term damage then?" Aelf's eyes shifted to Saewynn's thickening waist.

"None at all." Saewynn laughed.

"Now, there's a decent pair." Saewynn turned to see Thunor approaching. He rushed towards the fence, stopping abruptly and shaking his head, ears laid back and eyes rolling. Aelf stepped back in alarm.

"He likes scaring people. Don't you, boy?" Saewynn found a shrivelled apple and offered it to the horse. "Thunor is Byrhtnoth's horse." Aelf moved out of his range.

"And is his master similarly endowed?"

"Um, not quite." Saewynn blushed. "Although he is a big man."

"I know, he nearly broke my ribs." Aelf noticed Saewynn's annoyed expression. "When we were fighting, nothing else."

The conversation had gone far enough. Saewynn turned back to Thunor. Did she dare? She climbed up onto the fence.

"Warn me if you see Wulfstan coming. Byrhtnoth said I wasn't to do this." She wasn't wearing her new glove, so she dug her twisted hand into the horse's thick mane, then pulled herself up onto its back with the other. Thunor stood still as a statue, muscles twitching beneath the smooth coat. She leaned forward, "Behave, we have a visitor."

Thunor tossed his head, then proceeded in a sedate walk across the paddock. "Thank you," she whispered. It felt good to be on a horse again. She urged him forward and he broke into a trot. They made a circuit of the paddock and Saewynn realised how long it was since she had ridden. Thunor's back was wide, and her legs ached. Was she damaging the baby? The women had told her there was no danger, although they had no experience of a horse like this. She brought him back to where they had started. Thunor waited as she disentangled the coarse hair from her fist, then she stepped off onto the top rung of the wooden fence. Once she would have jumped to the ground. Aelf noticed her hesitation, stepped forward and lifted her down.

"Thank you." Saewynn smoothed down her rucked-up skirts. Thunor moved away, searching for fresh grass.

"How did you do that?" Aelf's eyes moved from Saewynn to the horse and back again. "He must be gentler than he appears."

"He's not. If you get too close, he'd probably kill you." Saewynn smirked. There was one thing she could do better than the other woman. She took a deep breath. "Do you think that I can learn to fight again? I don't know if the device Wulfstan brought will make a difference."

"It might help you to hold a shield, but you will have to use your left hand to hold a weapon. Byrhtnoth said you used to be good."

"I wasn't bad, although not as good as you."

"It will come back. Last night, at the meal, you used your left hand to cut the meat. You've made a start."

"I suppose I must have." She hadn't thought about it before. She focused so much on not being able to use her right hand that she hadn't noticed how much she now used her left.

"Let's go back to the hall and experiment," suggested Aelf.

"There will be people, I don't want to..." what? Make a fool of herself?

"We can use the chamber, we won't need much space. If it works, we'll find somewhere private outside to practice."

"It might," said Saewynn has they walked back to the hall. "We'll make it work."

Part III: Early Summer

Chapter 14

At last I was able to escape the land and all its problems. God willing the voyage would be calm, and soon we would join the army in the north. The sun shone, and with the breeze at our backs, we flew across the water, leaving a creamy wake that dissipated into the scattered white tops of small waves. The sail flapped. I checked the position of the other ships and adjusted the steering oar. It was easy enough to follow the leading boat, with Lord Elfgar on board. To my surprise, he was at home on the sea. He stood beside the local man steering the ship, his gestures suggesting that he was asking questions about the passing land.

  Behind us, Petroc was at the helm of his ship. It was slow but holding its own with the others, at least for now. I hoped it wasn't going to delay us. Our mast groaned under pressure and I shouted at the crew to slacken a rope. We had stopped not far along the coast for final adjustments and were now heading for the far western corner of England, before turning north. There had been much time spent studying charts and discussing the characteristics of the coast. The cliffs were taller and more rugged and waves hit us with more force. A lookout stood in the prow, staring intently ahead. He raised an arm, and I pulled on the oar, following the others away from the dangerous waters. Rocks could split a ship like a seax through butter. I didn't want to lose any, not after all our work.

When darkness arrived, we found a sheltered cove and beached the ships. Although the sea air had given us a thirst, I rationed the ale. Who knew when we would get more? As the men prepared to sleep, I took a final stroll around the ships, to check how they had stood up to the journey. I paid particular attention to Petroc's ship. Was there any way to increase its speed? I studied the hull, in particular, the new wood that had replaced the rotten planks. As far as I could tell, it was sound.

I leaned against the side of the ship, listening to the gentle lapping of the waves, the murmur of voices as people settled for the night. Something was knocking. A loose rope blowing in the wind, or the spear butt of a guard tapping the deck? I knew it would keep me awake until I found out. The guard was alert and helped me on board the ship. I walked along the centre of it, stopping every few steps to listen. Chests of weapons were stacked at the stern. The tapping, quieter now and slower, was coming from one of the boxes. I knocked on the outside and received a feeble reply.

Shouting for Petroc, I heaved the top chest out of the way and raised the lid of the next. Scared eyes gleamed in the darkness and cramped lungs gasped in air.

"What's the problem?" Petroc squeezed in beside me, and the guard peered over his shoulder.

"We have a stowaway. It's your son."

*

"I can't spare a ship to send him back." Lord Elfgar stood over the boy, who had recovered enough to devour some bread. He crouched beside the campfire, trying to make himself invisible. "You're sure you didn't hide him there yourself?"

"Why would I do something like that? I don't want him here, any more than you do." Petroc aimed a fist at his son, who ducked with a well-practised motion. "If Byrhtnoth hadn't heard him, he would have died. Why did you do it, stupid boy?"

"I didn't want to stay behind with the children and old men. How did I know you would pile everything on top of my hiding place?" he whimpered.

"We can't leave him here." Elfgar surveyed the beach, shining dull gold in the light from our fire. "Although I'm tempted. Get some sleep, and we'll decide what to do in the morning."

Young Petroc soon made himself useful. He was agile enough to reach the very top of the mast, looking out for enemy ships. Not that we encountered any, only the occasional merchant that we stopped, slipping silently up beside them, then leaving them grateful we did nothing more than search them.

*

After patrolling the seas, the date for our meeting arrived, and we rowed up the Dee to the ancient city of Chester. The docks were busy. We recognised some of the trading vessels we had stopped during our voyage. Lord Elfgar ordered Petroc to restock the ships. We were running low on water, and more importantly, ale. Fresh food was also needed.

"Don't let the men stray too far from the harbour. I'll find out what's happening. We may need to move on quickly," said Elfgar.

I followed him through the bustling crowds. We were directed to the church of St Werburgh, where the leaders of the army were meeting. Instructions had been received from the King, and excitement flowed through the streets.

The original wooden church founded by Lady Ethelflaed, the Lady of the Mercians, and her husband Ethelred, was in the process of being rebuilt in the same red stone as the town walls. We pushed our way past the scaffolding and into the church. Guards stopped us and asked our business, allowing us through when told the Ealdorman of Essex had arrived. Elfgar joined the other men assembled before the altar where he exchanged greetings and was received the latest news. I recognised Lord

101

Ealhhelm of Mercia. The man in charge of the meeting would be the local Ealdorman, but it was Mercia who held the floor. Men argued and, from my position near the door, it was difficult to know what was going on.

"You managed to get the ships here on time?" I turned to find Elfhere at my side. He had managed to creep up on me again. It was something we had learnt as boys, and one of the few things at which he was better than me.

" What's all the arguing about? Some of them aren't happy."

"It's the instructions from King Eadred. They keep repeating the same things over and over and never agree. Now Elfgar has arrived they'll go through it all again. Let's get some air, it's too hot in here." I followed him outside. The stone walls concentrated the early summer heat, and the inside of the church had felt stuffy after the fresh sea breeze.

"What's the problem? Aren't the instructions clear?"

"Very clear." He brushed the dust off a block of stone in a patch of shade and sat down. "The plan hasn't changed. It's just that some people don't agree with it."

"Why not?" I leaned against a post that marked the position of some part of the new church.

"King Eadred is asking us to destroy everything: men, houses, crops. Everything," explained Elfhere.

"I heard that. Does the king think that by laying waste to the country, he will make peace? He can't kill everyone in Northumbria." I shook my head. "It's impossible."

"I know," agreed Elfhere. "Some, those from the south, are in favour. Those closer to the border, and that means Mercia, fear it will only stir things up, encourage attacks that my father will have to deal with."

"I can understand that. It's insane."

"Some wonder if Eadred is fit to rule." Elfhere lowered his voice "You're not at court much. He's getting worse."

"He didn't look well at Easter. He ate very little at the feast." I remembered the comments.

"He has problems with food. Chews until he's sucked out all the goodness, then spits out the remains." Elfhere frowned in disgust. "His grandfather, Alfred, was the same, they say, and still ruled well for many years. We need a king like him now. Why did Edmund have to die so young?" He studied his nails, then glanced up at me. "Was Erik behind that? I'd count this campaign a success if we manage to get rid of him. Do you know anything? Didn't you get blamed for the king's death?"

"That was thanks to your father and Lord Elfgar. I did wonder if either of them was involved. Elfgar had no reason to kill King Edmund, he had just married his daughter to him."

"Have you seen his other daughter? Weren't you in love with her at one time?"

"A long time ago."

"You must be sorry you married what's her name. Without the money and connections you might have got from marrying Lord Elfgar's daughter, you'll never achieve anything." Elfhere gave a pleased smirk. With difficulty, I stopped myself from hitting him.

"Perhaps you should marry Elfflaed," I suggested. "She once mentioned how handsome you were. Sorry, you aren't any more, are you? Never mind, I expect you'll find some woman to marry you if they're desperate enough."

Although we both knew that any woman would be glad to marry the son of an Ealdorman, whatever his appearance, he still remained sensitive about his ruined face. It had been his own fault; he should never have tried to rape my sister. If he had succeeded, it would have been more than his good looks he would have lost, and he knew it. His hand moved towards his sword. I folded my arms and grinned.

He had second thoughts, pretending to pull his tunic straight, then gave me a sly glance. "I heard some interesting news recently."

I shrugged my shoulders. "I imagine there is much news exchanged at a meeting such as this."

"Someone has spotted Egbert."

"Where?" This time it was my hand that reached for my weapon.

"York."

I considered the options. It was impossible to leave, to abandon Lord Elfgar and the men. I forced the blade back into its scabbard. We would head for York eventually. I prayed Egbert would still be there. I had vowed to kill him. Whether it was in battle, or otherwise, I would face him soon and he would die.

"Thank you. I hope this time your information is more reliable than what you told me in Winchester." Men poured from the doors of the church "I think the meeting is over, I must go."

I walked away to meet Lord Elfgar.

Chapter 15

Everyone was suffering from the effects of the feast the night before. Although there had been little meat, there had been plenty to drink. I clung to the steering oar and vowed, yet again, not to drink so much mead. At least the river was flat. There was not a breath of wind, and the heat was unnatural. Early as it was, the rowers were sweating. Perhaps there would be more wind when we reached the open sea.

There were rumours of a storm, but the sky was cloudless. We were to travel north, to another river. The ships would sail upstream, as far as they would go, then land the men. We were to cut off any retreat by Erik Haraldsson, become the grindstone to the mill that would be York. We were to destroy everything in our path. Were Godric and the others marching north or had they already arrived, waiting to attack?

Someone shouted.

"Sandbanks ahead, slow down and keep an eye open." Lord Elfgar had found a local guide. He said the sands stretched all the way along the coast. They were dangerous, boats trapped by them disappearing without a trace. I thought it a story he told to justify his job.

It was close to noon when we escaped from the mouth of the Dee. I handed over the steering to Thurstan and took a seat at one of the oars. We appeared motionless, suspended between the sky and the sea, only the other ships hanging nearby. Sometimes the colour of the water changed as we passed the mouth of another river. The guide said he was able to tell one river from the next, by the colour and the debris suspended in it. It just looked like sand to me, the same as that on the long beach that was the only sign that land existed.

After a mouthful of bread and cheese and a large cup of ale, I found a place to lie down. The murmur of voices and the regular swish of the oars soon sent me to sleep.

I woke to a splash of water on my face; had someone missed their stroke? The view was unchanged, apart from a dark smudge on the northern horizon. It looked like a cloud, although the guide identified it as mountains. We were close to our destination. I took back the steering oar as land closed around us. The sea wrinkled at a sudden, welcome breeze.

"Should we put up the sails?" There was another puff of wind, stronger this time. The ships rocked. The wind blew from the land, and we watched as small clouds detached themselves from the peaks of the mountains. Sails would take us in the wrong direction, and instructions were given to row faster. Drops of rain fell on the deck, disappearing as soon as they hit the hot boards. Someone pointed to the river mouth ahead. The rain fell faster, and I shivered as clouds obscured the sun. The guide warned that the current was taking us in the direction of dangerous sands.

Instructions were given to raise the sails, abandon our efforts to reach the haven of the river mouth, and ride out the shower in deeper water. The crews leapt into action and oars were hurriedly drawn on board. Sailors hauled on ropes as the dusty sails rose, flapping in the boisterous wind. I heaved on the steering oar, and the ship swung around. A wave washed over the side. As the wind caught the sail, I told the crew to secure any loose articles on the deck. The ship resisted, then we leapt forwards towards the open sea. Behind, Petroc's ship wallowed, then the wind hit the sail, and he followed the rest of us.

"Stay together!" The words were snatched by the wind, which increased by the second. As we passed the enclosing arms of the bay, there was a flash, followed by a rumble of thunder. Had it hit one of the ships? Impossible to tell as the view became obscured by a solid sheet of rain. Then the wind and waves took us in their powerful grip.

*

I clung to the steering oar until my hands bled. They had long lost all feeling. Only the fact that I still gripped the wood proved my arms had not been torn from their sockets. I was drenched to the skin, and so cold that the previous hot weather seemed like a dream.

"A ship." They were the first words I had heard above the howling wind. I followed the pointing arm and spotted one of the other vessels. The rain slackened, and I saw lord Elfgar crouched in the bow. The curtain of rain closed again. Perhaps the others were close. I pushed wet hair from my eyes and peered through the gloom. Having survived the storm, I didn't want to die from a collision. I couldn't spot any empty spaces on the benches, although it was difficult to tell with the fighting men on board. White faces stared back at me as if surprised to be still alive. Someone stood and was knocked off his feet as the ship tilted. Water sloshed from side to side in the belly of the ship. I shouted to the crew to start bailing.

"Drop the sail until we find out where we are. Unship the oars." The crew struggled with sodden ropes. By the time the sail, heavy with water, was lowered, I had spotted two more ships. The rain slowed and was no longer hurled hard into our faces. Above us, clouds churned. It wasn't over yet.

"Where's Petroc's ship?" shouted Thurstan. This was what I had feared. Was it capable of coping with such bad weather? I passed him the steering oar.

"Keep us close to the others." I forced open my cramped hands and inspected the blistered palms. I dipped them in the seawater that lapped at my feet and then stretched to ease my aching back. Something moved against the turbulent sea. A bird struggling against the wind? Someone waving? It grew closer. It was a ship, half submerged. The bow and stern were above the waves and only the frantic rowers kept it from sinking. The sail hung in tatters, whipped by the wind.

"Over there." I pointed. Others saw the stricken ship and altered course. Could we reach it in time? How many were on board? Thirty? More, with the fighting men. As we drew closer, I made out Petroc's frantic face. The prow dipped. I held my breath until it rose again. Where was the boy? I scanned the row of terrified faces. Then I saw him, clinging to the top of the mast. Had they sent him up to escape the sea, or to search the horizon for the rest of us?

The mast swung. The boy's clothes flapped as the wind changed direction. I realised the danger and waved at him to get down. Oblivious, he loosened his grip to wave back. I caught the flash of a triumphant grin before a rogue wave caught the ship. The mast dropped. When it sprang back, the boy was gone.

I searched the white froth of the sea and spotted his head. He was being swept away. A shout came from the sinking ship. Petroc leaped from the bucking deck into the dark water.

"His father will save him," I said, with relief. Petroc was used to the sea, he would know what to do.

"He can't swim." One of my crew watched his friend in horror. Already, Petroc was struggling. His head disappeared, and then he bobbed up, further from his son than before. I ran and grabbed a spare oar. We were too far away to reach them. I lifted it to my shoulder, braced my legs, and measured the distance. I cast it towards the two bodies in the sea, aiming for the gap between. It was much heavier than a spear and badly balanced, but my aim was true. The wood plunged into the churning water, and I had time for a brief prayer before it bobbed up close to the boy.

I called for a rope, stripped off my cloak and anything else that would drag me down. I wore no shoes; bare feet are the safest footwear on a ship. I tied the end of the proffered rope around my waist and tugged to check it was firm.

"Give me plenty of slack." The man was used to ropes and played out a length. I nodded, climbed onto the edge of the ship, took a deep breath and, before I changed my mind, dived into the dark sea.

I was cold already, but this was far worse, the shock of the icy water drove the air from my lungs. I struggled to the surface, spluttering. No one could survive for long in this. I headed towards the oar. The sea was much rougher than it had appeared from the comparative safety of the deck. The heavy wood twisted and spun like a wisp of hay in a puddle. I ducked as it swung towards me and caught hold as it passed. The rope dragged at my body as I steadied the oar.

The boy was not far away. I reached for his hand. He drifted away. I let go and kicked my way towards him. He had done well to keep afloat, but now he was ready to give up. He hung in the water, and a wave tossed him high. I rose with it and grabbed him before he sank. Although small, his weight would soon drag me down. The rope tugged me back towards the ship, the oar was now an obstruction. Tucking the boy beneath my arm, I lurched towards it.

My fingers touched and slid off. I kicked hard and found a grip, then lifted the boy, and threw him over it. I thumped his back, more to keep him in place than anything else. Water spewed from his mouth, and he lifted his head. Scared eyes met mine.

"Wait there. I'll find your father." I scanned the churning waters. I didn't want to leave the safety of the oar. A wave washed over it, my weight was forcing it below the surface. Where was he? The waves rose, and I spotted a waving arm.

I let go of the oar. My ship was close, someone would retrieve the boy. By the time I reached Petroc, I knew he was done for. His hands flapped ineffectively at the surface of the water. With every wave, he drifted further away. Beyond was nothing, no land, just open sea. The only safety was the ship behind us.

I had reached the limit of the taut rope. I glanced back. It quivered in the flying spray. The sailor leaned over the ship's side, his hands clamped around the rope. A companion hung on to his legs. Thurston urged the rowers faster. I shouted to the man to drop the rope. He shook his head and pointed. Petroc was even further away. From the expression of resignation on his face, he had given up.

"The boy?" I read the question on his lips, rather than heard it above the howling wind. Was it getting louder?

"Safe," I replied. Petroc nodded and glanced up at the sky as if to check the weather. His eyes closed. The next wave filled his mouth, and he sank below the surface.

I shouted his name. I dived, down into the darkness, below the waves, where it was quiet. The sea was taking him. I tried, again and again, then, when I had no strength left, they dragged me back, pulling me onto the deck like a dead codfish. I lay still, exhausted.

Eventually, someone cut the rope and sat me up. A cup of ale was thrust into my hand. Although my stomach was already heavy with liquid, it tasted good. It wasn't so nice when I vomited everything up over the side.

"Where's the boy?" I asked. Someone pointed down the ship. I stood, legs shaking and made it to where he sat, wrapped in a blanket that somehow had been kept dry. He held a chunk of bread and glanced up hopefully.

I dropped down beside him, shivering. Thurstan put my cloak around my shoulders. It was wet but kept off the wind.

"I'm sorry," I told him. "I couldn't save your father."

Chapter 16

Elfgar's ship slowly approached Petroc's stricken vessel.

"Do we let it go, or try and save it?" shouted Elfgar across the gap of churning sea.

"Bring it closer. I'll check the damage." A few strokes of the oars and I was close enough to jump across. The ship listed under my weight and I moved towards the centre. My shoulder ached, and I rubbed it as I edged towards the water welling up between the boards. It was where the original leak had been.

"How was it repaired?" I asked. One of the men told me that the ship had been beached and a new section of wood nailed to the hull. I remembered seeing the repair on the beach, the night we had found Young Petroc. It had been low down, nearly buried in the sand. There was no way to reach it, and it would be impossible to make a repair from inside the ship with the sea pouring in. "Keep bailing for now," I told the tired men.

Petroc had worked hard to get the ship ready in time. Had he known the repair would not hold? No one could have had predicted a storm like the one we had just experienced.

"Is there space for these men on the other ships?" I asked Elfgar.

"There are too many men packed in already. Any more and the oarsmen will be unable to row."

"There's nothing else to do, we've got to keep it afloat." I scanned the sky. "Night is falling. Maybe we can make repairs tomorrow." I threw a rope. There was another twinge from my shoulder. I ignored it. "Get a ship either side and fix it between them. Keep the others close, in case we need support. We can't afford to lose three ships."

I helped tie the ships together before clambering across to report to Elfgar. "We'll keep men on board to bail her out. It will give them something to do, though they're fighting a losing battle. The rest can take refuge on the supporting ships, to take over when the others tire. Make sure someone has a knife ready to cut the ropes if she threatens to sink and take the support vessels with her. Where's that guide? Does he have any ideas of where we are?" We waited for him to be found. If it had been me, I would have kept well hidden. Luckily there were few places to hide, and he was soon dragged forward.

"I'm sorry, my lord. I was not to know a storm would arrive so fast."

"You know these waters," said Lord Elfgar. "Where are we?"

"We were blown west, my lord."

"I think we can work that out. Are we close to land?"

"I don't know." Elfgar raised a fist, and the guide flinched. "We might be close to Man, or we could have been blown as far as Ireland. These waters are enclosed by many lands, we can't be far from anywhere."

"Not much help if they aren't friendly," I said.

"It's possible we have passed all land, into the great ocean beyond," added the guide.

"And?" Elfgar glared at the man. He shrugged, and Elfgar waved him away in disgust.

"Should we restrict the rations?" I asked him quietly.

"Yes. Hopefully, we can find our way back in the morning," said Elfgar.

112

"I pray so, my lord." Would a prayer to St Petroc be appropriate? "What if there are other ships out there?" The cloud-draped horizon had faded into the darkness.

"Tell the men no lights and as little noise as possible."

"Yes, my lord." I passed the word to the crew.

"Shoulder troubling you?" asked Elfgar. I realised I had been rubbing it.

"I think I hurt it throwing that oar," I said.

"I'm not surprised, I don't know how you did it." Neither did I. "Go and get some sleep. You've done enough today."

Not everything. I returned to my ship and explained what was happening, telling the men to keep weapons to hand. Then I went to find the boy.

It had finally sunk in that his father was dead. He lay curled up in a small space at the back of the ship, sobbing silently. I picked him up and wedged myself against the sternpost. I held him against my chest, and we talked about his father. He cried harder when I told him that his father had given his life to save him.

"He wasn't able to swim. Why did he jump into the water like that?" he sobbed.

"Because he loved you. People will do anything to protect their family. That is your job now, to care for your mother and your sisters."

"Grandfather will help."

"Yes, your grandfather will help." How could I explain to the old man when I brought back his fatherless grandson? "Sleep now. Things won't seem so bad in the morning." I tightened my arms around him, and eventually, he relaxed. It was good to have someone to hold.

*

"There's the sun."

"Not quite." I rubbed my eyes. The mast was silhouetted against a golden haze, the sun was not yet above the horizon.

"Now we know which way to go." The boy wriggled out from beneath my cloak. I shivered at the sudden removal of warmth.

I had spent most of the night watching the stars, so I already knew our direction.

"Is your father's ship still afloat? Go and check. He ran lightly along the deck, disturbing some sleepers and earning a curse or two. I rose cautiously, testing my aching limbs. My shoulder should mend in a few days.

"It hasn't sunk." His face dropped. "It isn't my father's ship anymore."

"No, it isn't. It's yours now if Lord Elfgar agrees." I would make sure he did. Petroc had died in his service, his son deserved a ship with which to make a living. "Let's go and find out what needs to be done to make it safe." If we were unable to salvage it, not everyone would make it home.

"Some bread, my lord?" said one of the sailors. "Afraid it's a bit damp."

"Better than dry. Anything to drink?"

"There's some ale in that barrel." I identified the object that had been digging into my back all night. If I'd realised what it was, it would be empty by now.

"I remembered." The boy came hurtling back, waking a few more sailors. I poured a jug of ale and passed it along to the men. "Yesterday, when I was up the mast, before..." the excitement drained from his face, "during the storm, I saw mountains. They must have been the ones we saw before the wind got up."

"Which way?" I took a mouthful of ale. Seawater had breached the barrel and I spat it out. We must check all the supplies. The boy pointed, then frowned.

"I don't know which way the ship was pointing, I'm sorry." He sat down, picked up my piece of bread and gnawed at it.

"What do you remember? Was it in front, or behind? To the left, or right?" He closed his eyes, visualising what had happened.

"Behind, it was behind us." If he was right, it meant it would be a simple voyage back.

"It's a start. Let's go and repair your ship."

114

Chapter 17

"If we can't get it out of the water to make repairs," I crouched beside the leak, ankle deep in water, "it needs a patch. Pass me that sheepskin," I told a man nearby.

"Oi, that's my bed," his companion complained.

"I'll get you a new one." I measured it against the crack. His neighbours would be grateful to lose it, the stink was unbearable. At least the grease in the fleece would waterproof it. "Fetch some rope." I made holes in the corners of the skin with my knife and threaded the rope through them.

"How do we get it into position?" asked Thurstan.

"I'll take it down." I stripped off my clothes. They were still damp, but there was no point in soaking them again. "Slacken the ropes from one of the supporting ships, just this end." I watched until the gap was big enough for me to slip through. "Add a block to stop it closing, I don't want my head crushed when I come up. Make another gap, on the other side, wide enough to hand up the ropes." I watched as it was done, planning my future moves. "The skin needs to be held against the hull. Find a belt, several belts. Join them until they are long enough to go around the hull."

It was time. I stared down into the dark sliver of water. It had been one thing to dive in without thinking to save a life, quite another to enter knowing how the cold would chill me to the bone. A breeze touched my naked back. I shivered and handed the sheepskin to one of the watching men. "I'll check the damage first. Hand it to me when I'm ready."

I climbed over the side and lowered myself into the cold water. I took a deep breath and swam down the curve of the ship until I reached the problem plank. It was impossible to see anything in the darkness, so I closed my eyes and used my fingers to find the original repair. It was still attached, with one end loose, ripped apart by the sea. I pushed upwards, and the loose section slipped into place. I heard swearing as someone above received a face full of water.

I surfaced and took the sheepskin. "Hold the ropes. Keep well apart. Two this side. I'll bring the others up the other side." The ship rocked as they moved. I watched the block of wood that kept my escape route open. I noted the position of the men and tried to drag the sheepskin down. It refused to sink until I braced myself against the hull and pulled hard. A good sign, air trapped in the fleece would force it against the underside of the ship.

My breath was nearly exhausted by the time I returned to the faulty plank. I thrust the fleece against it and tugged the pair of ropes to the far side of the ship. I raised one hand, and someone took the strings. Lungs burning, I followed them to the surface. The gap widened. The block dropped. I took a desperate breath and sank before the ships clashed together.

Heart pounding, I located the sheepskin, arranging it so that it covered the hole. I banged on the wooden hull, and the ropes tightened. With relief, I found the gap where I had entered the water still open. I hung from the side, taking gulps of air until I was able to speak.

"I'll check it's in place. Have the strap ready when I come up again." I dived, patted the sheepskin, and made an adjustment to one of the ropes. "It looks all right," I gasped. "Has the water stopped rising?" Someone confirmed that it was now stable. "Good. Tie off the ropes, keeping them taut. Where's that strap?"

A tangle of leather dropped on my head and I pushed it back over the side. "Just one end."

An apology and Thurstan handed me the buckle end of the strap. I nodded and swam down, the leather coiling after me like a strange snake. I positioned the broadest piece across the centre of the sheepskin, a loose nail acting as a convenient anchor and hesitated under the narrow gap. The wedge had been replaced. I kicked upwards and placed the end in an exploring hand. Immediately the strap drew tight around the hull. It was done.

I checked the edges of the patch as I passed. Back onboard Thurstan put my cloak around my shoulders while I inspected the ropes.

"It will hold for a while. I don't know how long. Keep bailing and put someone to watch the repair. We must get moving." I dressed and returned to my own ship where I asked if anyone had worked out where we were.

Someone pointed to the mast. The boy was clinging to the top. I wanted to shout at him to get down but made do with asking what he saw.

"There's more cloud. That way." He pointed west.

I hoped it wasn't another storm, although a bit of wind would be useful. Did we have a spare sail for the damaged ship?

The boy spoke to the guide, who had positioned himself at the bottom of the mast. "It might be land."

Elfgar joined me from his own ship. "We don't want land in that direction. Do you know what land?" he shouted at the guide.

"From what the boy says, it might be Man."

"Then at least we know where we are. Ready the ships. You've all had a good rest, return to your oars," said Elfgar.

"We might need the sails after all," I said. "The boy has spotted masts. How far," I shouted up to him.

"A long way, close to the land. Are they coming to help us?"

"Only to death or slavery," I said to Elfgar in a low voice. He nodded. "You can come down. We know enough."

"Do we leave the damaged ship?" asked Elfgar.

"The men can still row. If we get enough wind, we can try towing it. Perhaps they haven't noticed us yet."

"If they haven't already, they will if we set sails."

"I know. Get the ships separated," I shouted as I regained my place at the steering oar. "Head east and keep your weapons handy. Keep the ships together. If an attack comes, it's every man for himself." The boy jumped the final few feet from the mast and raced to my side. Elfgar had already crossed back to his own ship.

"Wait, they can't leave me behind," said the boy in dismay. The gap was already too far for him to jump back to his own, doomed ship.

"You were too slow. You'll have to stay with me. I need some help. Did you steer your father's ship?" He turned away from the increasing chasm.

"Sometimes, when it was calm."

"Good, you can help Thurstan while I take a turn on the benches. I need some exercise to warm me up. Have you found something to eat?"

I would have given anything for a hot meal, but it would have to wait. I located my axe and propped it nearby. It was better than a sword for fighting on ships. How long would my repair last? The ship was keeping up with the rest, for now and there were no strange ships in sight. I pulled on an oar and refused to acknowledge the gathering clouds.

Chapter 18

"Sails!" The lookout pointed. It must be the ships we had spotted earlier.

"How many?" I asked.

"Two." I searched the sea ahead. Was that land on the horizon or just more cloud? If it was land, which land? I studied the repaired ship carefully. It wasn't falling behind, yet. We had removed as many of the extra men as possible to lighten the load, although they hindered the rowers on the other ships. If we were to outrun the approaching ships, we needed to use the sails, but the one on Petroc's ship had been shredded by the storm.

I hailed Elfgar and explained the problem.

"The ships may be friendly. They may be coming to help," he said.

"I don't think so. They are eager to catch us, but we might escape using the sails. The men are too tired to row for much longer."

"If we abandon the useless ship, it will divert the enemy while the rest of us escape."

"No!" I hadn't noticed Young Petroc was listening.

"The boy's right," I said. "I didn't come all this way to leave men to die, or worse. We started with five ships. We will finish with five ships. I'll tow the damaged ship and hope our own sail is sufficient for both. We might escape, if not..." Our ships were full of fighting men. Two against two were good odds. A plan started to form in my mind. "You flee with the other ships. We'll follow. Find a decent place to land, and we'll meet you later."

It didn't take long for Elfgar to make a decision. He nodded and gave instructions to raise the sails. As the gap between the ships widened, he shouted, "Good luck."

We would need it. I surveyed the nervous men resting on their oars. "Bring us close to the other ship, then prepare to raise the sail."

We manoeuvred until our stern was close to the other's bow, and we were shackled together. The rear of our vessel dipped with the extra weight. I exchanged a few words with the helmsman of the following ship. He was a good man, he would know what to do.

As we waited, I became aware of the deck rolling beneath me. My cloak flapped in the increasing wind, and the boy's hair streamed like a flag at the top of the mast. The boy! I should have sent him away with the other ships. Already they were far away. I called him back to the deck. He had hidden in one of the chests once, perhaps he could do it again.

"How far away are the enemy ships?" I didn't really need to be told. Already they were visible from the deck, and they were definitely not friendly.

The two dragon boats slid through the water with barely a ripple. They raced towards us like wolves homing in on an injured stag. Our sail filled with wind, accompanied by a spatter of rain. The mast groaned, and the vessel shook. The rope connecting us to the ship behind went taut. I prayed it would not break. The sudden jerk knocked me off my feet. I pulled myself upright and clung to the steering oar. Water surged past the boards of the hull, and the ship behind rode our wake. I handed the steering oar to Thurstan and explained my plan.

For a while, it seemed we would escape, but slowly the ships grew closer. Our own companions had disappeared, obscured by the squally rain. Standing at the stern, I watched the enemy come nearer. My grip tightened on the steering oar. Young Petroc crouched nearby. He had refused to hide. He wasn't stupid, and we both knew that if we were boarded, every chest would be plundered.

I gave him my seax. "If we lose the fight, use it. It is better to die than to suffer as a slave," I told him. He bit his lip and took it, then almost smiled as he admired the patterned blade.

Soon we would be within range of their spears, and I ducked down to make myself a smaller target. I was ashamed to act so cravenly, but must pretend to be a defenceless sailor. Petroc's ship was crammed with men, all waiting for my signal. To the approaching enemy, it would appear nearly empty. Would they attack there first? I returned my attention to my own ship. All eyes were fixed on me. My men crouched below the gunwales, clutching their shields. Spears lay beside them, and many had axes ready; my own lay close at hand.

Now the ships were close enough to make a rough count of their men. I gave a grim smile - we outnumbered them. Even better, one ship held back, leaving the other to make the first contact. I could see the captain, standing beside the steersman. He wore a helmet, but no byrnie. He drew a sword. I held up two fingers to Thurstan. He nodded. I would have cast the first spear myself, but my shoulder still ached, I couldn't rely on making an accurate throw.

I stood upright, Thurstan with me.

"Shieldwall!" I yelled, and every man rose together, shields locked. A quick glance showed the men on the following ship had done the same. A hail of spears sped across the narrowing strip of water. The captain was the first to fall, the force of Thurstan's spear through his chest swept him from his position into the sea beyond. I signalled one of the sailors. The angle of our sail altered and I pulled hard on the oar. Our ship swung towards the enemy. I had hoped to pull alongside and board them, but the trailing vessel upset our balance. We swung too far until our prow pointed directly at the enemy ship. I braced myself for the impact.

There was a tremendous crash, and wood splintered. There was another bang as the ship behind hit our stern. Luckily the turn we had made had put us at a different angle. It slid past before jerking to a stop. Should I cut the rope between us? No, we were safer attached. I told them to watch out for the other enemy ship. Where had it gone?

I looked back towards the bows. Our deck still seemed to be in one piece. The broken shafts of wood were from the enemy's ship. We were embedded in its side. Already my men were clambering through the wreckage to attack the enemy sailors. I resisted the urge to join them. An axe rose, then fell, biting deep into a shoulder, blood fountaining into the air. Thurstan attacked a man with long dark hair. Another enemy ran to assist. Before I could shout a warning, Thurstan spotted him. His axe struck, and a hand clutching a knife spun into the water. Thurstan swung back, ripped open the first man's belly. His guts slithered to the flooded deck.

Something tugged at my leg. Young Petroc pointed to the sloping deck of our own ship. In the excitement, I hadn't realised that the hostile ship was sinking. Its mast tilted dangerously. If we didn't break loose, it would drag us with it. I shouted a warning. Sailors rushed to the ropes.

The attackers were now more interested in escaping the sinking ship than fighting back. I screamed a warning to Thurstan. He glanced back, nodded and grabbed one of the younger men and pushed him back towards our ship.

The men who had been unable to join the attack rushed back to the oars. I ordered the crew of Petroc's ship to do the same, sending more men across to help. If it came to the worst, we might all have to take refuge there.

The second enemy ship was circling some distance away. Men from the sinking ship attempted to reach it, but most sank into the cold dark water, never to reappear.

I held my breath as my men laboured at the oars. I prepared to sever the bond between our two ships as the deck tilted further. Then with a scream of tortured wood and a roar of churning water, our ship was released, nearly pitching me from my place. I felt the boy's grip around my ankle as I righted myself. I smiled my thanks.

The attacker's mast tipped, and the sail spread across the surface. Could it be retrieved? Before I could even suggest it, the dying ship carried it down beneath the waves. Soon all that remained were a few shards of wood, soon swept away. A pity, we could have done with the extra ship. The second ship was beating a hasty retreat.

"Any casualties?" I asked Thurstan.

"None to speak of." He wiped his face with his sleeve and frowned at the blood.

"I don't think it's yours. You fought well." I told him.

"Thank you. They were so surprised by our sudden appearance, they forgot what they were there for until it was too late."

"Hope we haven't done much damage to the ship. Have you checked the bows?" I asked.

"Not yet, I need some ale before I do anything else."

"You've earned it. I'll do it myself. Petroc? Can you take over the steering until Thurstan's rested? Just keep heading east. We should catch up with the others soon. I told them not to go too far."

First, I checked the stern. There were a few scratches along the side, nothing serious. "Are you all right?" I asked one of the men in the ship behind.

"We're letting in a bit of water close to the patch. Nothing serious, it's under control."

"Perhaps the ropes have worked loose. I'll come and take a look later." I walked through the ship, congratulating the men on their

123

performance. "I don't think I've seen a shield wall formed so tidily, not even on land."

I broached a new barrel of ale and sent a jugful back to Thurstan. The men were soon relaxing around it. "Not too much. There may be more hostile ships about." I grinned as one of the younger men rushed towards the mast.

"We'll have to work on that manoeuvre," I told the sailor who had altered the sail at the vital moment.

"It was your fault, you pulled too hard on the steering oar."

"Probably. It worked out for the best though. Did I cause any damage?"

"Not to us. The prow doesn't look as pretty as it used to, but there's no water coming in, no more than usual." He shouted at a young sailor, not much more than a boy, to start bailing.

When I got to the bow, I wrapped an arm around the curving prow post and leaned over the side to inspect the damage. There had been a nice piece of carving I had liked but most of it had been sliced off. I would arrange for a replacement, once all this was over. I sat for a while, sipping a cup of ale. I had struck lucky; this one hadn't been spoilt by seawater. It started raining again, and the wind strengthened. I wrapped my cloak tighter about me. At least it was blowing us towards the mountains I could now see ahead. I was cold and wet. For once I would be glad to get onto dry land.

Chapter 19

"Ealdorman Athelstan is coming. He sent a message that he would collect the men personally. " Saewynn met Wulfstan as soon as he entered the hall after a day in the fields. "I don't know what to do. What do I say to him?"

"Calm down. You spent time in Lord Elfgar's service, and at the king's court. You know how these things are done. He won't expect us to be formal here. And it's not as if you don't know him, we spent Christmas at his hall last year."

Saewynn remembered the great feasts, the hunts and entertainment, the people. "How many will come with him? Where will we put them?"

"The fyrd is assembling at Medeshamstede. He'll bring his personal attendants, perhaps his son Ethelwine, you know him. When is he arriving?"

"Tomorrow. What about food?"

"Tell Hild as soon as possible. It will take her mind off Godric leaving."

"Yes, I wonder if the new batch of mead is ready?" She made for the door, then stopped. "Will he want to stay the night?"

"Depends how much mead we give him. Make sure the chamber is tidy, just in case."

"With Byrhtnoth away, it's tidier than usual. I'll clear my things." She headed for the chamber, remembered her original destination, shook her head and hurried towards the door.

*

"Welcome to Byrhtnoth's hall, my lord." Saewynn offered the horn of mead to Lord Athelstan. Hild gave an encouraging nod.

"Thank you, Saewynn." He took a sip and passed it to Ethelwine, who took a bigger draught. "You're looking well. You have recovered from your injuries?"

"Thanks to your wife's help. She is well?"

"Better now that spring has arrived." Athelstan turned to Wulfstan. "How many men have you got for us?"

"Godric is assembling them. There are a couple of boys, old enough to join the men this year. Do you remember Edward?" Wulfstan led him away towards the practice ground.

"Hello, Saewynn." Ethelwine attempted to give her a hug, but she moved away, handing the horn back to Hild. "Sorry, I suppose now you're a married woman that's not allowed."

"It's not that, it's just..." she looked around, was there anything she had forgotten?

"What's the matter? Is it the old problem, the fear?" Saewynn nodded. She had tried hard to hide it, but Ethelwine's approach had broken through her defences. "Come inside and sit down, nothing needs to be done for now." He found a seat and helped himself to a piece of cheese. Saewynn stood nearby, not too close. "I thought you would have recovered by now. Marriage must have helped." He studied her. "Byrhtnoth didn't waste much time. When is it due?"

"Around harvest." Saewynn blushed and wrapped her best cloak around her.

"We'll all be home by then, God willing."

Saewynn repeated a silent prayer and sat down. "Have you had any news?"

"Leif met Byrhtnoth in Exeter and helped find masts for the ships. He said he was well."

"Will Byrhtnoth be coming back here, before...?" She waved a hand towards where Wulfstan had disappeared with Ethelwine's father.

"I'm afraid not. The latest news from Winchester reported that the fleet had sailed. The weather has been good so they shouldn't have any problems."

"Unless they encounter enemy ships." Saewynn wished she was with him. She had enjoyed their voyages, learning to sail his ship. Once more, she regretted her current condition.

"He knows what he's doing." Ethelwine moved to pat her shoulder, paused and reached for the bread. "They're due to land somewhere on the coast and march south to meet us. I expect we'll join up in a few days. Is that why you're scared, you're worried about Byrhtnoth?"

"Partly. It's stupid, I know I'm safe here, even if he is away,"

"We won't take all your men away if that's what concerns you. Why don't you go to visit my mother? I'm sure she would enjoy making a fuss of you."

"Thank you, my place is here, while my lord is away. It's Egbert, he was seen at Winchester."

"I see. Winchester is far away, you know," Ethelwine reassured her.

"I know, but he sent me a message. He said he would visit. He knew about the baby. I don't know who told him. I felt helpless. I became suspicious of strangers again. I'm sorry, I know you're not a stranger, but sometimes even Wulfstan makes me nervous."

"Byrhtnoth shouldn't have left you on your own."

"He doesn't know. And don't you dare tell him. I'll deal with it myself. I know what to do, stop brooding and keep busy. At least your visit has given me something to distract me." Saewynn stood up and smoothed down her skirts. "And you can stop helping yourself to that cheese, there won't be anything left for your father." She forced herself to rest a hand on his shoulder, then went to meet Lord Athelstan who was congratulating Godric.

"You've got a good group of lads there, the best trained I've encountered for a long time. They are a credit to Lord Byrhtnoth."

"He sent us a new trainer from Winchester. It made all the difference." Saewynn pointed out Aelf, strolling across the yard towards them.

"I don't think I know him. Will he be coming with us?"

"I'm afraid she will be staying here," said Saewynn with a smile.

"Not another one. Where do you find these women?"

"We do it to confuse our enemies, my lord. Here's Hild with the water. Would you care to wash your hands before the meal? We still have a little food left after winter. You are welcome to what we have."

"Thank you. I'm glad at least some of your women dress like women." Athelstan gave Hild an appreciative inspection. She blushed, and a low growl emerged from Godric's throat.

"I'm sorry. Godric's not happy that you came so soon to collect the men and forced him to abandon his wedding plans."

"Like that, is it?" Athelstan grinned. "We'll have to think about what we can do. Now, where's that food?" Saewynn led him into the hall.

*

"Do you have to leave today?" Saewynn offered Lord Athelstan the plate of cheese. It had matured well over the winter.

"That was my intention. I don't want to impose on your hospitality. Your stocks must be running low." He tasted the cheese and cut off a larger piece.

"Since the men were away in Winchester for Easter we still have plenty." She picked up a jug of ale and poured some for the Ealdorman. "Perhaps you would like to pit your men against ours. A little more practice won't do them any harm."

Athelstan sipped at his ale and considered it.

"What are you two plotting?" Ethelwine handed his father the basket of bread.

"I think Ethelwine should challenge Aelf to a fight," said Saewynn.

"You mean that giant woman with the sword?" he asked, taking some bread for himself.

"She's not a giant, she's not much taller than I am."

"I remember what you did to me when I persuaded you to fight. Leave me out of this."

Saewynn grinned at Athelstan. "Are we agreed?"

He nodded. "What can I do?"

"Relax and enjoy the rest of your meal. Ethelwine, come with me." She led him away "Don't worry, you don't have to fight Aelf. Just find Godric and keep him busy for a few hours, then bring him to the hall, clean and tidy. He doesn't know it yet, but he's about to get married." Ethelwine grinned, grabbed another chunk of bread from the table, and hurried out.

*

"The Ealdorman will be staying the night," Saewynn told Wulfstan.

"Why are you so cheerful?" he said. "You were dreading it."

"I'll explain later. Kill that calf we selected and joint it; we haven't time to roast it whole." Saewynn's eyes drifted across the hall, making a rough count of the men enjoying their meal. "Find another and kill that as well. I wonder if we've got enough ale? Eels!" She rushed to the door without another word. Wulfstan, confused, watched her leave. He saw that Lord Athelstan was content and went to find a sharp knife.

As she hurried towards the kitchen, Saewynn spotted Aelf. "Come with me."

"What's going on?"

"Can you cook?"

"A bit. Why?"

"The Ealdorman is staying the night, and Hild will be too busy to do anything."

"What's happened?"

"She's getting married."

When Saewynn walked into the smoky kitchen, Hild and the women that helped her were relaxing with some ale. "Ealdorman Athelstan is staying until tomorrow. I want a feast fit for a king, by this evening."

"All right girls," Hild heaved herself to her feet. "Back to work."

"Not you. You're coming with me."

"What do you mean?" asked Hild

"They can manage on their own. Aelf will help. I've sent Wulfstan to kill the calf. I thought we might have some eels as well? You showed me how to cook them, I think I remember the recipe."

"Why?"

"I'll give you some time to give them instructions. There's enough flour for more bread. Edward." Saewynn nearly collided with him in the doorway. He had come to say goodbye to his sister. She grabbed his arm. "Put down that bag, you're not going anywhere today. You're to have a mock battle with the Ealdorman's men, but I need you to fetch some eels first. Hild will tell you how many. What next?" Saewynn frowned at the hearth. "Heat some water and bring it to the chamber. I'll be back later. I must have a word with Edith."

"Stop!" shouted Hild. "I know you're the mistress now, but I'm still in charge of the kitchen."

"Not tonight. I've got other plans for you."

*

"What about a priest? There's no time to send to Ely."

"It will be a simple ceremony," Saewynn told Edith. "The Ealdorman will act as a witness. If you, they, want it blessed, they'll have to wait until Godric comes back. The important thing is the bedding. That's where I need your help."

"What do you mean?" said Edith with a shocked expression.

130

"Nothing like that. Hild's room is behind the kitchen. I don't suppose it's very tidy." Or clean, she thought. "Can you sort it out? Clean bedding, flowers, that sort of thing?"

"I've a few candle stubs." Edith's face brightened. "They should disguise some of the cooking smells. What about a fire?"

"I think they'll be warm enough. Thank you, Edith." Saewynn reached forward and kissed the older woman's cheek. "I must check the Ealdorman is comfortable."

*

Saewynn was rummaging in one of the chests when Hild arrived in the chamber. She carried two buckets of water and a servant brought another.

"How much you want? Is this enough? Does the Ealdorman require a bath?" The chamber was in chaos, several gowns had been thrown across the bed.

"It will have to do." Saewynn leaned back on her heels and rubbed her back. "It's not for the Ealdorman. It's for you. Get those clothes off."

"But I don't want... You can't make me."

"I think this will do." Saewynn struggled to her feet with a dark green woollen gown. "It should fit you. I don't know who wore it last." She noticed Hild's stricken face. "You do want to marry Godric, don't you?"

"Godric? Of course. I thought... what the Ealdorman said about me..."

"I'm so sorry. I should have explained. Come and sit down." Saewynn led her to the bed. "You must know I would never force another woman to do that." She put a comforting arm around Hild's shoulders. "I knew how disappointed you were, not to have time to arrange a marriage with Godric."

"It took so long to persuade him."

"Lord Athelstan was dismayed he had upset your plans."

"Was he?" said Hild in astonishment.

"Well, he didn't disagree when I asked him to stay. You and Godric can make your vows and spend the night together before he leaves. Is that what you want?"

"Oh yes. It's such a rush though."

"Everything's under control," said Saewynn with a confidence she was beginning to regret. "Do you like the green? I'd lend you the yellow silk, but I don't think it would be big enough."

"The green is beautiful. I've got a new white shift that will go well underneath. I've been saving it for... my wedding I suppose." She grinned.

"I'll fetch it. Anything else you need?"

"There's a string of beads, they belonged to my mother. They're in my chest with the shift."

"We don't have time for a proper bath, but you can use the bowl," Saewynn pointed to the corner. "There's soap. Leave a little clean water. No, I'll bring a fresh jug. I'll wash your hair when I get back. I'll lock the door behind me, so you're not disturbed."

*

"Beautiful." Saewynn stood back and surveyed her handiwork. She was pleased with what she had achieved. She had rinsed Hild's hair in water scented with dried flower petals and combed it until it hung like silken gold down her back. It crackled at the slightest touch. The string of beads held it off her face, anchored by flowers from those collected by Edith. She imagined Hild's expression when she saw her bedroom. Edith must have scoured the whole village for blooms.

The green gown was thick wool, too warm really for the gentle spring weather. Hild had flushed when Saewynn commented that she wouldn't be wearing it for long. They found a strip of embroidery; wrapped around her waist, it emphasised her figure.

Saewynn poured wine into two cups and handed one to Hild. "To calm the nerves," she said.

"Yours or mine?" replied Hild, perched on the edge of the bed. Saewynn sat next to her and took a sip.

"I can't believe it," said Hild. "A feast is being prepared, and I'm not a part of it. I feel I should be checking things are ready."

"It's time you had a day off. Don't worry, everything will be back to normal tomorrow." They sat in silence, listening to the rising noise in the hall. Saewynn cleared her throat.

"Is there anything you need to know? I understand your mother died a long time ago, and..."

"I know all about that." Hild laughed. "although thank you for offering."

"Good," Saewynn said with relief. Have you and Godric already...?"

"Of course not, well, not everything," Hild giggled. "This wine is strong." She stared into the empty cup.

"No more for now." Saewynn took the cups and returned the jug to the table.

"I'm the village expert," admitted Hild. "I keep all the herbs and remedies, give advice to the girls and older women, sometimes men. Even Byrhtnoth came to me for help." Hild stopped when she realised what she had said.

"What sort of help?" Saewynn placed the jug carefully on the table.

"It's nothing. Are they ready yet?" Hild glanced towards the door.

"You had better tell me. How did you help my husband?"

"It was just before you married. He asked some questions."

"Questions about me?"

"Yes." Hild hung her head with embarrassment.

"What?" Saewynn gripped Hild's arm." Her left hand had grown stronger, and Hild flinched.

"It was about your... attack. When you were injured."

"He wanted to know if another man had had me." Saewynn felt a chill spread through her body. "So he had a reason to reject me."

"No, that didn't matter. Byrhtnoth was worried, afraid he would hurt you.

"You're sure?"

"He loves you. He would have married you whatever had happened. He would have forgone sleeping with you if that was what you wished. There are not many men who would do that."

"No, there aren't." Tears filled Saewynn's eyes. "I'm sorry, I shouldn't have forced you to tell me." She wiped her sleeve across her face.

"It's all right. I don't like keeping secrets."

There was a knock on the door and a loud whisper from Edith. "Are you ready?"

"Just a moment." Hild gave Saewynn a hug and wiped away a stray tear. "If I don't get a chance later, thank you, for today." Saewynn returned the hug.

"Don't forget the night." They exchanged a conspiratorial glance, and Saewynn led the bride out into the hall.

Chapter 20

We soon caught up with the other ships. Would they have returned if we had not defeated the enemy ships on our own? It didn't matter now. The mountains that had beckoned us darkened. Behind us, clouds covered the sinking sun. It was later than I thought.

"Does the guide know this coast? Do we have a destination?"

The reply was drowned by the flapping of the sail. The man tried again. I caught shreds of words, sand, a river, some kind of warning? I shrugged. We followed the others. If there were problems, they would encounter them first. Elfgar's ship took the lead.

I peered ahead and saw a pale line along the coast. Breaking waves or smooth sand? Either was capable of killing us.

Then the rain hit.

The other ships slowed. Sails were adjusted to run parallel to the coast. The hills were dark and foreboding in the torrential rain. I caught a glimpse of bare black rock, cleaved by a white streak of water, and then it was gone. There was no sign of dwellings, nothing formed by man, just bleak wasteland. The sand worried me. It ran along the coast, and out into the sea. Was it the same sand as the flat sandbanks through which we had threaded our way towards the river mouth, only the day before? Stories had been told of ships caught on them and disappearing beneath the waves, or held until the sea smashed them to splinters. I heaved on the oar, and we swung around, away from danger. The following helmsman had been watching and echoed my action. His ship was low in the water, and as the sail slackened, our speed fell. There was a vibration, and the deck tipped. Then the sail filled and with a grinding loud enough to be heard above the shrieking wind, we were free.

I looked back. The straps that had secured my repair were loose. Ropes thrashed in the wind. The sandbank had scoured the hull and torn the sheepskin away. Already the water was rising around the doomed men. I reached for my axe. One stroke and we would be free, but they would die. I couldn't abandon them.

I scanned the passing land. Was the rain decreasing? Along the coast, a patch of light appeared. The final light of day had broken through the cloud. Was that a gap in the unrelenting hills? A gap might mean a river. It was our last hope.

"Keep bailing," I shouted over my shoulder. The light moved. Now it illuminated the sea. I grabbed the boy and pointed. "Is that the mouth of a river?"

"It might be. The sail's in the way. Shall I...?" He pointed to the bow. I hesitated. There was no choice. The faster we moved, the longer the towed ship would stay afloat.

"Go." He would be safer there if we began to sink. "If it is a river, help guide us in."

He scampered away, giving a cheerful wave when he arrived. I aimed the prow towards the gap in the hills. The beckoning light had faded, but the sea was calmer there. Wind filled the sail. The other ships were scattered across the sea. One turned towards us, then another. They had noticed our change of direction. Was I leading them into danger?

The trailing ship was even lower in the water. Someone had pulled one of the sea chests over the hole and two men were sitting on it. One waved, and I acknowledged the greeting, before concentrating on our course. The boy pointed right and I steered that way. The water calmed. We headed straight towards the gap in the hills, beyond were more hills, much higher. My heart sunk. Had I made a grave mistake?

The boy pointed into the water. Was there a sandbank? The foam that rushed past was a different colour, no longer white, but a muddy brown. We had found a river. I ordered the ship to slow. The sail dropped, and the oars were readied. If the ship sunk now, the men had a chance of reaching land. The lookout threw a line into the water and pulled it up. The boy pointed the direction. Sandbanks appeared on one side, then on the other. A tuft of grass or were they reeds? We were close to land. Far behind us, another ship had found the river entrance. It dropped its sail and followed in our wake.

We were in a river now, shallow and winding between banks of black mud. Where did it lead? Did anyone live here? Our keel touched the bottom, and I adjusted the steering. The man behind was not as alert, and we jarred to a halt as the other ship stopped. In the sudden silence there came a gurgle of water as their hull was breached. Against the last rays of light from between the clouds, the mast tilted and the ship settled to one side, leaning against the bank with a sigh of displaced mud. It died, but at least the men still lived.

"Stay where you are," I shouted. "Someone make a light!" At least one of the other ships was approaching. A collision might damage it, blocking the entrance, or exit if we needed to escape.

"I'm not sitting here in cold water. I'm getting out" A torch flared, illuminating the shape of a man climbing from the ship onto the bank. He took a couple of steps and disappeared. There was a splash, a struggle. "Help! Get me out!" His words soon turned to panicked screams, to silence, then to a belch of satisfied mud. A foul smell drifted across the ships.

"What was that?" came a shaky voice.

"Monsters! They'll pick us off one by one."

I leaned over with the torch. It flared green, and the faces gazed up at me like dead men. "It's just the marsh. You'll be safe if you stay on the ship." I hoped I was right. Everyone knew the story of Beowulf and the monster who lived in a bog. I shivered; it was just a story.

"Move to the side, clear of the water. We'll wait for the other ships before we decide what to do. There's not much we can do in the dark. If you can find a dry spot, try and get some sleep."

"What about food? We've not eaten since this morning."

At the mention of food, my stomach gave a loud growl. "Don't worry, that's not a monster." Someone gave a nervous laugh. "I'll check what we've got. Has anyone tried the river water, is it fit to drink?" Someone scooped up a handful and took a sip, before spitting it out.

"Reckon it'll do if you're thirsty enough."

"It won't come to that," I told him. "Here comes another of the ships."

I shouted into the darkness and, to my relief, Lord Elfgar's voice replied, I warned him about the marsh, and we agreed to wait until light before making any decisions. We posted guards and settled down to sleep.

Chapter 21

Godric stood in front of the table. He gave the impression of awaiting execution. Saewynn didn't recognise his tunic. Had Ethelwine borrowed it from his father? She glanced at the Ealdorman and felt a stab of jealousy at the sight of another man in Byrhtnoth's chair. As her husband's lord, he had the right. She bowed her head and led Hild to stand beside Godric, before finding her own seat beside Ethelwine. The seats either side of Athelstan remained empty. The married couple would occupy them after the ceremony.

"Any problems?" she whispered to Ethelwine.

"I don't think he knows what's happening. The battle went well, a few bruises, but no blood spilt. Are you all right? You seem upset."

"A bit tired. I didn't know how much there was to organising a wedding."

"You've done well, she looks beautiful."

"She does, doesn't she?" Saewynn admired the couple. If only the food would be as successful. Lord Athelstan rose and welcomed everyone to the feast.

"I apologise to all the men who are eager to leave for battle, but when I discovered that the marriage of this couple was to be cancelled because of the man's departure, I agreed that I would wait. He deserves the opportunity to spread his seed in anticipation of a happy return to a productive harvest." Hild hid a smile, Godric looked confused. Laughter ran along the benches.

"This couple both serve Lord Byrhtnoth, who is away on the king's business. It is he who should give permission for the match. In his absence, I ask his wife, Saewynn, to confirm his wishes." Caught unawares, Saewynn struggled to her feet.

"I am sure my husband would approve," she managed before sinking back into her seat.

"And if he didn't, I am sure his wife would soon change his mind, judging by the organisation she has displayed here today." Saewynn's cheeks flared pink as cheers rang around the hall.

"Good, as Byrhtnoth's lord, I also agree to the match. Now, Hild isn't it?"

She lifted her head. "Yes, my lord."

"Hild. Are you willing to marry this man, Godric, before this audience and in the sight of God?"

She looked at Godric. "I am, my lord." She gave a broad smile.

"Godric. Are you willing to marry this woman, Hild?" There was silence as Godric studied the reeds on the floor with a puzzled frown. Hild stirred uneasily. Godric lifted his head.

"Of course, my lord." Everyone, including Lord Athelstan, let out a sigh of relief.

"Good. You are now man and wife. A toast to the happy couple." The colour drained from Saewynn's face. The mead. She had forgotten the mead. Where did Hild keep the horn? There was movement at the side of the hall. It was Edith. She carried the horn, brimming with mead, and offered it to Godric and then Hild. They each took a sip and then Edith passed it to Lord Athelstan, and it continued along the table. When it reached Saewynn, she took a large mouthful, nearly choking when Lord Athelstan said, "Where is the food?"

To her relief, the servants rushed forward with bread and jugs of ale for the men. She exchanged an expression of relief with Hild as she and Godric walked around the table to sit beside Lord Athelstan.

A dish of eels was placed on the table, and Saewynn searched the crowded benches for Edward. She had explained the recipe to him as she remembered it from Hild's instructions, then watched him cook the first batch. She spooned a portion onto her plate, tasted it and sent a smile in his direction.

"Ale?" Ethelwine lifted the jug, "or would you prefer wine?"

"Ale will do. I had enough wine earlier." Saewynn pushed her cup towards Ethelwine.

"Your hand!" He stopped; the jug poised in mid-air.

"What do you mean?" Saewynn glanced down at her hands. She had put on the gloves much earlier and forgotten about them, now her fingers were aching. There was a greasy mark on her left glove. How was she going to get rid of that?

"Your hand is straight. Did Wulfstan manage to mend it?"

"In a way. He went to the Abbot of Glastonbury. Dunstan made these gloves. They hold my fingers straight, for a while. I can't use my right hand; it just makes it look better." She hid it in her lap.

"You can use it. You pushed your cup towards me." He poured a little ale into the cup. "Can you pick it up?"

"I can't do anything like that," she raised her hand to demonstrate. The cup was small, with straight sides, made of clay with a painted design of flowers. She positioned her hand and relaxed. Her fingers closed around it. "I can grasp but can't release it again." She lifted her hand and the cup with it.

"When it's ale, you don't need to let go. Drink it." She lifted the cup higher and leaned forward until her lips touched the rim. She twisted her wrist and the cup tilted. Some ale went into her mouth, most dribbled down her chin.

"I'm sorry." Ethelwine found a cloth and dabbed at her face. Saewynn ignored him and stared at her hand holding the cup. "You need practice, but you can do it. Can you let go?"

Saewynn lowered her hand to the table, and with her left hand pulled her fingers straight. The cup dropped, spilling ale on the table. Ethelwine mopped it up. "Needs a bit of work." He stood the cup upright and refilled it. Saewynn took it in her other hand, downed it in one gulp and held it out for more.

"What's going on? Not attempting to get my lord's wife drunk?"

"Hello, Wulfstan. Saewynn has done something amazing."

"I know. Who else could have arranged a wedding in a matter of hours?" Wulfstan slipped onto the bench beside her.

"Not that. She picked up a cup," said Ethelwine.

Saewynn ignored him. "Where have you been? You missed the wedding."

"We watched from the back. I was helping Aelf prepare somewhere for you to sleep. Or were you thinking of sharing a bed with the Ealdorman?"

"Shush." Saewynn giggled and glanced along the table. Lord Athelstan was busy paying compliments to Hild. "I hadn't thought about that. Where?"

"The storage room next to the chamber. We need the extra bedrolls that are kept there, and I didn't think Aelf was safe in the hall with all the extra men. You can share it for tonight. I collected your things from the chamber and made it tidy for the Ealdorman."

"Thank you. Do you want some of these eels? Edward cooked them."

"Edward? I'll have some of the calf meat, since I had to kill the animal myself. Who cooked that? You?"

"No, they can manage perfectly well in the kitchen, although I'll be glad when Hild takes charge again."

"Perhaps she'll go to war with her husband." Ethelwine broke into the conversation.

"I hope not," said Saewynn fervently. "Pass me more of those eels. Those burnt pieces of skin give it a special flavour."

*

"I'm glad that's over." Saewynn stretched out on the hard mattress. At least Wulfstan had thought to move the wolf skin from the chamber. She had disliked the idea of someone else sleeping beneath it. "I hope we haven't made them so comfortable that they won't want to leave."

"They're off to war, they won't want to delay." Aelf slipped out of her tunic and folded it carefully. "Are you ready to sleep? I'll douse the candle."

"Do you regret not going with them?" Saewynn pulled the fur up to her chin and sighed.

"Why? Do you?" The room was plunged into darkness.

"I went last year. It was exciting, at least to begin with. And I was with Byrhtnoth, some of the time. Then... People get hurt. Some die."

"That can happen anywhere." Aelf pounded at the hard pillow.

"Don't say that."

"I enjoy fighting. I'm good at it. But go to war? I prefer to stay comfortable at home."

"Me too." It would be better if everyone stayed at home, Saewynn thought, out of danger, although she knew that Byrhtnoth sought glory in battle. Silently she said her nightly prayer for his safety and settled down to sleep. She listened to the regular breathing beside her.

"Did you bring the pot?" she whispered. "Some of that meat wasn't cooked properly. Mine was bloody in places. I don't feel right."

"Is it urgent? I'll make some light." Aelf fumbled for her bag.

"Don't bother, it's going off now. It was a strange feeling."

"What was it like?"

"I don't know. Like the fluttering of a moth."

"I think," Aelf paused, "I think it might be your baby."

143

"The baby!" With all excitement of the day Saewynn had almost forgotten about it. Had she damaged it? She pushed back the wolf fur and sat up.

"What have I done? Is it...?"

"Don't worry." A friendly hand reassured her from the darkness, "It happens around this time. You said he was expected in the autumn?"

"Months away."

"I remember the feeling, just as you described." Aelf was silent a moment. "It is your baby saying hello. He is telling you he is there, that everything is all right. It will get stronger. Towards the end, he will keep you awake with his kicking." She laughed. "It is perfectly normal."

Saewynn lay down, her hand resting on the small mound. She felt the movement again, like nothing she had ever felt before. "Hello baby," she whispered.

Chapter 22

"Wake up." The sky was bright. I had meant to rise at first light, but the guards hadn't woken me.

"Quiet, there are men." The boy thrust the hilt of my sword into my hand.

"What men?" I whispered. He shook his head. I concentrated on the sounds that reached me in the space beneath the ship's stern. Lord Elfgar was complaining, that was clear. Someone asked a question. Elfgar shouted that he didn't understand. I recognised the language, it was similar to that spoken in Northumbria. Where was the guide? He should be able to translate.

"What's the problem?" I didn't raise the sword, letting it hang ready in my hand. I pushed the boy down into the bottom of the boat. The ship was surrounded. Men trained arrows on us from the banks. The man I had left on guard was slumped in his place, a shaft protruding from his chest. Blood pooled at his feet. He must have fallen asleep.

"Who are you?" The man haranguing Lord Elfgar walked along the bank towards me. He kept to the course tussocks of grass, avoiding the smooth, deceptive ground between. He hesitated when he saw my sword.

"We are travellers, driven ashore by the storm. When we have repaired our ship," I pointed at the other vessel, which had sunk lower into the mud during the night, "we will leave."

"Many of you bear arms." The man had no sword, only a spear. Even at a distance, I saw it bore traces of rust. I picked up my axe and rested it casually on my shoulder.

"The world is a dangerous place. Who is your lord?"

"I serve Lord Hrafn. He rules this land." He waved his spear towards the encircling hills. "I will take you to him." I could have killed him easily with my axe. I looked around and caught Thurstan's eye. He gave a slight shake of his head. I realised arrows were aimed at my back.

"I will be happy to meet such a powerful lord, but first, I must care for my men. Some were injured in the storm. We must make repairs." I leaned the axe against to side of the ship and bent to retrieve my sword belt. I slid the sword into its scabbard and belted it around my waist. The man watched, searching for a reply.

"You will come now."

I raised a foot to the side of the ship and jumped, landing on the same patch of grass, forcing the man to step back. His foot landed in the sucking mud. He stumbled and fear crossed his face before I seized his arm and pulled him to safety.

"Lead the way." I rested my hand on my sword hilt and waited. A nearby archer grinned.

"All of you." The man waved towards the other ships.

"All? You will allow us to post a guard at least. Although I know Lord Hrafn will welcome us, you never know who else might be out there." I looked towards the sea, noticing how far away it was now. We would never escape without help. "I wouldn't want to come back to a smoking ruin," I added the hint of a threat to my voice.

"Organise guards," I shouted to the rest of the ships. "Everyone else come with us. We have an invitation to Lord Hrafn's hall. I expect there will be a feast in our honour." I looked enquiringly at the man. His face blanched. He moved to higher land, there must be a path there. His men helped ours out of the ships. One escorted Lord Elfgar towards me.

"What's going on? Do you know these men?" he asked suspiciously.

"Not at all." I kept my voice down; someone might speak our tongue. "We can't get out of here without help. If we fight, we're stuck, even if we win. We might as well try and make friends. Where's that guide of yours? He must know of Lord Hrafn."

"I haven't seen him since last night. He must have slipped away from the ship."

"Then he is dead, swallowed by the marsh. Unless he knows more than he told us." I hoped he was incompetent rather than a traitor. I told Young Petroc to stay on board. He would have a chance if we didn't survive Lord Hrafn. It was a Viking name, a people not noted for their hospitality.

*

There was an open space where water and land met. After the heavy rain, it was thick with mud. It was surrounded by ramshackle buildings and from them emerged a distinctive smell.

"Slaves?"

Lord Elfgar nodded, "Empty, for now."

"Where do they come from?" The surrounding hills appeared devoid of life.

"Wherever there is trouble. I expect we shall be sending some this way in a week or so. It's not far across the sea to the Irish slave markets." He pointed back the way we had come. "Be grateful we have arrived in numbers, otherwise it could be us."

It was not something I had considered. I studied the pens and buildings with new eyes as we left the market area.

"Of course, it might be used for animals, most likely is. How much further?" Elfgar shouted at the man who had captured us. He ignored the question.

147

We joined a wide, paved road. It ran straight as an arrow towards what was obviously our destination: a large rocky hill, emerging from flat green fields like the back of a dragon.

At the entrance our captor spoke to an armed guard. There was an argument, and we were allowed to enter. We were directed to an area of barns and stockades.

"Wait here. Food and drink will be brought. Lord Hrafn will receive you," he assessed our numbers, "some of you, later."

"Bring water," I demanded. "We have been at sea, we need to wash before meeting your lord." The man was confused. From his smell, he was unfamiliar with washing, or perhaps he spent too much time in the marsh.

"I'll see to it." He hurried away, leaving his men stationed around the fence. We explored the empty buildings, allocating sleeping places. One hut, solid and with a door barred on the outside contained a pile of chains. I exchanged a glance with Elfgar, and we shut the door, leaving it empty. At least they hadn't removed our weapons.

The light was fading when they came for us. We were tired and hungry. A few loaves of bread had been delivered, not enough to satisfy, and no ale. Some of the men complained, wishing themselves back at the ships.

"If you want to return to the marsh, I'm sure it can be arranged." They remembered the eerie night before and grew quiet. The wait had made me nervous too, but I made ready to meet Lord Hrafn.

*

The hall was packed with men eager to inspect the visitors. It was not large, and most of the light came from the hearth. If the beast dripping fat into the flames had been killed for our benefit, the feast boded well. My eyes were drawn to the far end. The occupant of the large chair was thin, neither young nor white-haired. He was plainly dressed, displaying little wealth. Dark eyes shone with intelligence. Not a warrior. Someone much more dangerous, a man powerful enough to have no need to display it. I bowed deeply, and with reluctance, Lord Elfgar followed my example.

"Welcome to my land. I understand one of you speaks our tongue."

"Yes, my lord." I stepped forward. "I spent several months last winter with Lord Osulf in Bebbanburg. Your speech is similar."

"I have met Lord Osulf. Did you enjoy your stay?"

"I did, my lord. He was very hospitable." A young man sitting nearby laughed and was silenced by a glance from Lord Hrafn.

"He is not known for his hospitality. You are a friend?"

"I hope I became his friend," I said.

"You serve this man?" He had noticed the way I deferred to Lord Elfgar. "Who is he, and why is he here?"

"May I present Lord Elfgar, Ealdorman of Essex, father to the wife of the late King Edmund."

"I asked why he is here."

I planned my words carefully. "This place, wherever it is, is not our destination. Our ships carry men, ordered by King Eadred to attend his meeting with Erik, so-called King of York."

Lord Hrafn nodded and smiled. "Welcome. I apologise for the questioning. We receive many visitors, but none of such high rank as the Ealdorman of Essex. Lord Elfgar, please sit." He made room beside him. "Join our meal. Drink."

A servant brought the mead horn. She offered it to Lord Elfgar, then to me. I remained standing, took a small sip, and passed it back.

"This man who translated your words so well, is he your son?" Lord Hrafn spoke our language. I should have realised.

"I do not have that honour. My name is Byrhtnoth, son of Byrhthelm. I serve the Ealdorman of East Anglia, and the King."

A man close to Lord Hrafn leaned over and whispered in his lord's ear. I thought I recognised him. Lord Hrafn studied me with interest as the man spoke.

"My nephew was at Bebbanburg last winter. He heard tales of a warrior called Byrhtnoth who killed a great wolf." I knew the man now, one of the visitors at Lord Osulf's table. "We have many wolves that roam our hills, perhaps we can persuade you to help us dispose of a few."

"It would be my pleasure, my lord. However, generous as you are, we must travel onwards. We would not expect you to feed such numbers for long."

"Indeed." He laughed. "I'm sure you must eat as much as two, or even three men."

"It's true," said Lord Elfgar, "he is always hungry."

"Find a seat and help yourself to meat."

"Thank you, my lord." The man who had recognised me, Lord Hrafn's nephew, invited me to sit beside him. A plate of food appeared, and a brimming cup of ale. I took a draft and relaxed.

"You disappeared suddenly from Lord Osulf's hall," the young man said. "Some were worried. Young Uhtred accused his father of having you killed."

"That was brave of him." I was pleased the boy had stood up to his father. "I regretted I was unable to say goodbye but I had received news that Osulf's elder son was returning. I met him once and didn't want to do so again." I didn't mention the fight we had on the beach before I left.

"He makes trouble for the sake of it. We're lucky to have the hills to protect us."

"Where exactly are we?" I asked my neighbour. It turned out that we were not that far north of our original destination. "Is there a road along the coast?"

"Not really, it is easier by ship."

I explained how one of our ships had nearly sunk, the others needed repairs.

"You can leave the ships here; we can help with repairs. If you are in a hurry, you can continue on foot through the hills."

"Is there a path?" They had looked impassable.

"Not in winter. It is clear this time of year. Traders use the route regularly. The Romans built a road, although little remains of it." That explained the good path from the sea. "It is how we survive, by taxing the goods that pass through our port." He was telling me that we had a way out, although we would have to pay for it. Negotiations would be tough. How much gold did Lord Elfgar have left?

"I'm telling Lord Hrafn about our arrival on the coast," Elfgar called across the table. "How did you find the river? I thought we were doomed until you led us to safety."

I struggled to remember what had happened. "It was the light," I explained. "The sun found a gap in the clouds and it reflected the smooth water from the river. The ship we towed was sinking, it was our only hope."

"It was a miracle," said Elfgar.

"A sign from God," agreed Lord Hrafn." He must be a Christian. I had feared that they worshipped the old gods. Would it make them more likely to help us?

"More meat?" Someone offered a loaded platter.

"I hope there will be some left for our men," I said.

"There is plenty, we have already sent some to them. Now you are our friends.

Chapter 23

We returned to the ships next day with small boats and workmen, timing the arrival for high tide. Our supplies and weapons were moved to my ship, and it was brought up the river and moored beneath the rock. Hrafn had agreed that we could leave the ships there, with enough crew to man them when they were fit to sail.

There was much argument about the fate of the wrecked ship. Hrafn wanted it cleared as soon as possible since it was blocking the channel. Someone suggested it be burned, and Young Petroc, just Petroc now his father was dead, insisted it was repairable. I told him that if he were able to repair and move the ship before we returned, he could stay with it. It would keep him busy and away from the fighting. As I walked up the path to the hall, he was already discussing plans with Lord Hrafn's nephew, something about digging a ditch to get around his ship.

Lord Elfgar watched our men sort the equipment. "That's too much for one pony. Split it and add the bundle of spears to the next."

I sat down on a chest and stretched. The ache in my shoulder had healed, just an echo of the pain remaining. A few days and I'd be fit enough to fight. "Petroc will remain to get his father's ship sailing again. How many men should we leave behind to get the ships away?"

"Lord Hrafn won't let them go until he's extracted enough money from us."

"Do we have enough?" I asked

"Probably. It's better than the alternative."

"Do you think that he would have taken us as slaves if there had been fewer of us?"

"I'm sure of it," he said.

"Will the men on the ships be safe when we've left?" Perhaps we should abandon the ships altogether.

"He's given his word."

I was unsure how reliable that would be. "We must be careful through the hills, Hrafn might change his mind." I found a rag and started to clean my axe. "He's providing a guide?"

"Yes. Tie those barrels together. They'll balance once we get them over a pony's back. How many have we got left?"

"I·hope he's a better guide than the one on the ship. Any news of what happened to him?"

"None. He disappeared off the face of the earth." Elfgar straightened and waited for the next load. "You had a long talk with Hrafn's nephew. Did he tell you what Osulf will do? Should we worry about an attack once we head for York?"

"He said not, and I tend to agree with him. Osulf of Bebbanburg is unlikely to cause problems unless he's attacked. I met Elfhere in Chester. He said it was all arranged. Not that I believe everything he says." He had lied in Winchester when he had told me Egbert was far away. Was it true that he had been seen in York? I raised my head and stared around at the bleak hills. At least Egbert was unlikely to be out there. I dismissed him from my thoughts; I was becoming obsessed with the man.

"Osulf was paid enough last year," I said, scrubbing at a particularly stubborn stain.

"Exactly. And no doubt we'll pay him more with what we take from Erik."

"Then he'll walk straight into the devastated lands."

"At least he's someone we can do business with, like Hrafn. Leave this for now." He pointed at the packs. "It's getting dark. We can do the rest before we leave in the morning."

"We're going tomorrow?" I wrapped the axe in oiled cloth and leaned it against the chest.

"He was very polite, but he wants us out of the way as soon as possible."

"Is he expecting ships from Ireland?"

"I hope not. Let's get some food. I don't plan to die on an empty stomach."

I buckled on my sword. Neither did I.

*

I studied the hills as the packhorses were assembled. There seemed to be no way through. Were we doing the right thing? I had spoken to the men we were leaving with the ships. We set a date to meet at Chester. If that passed without a message from us, they should sail back to Exeter. I wished Petroc good luck with his ship and gave him money for his family. He wanted to come with me, but I insisted he stay with his ship. I hoped he would be safer here than accompanying us. Perhaps one day we would meet again

I picked up my shield and moved out of the way of the packhorses, so many of them. Lord Hrafn had forced us to buy them from him. He gave us the name of a buyer so we could sell them later. I knew we would receive a lot less than we paid for them. Eventually, they would then be sold to other travellers and return home and Lord Hrafn would receive his profits from both ends of the transaction. Elfgar had suggested we keep the ponies for the journey to York. There would be much plunder, he explained. He also knew how to make a profit. I preferred fighting to trade. I rested my hand on the hilt of my sword.

"You have an interesting sword. Is it old?" Lord Hrafn had come to see us off.

"The hilt is old, the blade is new."

"May I see?" It was impossible to refuse his request. I slid it out of the scabbard and handed it to him.

"Its name is Wolf's Claw," I told him.

"It is a good blade, well balanced." I watched his face as he inspected it. I knew that expression, the lust of a man for a sword. I must have worn it myself when I had first laid eyes on my father's sword. Did Egbert still have it? If so, God willing, I would soon retrieve it from his dead hand. My concern now was for my men and the boy. Surely the gift of a sword would guarantee their safety?

"Take it. It is yours."

Lord Hrafn looked at me with surprise. I did not ask for anything in exchange, but he must have guessed my concerns. Elfgar frowned. Hrafn grasped the hilt tight and swung the blade. I took a last lingering look and walked away. It was my duty to protect my men, especially the innocent boy whose father I had been unable to save. That was what a sword was for. The sacrifice was worth it, although I would mourn its loss.

"Why Wolf's Claw?"

I paused before replying. "It is for the scars I received from the wolf I killed in Northumbria last year. My wife named it on our wedding night." I ignored Lord Elfgar's startled expression. "She gave it to me on our marriage day, to protect her and our children. She has no family, no father or brother, the sword..." I cleared my throat. "The hilt of the sword is old, taken from an ancient barrow. It is worn smooth by the hand of some great warrior." Lord Hrafn studied the hilt and nodded. "My friend nearly died retrieving it. He did it for me." Why had he done that? I still didn't know.

"The blade?"

"The blade was forged at the command of the Ealdorman of East Anglia. It is long, made for my arm. A reward for my service. He will wonder how I lost it." I shrugged. "It is just a sword."

"It is not just any sword, it is the sword of a great man, a sword to achieve great deeds. It is your sword and can be lost only in battle, which will, I hope, be a long time in the future. I cannot accept it." He reached forward and pressed the hilt into my hand.

"But..."

"Don't worry, my friend. I will protect your people as if they were my own." He leaned close and whispered, "The blade is too heavy for me, anyway." He stepped back.

"Thank you."

"Get on your way. I can't afford to feed you for another night."

"Thank you for your hospitality." I walked briskly to the head of the column, ignoring the conversations buzzing through the crowd. I stepped onto the well-worn path, and the men fell in behind me, the hooves of the ponies clattering on the rounded stones.

My hand rested on the hilt of my sword as I questioned what I had tried to do.

Chapter 24

About midday, we stopped at a bend in the valley to rest the horses. The rocky hills had closed in on either side, a perfect place for an ambush. As the animals were watered, I splashed through the stream, stopping to dip my hands to scoop up the cold fresh liquid. I climbed the slope until I had a good view of the surroundings, then sat on a rock and bit into a piece of bread. Although everyone was spread out below, all talk was drowned by the sound of water. It rushed through a narrow gate of rock, leaping from side to side from high above, its course traced by a scattered line of trees. There was movement, and I narrowed my eyes against the drizzle - a sheep. What did it find to eat up there? At least it would never lack something to drink.

How did anyone survive here in this land of rock and water? So many streams, pouring from the hills, meeting and separating. Pools, impossible to reach beyond squelching bog. Try to shelter beneath one of the tortuous trees and the water still found you, dripping from slick leaves. Down the valley there had been fields, surrounded by rocky walls, where cattle grazed on the fresh green grass.

Someone must have lived here once. I studied the scattered piles of stone. There had been houses here. That dip in the hillside was a path between them. Once noticed, I saw other marks of life, signs of digging, not wells, surrounded as they were by abundant water. Burials? I shivered, sensing the long-dead inhabitants around me.

I needed to get back to the others, swallowing the last of the bread, I made my way downhill. As I stopped at a pool for another drink, I studied the waterfall. Was that narrow channel natural, the sides carved smooth by the water, or by man? Were those scattered stones the remains of a building? It was a choice spot for a mill.

Someone shouted above the sound of rushing water. We were about to leave. I took my place at the end of the line of horses. From there I encouraged the laggards, to keep the column together. If we were attacked, I was ready to defend. I thanked Thurstan, who handed me my shield. It got heavier with every step.

"Blood!"

"Where?" I swung around and saw nothing to cause alarm.

"There." One of the men pointed at the ground. "Blood on your feet." He backed away, fear on his face.

"An omen of death," said another. "We will all die."

Had I stepped on something sharp? I hadn't noticed but the cold water had chilled my feet. He was right, my boots were covered in blood, thick red blood. I felt no pain. Perhaps I had stepped on some dead animal. Thurstan bent and touched the glutinous mess with a finger.

"It's not blood, it's mud," he said as he stood up.

I smiled with relief. On closer inspection it looked nothing like blood. The men were more nervous than I thought. I wiped the side of my boot against a tuft of grass. The mud smeared, sticking fast to my foot. It would dry as I walked or, if the rain continued, wash off. "Let's get going, we'll get left behind. It's only a bit of mud."

160

"Why that colour? Why just you? No-one else has it." The man was right. All the men's boots were covered in mud, but none of that violent blood red hue.

"Did anyone else cross the river?" asked Thurstan. Heads shook. "That's it, the soil is different over there." He pointed to a puddle. From a distance it resembled a pool of blood. The man exchanged a glance with his companion.

"It might still be an omen. Only the lord will die." A shiver ran down my back. I knew I must stop this here, now. If rumours spread through the men, everyone would believe our campaign was doomed before it had even started.

"If it is an omen, it is a good one. The blood is not mine. I will kill so many of the enemy, I will be wading in their blood." I watched as fear changed to relief.

"That makes sense." The man nodded to his friend who raised his spear in the air and shouted.

"All right, get a move on, or it will be your blood I wade through."

"Yes, my lord." He pushed the others into line and trotted to catch up with the others. I adjusted the load on my back before following. Every time I looked down to check my footing, I saw the red boots. Was it a sign of triumph, or death? I caught Thurstan's eye. He gave me a noncommittal shrug, before following the rest of the men.

*

The rain stopped and the valley widened. Cloud clung to the tops of the surrounding hills, disguising their height. Perhaps they reached to the sky. An eagle circled overhead. We must have looked like a line of ants crossing the bottom of an empty bowl. The bird dismissed us as a source of food and disappeared to hunt the misty peaks. The landscape was forbidding, similar to the hills near Bebbanburg where we had hunted the wolves. Were there wolves up there now, watching us?

We crossed the river, yet again. The men who had built the road had added large rocks to keep the feet of travellers dry. At this point, it made little difference and many ploughed oblivious through the water.

The valley veered to the left, the path must lead that way, following the river. I hoped we would stop soon, the men were tired, their chatter dwindling into silence. It had been a long day and many men, particularly those sailors who had accompanied us, would not have walked such a distance for a long time.

From ahead came raised voices. This had to be where we were to spend the night. Then news filtered back that we still had a way to go, and it was uphill. Someone pointed to the mountain ahead. It rose like a wall blocking our path. "The road goes up there."

There was a dip on the horizon. "We'll never cross that before night," I said. We needed food and rest. Earlier, the guide had disappeared, coming back with a dead sheep across his shoulders. Now, it hung over the back of the pony just ahead of me. One of the animal's legs was broken, and its eyes were missing. It had been dead a day or so. The guide was clearing up the hills and feeding us the leftovers. At least we hadn't been made to pay for it. Or had we?

"There's a camping place higher up. Not far now," the guide explained.

The wind increased. Blankets of cloud tore themselves to shreds like the sails of the damaged ship. I hoped there would be some shelter; it was getting cold.

*

There was shelter, of a sort. By the time we staggered up the final path to the walls, the cloud had disappeared and it was very cold. Behind us the valley retreated, trees and rivers glowing in the light of the setting sun.

"It was built by the Romans," Elfgar explained as I passed through the impressive entrance. The men were making camp. There was a square area in the centre of the enclosure, a large building, only the base of the walls surviving. We tethered the ponies there and removed the packs. I found the highest

162

surviving wall, out of the prevailing wind and gathered my crew. Thurstan lit a fire and I was glad we had collected fallen branches as we walked as there were few trees up here. I hoped it would last long enough to cook the sheep. I had been dreaming of the roasted meat for several miles. The fleece had already been removed, and someone cut chunks of meat from the bones. Thurstan tossed them into the cauldron. Water was fetched and soon the food was bubbling over the fire. Boiled mutton would do.

*

I moved to avoid a draught that had weaselled its way through the stones at my back. With my stomach full of warm food and an empty cup of ale in my hand, I could have fallen asleep without moving. Stretching my feet towards the fire to catch the last warmth before it died, the mud on my boots glowed red with each flicker of the flames. I had laughed off the bad omen, but as shadows collected in the base of the walls and darkness fell, I asked myself if there was something in it. Soon we would meet the enemy. Some might die. What would happen to Saewynn if I didn't return? I had planned to be away only a few nights, now it was weeks later, months. We hadn't spoken about what might happen, nor properly said goodbye. She would be looked after. Wulfstan would make sure of that. Who knows what the future held? In the darkness of this haunted place, it was impossible to ignore the signs and sleep in peace.

"I won't be long." A sleepy acknowledgement emerged from a bundled-up body as I walked into the darkness. Away from the fire it was easier to observe our surroundings. The sky was clear and a band of stars spread across the heavens. I stopped to identify some familiar constellations, before finding a clump of long wet grass and cursing quietly as my hand discovered it contained nettles. Sitting on a low wall, I removed a boot. I held it up to the starlight and scrubbed, rotating it this way and that until it was clean. It was damp inside. If it were dry come morning, perhaps I would rub in some of the leftover mutton fat. I put it to one side and reached for the other.

"Byrhtnoth? Is that you?"

"Yes, my lord." What did he want now? To complain I'd done something wrong? I grabbed another handful of nettles and squeezed them hard, imagining they were Lord Elfgar's neck.

"What's all this fuss about blood and omens? It's unsettled the men."

"It's nothing. I strayed off the road and stepped into some red mud." I held up my boot. "I'm cleaning it off now. I hope I convinced them that it was a good omen, not bad."

"You're good at that, aren't you?"

"What do you mean?" I found my knife and levered out a stubborn stone embedded in the sole of my boot and threw it into the darkness. It had annoyed me during the latter stages of the march. I would be more comfortable tomorrow.

"Telling people what to think. Diverting them from what you don't want them to know. Can I sit down?" I shuffled along the wall, to give him space.

"How did you think up that fantastic story about your sword? You even had me believing it for a while. It took in Hrafn, though. Hope he doesn't take it out on the men when he discovers he's been fooled."

"He wasn't."

"What do you mean?

"It was true."

You don't have a wife." He stopped and stared at me. "You didn't say anything."

"You didn't ask," I snapped.

"You let me think that you had ambitions to marry my daughter."

"I did once. That was long ago, things change." I gave my boot a final rub with the nettles and put it down.

"You must have known that was why I chose you for this venture."

164

"You? I thought it was King Eadred who made that decision."
Well, he gave the orders, I only made the suggestion. I have
been talking to the Ealdorman of East Anglia. He was impressed
with your efforts last year. I didn't realise you were connected to
his family."

"I didn't know myself until recently. I met my sister just after
we rescued your daughter. She told me more about my parents.
My mother was some sort of cousin of Lord Athelstan. Is that
why I am now a worthy suitor to your daughter's hand?"

"One reason. These things have to be considered. You did well
on that expedition, and you succeeded in getting the ships ready
in time. I think you have a great future ahead of you, with the
right support, and the right wife."

"Your daughter didn't think much of my prospects. Anyway,
you're too late, I'm married now."

"A pity. Elfflaed noticed you when you were at Winchester. I
think she might have been persuaded." I glanced at him in
surprise. What would he say if I told him I wouldn't marry his
daughter even if I was free to do so?

"Who is she, anyway? One of Lord Athelstan's relatives? I
hope she came with a decent fortune. That's what you need to
get on in this world."

"She came with nothing." I sensed his confusion. I had to tell
him now. "You know her, knew her, quite well."

"A friend of my daughter? I can't think who you mean."

"Her name is Saewynn."

"The name's familiar. My daughter had a slave of that name,
but it can't be her. We got rid of her, a bit of a troublemaker.
Who did we palm her off on?"

"Lord Athelstan?"

"That's right." Elfgar realised what I had said. "You can't have
married someone like that." He gave a relieved laugh. "I
understand, she's your concubine, to be put aside when you're
tired of her. My daughter will be pleased. She needs a man with

a bit of ... experience." He nudged my arm. "You nearly had me fooled there."

I slipped on my boots. They were cold, but my feet were just as cold. I was tempted to leave it there, leave Elfgar thinking that I would still make a suitable husband for his daughter. I owed it to my wife to tell the truth. I stood up and rubbed my stinging palms.

"Saewynn is no longer a slave. Lord Athelstan freed her. It was at the Christmas feast, everyone witnessed it. She wanted to learn to fight, she became one of my men. Last year she..." I refused to tell this man what she had suffered. "We married before a priest and she is expecting our child in the autumn, and if it wasn't for your interference, I'd be with her now, not in this godforsaken place. Now, if you'll excuse me, my lord, I'm off to get some sleep."

Chapter 25

Saewynn woke early. As soon as the first light filtered between the wooden boards, she rose and dressed. She slipped out into the hall, closing the door quietly behind her. Although the men were due to leave, most were still asleep, grey shapes in the dim hall. She shivered; it was too early for anyone to have stirred the hearth into life. Hild had better things to think about. Saewynn hoped she had enjoyed her wedding night.

Stealthily she made her way to the alcove where Wulfstan slept. She bent over the bed and called his name. He didn't stir. Worried that someone would hear, she touched his arm. He groaned and rolled over.

"Saewynn?" He squinted into the darkness. "Is something wrong?" He struggled into a sitting position.

"No. I want to write a letter."

"A letter? Who to? Can't it wait?" He rubbed his eyes.

"To Byrhtnoth, I want to tell him... something."

"All right, but you'll have to wait until I've got up." He yawned. "I'll bring my writing things when I've dressed."

"I don't need you, just a pen and a piece of parchment. I'll write it myself."

"You? I've taught you a few words, not enough to write a letter."

"I'll manage. Just give me what I want, and I'll leave you to sleep."

Wulfstan peered out into the hall. "Is it even light yet?"

"Not really. Is this what I need?" She picked up a leather bag from the corner.

"Yes." He slumped back on the bed. "Please, don't make a mess."

"Thank you."

"And put everything back where you found it." Saewynn was already gone.

The main door creaked as she pushed it open, she halted, no one stirred. She needed to find somewhere flat, the rocks beside the river where the women cleaned cloth would do. The light would be better there, and she would not be disturbed.

She unpacked the bag on the largest, flattest rock she found. It was where she had tried to wash Byrhtnoth's tunic long before. She remembered his body as he lay on the grass after swimming in the river. How she had wanted to touch it. Now she knew every inch, but she still ached for him. She dismissed the distracting thoughts. The only way to touch him now was with words. Did she have enough?

She got out a pen and a pot of ink. She removed the stopper and peered in, there was enough ink for her purpose. She placed it carefully on the rock. Was there any parchment? She pulled out several sheets, full of neat black writing. She tried to read them but they were too small and cramped. Why did she think she was capable of writing a letter? There was another sheet: a list of names and figures, crops? There was space at the bottom of the sheet. She smoothed it out on the rock. There was a knife in Wulfstan's bag, and she cut a strip off the parchment. Was it big enough? It would have to be. She returned the other sheets to the bag, she knew how much mess she made with a pen.

She knelt beside the rock and thought about the words she had spent the night assembling. She dipped the pen into the ink and started to write.

It took a long time, finding words and deciding how to spell them, forming the letters into the correct shapes. Wulfstan had shown her how to do it. She knew parchment was expensive; he was always complaining about the cost. She had practised on the wax tablet that he used to make notes, but that didn't involve ink. How did he make it look so easy? The ink fought her every attempt to write the words, refusing to flow at all, then flooding the page with blotches. When she reached the end and studied what she had written, she wanted to cry. She had known what she wanted to say, now it was a sprawling mess. The words were almost unreadable. It was her best attempt and would have to do. She stretched her aching fingers and waited for the ink to dry.

The light was stronger, sounds of morning drifted from the village. Saewynn realised the letter had no signature. How would Byrhtnoth know it was from her? Wulfstan had taught her to write her name, but there was no space left. Perhaps she should give up, let Wulfstan scrape away the ill-formed words and write a proper letter.

No, it was private, and although Wulfstan was her husband's best friend, she wanted Byrhtnoth to read the news, no one else. Was there room for another letter, in the corner at the very bottom? Her hand was tired. At the feast Ethelwine had encouraged her to pick up the cup. She hadn't put on the glove when she had risen and her fingers were bent, the way they had been since she was injured, although the pressure of the glove had caused them to loosen slightly. She imagined them straightening on their own. No, that would never happen.

She picked up the pen and pushed it between the twisted fingers and the thumb. For the final time, it dipped into the pot of ink, there was not much left, Wulfstan would have to make some more. Holding the scrap still with her left hand and twisting her wrist she produced a swirling letter at the bottom. It was perfect, like a small snake. She considered adding an extra curl to the tail, but footsteps were approaching. She blew on the letter to dry it and folded the parchment. It sprang open, so she folded it again and put it to one side.

Saewynn wiped the pen on a piece of cloth and replaced it in the bag with the ink. She dipped the rag in the river and scrubbed at the rock. The women would have to be warned before they next brought clothes to wash.

"There you are. Have you finished?"

"Yes, thank you, you can have your bag back." She handed it to Wulfstan.

"Do you want me to check your words?" He bent to pick up the letter.

"No!" Saewynn snatched it away and stuffed it in her pouch.

"All right," said Wulfstan, humouring her. "Come and get something to eat. The Ealdorman will be leaving soon. Do you want him to deliver your letter?"

She shook her head. She had thought about that. There was only one person she could trust.

Back in the room where she had slept, she attempted to tidy herself. Her hair had come loose. There was no one around to plait it, so she combed it through. With a scarf over the top, it would do until the men had left. She glanced at the letter. It still refused to close. Anyone would be able to read what she had written. There was nothing suitable in the small room. A piece of thread would do, but the sewing basket had been left in the chamber. She heard Lord Athelstan moving about in there. She pushed an annoying strand of hair behind her ear; she must tie it out of the way. Perhaps the strip of leather she used for her hair would secure the letter, or was there a better way?

She ran her hand through her hair. It was nearly a year since it had been shorn off. It had grown back, although it not yet as long as that of the other women. It must be longer than when Byrhtnoth left. She hung her head forward, combing with her fingers, searching for the longest strands. She took out her knife and cut them, close to her scalp. She held them up, they would do. She twisted the hair to make a thin cord and with difficulty, knotted it at either end. She wrapped it around the folded letter and pulled it tight. All it needed was to tie it off, but with one good hand, she was unable to hold the letter and tie the free ends at the same time. It was as if someone was trying to stop her from sending this letter.

The noise in the hall became louder as final instructions were given and farewells made. There was a cheer. Godric and Hild must have appeared. Saewynn burst into tears. It wasn't fair, they had spent the night together, and she couldn't even send a message to her man.

"They're about to leave," Aelf pushed open the door, "aren't you coming to ..." She stopped. "What's the matter, is something wrong? The baby?"

Saewynn pushed back her hair, wiping away the tears as she did so. "I've got to fasten this letter, and I don't have enough fingers."

"Let me help. Give me the ends." Saewynn held the letter as Aelf nimbly tied the knot. "Another to keep it secure?" Saewynn nodded.

"Thank you." The untidy package wasn't much, but at least it might now survive the journey. She hurried towards the door.

"Stop. They will wait long enough for you to get tidy." Aelf bundled up Saewynn's hair, gave it a twist and covered it with the waiting cloth. "A letter?"

"I wanted to tell Byrhtnoth about," she lowered her voice, "about last night, the baby."

"I see." Aelf grinned. "Do you think he'll know what you're talking about?"

Saewynn stopped, ran through the words she had written. Would he understand?

"Don't worry. I'm sure he'll work it out. Who will carry it for you?"

"Edward." She slipped the letter into her sleeve, took a deep breath and led Aelf out of the empty storeroom.

"I hope I haven't delayed your departure," she apologised to Ealdorman Athelstan. "All the excitement yesterday, I must have overslept."

"I was finishing some of your excellent ale, something to remember when we are in the north." He drained the cup. "Thank you for your hospitality. I will congratulate Lord Byrhtnoth on your abilities." He walked out into the bright sunshine and surveyed the assembled men. "I must admit," he said, "I had my doubts when I heard about your marriage, but he made the right choice."

"Thank you, my lord," said Saewynn, blushing with pleasure.

"Sorry to drag you out of bed." Athelstan had spotted Godric among the men. "I hope you managed to get some sleep; we've got a long journey before us."

"Yes, my lord." Godric kept his head down.

Saewynn noticed Hild at the back of the crowd. She had a satisfied smirk on her face, and Saewynn sighed with relief.

Lord Athelstan raised his voice and spoke to the men. "We go to harry the north, to persuade them to submit to the lawful king. It is not a dangerous task. You will not be away for long." He reassured Saewynn. "He will be home long before harvest time. I promise you."

"Thank you, my lord. If you'll excuse me, I must check Thunor."

"Thunor?"

"The horse, my lord."

"That savage black animal that kicked my stables apart?"

"I'm sure he wouldn't do something like that, my lord. Byrhtnoth will want him. You are planning to meet him?"

"At York, or outside it. Depending on how thing go."

"Good Luck, my lord."

"We're going to need it." He frowned, realised everyone was watching him and changed to a confident expression. A servant brought his horse, and he climbed into the saddle.

Saewynn sped across the yard to where Edward stood with Thunor. She gave him strict instructions and handed him the letter.

"Why don't you want anyone else to know?" he asked.

"I don't want any fuss, and it's private, about the baby." She blushed and turned her attention to Thunor. "There's nothing wrong, I just wanted..." She buried her face in the horse's neck, "Look after him."

"I'll do my best."

"Not you, I was talking to Thunor. You take care, keep away from the fighting."

"But that's why I'm going, I'm old enough to join the men now."

"Are you?" She studied the boy. He was right, he had grown taller over the last winter, although he still looked so young, "In that case, enjoy yourself. I wish I could come with you. Looks as if Lord Athelstan is leaving." She watched as Edward tucked the letter away, and mounted his own horse. She handed him the leading rein and stood back as they moved away.

"Behave yourself," she shouted. Edward turned and waved.

"Do you mean me, or the horse?"

"Both." Saewynn's encouraging smile faded as they followed the other men towards the road. Would they all return alive, and uninjured?

Part IV: Summer

Chapter 26

"I didn't come here to kill innocent people."

"Why did you come?"

"I came..." In my anger, for a moment, I couldn't remember why I had come. "I came because the king ordered me to mend your stinking ships. Not this." I swept an arm towards the pile of tangled bodies. It was difficult to look at what we had done.

Lord Elfgar sat on a stool that we had dragged from the hall before setting fire to it. Someone thought it might be valuable; it was just a stool. He inspected the blade of his sword, wiped it clean and slid it away.

"You attended the Witan. You heard the king's instructions. You would be here, whether you came by ship, or walked every step of the way. We are to destroy this land, whether we like it or not."

The problem was, it seemed to me, that he enjoyed it too much.

The day had started well. The long journey through the hills had ended and the flat, fertile lands of York were laid out before us. The sun was bright, and there was a gentle breeze. From the heather clad hills behind us came the sound of a lark. It flew high until it was beyond sight, but the echo of its song lingered in the space between sound and silence. Elfgar's words interrupted the call of a second bird.

"That one." He pointed out a settlement, no more than a small hall and a handful of farm buildings. It lay in the sheltering arms of the hill. Beasts grazed in a meadow beside a stream. Fields of crops, still green and studded with summer flowers, rippled like the sea.

We left the baggage in a sheltered spot and we rode the horses. Elfgar was insistent we move fast.

"Circle round, drive the animals back towards the farm. No need to hide, we want to cause as much fear as possible."

A worker in the fields stood upright to ease his back. I remembered the feeling, the dull ache caused by trudging between rows and pulling weeds. The wind snatched his shout of warning and flung it in our direction before he ran off.

"Off you go. We need meat." Our rations were low, and anticipation replaced the apprehension on men's faces. I craved the taste of fresh meat myself. "Herd them through the crops, it will save having to destroy them ourselves."

It seemed to make sense. I kicked my pony into action, one of the larger animals, although I still had to keep my legs bent to keep them from dragging in the dirt. Half the men followed Elfgar leisurely down the dusty path while I took the others, faster, cutting off any escape.

For a while it was fun, trampling the stems of grain, like children breaking the surface of freshly fallen snow. The cattle panicked. We used the butts of our spears to force the fleeing cattle back towards the buildings. One cow stopped and confronted me, defending a young calf. I could almost taste the succulent flesh. I aimed my spear, expecting her to run in fear, but the stupid animal stood firm. The blade entered her throat and she dropped. As I withdrew the spear, the calf tottered towards me, lowing plaintively. I hit it on the side of the head with the shaft of the spear, and the noise stopped. Should I bring the calf? I could come back for it. Shouting at another confused animal, I chased it up the slope towards the farm.

Weapons clashed as I entered the yard. Elfgar's horse screamed. His men were huddled close to the entrance to the hall, trapped by a shouting mob. I drew my sword and yelled at my men to abandon the cattle.

I had trained them well. We hit the back of the crowd hard and bodies fell beneath our weapons. Almost immediately we were through.

"Are you all right?" I asked.

"Yes," said Elfgar, brushing himself down." My horse was startled by a squealing pig and threw me. Half brained me on the corner of the roof. Calm it down, someone. Where are the beasts?"

"We left them. I thought you were in danger."

"From that rabble?" He nodded towards the heap of bodies. "They didn't want us to take their pig." I stared at him, at the pig, its lifeblood draining into the mud of the yard, and then at the bodies. It was a group of ceorls and slaves, the men who had run from the fields. One still held a spade, the only thing close to a weapon.

" I thought..." I no longer knew what I thought. "I'll round up the cattle. How many do you want for tonight?"

"Kill them all. We'll take what we need. Once we get into the hall, we'll soon have a fire going." One of the men was attacking the door with an axe. "Haven't you got that door open yet?" he shouted. The man was spared a reply as, with a crack, the door fell open. "Kill anyone inside, then I'll search for valuables." He noticed me waiting. "Are you still here?"

"No, my lord." I climbed back onto my horse, and forced my way out of the yard, my men following. I praised their action, although we had done little. As we passed another building, smaller than the hall, I heard a muffled scream and a curse.

"Wait here." I dismounted and drew my sword. It stuck in the scabbard and I remembered that I hadn't cleaned the blood from

179

the blade. I tugged it harder and pushed open the door. In the dimness after the bright sun, I stumbled over a body lying on the threshold, an old man, white hair sticky from the blood that still dribbled from the yawning hole that had been his throat.

"What's going on?"

"Sorry, my lord, I didn't notice you there."

I saw three of our men. I knew them, had spoken to them, eaten with them, although now I didn't recognise their expressions, full of excitement and lust. One held a woman, a girl really. She clutched a young boy, brother, son? One of the men tore him away from her. By the gaping hole in his stomach, he soon would be dead, if he wasn't already. They tossed him into a corner and his guts unravelled across another still figure. All that was visible was sallow skin and a long skein of grey hair.

"Lord Elfgar told us to kill everyone. Thought we'd have a bit of fun with this one, she's quite a wild cat." One of the men sucked at his hand, bloody teeth marks showed against the dirty skin. They tore at her clothing until she was naked. She shrunk back, eyes wide, trying to hide. She was beautiful.

"Perhaps I'll take a bite of her flesh in exchange." The man with the bitten hand reached to touch the pale skin, bent towards one of the barely formed breasts.

"No!" I had a sudden vision of Saewynn's body. The girl's hair was dark like hers. For a moment it was Saewynn. I erupted into motion, pushed the men aside and seized the girl.

"Do you want her first, my lord? Shall we wait outside?"

I shook my head, unable to speak. I felt the soft, warm skin of her quivering body beneath my hands.

"She's got a knife!" I jumped back. She was clutching my seax. She drove it deep into her belly. I grabbed her hand but she was stronger than I'd thought. She stared into my eyes, blue, not dark like Saewynn's, as her life ebbed away. She whispered something in the final moment. Thank you?

I laid her gently on the floor and closed her eyes, averting my gaze as I pulled the blade from her tender flesh and covered her with the remnants of her clothing.

"I'll speak to Lord Elfgar about this." I looked from one face to the next.

"What does it matter? He wanted them all dead," said one. He stepped back when I moved towards him.

"You will dig a grave, and give these people a proper burial."

"No need, they will burn with the building."

I glanced at the ceiling; the thatch was dry and it would burn quickly. I grabbed the man's wrist, twisting his arm behind his back. I pulled harder, lifting him until I was able to whisper in his ear.

"Do as I say, or you will have no arm left to harm anyone." I let him fall. "Get it done," I told the others, "or you will join the dead in the fire."

"What happened?" my men asked as I emerged blinking into the daylight.

"Nothing. Let's find those cattle."

Chapter 27

I sat beside the stream, my back to the ravaged farm and my face towards the high hills. It took a long time to clean the blood from my weapons. I had carried the seax since King Edmund had given it to me. How long ago? Although it had spilt blood in the past, never had I felt such shame as when the girl had snatched it to kill herself. However much I scrubbed the blade, I still saw it, thrust deep in her pale belly. The vision might fade, although I knew I would never forget her.

I picked up my sword. In my anger, I had thrust it into the scabbard without cleaning it. How did one remove the stain from the soft sheepskin of the lining? I shook my head. Everything was spoilt. The blade had been new, unused, the first I had ever owned. I had wanted it to be special, to kill fierce warriors in great battles, to become renowned for its actions. Instead, I had dishonoured it, killing a rabble of unarmed slaves, innocent of any crime except that of being in our way.

I wiped a smear of blood from the hilt. My hand must have been covered in gore when I drew it. Who had held it and used it so many years ago? Was he angry that it had been stolen from him? Would Wulfstan suffer for its theft? He had almost died to retrieve it from one of the mysterious mounds. Perhaps it was cursed. I remembered the red stain on my boots. Perhaps I was cursed too.

A few months before I had sworn to use it to protect my family. Would my unborn son suffer because of my dishonourable act?

I scoured the blade, plunging it into the gravel of the stream. I cleansed it again, and again. I oiled it until the patterns on the blade glittered like the skin of a dragon.

Cenwulf brought me a chunk of meat, cut from the hindquarters of one of the dead cows. Earlier I had dreamed of the taste, now the burnt blood smell of it made me sick.

"Take it away." He had been left, like the rest of the younger men, with the baggage. He probably thought we had done something courageous. "I'll have that though."

Relieving him of a heavy jug. I tipped it and drank. The ale had to be from the farm and I gagged remembering the old woman, dead on the earthen floor of the barn. She would make no more ale. I forced down another mouthful.

"Go away." I scowled at Cenwulf, and he scuttled back to the celebrations of Lord Elfgar and the men. I drank as my sword faded into the darkness. I drank to forget the death I had dealt that day, and I drank to drown the knowledge of what would come tomorrow.

I must have slept because when someone shook me it was light, and the smell of burning filled the air.

"Drinking doesn't help." Thurstan sat down beside me and passed me a jug of water.

"What do you know about it?"

"Remember? I rode with Elfhere, Egbert and the others. Drink, it's from a spring, high on the hill."

I sipped the water. It was cool and refreshing and I gulped down more. Thurstan passed me a piece of bread. It was dry, and I bit off a mouthful swallowing it with more of the water. I glanced at him.

"You must be used to this."

"I don't think you ever get used to it, you just become hardened and learn to accept it."

"I'm not sure I want to accept it." I knelt down by the steam and scooped handfuls of water over my head. When I sat down, I felt, if not better, a little less like wanting to die. "What was it like, travelling with Egbert? How did you come to be with him?" I took a bite of bread and wondered if there was any meat left from the previous night.

"At times like this," Thurstan waved an arm towards the burning farm, "like it was that summer, a man cannot survive alone. You have to take what you are given."

"Why were you alone? You're from Northumbria, aren't you? Near here?"

He shook his head and stared into the distance. "Far from here."

"What about your family?" I asked him.

"I have no family. Not now."

"I'm sorry, I didn't know."

"Why should you?" Thurstan glanced towards the buildings and stood up. "They're ready to leave. What are you going to do?"

"I have a choice?"

"I suppose not. What you do with it is important."

"What do you mean?"

"What do you want to do?"

I looked down at the empty jug in my hands. "I want to leave, return to the ships and sail away."

"You can't do that."

"I know. I suppose I have to go on." Reluctantly I stood up.

"Yes, but you can choose how to continue. What does Lord Elfgar want?"

"Want?" I thought about it. "Wealth, more gold and silver."

"Exactly. He doesn't really want to kill all these people. Not many men want to kill, especially not innocent people. Perhaps there's another way to get what you want, and also what he wants. Don't despair. Think."

185

Thurstan walked away towards where Cenwulf waited with my horse. I ran a hand through my damp hair, buckled on my sword belt and followed him.

By the time we rode away from the smoking remains of the farm, Lord Elfgar and I had come to an accommodation. I threatened to leave, and eventually he agreed to moderate the killing. I knew that in the long run most of the people would die, starving after the loss of crops and animals. They would be encouraged to head for York, to flood King Erik with mouths to feed and backs to clothe. That was what we were here for.

Once Elfgar realised he was able to make money, I knew I'd won. Men would be killed only if they fought back. If they were rich, they could pay: for a field undamaged, a milking cow left alive, a thatch not fully burned. Although it was against everything I believed in, fewer innocent people would suffer.

We split the men into smaller groups that could move faster, cover more ground, more farms. We kept in touch, meeting occasionally at some large hall to feast and plan our raids. As we rode south, we encounted others from the King's army. Sometimes we saw columns of smoke in the distance and diverted to fresh pastures.

At one farm, as we searched the outbuildings for valuables, I found a horse, a mare. She turned her head towards me, unconcerned by the burning torch in my hand. I led her outside. She was a tall horse, calm. I found a saddle and rode her around the yard. She was a comfortable ride, and for once my legs weren't dragging in the dust. I could have taken her, but I gave the owner a few coins. Perhaps it would help him survive the winter. He told me her name was Smoca, for her dark grey coat. It was an apt name as smoke was our constant companion. Our food and drink tasted of smoke, the flowers we trampled underfoot smelled of smoke, and our clothes reeked of it.

Wulfstan had asked me to search for breeding mares. As far as I could tell Smoca was ideal, although I hadn't paid much attention to what he had said. I instructed the men to keep an eye out for more, and they competed to find the best. Soon we had assembled a small herd, and everyone was well mounted. The pack ponies were laden with other spoils, bolts of cloth, gold and silver. It all added up. I was becoming rich.

I was careful to maintain discipline. A guard was posted at all times, ready to defend us from competing gangs. I knew that sooner or later Erik would appear to defend his land. Whenever we met the others, we exchanged rumours. There was not a whisper of assembling soldiers. As we moved towards York, the countryside became empty. News of our coming had spread. We found farms abandoned, empty of stock. People should be in the fields, collecting hay. Now the grass stood neglected, wilting in the heat until we came with our torches. It made the job easier. A quick search, a glance at the wind direction, a tossed brand, and the yellow grass was transformed into sheets of red flames. Fire rolled across the land, and the sun was obscured behind the smoke.

With the animals gone, there was nothing left to feed us. Not that I worried. As long as I found enough ale to drown me into unconsciousness each night, I was content.

One day, we found a cask of mead hidden beneath the floor of a rich hall. Next morning, I swayed in the saddle, speculating whether it would be better to dismount to be sick, or easier to do it from Smoca's broad back. When the men were not close, I talked to her. She seemed to understand. There was no one else I dare reveal my thoughts to.

"Fire!" We were surrounded by fires; what was so special about this one? I swallowed and raised my eyes.

Thurstan pointed, and then I saw it. A thick black column on the horizon, far larger than anything we had produced. "Where is it?"

"Ripon, my lord. Rumours are that the local people fled there."

"I thought we were chasing them to York."

"I expect they thought they would be safe at the monastery. It's the largest in the area, bigger than York."

187

"Isn't it built of stone?" I remembered someone talking about it. "That can't be burning."

"I went there once," said Thurstan. "Only the church is stone, the monastery and the rest of the town are wood."

"And it's been dry," I said, remembering the speed with which the fields had burnt. "We should go and find out what's happened. It might be an accident, or started deliberately."

Was King Eadred to blame? Surely Erik wouldn't do something so drastic unless to blame us for it. An attempt to burn such an ancient and revered monastery would be like hurling a bee skep onto a bonfire, not the minor stings we had inflicted.

"Let's go." I dug my heels into Smoca's side. She looked around to check I was serious. When I shouted, she knew I was, and we galloped towards the towering column of smoke.

We met Lord Elfgar and his men. They knew nothing about the cause of the fire and we joined them. If Erik's army was in the area, together we made a formidable force. Too large. I pointed to the loaded packhorses.

"Should we leave them behind?" They slowed us down and were a temptation to anyone powerful enough to relieve us of them.

"Good idea," said Elfgar. "I should have thought of it myself. We're getting careless. There was a thick forest a way back, big enough to hide an army."

"I hope there wasn't one."

"I'd have noticed." He gave me a sour look. "Might be a good time to split our rewards."

I nodded. We had passed a farmstead which I had in mind as our next target. It was on the river, out of the way and surrounded by trees. I separated the luggage and the extra mares from the main force. I spoke to Thurstan.

"If it is like the others, there shouldn't be anyone there. Take a couple of reliable men and hold it. There will be water and grass for the horses, enough food to keep you until we come back. If we don't return, head south. Find Lord Athelstan, he shouldn't

188

be far from the king. He'll sort things out. The horses are for my herds, tell my wife... Never mind. Good luck."

I watched them separate the ponies and leave. Once they had left the road, I followed Elfgar towards Ripon.

Soon we met people escaping from the town. They knew nothing or were unwilling to answer questions, just that the town was ablaze.

"Who started it?"

"The English." A large man spat onto the dusty road. He was a blacksmith who carried a large hammer among his belongings. "Where are you from?"

"We've just arrived from the north," I told him. Elfgar glanced at me and nodded.

"Where is the army? We have come to support King Erik."

"Thor only knows. In York, I expect. You sure you're Northumbrians?" He gave us a suspicious look.

"I might ask you the same question." Elfgar stared down at him and frowned. "Get out of the way." He urged his horse forward.

The man stood motionless. I tossed him a coin and he stepped aside. He glowered as he watched us ride past.

Chapter 28

When we reached the outskirts of the town, we had to fight against the crowds pouring in the opposite direction. We threaded through narrow alleys, changing direction as we found the way blocked by burning buildings, heading towards the column of smoke.

"Do you think this is a wise thing to do?" Elfgar brushed a spark from his cloak and calmed his nervous horse. "Perhaps we should get out while we still can."

"Somebody might need help." I patted Smoca as she picked her way through the refuse-filled streets, untroubled by the surrounding chaos. "And we need to find out who caused the fire."

We passed through the abandoned stalls of a market place. I plucked a couple of loaves from the back of a cart, tossing one to Lord Elfgar. I tore off a piece and passed the rest to the riders behind me. Down a narrow lane, under a stone archway, and then we were hit by the heat from the inferno that had once been a monastery.

There was nothing left of the buildings that had surrounded the church, except a row of blackened patches in the ground. As we watched, a large wooden cross toppled from its base and burst into flames. A huddle of monks took a step backwards. I urged Smoca closer.

"Is there anything we can do?"

One of the monks turned to me in anguish. "It shouldn't burn. What have we done, that God has punished us like this?"

"How did it happen? An accident?"

"No one knows," replied another monk, a novice, still young enough to be excited by the fire. "All was well at the night office, but when we entered the church for matins, the fire was raging."

"Someone must have knocked over a candle," said the first monk.

"No, it was alight when we arrived. There was a great whoosh, and flames leapt to the roof."

"Nothing to do now, except watch it burn itself out." Elfgar had been listening to the conversation as he chewed on the bread.

"Did everyone get out safely?" I joined the audience, fascinated by the roar of the flames.

"I think so." The novice muttered, then gasped as a single flame shot from the roof into the sky, followed by a spray of sparks.

"Fetch water, we don't want the fire to spread further than it has. Have you taken a roll call, counted heads, checked no one is missing?"

"That's Brother Elfrid's job. He's in charge of the scriptorium, keeps all the lists," the older monk told me.

"Where is he?" The question rippled through the group of monks.

"Has anyone seen Brother Elfrid?"

"He went back to fetch something from the church."

"Yes," said someone else. "The book. He only finished it recently."

"Spent his whole life on it," said the novice, eyes wide.

That might cause someone to enter a burning building. I checked again that Brother Elfrid wasn't amongst the monks. "Would he go anywhere else?"

"There is nowhere else to go."

I dismounted and handed the reins to the novice. "She doesn't bite," I reassured him. "Where would the brother be? Which door is closest?"

"In the apse." Several monks pointed towards the east end of the church. There was a door nearby.

"Where do you want this?" Someone put down a bucket of water. I dipped a piece of cloth in it and wrapped it around my face, then tipped the rest of the water over my head.

"Where are you going?" said Lord Elfgar, staring at me in astonishment.

"To find Brother Elfrid." I headed towards the door.

"Why you?" He shouted after me.

"Because no one else will." I took a deep breath and opened the door.

It was quiet inside the church. At first it appeared untouched by the fire until I found myself stepping on the burnt reeds. They must have helped spread the fire. Sooty shadows climbed the walls. Had they once been hangings, painted cloth or tapestry? There was nothing now. A chunk of wood, burned black fell and hit the floor, exploding in a cloud of ash. I squinted up at the beams that crossed what had once been a ceiling. The latticework was silhouetted against thick churning smoke. The roof was gone and the beams glowed red from the fire. One shifted and broke my frozen hesitation. I ran towards the apse. On the curved walls painted scenes of hell were being covered with the soot of real fires.

"Brother Elfrid?" There was nothing but the roar of flames and thick swirling smoke. I coughed, aware of the heat that surrounded me. I plunged into the darkness, calling. Then I heard words of prayer and followed their sound. A dark shape kneeled before the altar.

"Brother Elfrid?"

He turned his head. "You came." He was old, a fringe of white hair circling a tonsure brown with the scattered spots of age. His

193

face was thin and his eyes squinted up at me. "I knew you would. Take it." He thrust a book into my arms. The weight nearly caused me to drop it. How had he managed to lift it? "Go. Keep it safe."

"I didn't come for a book, I came to get you." I tucked the book under my arm and pulled him from his knees. A scream rang round the walls. I backed away, heart pounding. "Are you hurt?" Sweat stood out on his forehead and he knelt in silence until his breathing returned to normal.

"You caught me unawares. I tripped in the darkness and cannot walk. That is why you came, isn't it? My life is over. I will live again in my life's work. Pride is a sin. Perhaps that is why God has punished me."

I glanced back towards the door. There might still be time to dodge between the dropped beams to freedom.

"How are you hurt? May I look? I'll be careful."

He gave a long-suffering sigh and lifted the hem of the robe that had gathered on the floor around him. His knees were bruised and bloody, he must have crawled to reach the book. I saw the problem. One bare foot was twisted, the joint swollen. The pain it gave the old man suggested that it was broken. I touched it gently and he flinched. He was silent, although I heard bones grind together.

There was another sound, a regular groaning. Above us hung a crucifix. The figure of Christ was larger than life and gleamed in the light of flickering flames. Metal? Gold? The draft from the fire had set it swinging to and fro above our heads. It hung on chains, fixed to hooks embedded in the stone. As I watched, a crack appeared in the wall. The crucifix juddered, and a shower of mortar fell to the floor.

"We've got to move. Now." There was no time to strap the ankle. A sturdy leather bag lay on the floor. I slid in the massive book and it fitted exactly. I lifted the strap over my head and adjusted the weight on my back. The cross was moving.

"I'm sorry, this is going to hurt." I slid one arm around his shoulders, the other beneath his knees. He was lighter than I expected, like a bag of bones. I hurried towards the door.

More beams fell. The way was blocked. One of the hooks ripped from the wall, and the crucifix spun. It crashed into the opposite wall with a sound like a great bell. Cracks spread from the impact point like a giant spider's web. Another chain broke free dragging large stones from the wall. The whole of the apse was about to come crashing down, bringing the burning beams with them.

"Is there another door?" The old man shook his head. We might be safe at the far end of the church. More beams fell, great lumps of solid oak smouldering with fire.

"The crypt." The old man pointed. A flight of stone steps led down into the earth. Another boom from the metal cross was followed by the crash of falling stone. I dived for the entrance. The leather bag broke my fall and I slid backwards down the first few steps. I slithered to a stop.

"Door," gasped Elfrid.

A trapdoor stood open, ready to funnel any debris down on top of us. I reached to grab the handle. The monk's body shuddered against me. I heard the rumble of falling walls. The door slammed shut, and we were plunged into darkness. We clung to each other as the world shook.

Into the silence that followed, Elfrid spoke. "I'm alive." He sounded surprised.

Chapter 29

"Are you all right?" We were in total darkness. I couldn't tell how many more steps were below us
 "No worse than I was. We are alive, aren't we?"
 "I think so. Where do these stairs lead?"
 "To the grave of St Wilfrid. We will be safe down there. There should be a light, it is always kept burning. Let me go. I can get down the steps without further injury."
 "Sorry." He was still cradled in my arms. The passage was narrow, and I laid him on the step beside me. He slid away, down into the darkness. I sat up and hit my head on the stone above.
 "The roof is low." His voice echoed in the darkness. I crawled down the steps after him. He was seated on the bottom step.
 I squeezed past and stood up carefully. The height was adequate for a normal man, but not me. The roof was flat, large slabs laid across it. I felt the joints beneath my fingers as I shuffled forward. The passage was narrow, the rock smooth with the passage of many bodies. The walls pressed in, like the sides of a grave. I imagined myself trapped forever in the cold and dark. My questing hands encountered a blank wall ahead, and I felt myself begin to panic.

"The corridor bends to the right." The monk's calm voice came from behind. It sounded far away. I stretched out an arm into empty space.

"I'm there." I tried to hide the tremor in my voice.

"Carry on. Watch out for a step just before the end of the corridor. There should be a lamp there and a flask of oil."

Although I moved slowly, I tripped on the step and fell against the rough wall. I waited for my heart to slow before finding the lamp in a niche together with a bowl of sweet-smelling oil. I fumbled in my pouch for my flint and blinked as the spark ignited, then lit the wick of the waiting lamp. Light flooded the corridor. I hurried back as shadows flickered across the walls of a large room just visible through an arch.

First I needed to fetch Brother Elfrid. I turned the bend, and the light illuminated the passage. Had it really been that short? The old man sat on the bottom step, the stairs disappearing into the darkness above him. He was so still that I thought he was dead. "Amen," he said and lifted his head to smile at me. There was a niche in the wall beside me, I placed the lamp there.

"I'll have to carry you again."

"Thank you." He lifted his arms, like a child waiting to be picked up. His face was pale, or perhaps it was the light from the lamp. "You still have the book?" I felt the weight of it on my back. I had forgotten about it.

"It's safe." I carried him along the passage and stopped at the archway.

"Two steps." I negotiated them successfully and deposited him on the floor, close to an altar. I lit another lamp, found a box of tapers and lit other lamps until the room glowed with light.

"I'll deal with that foot now." I lifted the strap of the heavy bag over my head and searched for somewhere to put it.

"Lay it on the altar. St Wilfrid will protect it."

I placed it carefully. Behind the altar, there was a small enclosure marked by stones.

"Is that...?" I asked in a whisper.

Elfrid nodded. "This is a sacred place, we are blessed." He looked up at me, puzzled. "Are you a manifestation of St Wilfrid? You appeared in answer to my prayers and saved the book from the fire."

"Afraid not. My name is Byrhtnoth, I serve the Ealdorman of East Anglia." There was a noise, a rustle of cloth? Probably just a draught as something settled. "Tell me about St Wilfrid."

I inspected the monk's swollen ankle without touching it. I was right, a glint of white bone appeared amongst the puffy flesh. Should I move it back into place, or bind it until I could find someone who knew about these things? That would be safest. I needed something to keep the foot steady. I searched the space. At least the ceiling was high enough for me to stand upright. Opposite the altar was an archway, leading into another room, empty apart from an abandoned monk's habit. I picked it up. Stairs at the end of the room led upwards into darkness. A breeze touched my cheek. Was there another way out? I would check when I had dealt with Elfrid.

The monk's eyes were closed. He was still talking about St Wilfrid who had evidently spent a long and eventful life.

"Do you have anything I can use as a splint?"

Brother Elfrid rummaged in the depths of his habit and brought out a book. It had worn wooden covers. "Will this do? The prayers it contains will act as extra medicine."

"That's ideal, but don't you need it?"

"My eyes are too dim to read; it lives in here now." He tapped his forehead.

"I'm sorry."

"It doesn't matter, my life is near its end."

"I meant, I'm sorry, but this is going to hurt." I prepared the bindings. I felt his hand rest on my head and heard the words of a blessing.

"St Wilfrid will help you." He closed his eyes. "Continue."

By the time I finished, we were both covered in sweat, despite the chill of the underground chamber. I had opened the book and folded it around his heel, padded by a strip ripped from the abandoned robe. More strips swathed his foot.

"Not very pretty but it should hold it steady until we can get out. Can we get out? I saw more steps, I'll check. Is there anything to drink?" I had checked the leather bag at my waist. It was empty. When was the last time I had drunk anything?

Brother Elfrid opened his eyes. "There might be some wine." I searched behind the altar where priests usually hid their valuables. There was nothing there. My throat was dry and I could taste the smoke from the fire. I found the piece of bread that I had taken from the market and offered it to Elfrid. He declined. I took a small bite and put it away.

The excitement of the rescue had drained away, and the headache from the previous night's mead had returned, reinforced by the blow from the ceiling.

"I'll check those steps, there may be a way out." I stood up and stretched to ease the stiffness. I must have received a few bruises falling down the stairs.

I checked the level of oil in the lamps. Many were getting low. Brother Elfrid said that there should be plenty of oil in the corridor, but there was none. There had been nothing in the adjoining room either, perhaps it was stored near the door. I took a lamp and ducked through the archway. The second room was vaulted, more like a wide corridor. At the far end a step led to another bend. I peered around it. Beyond it was another archway and a corridor, the twin of the one by which we had entered. Steps rose upwards leading, I hoped, towards another entrance.

I raised the lamp. The stairs disappeared into darkness. I hurried forward. There was movement in the fluttering shadows. I slowed, and something flashed out of the darkness.

I jumped backwards, dropping the lamp. I felt the breeze from a swinging blade as I stumbled back to the room, missing the corner and crashing into the wall. Light filtered from the next room. I stopped to draw my seax. I had removed my sword belt.

Out of the corner of my eye, I saw it leaning against the altar. Could I reach it before the man behind the sword appeared?

Something snagged at my memory. As the blade had caught the lamplight, it had looked familiar. My opponent slipped on the patch of oil and swore. I recognised the voice. A figure stepped from the darkness.

"What are you doing here, Egbert?" I raised the seax, ready to defend myself.

"I might ask you the same question." He held the sword low, loose in his hand, but I knew how fast he could move.

"You haven't been caring for my sword," I said, ready to respond.

He lifted the sword, rotating it, so it glittered in the half-light. There was a touch of rust near the hilt, and the blade bore several nicks.

"Your sword? Yes, I remember now, you did own it, until I took it from you. Then you let me keep it." He jumped forward swinging the sword. I blocked it with the seax.

"I didn't let you keep it, you forced me." I remembered the forest, Saewynn's body covered in blood.

"Sorry. Didn't you enjoy her after I'd loosened her up for you."

"You didn't..." He was trying to make me angry. I had thought about this meeting for so long that my anger was well tempered, like the blade that he had stolen.

"That's what she told you, was it?"

I bared my teeth in a grin. "I know the truth."

I tossed the seax from hand to hand, watched his eyes follow the movement. "She told me you couldn't even get it up."

As anger flashed across his face, I threw the seax and dived through the archway landing close to my sword. By the time he followed, it was in my hand. I attacked, slashing at his belly. He dodged to one side. There was little room to fight. I had to keep clear of the old monk who had pulled himself to the shelter of the altar. I kept my body between him and Egbert. The sound of crashing blades echoed around the space. Elfrid shut his eyes and put his hands over his ears.

My seax had struck Egbert in the upper arm and was lodged there. Blood welled from the wound, spraying the walls of the room whenever he lifted his sword. I moved fast, testing his sword arm again and again. There was nowhere to hide. Nowhere to go. No time to rest. Were his blows weakening? The smell of our sweat drowned the sweet scent of burning oil. He backed me against the wall, a lamp hot on my back. I reached for it and hurled it into Egbert's face.

He ducked, and burning oil dripped down his tunic. He brushed at the tiny flames that took root there. I jumped forward, grabbed the handle of my seax and twisted. He screamed and backed away. I tasted victory. I pulled out the seax and prepared to drive it into his chest. He punched the pommel of his sword towards my face. I saw it coming and jerked back my head, hitting the stone wall, and the room seemed to tilt.

I fought the darkness as Egbert retreated. He noticed the book bag on the altar, and must have guessed it contained something valuable. He picked it up. The monk caught the trailing strap and hung on. I staggered forward to help. Egbert's blade swung. He had the bag, the monk's severed hand still clinging to the strap. Feebly my hands closed around his neck. I was still faint from the blow to my head. He swung the bag and struck me with it. I grabbed it and pulled. I had the book, although Egbert was now free.

He dashed to the archway and looked back. I was on my knees now, trying to staunch the blood that spurted from the monk's arm.

Egbert still held my sword, my father's sword, but his arm hung loose, his other hand clasped to the bloody wound.

"Better luck next time."

The last I saw was the blaze of his bright blue eyes. Then he disappeared. As I nursed Elfrid's arm, I heard the hollow steps on the stairs, the creak of a heavy door followed by a slam and the dropping of an equally heavy latch.

Chapter 30

I slid the belt from my scabbard, wrapped it around Elfrid's arm and pulled it tight. The spurting blood slowed. I pulled the belt tighter until it stopped completely. I checked my efforts had not been in vain; he was very pale, his lips blue, but he was still alive. I sat back to think. The book bag lay on the floor, speckled with spots of blood. Wearily I picked it up and placed it back on the altar. The monk's hand still clenched the strap, and I laid it gently beside the book. The room was splattered in blood. I moved Elfrid to a more comfortable position. He smiled at me.

"Saved me again." His voice was a thready whisper. How long would he last? The wound needed to be cauterised. We needed help, and quickly.

"He's gone. There must be a way out." I rested my hand on his shoulder. "I won't be long."

I took one of the surviving lamps. Would they last until we got help? A trail of blood led across the stone threshold, into the next room, and up the stairs. At the top, another archway was blocked by a solid wooden door. There was no handle. I pushed hard. It didn't move. I laid my ear against the rough surface. Silence. Either nothing was happening outside, or the door blocked all sound. I shouted and hammered on the door with the hilt of my sword. There was no response.

I searched the things Egbert had abandoned. A leather bag of water was half full. I took a sip and swilled it around my parched mouth, before swallowing. There was a jug of wine, nearly empty. I had smelled it on Egbert's breath when we fought. It must be the wine that Elfrid had mentioned. On a lower step was a large empty jar. I sniffed it: oil and it still contained a dribble. If we were careful, it would lend us more time in the light. I hurried back to the monk.

"I found the wine, take a drink." With the loss of so much blood, it was vital that he drank more liquid.

"No," he averted his head, "not allowed."

"It is allowed if you are sick and I think that losing a hand counts as sickness." He lifted his arm and stared at it.

"Oh." He accepted a mouthful of wine, and I put it carefully to one side. I inspected the strap. It would do for now, but I knew it would have to be loosened at some point.

"I wonder what time it is?"

"Just past vespers. It will be dark soon," said Elfrid.

"How do you know?"

"In a monastery your body knows the hours."

"I have a friend who does that. He only spent a few years there." How I wished Wulfstan was here. He would know what to do.

"My whole life. It will soon be over."

"Certainly not. You have many years left."

"Knew it today. My work was finished."

"The book?" He nodded. "What is it? A bible?"

"The life of St Wilfrid. It was written down long ago. I copied the words and painted pictures. Do you want to see?"

All I wanted to do was sleep, although I knew I must stay awake.

"I'll tidy up, we'll eat, and then we can study it."

I found my seax and wiped off the blood. I cleaned my sword; there was less blood on that blade, but at least, this time, it had been earned with honour. Would Egbert survive the wound I had given him? If he had collapsed outside that door, his body would draw attention to our refuge. Perhaps he had found only flames. I hoped he had died in agony, but knowing him, he had escaped and I would have to fight him again. My vow was not yet fulfilled.

"He must have been here all the time, hiding in the darkness," I said

"I suspected something," said Brother Elfrid. "When we entered, although it was dark, I caught the scent of burning oil."

"Why was he here?" It was the first time I had thought about it. "If he was sheltering from the fire, why hadn't he escaped with the others? Why was he in the church to begin with?"

"He started the fire." Elfrid was right. Egbert had used the oil, that was why the jar was empty. Had he been trapped by the flames and forced to shelter, or did he intend to hide and emerge later? It didn't matter. He had been here, and now he was gone.

"Why would he burn the church?"

"Your king has been burning the country, why not a church?"

"King Eadred ordered him to do it? He would not have needed much encouragement."

"You know this man?"

"I have met him before." I slid the clean blade into the scabbard. "He does evil for the pleasure of it. One day I will kill him."

"Not today."

"No." I found the remains of the bread and broke it in two. I handed the largest piece to Elfrid. "How is your arm?"

"The belt is tight. Otherwise I feel nothing."

"It will do for now." I sat down beside him. "More wine?"

After we had eaten, I removed the book from the bag. I rinsed my hands in some of the water before touching the rich, tooled leather cover.

"Did you make the binding as well?"

The monk nodded. "It took a long time to learn to cure the leather and then carve the wood to make it beautiful."

"It was worth it." I rested the heavy volume against my raised knees and opened it. I gasped at the colours. A whole page covered with pictures, and a few words, writ large: The Life of Saint Wilfrid. On the next page there was more writing.

Elfrid peered over my shoulder. "It is the story of his birth. He came from Northumbria, a rich and powerful man, a relative of the king."

"Is that Bebbanburg?" I pointed to a small picture in the border.

"It might be, I forget the details."

"I was there last year, I recognise it."

"Did you burn it?"

"Of course not. Why should I burn it?"

"You come from the south, like the other man. I can tell by your voice. You came to burn our land."

"I'm sorry. I didn't want to do it, but a man must obey his king."

"I know, sometimes I have disagreed with the abbot's commands, and suffered for it. You must bow your head and accept your fate. You have redeemed yourself today; you have rescued the book. Turn the page, I want to remember."

We sat there for a long time, examining the book, talking about St Wilfrid and our own lives until Elfrid's eyes closed. I checked the strap. It had worked loose, and blood dripped from the wound. He couldn't afford to lose much more. I pulled the strap tighter. I doubted he would last the night. Should I try and cauterise the arm? How to make a fire hot enough to do it? Burn the book? He wouldn't let me, the injury to his soul would be worse than the physical pain, or even death.

I would leave it to God and St Wilfrid. I extinguished all the lamps except the one that flickered above St Wilfrid's grave. The floor was cold. I laid down my cloak and lifted the monk onto it, covering him with the remains of the abandoned monk's robe. I lay down close beside him.

For the first time in weeks, I was at peace.

Chapter 31

Where was I? A light flickered, and I recognised the stone walls of the crypt. I rolled over, expecting to find the monk dead beside me. He was white, still and just alive. The cloth I had wrapped around the stump was damp with blood, but there was little pooled beneath it.

How long had I slept and what had woken me? Faint voices was Egbert back? I picked up my sword and walked silently into the adjoining room and listened. Several voices discussing what to do. I heard the sound of weapons being drawn.

"Is there anyone there?" Light and shadow played on the walls leading to the steps. Someone called my name. I recognised the familiar voice of Lord Elfgar.

"I'm here." I walked quickly to the corridor. Bright light streamed through an open door; it must be morning. Dark shapes descended the steps, Elfgar, followed by several monks. I lowered my sword.

"Come quickly, Brother Elfrid is here. He is injured, bleeding. He needs attention. Mind the oil on the floor." I led them to the chamber where we had slept.

"What happened?" The light from a torch revealed the blood splattered walls.

"Egbert was here."

"Who's Egbert?" asked Elfgar.

"He rode with Elfhere, last year, kidnapped Saewynn. He started the fire."

"It wasn't an accident?" asked a monk standing behind the Ealdorman.

"We found an empty jar of oil. Please, look after Brother Elfrid. He injured his foot when he came to rescue the book. We made it down here before the apse fell. It's broken, I bound it up. Egbert was hiding in the dark. He attacked, we fought, and he was injured."

"You must have seriously hurt him," said Elfgar. "That was how we found you. He escaped in the dark. When daylight came, we saw the blood. Everyone thought that the crypt had been destroyed with the rest of the church."

"Egbert cut off Brother Elfrid's hand when the monk tried to stop him from taking the book. He might have done it to stop me following. He enjoys forcing people to make impossible decisions. Please, the monk has lost a lot of blood. I tried to stop it..."

"We'll take care of him now." The monk bent over Elfrid. He glanced at the hand on the altar and nodded. He gave instructions to the young monk I had met when we arrived, who hurried away to fetch bandages and fuel for a fire. "Some beams are still burning," the first monk called after him. "Bring one of them if you can; it will save time. We will treat him here," he reassured me. "There is nowhere else. You did well. He would have died without your help."

"Our prayers to St Wilfrid must have helped," I said.

"Of course."

"Give them space." Elfgar took my arm. "We need to talk."

I picked up my scabbard; I would have to find a new belt for it. I followed him up the stairs and out into the daylight.

I was disorientated. It was not just the apse that had fallen, the whole church was gone. All that remained was a heap of broken stone. A haze of dust and ash hung in the air, and smoke rose in thin trails from the red glow of charcoaled wood.

"The other entrance to the crypt is over there." Elfgar pointed to where the tumbled stone was deepest. There was no sign of the trapdoor that I had slammed shut behind us. St Wilfrid must have protected us.

"This is how we found you." Near the open door the latch that had held the heavy wood in place had been abandoned. It was marked by a bloody handprint. I noticed a scattering of blood spots on the ground. I started to follow them.

"Don't bother. Too many feet have passed this way. Stones fell and blocked the door." His hands were scratched and grey with dust. He dusted them off with embarrassment. "We were searching for your body."

"To prove I was dead so you could claim all the booty?"

He gave a grunt. "Are you injured?

"Nothing serious. Let's get clean and find something to eat."

*

"Why did Egbert set fire to the church?"

Elfgar's men had set up camp beside the river. Smoca was there, calmly cropping the fresh grass as if nothing had happened. A quick dip in the shallow cold water revived me, and with a cup of ale in my hand and some fresh bread, I felt more myself.

"He must have been working for King Eadred." I had spent much time in the crypt thinking about it. "The destruction of crops and burning of villages hadn't provoked any reaction from either Erik or the Archbishop of York. We both know how impatient the king is." Elfgar, his mouth full of cold meat, nodded in agreement. "The fyrd can't be retained for much longer. He had to force the Northumbrian's hand."

"That sounds about right." He wiped his mouth on his sleeve and picked up a jug of ale. "There'll be a battle soon."

"Where?" There had been no trace of the enemy army. "Is Erik still in York?"

"He must be. It's the obvious place. Our army is gathered nearby." He took a deep draft and passed me the jug. "No doubt you'll find your friend Egbert there."

"If he's not dead in a ditch." I hoped he was, but I couldn't rest until I knew for sure. "We head for York?" I emptied the jug. "What about the packhorses? Do we wait for them?"

"I've heard that people are gathering to take their spoils south, to get the valuables out of the way before the battle begins."

"Sounds sensible. I'll send someone to tell the men to head in that direction."

"I've already done it." Lord Elfgar stood up and brushed down his tunic. "Let's go."

I was preparing to mount when the young monk appeared.

"I was told to give you this, my lord." He handed me my sword belt. Someone had attempted to clean it, but it was stained with blood, and the stink of burning flesh permeated the leather. "They stopped the bleeding. Brother Elfrid is alive. With time, he should recover."

"Thank you for coming to tell me. Perhaps one day I will return, and we can continue our conversation about St Wilfrid."

The boy grinned. "I'll give him your message." He waved as we splashed through the river and headed for York.

*

"Where is the king? We bring news from Ripon."

It was late when we reached the outskirts of York, and the camp was quiet. When told that the Ealdorman of Essex had arrived, men on the gate directed us to the king's hall. The room was not large, and tables still carried the remains of a meal. A few men watched our arrival in silence. Others were sleeping, wrapped in blankets around the dying embers of a hearth.

"The king is asleep. He must not be disturbed," said a guard. "What message do you bring?"

"It is important," announced Lord Elfgar. "The Minster at Ripon has been destroyed, burnt to the ground."

"The king has already received this news. If you have anything to add, return in the morning."

"What is all this commotion?" A priest emerged from the inner room. "The king is not well, he must rest."

"I'm sorry, we bring news from Ripon."

"We heard the church was burning. Was it saved, by God's mercy?"

"I'm afraid not," said Elfgar. "It was totally destroyed."

"What of St Wilfrid's shrine? Surely that was not ruined?"

"No, my lord, the fire did not touch it. I was there," I told him.

"And you are?"

"This is Thegn Byrhtnoth. He sailed with me from Exeter. We have been harrowing the lands to the northwest. We saw the smoke of Ripon and rode to investigate. Byrhtnoth entered the building to save one of the monks. They sheltered in the crypt."

"I see." The priest studied me with a frown. "I have heard that name before. Wait here, I will consult with the king's servants."

He retired, and we waited. I glanced at Lord Elfgar, and he shrugged. From behind the door came the murmur of voices. The men watched us with suspicion. One spat in our direction before taking a mouthful of ale. Had we been right to come straight to York?

When he returned, the priest glanced nervously towards the guards.

"I don't know what you hoped to achieve by coming here," he said, avoiding my eyes. "Thanks be to God the truth has already been revealed." He pointed at me. "Seize this man!"

The guards leapt forward and grabbed my arms. I struggled, but we had surrendered our swords before we had entered the hall and I was unarmed.

"Take him away. And keep him under close guard. Ealdorman Elfgar, you will return tomorrow to give evidence before the king. We have a witness who will testify that this man is responsible for the burning of the church at Ripon; a sacrilegious act.

"No, it was..." I shook my head as they dragged me towards the door.

Elfgar stepped forward to intervene.

"Leave him, my lord, or you will join him."

Elfgar paused and glanced at me. "Don't worry. I'll sort this out."

I tried to fight the guards, but they were well trained. My arms were tied tightly behind my back. I was dragged through the camp to a small hut and pushed through the door. One man punched me, and I fell to the floor. The other gave me a kick in the ribs and slammed the door. I lay still in the darkness, recovering my senses. The sound of running water indicated that I was close to the river, so close that it flowed through the hut. The smell of it told me that it had flowed through the latrines first. I struggled to my feet and propped myself against the wall. It didn't take long to work out what had happened. Egbert was not dead in a ditch. He had reached York before us. Whether King Eadred had planned the burning of Ripon or not, he had found himself a scapegoat, and I was to pay the price. Elfgar had said he would help. Could I trust him?

Chapter 32

It was a long night. I couldn't sleep standing, and I refused to lie down on that floor. I needed to be on my feet when they came for me. My shoulders were strained by the tightness of my bonds, and my ribs ached. I fought the ropes, but the guards were experts at their job, and all I achieved was to rub my wrists raw. When was the last time I had eaten? Before we left Ripon, and then not much. I was hungry and thirsty, made worse by the continual trickle of water.

Morning dawned, and no one came. Had I been forgotten? As the camp woke the volume of liquid from my neighbours increased, soon it washed around my ankles, and I retreated to the highest part of the floor. The smell became worse as it got warmer. The scent of new lit hearths filtered into my small space. Someone was cooking bacon. Perhaps it was the guards, doing it to torment me. The combined smell of food and the latrines caused me to heave. Now I had the smell of vomit to contend with; I couldn't even wipe my mouth. I closed my eyes and tried to ignore where I was, but my imagination conjured up bloody visions of what was to come.

The king's monk had accused me of sacrilege. It was not a crime that was often dealt with by the courts. It was only pagan raiders who burned churches, and they were rarely caught. If I was found guilty, what would they do to me? Hang me, I expect. I remembered the scaffold we had seen at the mounds near Rendlesham, the body left to hang and ripped apart by scavengers. I hoped they would build it high so that I would die quickly.

First, there would be a trial. Would the court believe me, or Egbert? He had the king's favour, and I did not. I was at a disadvantage to begin with. I knew that Egbert had started the fire. Why would he do it unless the king had given the order? Eadred was a religious man, surely he would never encourage someone to burn a church, and not just any church, St Wilfrid's own minster at Ripon. Just to bring Erik Haraldsson to battle? I knew that he had arranged the death of his own brother to take the throne. I almost laughed. He had tried to blame me for that crime as well.

Sweat trickled down my face, it must be near the middle of the day by now, and no one had come near me. I shuffled to the door and pressed my ear against it. Someone was snoring close by. One of the guards? Perhaps I could find a way out, escape. I edged my way around the walls, searching for some weak point, a rotting board that I could attack. Although I would achieve little with my hands tied behind my back. There was nothing. Considering the dampness, it was remarkably sound, only a small knot hole in one of the planks. It gave a view of the river and little else. I snatched a breath of fresh air, but the thought of fresh water so close and unavailable drove me back to prowling around the small space. Less than four paces across from wall to wall, not even far enough to stretch my legs.

I was dozing, leaning against the wall close to the only ventilation when the door opened. I rushed forward, only to be stopped by a spear pointed at my chest.

"Keep away, or you don't get any food."

I stepped back. The guard threw a piece of bread onto the floor in front of me. By the thump, as it hit the ground, it was very stale. It would have to do. The guards backed away. Was that all?"

"Water," I croaked.

"Sorry, the water's not fit to drink around here," said the guard who had thrown the bread. "We've only got ale." He held up a jug. "Do you want some?"

I nodded.

"You got a cup?" he asked the guard with the spear, who rested the butt of his weapon on the ground and handed over a dirty wooden vessel. I watched as he poured out a generous portion of the amber liquid. He held it out to me. I bent forward to take a sip, and the heavenly scent of the ale filled my senses.

The man snatched it away, the liquid slopping over the edge and spilling onto the floor. "What do you think you are? An animal? Take it like a man."

I frowned. "Untie me." I twisted to show my bound wrists.

"Oh, we can't do that, dangerous prisoner that you are." I stared at him in confusion, what was going on? The other guard laughed, and I realised this was a practised routine. The first man held out the cup again, and I watched it, as I had never watched anything before.

"Don't want it then? Well better not let it go to waste." He lifted the cup to his own lips and took a healthy swig. I watched the motion of his throat as he swallowed it. He smacked his lips and wiped his mouth on his sleeve before taking another sip. "Not a bad drop of ale." He offered the cup to the other guard, who shook his head. "Too bad." Slowly he tipped the cup, and the ale tricked out onto the floor. As he did so, he looked straight at me, with a triumphant grin on his face.

"Better luck tomorrow, mate," the other man said with a course laugh. As they prepared to leave, I launched myself forward, I don't know why. To catch the last few drops of ale? The butt of the spear caught me on the side of the head. I fell to the ground. I was aware of a boot kicking me out of the way of the door as I collapsed onto the floor.

It was some time before I found the energy to move. I searched for the chunk of bread in the darkness. It had fallen into a pool of the noxious liquid, but I paused only an instant before consuming it. At least I didn't have to make the difficult choice as to whether to drink. If I was to survive, I had to eat and drink, and I no longer cared what.

I tore at the softened bread with my teeth, bent forward like the animal they had named me. When every crumb had been consumed, I lapped at the liquid before recoiling in disgust. I huddled in the corner, hoping I would not need to do it again, although I had done it once, I could do it again if it were a choice between that or death.

Had they even intended to put me on trial or did they mean to leave me here until I died, alone and forgotten? Was I foolish to have put my trust in Lord Elfgar? Who else knew where I was? I had left Thurstan and the other men with the horses. Wouldn't they question where I was or had Elfgar given them some plausible excuse? Perhaps, in time, questions would be asked. It would be too late by then. Survival depended on my own actions. I would only get one chance, so my plan had better be good. I located the door and recalled where I had fallen when the guard had hit me with the spear. I arranged my body into a relatively comfortable position and prepared to wait.

As the heat of the day faded, my body grew cold as the damp soaked into my clothes, and I started to shiver. I tried to ignore my predicament. What would Saewynn be doing? I had no idea how late it was. Perhaps she would be sitting in the hall, lingering over the evening meal. The place would be half empty, most of the men would have left long ago to travel north. Where were they? Camped only a few paces away, oblivious to my condition? I mustn't think about it.

I hoped Saewynn and Aelf had become friends. Had my wife started training again? I had suggested she learn to use her left hand. Would I ever use my hands again? I no longer felt them. I attempted to bend my fingers, felt a stab of pain, not dead yet.

What would Saewynn do if I never returned? Who would look after her? I had arranged at our wedding that if I died, she would have the village. Wulfstan would help her. Perhaps they would marry. I pushed that thought away, it was still too raw. What about my son? I had almost forgotten about the child. How long until it was due to be born? Several months yet. I wished I could be back with them.

Would they be safe from Egbert? I had promised to kill him. I had failed in that endeavour, as I had in many others. I regretted that I would never meet my father. If he were dead, as I had thought for so long, perhaps we would meet soon. That was something to look forward to. I imagined what he would say to me.

Despite the long wait, the creak of the door almost caught me unawares. Light streamed into the hut, together with the early morning noise of the camp. It was easy to pretend to be dead, I was already halfway there. I listened to the exclamations of the guards, the accusations and then the triumph of a job well done.

"I thought he would last longer than that."

"It must have been that blow with the spear. I told you it was too hard."

"It was just a light knock, to stun him. Is there any blood?" A hand gripped my hair and turned my head roughly from side to side.

"I can't see anything. Drag him outside, where the light's better." I forced myself to stay limp as they each grabbed a leg and dragged me out of the hut and into bright sunshine. Should I wait until I became accustomed to the light or attack now? My head bounced over the threshold, and I tasted blood.

"What we going to do with him? Straight into the river?" Could I survive with my hands still tied? If I struggled, they would just pull me out again.

"Better not, it's light now. Put him back in the hut until tonight?" I refused to be returned, better to die now. I prepared to act.

219

"S'pose we'd better let someone know. They're all ready for the trial. Will they want to inspect the body?" There was to be a trial. I might have a chance. "Someone will check. There's some blood on his face, better get rid of that, or we'll get the blame."

Before I could decide how to pretend to wake up, a bucket of water was tipped over my head. Coughing and spluttering, I was still able to see the look of consternation on the faces of the guards. I managed to swallow a few drops of water before they dragged me to my feet.

"Didn't you check he wasn't alive?"

"You said he was dead and I believed you."

"We're lucky he didn't get away."

"In that state? He wouldn't have got far." He was right. I was weaker than I had thought. I could have attempted to walk but decided to save what little strength I did have and let them drag me towards the town. The pressure on my arms was agony, but the pain told me I was still alive.

Chapter 33

We entered a large building, the hall we had visited the previous night. The room was crowded now, hot and airless. Men craned forward to watch what was happening. I caught a glimpse of Lord Elfgar, looking serious. I managed to walk the last few steps and raised my head to stare into the eyes of King Eadred. I stood as straight as I was able, ignoring the filth that coated me. The king wrinkled his nose and waved me away.

"Am I dismissed, my lord?" I spoke more to test my parched throat than to expect a reply. The king frowned. Perhaps it had been a mistake.

"Certainly not." There was a titter from the audience. "Silence. A serious crime has been committed. Who makes the accusation?"

"I do, my lord." I had been aware of Egbert's presence from the moment I entered the hall but refused to acknowledge him. His voice was feeble, as if from his deathbed. His arm was strapped across his chest, and his body swathed in bandages. He reclined in a chair, the only person apart from the king to remain seated. His face was white, and his eyes closed. Then he opened them and I caught a gleam of amusement before his lids subsided. As I suspected, it was all an act.

"Are you strong enough to make your oath?" The king asked, patting his uninjured arm. Egbert murmured and nodded. The priest, the same who had spoken to us last night, no, the night before, brought a bible, and Egbert placed a hand on it.

"By the Lord, I accuse Byrhtnoth of burning the great minster at Ripon. I also accuse him of the callous murder of a monk of the monastery there and an unprovoked attack on your plaintive, bringing me close to death." He slumped in the chair, and his hand slipped limply from the book. I heard shouts of outrage and kept my face expressionless. He had made a serious mistake. Did I have a chance?

"What do you say to this accusation?" I stepped forward. The king shrunk back and waved me away. "They will bring you the book." I bowed my head. The priest held the bible out to me. I stared at him, then back at the guards.

"Untie him," snapped the king.

A knife sliced through my bonds, and my arms dropped. I rolled my shoulders to release cramped muscles. I raised my right arm, the hand had no feeling, although I knew it would be excruciating when the blood returned. For now, my fingers were white and swollen, useless as dead meat. I placed it on the book. Egbert had used his left hand to swear, was his oath valid? It didn't matter. I stared the king in the eyes.

"By the Lord, I am guiltless both of deed and instigation of the crimes with which Egbert charges me. I was many miles from Ripon when the fire started. Egbert was already there. I admit to fighting Egbert. He attacked me and the monk, Elfrid, whom I defended. The monk survived the attack by Egbert, and can be brought to this court to swear to the fact." I saw the alarm, rapidly hidden, on Egbert's face. The king frowned.

"Do you bring oath-helpers to support you?" Would Elfgar stand by me? If I had no one to speak for me, my testimony was useless. Sweat trickled down my back. Whispers ran around the hall.

"I will swear." I breathed again. "I am Elfgar, Ealdorman of Essex. By the Lord, the oath is pure and not false that Byrhtnoth swore. He was far from Ripon when the fire was set. He has served me well and always obeyed the king's commands, regardless of his own wishes." I gave a wry smile. We had had our differences, but in this, he had not let me down.

"I will swear." Another voice broke the silence. "I am Athelstan, Ealdorman of East Anglia. By the Lord, the oath is pure and not false that Byrhtnoth swore. This man has served me for several years. He gave me his oath, and he receives my protection."

I hadn't noticed him in the hall. He must have arrived with my men. I craned my head and saw Godric at his shoulder. He grinned at me.

"Thank you, Lord Athelstan." The king gave Egbert a sour glance, and my enemy's face grew even paler. "Does anyone else wish to speak?" He surveyed the hall. There was movement at the far end, and someone new stepped forward. For a moment I didn't recognise the man, then I saw Elfhere standing beside him. My stomach dropped, and I felt sick.

"Lord Ealhhelm. What does the Ealdorman of Mercia have to say on this matter?" said the king. I asked myself the same question.

"By the Lord, I have no opinion on the oath of Byrhtnoth, I do not know him. I wish to speak of the accuser." Did he support Egbert? I had two oath-givers, perhaps what he said would make no difference. Egbert stirred nervously in his chair. "I am ashamed to admit that the man Egbert once served me. He is the most untrustworthy person I have ever met. I dismissed him from my service last year, and I am surprised to find him in this place, so close to the king." He turned on his heel and left the hall.

Silence fell, then Egbert made a miraculous recovery. He leapt to his feet and freed his injured arm. It held a sharp knife. He grabbed the king and held the blade to his throat. King Eadred's face blanched and he scrabbled against Egbert's grasp.

"Keep still, or you die," said Egbert.

The king froze. They stepped from the raised dais and down into the main body of the hall. Egbert stared straight at me, a smile on his lips. I was the only person in his way. Before I could decide what to do, I was pushed aside as my guards rushed towards the king and his captor. I stumbled and nearly fell. By the time I had regained my balanced, I knew that the situation had worsened. The guards were not there to rescue the king but to protect Egbert. I should have known that they served my enemy. They ranged themselves on either side of Egbert and the king, swords pointed towards the shocked audience. Nobody in the room was armed; as usual, all weapons had been left at the door.

I looked around. No-one stepped forward, most were afraid that the king would die in the attempt, others hoping, perhaps, that he would be killed. I was closest. I had no weapon, not even my bare hands. I felt the prickling that told me the blood was returning, but they would be useless in a fight. Egbert grinned at me in triumph, once more he had placed me in an impossible position.

He was wrong. He thought I would fear causing the death of the king. I didn't. All that concerned me was that Egbert would escape. If the king died, I didn't care, another would be found, he couldn't be worse. I grinned back, and Egbert's smile faded. He moved the knife closer to the king's throat. A drop of blood dribbled down the king's neck, then another. King Eadred's pleading eyes met mine. I was close enough to see the sheen of sweat on his face. I shifted my balance and kicked out.

My foot hit not Egbert or the king, but the closest of the guards. I caught him on the wrist. He shouted, and his sword clattered to the floor. I ignored it, perhaps someone else could make use of it. I lowered my head and charged straight at Egbert. Ignoring the knife, I hit him hard in the stomach and the breath was forced out of him. Straightening, I caught his chin with my head. It jerked backwards, and his body followed. The knife skittered across the floor, and Godric stooped to pick it up. I pushed the king out of the way and faced the other guard. He hesitated, then his gaze flickered to something behind me.

"Mine, I think." I stepped to one side, and Lord Athelstan surged forward with the discarded sword. The man died instantly.

The first guard was on the ground, nursing his injured wrist. I kicked him again, in the chest and his arms spread wide. I stamped on his left hand, and he screamed. I placed my foot on his other hand, was it already broken? I didn't care and put all my weight onto the wrist, watching his face as I did so.

"Please," he begged. I shook my head and ground my foot as if crushing an insect beneath my heel. I continued until I felt the shattered bones crumble. Finished, I sank to my knees, clutching my swollen hands to me as jagged pain surged through them.

"Are you all right, my lord?" I looked up to find Edward standing beside me.

"Thirsty. Can you find me a drink?" He dashed away between the surging crowd. I looked up. The king had disappeared, whisked away by his attendants. Lord Athelstan was directing the binding of Egbert's hands. I noticed blood seeping from his bandaged arm; from the wound that I had given him in the crypt.

"Shall I finish this one off?" Godric crouched over the injured guard, who lay whimpering on the floor.

"No, let him live," I said, "he'll never use a weapon again," or hold a cup of ale in his hand, I thought.

"Will this do?" Edward tried to hand me a jewelled cup, realised his mistake and held it to my lips. Rich red wine slid down my tortured throat.

"Where did you find that?" I took another sip. "It's all right, I don't want to know. Ale would have been fine."

"I found this, as well." He produced a piece of soft white bread, tore off a piece and fed it to me.

"Can you stand?" asked Godric. I nodded, and he pulled me to my feet.

"I assume the trial's over," I said as we watched the hall empty. "Where's Lord Elfgar? I must thank him for his help."

"I think he left with the king."

"Of course." I saw Lord Athelstan watching. "We'll speak later," I told Godric. I approached Lord Athelstan and bowed. My head spun with relief and the wine. "Thank you, my lord. Lord Elfgar managed to find you?"

"I came as soon as I heard." He smiled. "Saewynn made me promise to look after you, and I couldn't let her down."

"You've seen her? Is she well?"

"She was very well when we collected the men. How are you?"

"I'll be all right when I've had a bath."

"Yes, I noticed the smell. Where have you been? We looked for you, but no one had seen you."

"Somewhere down by the river. The guards belonged to Egbert. I should have known by the way I was treated. There was a time there when I didn't think I'd survive." We walked out into the bright sunshine, and I lifted my face to the lifegiving warmth.

"You've cheered up." Lord Elfgar joined us. "I was sure things would go all right, with both of us speaking for you. That Egbert is a slimy piece of shit, isn't he? He almost had me believing his lies."

"Where is he?" I hoped they would put him in the hut where I had spent the night.

"Safe. It happened so quickly, No one expected him to move so fast," said Lord Athelstan.

"I did. It was only a minor flesh wound. I probably came off worse in that fight in Ripon than he did." I suddenly felt very tired. It had been a rough few days.

"I'll leave you with Lord Athelstan," said Elfgar. "Your service with me has come to an end. Thank you for your help. I'll send your horse to you. We can discuss everything else when you've recovered."

"All the mares are mine, remember." I wasn't prepared to let him get away with anything.

"I know, and half the rest of the treasure," he replied, "if the king leaves us anything."

"I'm sure you'll find a way to hide a few bits and pieces. It's been an education riding with you."

He snorted and asked Athelstan where he was camped.

"We're south of the river." He rested a hand on my shoulder. "We'll dump you in the water as we cross. I'll send ahead to prepare some food. I should imagine you're hungry."

My stomach replied for me, and everyone laughed. "I'll swim across the river if it means I get across quicker."

*

I wiped the last of the stew from the bottom of the bowl with a piece of fresh bread and leaned back with a sigh of contentment.

"How long have you been here?" I asked Lord Athelstan.

"Not long." He sat sipping a cup of wine. "The king has had us running all over the countryside, burning crops."

"Me too. Do you think it's done any good?"

"Apart from bringing in plenty of treasure?" He poured some wine into another cup and passed it to me.

"Not too much. I'm half asleep already." I took a small sip and put it down. "What was it all for? Did King Eadred think it would bring Erik to battle, or was it just punishment?"

"I don't know. Rumours are circulating that Erik is ill, close to death. Others say he's afraid. Most likely he's too comfortable, enjoying the bribes we paid last year. He's not concerned that his people will starve next winter. York survives very well on trade."

"If he has nothing to trade, they'll stop coming. How long does the king intend to stay?"

"Most of the troops that have been scouring the country have returned. That's why this place is so crowded. Eadred is either planning an attack on York..."

"That would be a big job." I yawned. All I wanted was to lie down in the sun and sleep. "Would it work?"

"I doubt it. Time's running out. The fyrd will leave soon unless he's planning to use some of the silver that we've collected to raise another. That can't be arranged overnight. With this hot weather, the harvest will be ready. Everyone wants to go home."

"Why burn Ripon? Was that a final taunt to Erik?" I picked up the cup and stared into it.

"Did King Eadred arrange it?" said Lord Athelstan

"It must have been him. Egbert was responsible, but even he must have been given instructions. You've not had a chance to question him?" I asked. "Not that he would tell the truth if his life depended on it."

"The king's guards took him away, so I suppose we'll never learn the truth. Is that your horse?"

"Where?" I sat up and squinted into the sun.

"Over there, a great grey mare, she's your size."

"Oh yes, Smoca. I found her on one of the farms we burned. I had an idea she would be good for breeding. Wulfstan told me to keep my eyes open for anything suitable. I've collected quite a herd. God knows how we're going to get them home."

"You'd better go and introduce her to Thunor."

"I'd forgotten he would be here."

"Your wife insisted we bring him. With no one to exercise him, he was getting fat." I hoped she hadn't tried to do it herself. "She's quite a determined woman, she even bullied me."

"Saewynn did? I apologise, my lord."

"Don't worry. Here's Godric, he'll tell you what's been going on." I realised I was neglecting my own men.

"I'll go and talk to him. Thank you again for your help." With a groan, I struggled to my feet.

"You're my man. I have to support you, whatever you are accused of."

Chapter 34

"What do you think? Wulfstan told me to find some mares."

"At first glance, she appears to be satisfactory." Edward studied Smoca. "I'll give her a more detailed inspection when I groom her. She's big. Is he planning to breed large horses?"

"He will if I have any say in the matter. There are more coming. I collected saddles and other equipment as well. I didn't enjoy burning farms," I frowned at the memory, "but the rewards will be welcome. How are we going to get them all home?"

"So long as you ride Thunor, we'll manage."

"I'll go and find him. How is he?"

"He needs exercise." I followed Edward towards the area where the horses were kept. "I hope the new horses will bring fodder with them. With the arrival of more men, it's getting difficult to find enough for them to eat."

"Perhaps we should start moving some of them south," I said. "Lord Athelstan thinks we'll be leaving soon."

"Well, we can't stay here for much longer. What do you think?"

Thunor had been dozing in the sun. When he heard our voices, his ears pricked, and he tugged restlessly at the rope. As usual, I approached with caution, but I thought he was pleased to see me.

I told him we would have a ride later, and he turned his attention to Smoca whom Edward had tethered nearby.

"You've cared for him well." I congratulated Edward.

"I wouldn't dare do otherwise. Saewynn gave me a long list of instructions. That reminds me, she sent you a letter." He rummaged in his bag.

"A letter?" Why would Saewynn send me a letter? Was she unwell? By the time he handed me a small package I had imagined a hundred disasters.

"She told me that you were not to worry. It is good news." Godric was hurrying towards us. I thrust the letter away, I would read it later. "He's got some news as well," said Edward.

"I've been searching for you. I knew you'd be all right with the support of Lord Athelstan, although for a while I was worried. You must have got on better with Lord Elfgar than when we accompanied him on that trip to save his daughter."

"Most of the time," I told him. "Why did Lord Ealhhelm support me? That was a bit of a surprise."

"It surprised everyone," said Edward. "He was arguing with Elfhere before the trial."

"Have you forgiven Elfhere for his attack on the village?" Godric asked me.

"Not really. I've met him a couple of times. In Winchester, remember? And..." where had it been? "in Chester. He apologised. I still don't trust him. If he persuaded his father to speak up, it was more that he was against Egbert than for me. Enough of that, Edward says you have news for me."

"Yes." Godric shifted from one foot to another. What had he done now? "I know I should have got your permission, but you weren't there, and we were about to leave..."

"Just spit it out Godric," I said.

"I've married Hild."

"About time too. I thought you'd never get around to it. Was she...?"

"Certainly not, my lord." Was he blushing? "It was Saewynn who organised it." Saewynn? What had she been getting up to while I was away?

"It was Lord Athelstan's fault," said Edward. "He arrived early."

"Yes," agreed Godric. "I'd left it too late, there was no time. Hild was upset."

"I don't blame her," I said.

"It was Saewynn who persuaded the Ealdorman to stay, and we had the wedding that night. She organised it all. Hild had to get ready, so your wife arranged the food and everything."

"She made me cook eels," added Edward with a mixture of shame and pride.

"You're sure about this? Saewynn took charge of everything? Even Lord Athelstan?" I looked in the direction of his tent. "It must have been Wulfstan who organised it."

"Oh no, my lord," said Edward, with a broad grin. "He was given orders to kill and prepare the animals for the feast."

I shook my head. What had happened to Saewynn? She had been so quiet, nervous about everything. Was it something to do with the baby? Was it because I wasn't there? Was she stealing my authority? The letter would give me an answer. I needed some privacy to read it.

"Saddle Thunor," I told Edward, "I'll give him some exercise."

Edward held Thunor steady while I mounted. The quiver of excitement that ran through his body matched my own. He took a step towards Smoca, then with a toss of his head that nearly unseated me, he wheeled and headed towards the edge of the camp. "That's right," I patted the glossy black neck, "We don't need women while there are enemies to destroy."

*

We were miles from the camp when Thunor slowed. We entered a wood to find some shade. There was a river, the same water in which I had washed away the filth of my imprisonment? If it was, it was much smaller here. There was no one in sight. I rubbed down Thunor and led him to the water then tethered him

233

to a branch, close to a patch of fresh grass. I sat down beside the river and, for the first time in a long while, relaxed. There was no fire or smoke. No people to give orders or need telling what to do. The wood was quiet, the birds silent. Overhead the sun shone through leafy branches. A fish jumped in the river and somewhere close, bees hummed.

I watched the sparkle of the sun on the river for a while until the letter called to me. I took it out and studied it. A scrap of parchment, folded several times, smaller than the palm of my hand. There were no words on the outside, no direction to its recipient. The edges were grubby, and it was fastened with a length of twisted thread. I drew my knife to cut it, then paused. Was it a thread? I touched it. It was smooth, with a shine. Hair? It was dark, like Saewynn's. I lifted it to my nose. Was there a hint of the perfume of her hair? The letter had spent a long time in Edward's bag. Perhaps it was the smell of the trees, but something brought back the memory of her, of running my hands through its dark softness. When I closed my eyes, I saw the strands spread across the pillow, remembered that smile of sleepy satisfaction that only appeared when we were alone.

There was a noise, and the image fled. Just the horse reaching for some succulent leaves, but I was angry. It had been so long since I had held her. Her hair must be longer now.

I struggled with the knot. Finally I managed to remove it without breaking the strands. I wound it into a curl and placed it to one side. The parchment unfolded slowly. I smoothed it out on my knee. There was a handful of words, badly formed and with plenty of ink blots. Was this Saewynn's writing? She had never had a need to write anything before. Wulfstan had mentioned teaching her a few words. How could she write with her injured hand? Perhaps she had used her left. I had encouraged her to practice with it, but she told me firmly she would never fight again. I had pretended not to notice the tears in her eyes as she said it.

At first, the words were illegible. I laboriously traced out each letter, and the first words became clear, 'Myne Leofe', My Love. I smiled. No one else would have used those words to me.

The next words were 'This Day'. What day? There was no indication of when it was written. I guessed sometime close to when she had given the letter to Edward. I would have to ask him. Did it matter? The next words were 'The Child'. It must be from Saewynn, no one else would write to me about a child. Unless it was a reference to Edgar, the son of the last king. Saewynn had helped to rescue him, hid him at the village before I arrived with Edith. Why would she write to me about him?

I puzzled long over the next word. Something about movement, a child walking? No, a child moving. Was the baby moving? What did it mean? Was it important? Did it mean the birth was close? It was a long time yet, I thought. What if it was too early? No, Edward had said it was good news. It must be something that women know about, something significant and good. I would have to find a woman to ask. How? It didn't matter, Saewynn thought it was good.

I recognised the last words, 'Be Safe'. I sat up and stretched my back, reading was hard work. I thought I understood the message now. 'My love, this day the baby moved, be safe.' Then I saw the initial. It was squeezed into the corner as if she had run out of space, an 'S', just like a snake. She must have thought so too, as she had added a tiny forked tongue at one end. I laughed out loud. It was if she were there beside me, sharing the joke.

I marvelled at her determination. She had wanted to tell me something. She had laboured in forming the words, used her own hair to bind it and chosen the best messenger to deliver it. Had she kissed it before she sent it? I hoped so, because I kissed it too. I lay back in the grass. I imagined her there beside me. I told her what I had been doing. I held her in my arms and promised I would soon be home.

I woke to find the sun had moved. It would soon be dark and Thunor was restless. We must leave. I folded the letter around the lock of hair and placed it in a safe place in my pouch. I clambered onto Thunor and headed back through the wood. The sun cast long shadows across the fields, and we lingered, enjoying the peace. By the time we arrived back at the camp, it was night. Godric had been worried, but I dismissed his concerns. We ate together around a campfire, just like old times. As I prepared to sleep, I remembered I had meant to ask Edward when he had been given the letter. It could wait. Saewynn was safe, and I would see her soon.

Chapter 35

Rumours spread through the camp like wildfire. One day we were about to attack York, the next we were packing to leave. Reports were received that Erik's army was gathering, then that a truce had been sealed.

I spent the mornings at the practice ground. Many of the men camped nearby mocked us. They spent their time drinking and talking about home. I insisted that all my men kept fit and ready for war. Lord Athelstan's men joined us when they got bored enough.

"They've come on a lot since spring," I said, joining Godric after a bout that had pushed me hard.

"It's that woman you sent, Aelf. She's good with the younger ones. Several boys were good enough to come if they had been old enough to leave their mothers. We've even had approaches from other villages to train their boys."

"How has she settled? Does Saewynn get on with her?"

Godric shouted some instructions to one of the boys before continuing. "They were wary to begin with. I think Saewynn suspected she was an old girlfriend of yours.

"What? I hadn't seen her for years until we met in Winchester."

"They didn't come to blows and now they have become good friends. Hild told me they are training together, in the chamber where no one can watch. Saewynn is using her left hand more." That explained why she had been able to write the letter. "Isn't that the Ealdorman of Essex?"

"What does he want? We'll continue later, Godric." I congratulated the boys on their progress and walked over to meet Lord Elfgar.

"Hello, Byrhtnoth. I don't know how you find the energy to run around in this heat."

"Welcome, my lord." My linen undershirt clung to my sweat-soaked body. "I'll wash, then we can find some shade. I suppose you want to discuss the division of the spoils."

"That, and a few other things." He followed me down to the river, where I scooped water over my head. I ran a hand through my hair, it was getting long.

"Let's walk by the river, there might be a breeze there." The last of the trees had been cut down for firewood that morning; there was no shade left. "We're going to have to move soon," I said. "I remember the conditions in the camp last year."

"Yes, you were up here when the truce was agreed, weren't you? What a waste of time that was." He fanned his face with a sheaf of parchment. "You must know the area well?"

"Not really, we were further south. I guarded the bridge. I encountered Bloodaxe there."

"Of course. Have your ponies arrived? I haven't noticed them here."

"I found a place to the west. There was no grass left here for horses."

He nodded. "Are they well-guarded?"

"I sent men to look after them. You'll want your own men back, and the ponies. I was planning to go over there later, if you want to come with me?"

"I will." He checked no one was within earshot. "The king has made a decision. We're leaving."

238

"Thank God for that. Will you head north, to collect the ships?"

"I think so, the roads south will become very crowded when the news gets out. Do you want to come?"

"Lord Athelstan needs me here," I said.

"Of course. At least I won't have to cross those mountains again. The ships should be waiting at Chester." I hoped Petroc and the others had managed to escape Lord Hrafn. At least Elfgar had plenty of treasure to pay any bribes.

"I'll fetch my horse. We can ride out there now. There's plenty of shade," I added.

"That's the best suggestion I've heard all day. I'll find some ale to take with us."

"I heard other news, from someone close to the king, that might interest you," said Elfgar as we walked the horses slowly through the forest, "about Ripon."

"Brother Elfrid?" I had thought a lot about our time in the crypt and hoped the monk had survived his injuries.

"It's about St Wilfrid himself. Now the Minster has been destroyed, the king has decided that the saint's bones are no longer safe."

"Are they taking him to Beverly?" I had heard that some of the monks were to be sent there.

"No," he lowered his voice, "Canterbury."

"Why Canterbury?" "Wilfrid is a local saint, he should stay in Northumbria."

"They say it's a temporary arrangement, but we know what will happen once Archbishop Oda gets his hands on them."

I nodded, distracted by a movement in the trees. A spear sped from the thick foliage and landed with a thump in the path ahead. Thunor reared, and for once I was ready for him. Lord Elfgar reached for his sword.

"Very funny," I shouted. "If we were an enemy, you would be dead. I saw the glint of your spear way back.

"Sorry, my lord." A branch shook, and a face appeared. "You told us to keep the equipment clean."

239

"I should have known it was you, Edward. Not when you're hiding. Smear some soil on the metal. Any problems?"

"We've not seen a soul since I arrived."

"Good." I pulled the spear from the path and handed it back to him. It had sunk well into the ground, a powerful throw. "A bow is better if you're clambering round in trees, easier to hide. Stay there in case we've been followed; I'll send someone to relieve you later." I urged my horse on.

We pushed aside a disguising branch and followed a narrow path, riding in single file until the trees opened out into a hidden glade. Someone rushed to take our horses. I noticed with approval that the men were alert. Weapons were piled ready for use, and some of the horses were saddled. Men guarded a pile of bags and boxes, covered with makeshift shelters of branches.

"Welcome, my lord," said Thurstan, "Lord Elfgar. Are we to move the horses? Most of the grass has been consumed, and we have to travel further for more. Someone's bound to stumble across us sooner or later."

"The whole army is to move soon. We're going home." There was a subdued cheer. I had told them to keep the noise down. "Lord Elfgar has come to collect his men, they will return to the ships."

"Through the mountains?" asked one of the sailors, who had complained throughout the journey.

"With luck they should have reached Chester by now," replied Elfgar. "We'll head there."

"Do we have to return on the ships?" It was one of the soldiers who had sailed on Petroc's ship, he had been terrified by the experience.

"We'll judge the situation when we get there," snapped Elfgar. "Now, who owns what?"

I had not interfered with the men. We had split the plunder as we travelled. I had allocated each man a pony, which had become his responsibility; some had become fond of the small animals. Each man collected his possessions from the pile.

240

There had been plenty of free time for games of chance and betting. Valuables had been won and lost. There were a few arguments until I threatened to take everything. The men who had come north with Lord Athelstan watched enviously.

"Didn't you get a chance to plunder?" I asked one of them.

"The Ealdorman took it all, said he would distribute it when we got home."

"That's the usual way. I'll have a word with him, make sure you get your share." I had not paid much attention to what I had taken, apart from the mares. Lord Elfgar looked at the large pile with suspicion.

"You didn't let your scruples prevent you from grabbing what you wanted."

"We agreed to separate, I'm sure you collected plenty yourself," I told him. "It's mostly equipment for the mares. Is everyone content?"

There were a few grumbles, but everyone knew they had done very well from the expedition.

"You can keep the spare ponies," said Elfgar. I was glad he offered them; they would be useful, as carts would be difficult to find when the army left. I sent someone to guide him from our hiding place and to relieve Edward.

I decided to send the mares on ahead. The riders would act as scouts for the slower packhorses. Lord Athelstan wanted to know if there any bridges this far west. At least with the lack of rain, the river should be easy to cross. Who should I send with them? Some of the experienced men in case of attack, or the younger ones, to get them to safety if anything happened to delay the rest of us? Should I send some of the treasure with them?

"I'm sorry about the spear, my lord."

I stood and studied Edward. He had grown, his tunic was tight across his shoulders, and his wrists stuck out from his sleeves. I would have to find him something larger.

"It doesn't matter, the throw was accurate, and there was power behind it. I have a job for you."

"Is there going to be a battle?" His eyes lit up with excitement.

"I'm afraid not, although it might be dangerous. That's why I need someone I can trust."

"I won't get a chance to fight?" His shoulders slumped.

"Don't tell anyone, but the army is returning south. The roads will be busy. I want to get the new horses out of the way. We need to know if the road to Castleford is safe. There's a ford, and there may be other places to cross the river. Ride south with the mares, scout out the area, send back a messenger, then continue with the horses. Can you organise that?"

"Yes," said Edward after some thought. "Do you want us to take some of the treasure?"

"Sort out some of the smaller items. I'll take the bulky stuff on the remaining packhorses to Lord Athelstan's camp. Who do you want to take with you?"

Edward looked around the clearing. "We don't need many men. There should be enough here." He counted heads and checked the mares. "When do you want us to leave?"

"It's late now. Get a good night's sleep and set off first thing in the morning, you should make it to Castleford without a stop. Do you want Godric to go with you?"

"No," Edward replied immediately, "unless you think he should come." He opened a leather bag and stared into it. "Do you want this to go?" He passed me the bag. I saw the shine of metal, knives. They were valuable.

"Put them in a saddle bag. If you're happy to go on your own, I need Godric myself."

He smiled with relief. "He has been a real nuisance since he married my sister. Thinks he should act like my father."

"I suppose that means he's your older brother now. At your age, he should be leading you astray, not acting as a nursemaid." I lifted the cover of a large package. Cloth. That could go on one of the ponies.

"That's what I've been trying to tell him."

"Did it work?" I added more cloth to the pile.

"No."

"Give it time. Do you like this colour?" I showed him the cloth. He shrugged. "It's good quality. Give it to Hild when you get home, to make you a new tunic."

"For me?"

"You can't wear that one much longer," I remembered wearing a tunic too small because I had no other. "You're getting tall, perhaps you'll be as tall as me eventually."

"I don't think so, my lord. I wonder if your son will be tall."

I hadn't thought about my son other than as a baby. I tried to imagine him as a boy, growing up, as a man. Had my father felt like this? Had he missed me when he went away? Where was he now?

"Of course, it might be a girl." Edward tied the load onto one of the ponies. "You wouldn't want a daughter as tall as you."

The thought of a daughter terrified me. I opened another bag. "This can go as well." If I had a daughter, it seemed she would have a rich father. I thrust away the thoughts, all would become clearer in a few months.

"Do you want to send a reply?" Edward was organising another bundle for the ponies. Skins now: snowy white fox from the north and something spotted grey, seal?

"A reply?" I stroked the soft fur.

"To the letter I brought you." My hand moved to my pouch, where I had hidden the precious piece of parchment.

"I don't think so. I'll be close behind you. If I travel with Lord Athelstan, I might even beat you home." A breeze ruffled the fur and chilled my back. We must hurry, or I wouldn't make it back to the main camp before dark. "If anything happens, tell her..." What should I tell her? "Tell her I love her and..." I remembered my own childhood, "tell my son about me. Don't let him forget me."

243

"I won't need to," I felt the pressure of his hand on my shoulder, "you'll have years to tell him yourself."

"Of course. Are the ponies loaded? I'll leave the rest to you. You understand what to do?"

"Yes, my lord. I'll fetch Thunor. He's getting a bit too close to the mares. Or do you want them to arrive with extra value?"

"Wulfstan will be angry if I interfere with his breeding program." I took the reins and mounted. "Don't worry," I whispered in his twitching ears, "you'll meet her again soon." I wished Edward good luck. Before I was able to say anything more, Thunor was off. I hoped he knew the way back.

Chapter 36

"You did what?" Godric was as angry as I had expected. "If I leave now, I'll be in time to accompany him."

"No, you won't." I held his arm. "It's too dark to go anywhere. You don't even know where they are."

"I'll go tomorrow, I can soon catch up."

"I know Hild told you to look after him, all those years ago, but the time has come for him to go his own way."

"He's only a boy."

"It was you who decided he was old enough to come with the men this year," I pointed out. "He's grown, he needs some responsibility, and he's the best person to care for the horses."

"What if they're attacked?"

"They can look after themselves. Do you really think your presence would make any difference? Let him go, he's in the safest place."

"What do you mean?"

"I don't know." I worried that I had made the wrong decision, but there was something else. "We don't know where Erik is."

"He's hiding in York, afraid to face us."

"Exactly. So, what does he do when we turn our backs and run away?"

"Chase us?"

"Yes, and he won't just nip at our heels like a dog herding sheep. He will want revenge. He will attack like a wolf, and we're the sheep."

"Doesn't the king understand that?"

"I don't know. He expected Erik to come out and fight as soon as we arrived. Now he thinks he's too scared to do anything. King Eadred has misjudged him, he's old, but he's not stupid. He's only survived with the support of the Archbishop of York and now the king has stolen the bones of St Wilfrid. The burning of Ripon was bad enough; the Archbishop won't be happy losing the bones. Erik Bloodaxe will be forced to take action."

"What can we do?" Godric reached for his sword.

"Nothing, except be prepared. Make sure weapons are sharp and armour ready. Once we move, everyone who has mail is to wear it, however hot it gets. You know what to do. You're more use here, than charging around the countryside with a group of boys. I'll talk to Lord Athelstan. He should know what's going on."

"There are rumours that the king has already left," said Godric.

"I hope not, for all our sakes."

*

"It's true, or at least it soon will be." The Ealdorman paced from his tent to the campfire and back again. "There was a meeting this afternoon. He wants to travel south with the churchmen and the saint's bones. We tried to persuade him to wait, organise an orderly withdrawal, but he insisted on leaving immediately."

"Can we keep it quiet?"

"I doubt it, word is already getting out. It's every man for himself." Through the open flap of Lord Athelstan's tent, I saw servants packing chests by lamplight.

"I've ordered Godric to prepare the men. When do you want to leave?" I asked him.

"I'll follow the king, first thing tomorrow. Can you wait here and organise the retreat? You can get across the river?"

"I should have news by the time we're ready to leave. I don't believe there will be any problem. It will be impossible to get everyone across the bridge." I remembered guarding it with a handful of men the previous year. "If Erik attacks anywhere, it will be there. We will be miles away."

"You think he will attack?"

"He won't be able to resist. It's almost as if..."

"What?"

"Please, tell me there is a plan. Troops ready to attack Erik when he falls into our trap." Perhaps everything would be all right after all.

"If there is a plan, no one's told me." We watched the flickering flames of the fire.

"Has Leif brought ships up the river, like last year?" We should be able to get the baggage away that way.

"The king ordered them to stay at sea, attacking the coastal settlements. It's too late to bring them inland now."

"We can only pray we get across the river before they attack " Athelstan didn't reply. "I'll go and prepare."

"Thank you. There's just one more thing." I stopped and looked back at him. I didn't think I was going to like what he was about to say. "There's a rumour going around that Egbert has disappeared."

I nodded with resignation. "Escaped or set free?"

"No one knows, and as I said, it's only a rumour, but nobody has seen him since the guards took him away after the trial."

"I can't say that I didn't expect it. Thanks for letting me know, I'll keep a look out for him." He was probably miles away by now, but it was another thing to worry about.

"Good luck."

"You too, my lord."

*

Why did people travel with so much stuff? Wagons loaded with tents and furniture, pulled by teams of oxen, moved slower than a walking child. I was tempted to abandon them, but someone was sure to complain. Whole families, women and children walked patiently together. The procession was becoming stretched to a length that was difficult to protect. By the time we stopped for the night, we were barely out of sight of the camp by York.

I asked Godric if this was normal. He told me it was. I had been lucky, he said, to travel north by ship. I told him about our near shipwreck.

"At least we don't have rain to contend with," he said. "When the road gets wet, everything slows down."

"I wish it was cooler. This heat isn't natural." I had soon regretted telling everyone to wear protection. The sun beating down on my helmet made my head boil. I hoped it would be the worst of our worries.

Next morning, a messenger arrived from Edward. They had encountered no problems and were continuing south. He told us to keep to the higher ground. The land was damp close to the river, although the water level was low, and it was possible to cross almost anywhere on horseback. I watched a wagon creak into motion, how would it manage? I shouted at the driver to get a move on.

Numbers increased. The line of Elfgar's ponies trotted past and I rode over to say goodbye. They were heading west, hoping to cross the river high in the hills, before travelling south to Chester. Lord Elfgar had joined the other leaders on the main road. They would be safe by now.

"Any sign of the enemy?" I asked.

Nothing, I was told, just the mass of our own army spread across the countryside. Thank God the ground was dry.

By the time we stopped that night, our destination was visible. The river snaked across the fields and beyond it, the town silhouetted against the darkening sky. To the west, the sun coloured a few clouds pink. I sat and watched them until they faded into darkness. I had wanted to press on through the night, but the animals needed to rest. With the setting of the sun there was no diminishing of the heat. If anything, it was hotter, a muggy heat that stopped many from sleeping. How long would it take to get home at this speed?

*

"The river will cool us down," said Godric. He wiped the sweat from his face and replaced his helmet. Even Thunor was reluctant to move, frustrated by the slow speed.

"We might get rain." I pointed west where clouds were gathering over the hills. More joined them as we watched.

"Come on, not much further," I shouted.

I passed a family. A soldier, spear resting wearily on his shoulder, his wife and several children. The woman held a child in her arms, too young to walk, and almost too heavy to carry. She walked, oblivious to everything except putting one foot in front of the other.

"Can I take the little one for a while?" I had got in the habit of helping some of the slower walkers. I reached down to take the child.

"Get away, they're mine." The man pointed his spear towards me.

"I'm sorry." I backed Thunor away. "I thought your wife needed some help."

"Not my wife, just a slave. Killed her husband, now she's mine. They're all mine. Wanted to get rid of the baby, it's too small to work, she insisted on bringing him."

The woman kept her face lowered, her dull eyes without expression. There was nothing I could do to help. I had taken my plunder in horses and cloth rather than human flesh. Who was I to complain?

There was a rumble in the distance, and it started to rain. I tipped back my head to catch the cooling drops. Overhead black clouds gathered. The temperature fell. I knew that if there was much rain, the river would become dangerous.

"Get a move on if you want to cross the river, " I shouted to the man and his captives, then left them to encourage more people to speed up.

There was a flash of lightning, and thunder rumbled soon after. As the rain increased, the solid ground became damp, then sodden underfoot. Thunor quivered as lightning struck close. The noise was louder, and then the heavens opened. The rain was no longer single drops but a solid sheet of water.

I rode on, telling people to hurry. There would be shelter in the town. We were close to the river now; I saw my ponies cross with a group of others. They were tied together, and when one lost its footing, it was pulled along with the others. Would the water ruin the cloth? I rode along the bank and saw a group of children hesitating as their father encouraged them into the now foaming river. I hoisted one up onto Thunor's broad back, then another, shouting to the father to cling to the saddle, and urged Thunor into the water. I set them down on the far side and crossed back to help more. A cart had stopped in the middle of the river, screaming horses tangled in the harness. I drew my sword and sliced through the wet leather. Once free they would find their own way out. We struggled up the bank, sliding in the mud. Thunor's hoof dislodged a clod of earth. It was torn from the bank and spun away.

I watched the water divide around the cart. What if we made a bridge, for people to cross? Nearby was the ox cart that had slowed us down the previous day, its wheels sinking into the soft ground. I urged the driver to enter the river. He shook his head. I swung my sword and hit the hindquarters of the nearest ox with the flat of the blade. He jerked forward and the wagon followed, then stopped. I snatched the whip from the driver and applied it to the other ox. They both moved and the wagon slid into the water. I followed, dragging boxes from the bed of the wagon into the water. The driver screamed at me, but I hardly heard him above the pouring rain and rushing river. I encouraged people across the makeshift bridge. Another driver saw what I was doing and drove his own cart into the swirling water to fill the gap. I waved my thanks and continued along the bank to help more people.

The rain began to ease, although it was still heavy and the thunder continued, an incessant rumble. The press of people on the bank became thicker and more frantic. Women were screaming and children crying. I confirmed Godric was still with me and went to check what was happening.

The sound was not thunder, but the beating of spears on shields. Erik had arrived.

Behind us, along the high ground, stood a line of warriors. I shouted at Godric to round up our men and prepare for battle. As I returned to the river, spears fell around me. Thunor sensed them better than I, and we reached the bank unscathed. I shouted a warning and directed all able men to the rear to defend those still trying to cross. People were no longer nervous about entering the water. They threw themselves into the white foam and were swept rapidly away downstream.

One huddle still lingered on the brink, the slave woman and her children. The man was dead at their feet with a spear in his chest. It looked like the spear he had been carrying. I slid off Thunor and the woman met my eyes with a challenge.

"What do you want? Stay here or go across?" I asked as she caught sight of the approaching army. "Go across, you can always come back when the water goes down." She nodded. I boosted her up into the saddle and passed up the younger children. I instructed the older ones, a boy and a girl, to hang onto the bridle while Thunor stood patiently. I handed the reins to the woman.

"Wrap them around you and the babies. Hang on. When you get to the other side, take care of the horse. His name is Thunor." I noticed a shield wall forming. I removed my axe and shield from the saddle. "If I don't find you after... go to the Ealdorman of East Anglia. Tell him it is Byrhtnoth's horse, and I demanded that he gives you a reward. Do you understand?"

"Byrhtnoth's horse. Reward."

"That will do." I slapped his rump. "Look after them." Thunor shook his head, swinging the girl off her feet, then slid down the bank into the water. As I reached the shield wall, I glanced back once. My horse stood on the far bank of the river, surrounded by children. I took my place beside Godric.

Chapter 37

"Where's Erik?"

Godric pointed left. Sheathing my sword, I wiped the rain from my eyes and concentrated on the men opposite me. I hefted the axe and beat it against my shield in time with the rest of the men. I don't know what we shouted, but it felt good.

I picked my target, an ugly man with a bulbous red nose and imagined my axe splitting the nose like an apple. Beneath my feet the solid ground had become soft. We would be fighting in a bog.

Nobody moved. The noise diminished. I glanced at Godric. He shrugged. A voice rose above the song of the shield wall and the pounding rain.

"Quiet!" Gradually the shouting stopped. "Who leads this army? What is the name of the man I must kill?" It was a good question. Who was leading our army?

"I think he means you." Godric's whisper confirmed my suspicions. I thought about it while the threats drifted overhead. We were no army. There was no leader. I had been forced into that position when the mass of fleeing people needed direction. I lowered my shield and stepped out of the line.

"To the left?" Godric nodded and stepped out to stand behind me. The shield wall closed behind us. "Let's go."

I forced myself to walk between the lines, exposed to the enemy opposite. Godric told our men to maintain the shield wall. They formed only a single line. There was no one to support us. Towards the riverbank, people continued to cross. If we had to retreat, we would stop there, backs to the foaming water. If we still lived.

I reached Erik. He was surrounded by his attendants. Overhead his raven banner hung limp in the downpour. I stood straight and faced him. He was less impressive without his horse. Once he would have topped my height, but time had diminished him. He leaned on a long-handled axe, although when he noticed I stood taller, he raised it to his shoulder and stepped back, to where the ground was higher. I smiled.

"My Lord, we have no leader. We are just ordinary people crossing a river. If you come to help, you are welcome."

"What's your name?" he growled.

"I am Byrhtnoth, son of Byrhthelm. I serve the Ealdorman of East Anglia. May I ask your name?"

"You know who I am." He thrust out his chest.

I cocked my head and studied him from head to foot. "Someone's grandfather? Sent to safety, while the proper warriors get on with the fighting? Don't worry, we'll protect you until the battle is finished." I offered a supporting arm. He slapped it away.

"You must be mad, or stupid. Don't you recognise the King of York?"

"Which one would that be? I know King Eadred, and you're not him. Are you the Irish one or the Norwegian one? Are there any more?" I asked Godric, who stared back open-mouthed. "Never mind." I swung back to Erik. The longer I kept talking, the more people could escape across the river. They would have a chance.

"I am Erik Haraldsson, king of Norway, Ireland and York." His face was flushed red with anger, although it was difficult to tell under the mass of wet hair.

"I met someone of that name last year. He was trying to cross a bridge to get home to his wife. I was forced to turn him back." A snort of laughter emerged from the men behind him. Erik turned and glared, searching unsuccessfully for the culprit.

"I recognise you now, Byrhtnoth. Your name was mentioned recently. You are the man who burned the Minster at Ripon, who stole the bones of St Wilfrid."

Who had told him that? Egbert? Threats emerged from the enemy shield wall.

"It was not me. Men swore my innocence before the king."

"What king?" he snapped.

"Eadred, King of all England. You still haven't answered my question, why are you here?"

"I have come to kill you. You invaded my country, killed my people, devastated my lands." His hand tightened on the handle of his axe.

"Perhaps. But now we are going home. Where were you when we arrived, eager to give battle? You showed no concern when your people were killed. Why didn't you defend them, protect their land, like a proper king should? Why attack now, when we are leaving? Why attack us, ordinary people who are no threat to you? Because you are a coward, scared to face King Eadred and his Ealdormen. Even now they escape, taking with them the bones of St Wilfrid. You are lazy, cowering behind the walls of York with your wife. Many people have told me how... hospitable she is."

"I will kill you." He hissed the words from a clenched jaw.

"Why don't we make it fair? Are you familiar with the word?" I spoke loudly, so all men, on both sides, could hear. "Everyone is getting very wet." I was soaked to the skin, and rain poured from my helmet, straight down my neck. I ignored it. "I challenge you to battle, just you and I. If I win, you retreat back to York. If you win, well, you will kill a lot of innocent people. I'm sure it will enhance your reputation."

I waited, shifting my feet to free them from the clinging mud. Erik could not refuse to fight. I had called him a coward, questioned his honour.

"Mark out the area." The opposing lines moved back. Men laid spears to measure out the ground. Erik shrugged off his bearskin cloak. It kept him dry but restricted movement. It dropped to the ground. I removed my cloak and handed it to Godric.

"What are you doing?" he asked.

"I don't know. Preventing more deaths?" Or did I fight for glory? In a few minutes, I would find out. Why had he dropped his cloak in the mud?

We met in the centre of the space, men clustering around, their own fight forgotten. The first blow, from his axe, was fast, faster than I expected. I dodged, replying with my own weapon. He raised his shield, and the blade slid off the metal boss. Already his axe was falling again and I stood firm as it thudded into the surface of my shield. I pulled, to drag the weapon from his hand, but he followed, driving me backwards. Godric shouted a warning. I was close to the edge. I dropped, raising my shield above my head and Erik stumbled. With a sound of splitting wood, my shield released his blade. I swung my axe, and it slid across the back of his byrnie. Stepping back I massaged my shoulder. It had twisted painfully.

My axe had nicked the rings of Erik's mail shirt, and blood welled from the wound. I scented success.

"First blood," I shouted. "My victory."

"To the death," Erik snarled and swung his weapon low, searching for my ankles.

I jumped, and it passed beneath me. As I landed, one foot skidded in the mud but I recovered. We circled, trading blows, searching for an opening. Splinters spun from the shields. Mine was already split. As more disappeared, it became useless. I hurled the heavy boss at Erik's face. He ducked and it sailed over his head, hitting someone in the baying mob. I moved my axe into my left hand. He grinned, tossed the remains of his shield in the air, transferred his own axe to his left hand and caught the shield in his right. His blows were just as powerful. His energy should have diminished as the fight lengthened. His breathing was even. He had been fighting all his life, he knew all the tricks. I had thought my youth would defeat his age. I was running out of ideas.

He stepped back and I followed. The speed of his blows increased. I moved faster. Every step was dangerous as the ground slid beneath me. Erik stepped back onto the discarded fur cloak. His stance was firm. Why hadn't I realised? My left arm was aching. How long could I continue? I returned my weapon to my right hand. He threw the remains of his shield at me. I fumbled the handle of my axe as I ducked, but saw the edge of the cloak lift. As he raised his axe once more, I jumped forward, grasped the fur and pulled. It didn't move, it had sunk deep into the mud under Erik's weight. I backed away as the axe dropped towards my arm. Mud sprayed my fingers as I snatched my arm out of the way. Unbalanced, I fell backwards, drawing up my legs to avoid the next chop of his axe. I twisted to escape but found myself wallowing in mud. I lost my grip on my axe and tried to stand. I managed to get to my knees as Erik's axe descended toward my head. I had become the perfect sacrifice.

The world exploded into pain. I was on the ground. A kick in the stomach drove all air from my body. A foot landed in the centre of my chest and pressed me into the liquid mud. I fought for breath.

My head jerked upwards and pain shot down my neck. My hands reached out, for a weapon, for something to cling to, found nothing. There was a terrible grinding, a deafening screech of tortured metal. My head fell back with a splash. Blood gushed across my face. I was unable to move. My eyes were blind. My ears deaf to everything but the rush of water, or was it my blood?

I fought to catch a final glimpse of light. Cold rain washed my face. The darkness cleared. I saw a boot, covered in blood, my blood. I closed my eyes. So that was what it had meant.

"Kill them all!" shouted Erik.

I heard Godric scream. Sound and sensation faded until all was silence.

Part V: Autumn

Chapter 38

The river was low. Saewynn wondered what would happen if it dried up altogether. The last rain had fallen just before Edward had returned with the mares. Where had they found such animals? Edward said that Byrhtnoth would explain; he was just a few days behind them. The days had become weeks, and he and the rest of the men were still not back. There were rumours of more fighting in the north, although Edward had told them that the army had been on the way home.

She shifted her position; it was impossible to get comfortable, the child kicked whenever she tried to rest. Her back ached, and the heat didn't make it any easier. There was shade beside the river, and the sound of the water was restful. Everyone insisted that she do nothing. She felt guilty, especially with the harvest about to begin.

Wulfstan had gone to the fields to check the crop. He was worried. Although the sun was ripening the grain, rain was needed to swell the heads. But if too much rain fell, it would flatten the crops.

Her thoughts were interrupted by Leola. She had been asleep in the shade nearby when she suddenly jumped to her feet, ears pricked.

"What's the matter? Is someone coming?" As always, her first reaction was fear, then as the dog's tail started to beat, she felt a flash of excitement.

One blast of the horn warned of visitors. A second indicated they were friendly. She heard horses, their steps were slow, tired from a long journey. Byrhtnoth was coming home! Already Leola was moving, racing back towards the village.

"Wait for me," Saewynn shouted after her. She gave a wry smile, knowing her plea would be unsuccessful. She would always come second to Byrhtnoth in the animal's affections.

She wanted to leap up and run like the dog, but could only struggle to her feet, back arched to balance the bulk of the baby. She wrapped a scarf around her head to cover her hair. Having rinsed it in the river the water had trickled down her back to keep her cool. It was nearly dry now. It was too hot to wear anything more than her shift and anyway, nothing fitted. She groaned as she bent to pick up her cloak and wrapped it around her swollen body. She grinned as she thought of the jokes he would make when he discovered her only half-dressed.

Why was there so little noise? Usually visitors produced a hubbub of interest as people gathered to find out who had arrived and seek news. She paused to catch her breath and continued at a slower pace. Leola returned to her, her tail now tucked tight between her legs. She pressed close to Saewynn and whined.

"What's the matter?" She had never seen the dog act in such a way. "Careful, don't trip me up."

The silent crowd parted as she reached the space before the hall, Leola trailing at her heels.

Godric had dismounted and was clinging to his horse. Blood stained bandages swathed his leg. His face was white and strained. Her eyes moved on, searching. Familiar faces were missing, many were injured. She spotted Thunor, his head low, his neck streaked with blood and dust. He had no rider, just an empty saddle.

Anxious, Saewynn searched for a litter, nothing, no shrouded body either. He must be injured. They had left him at some monastery for treatment. She must arrange for him to be brought home, to be nursed properly. She would send a ship; most places were close to the coast or a river. She turned to Godric.

"I'm sorry. There was nothing to be done." The tracks of tears ran through the dirt of his face, and she understood the truth.

"No!" She wanted to scream a protest, but the word emerged as a whisper. The figure of Godric faded. Her head spun, and darkness closed in. A dream. Yes, she had fallen asleep beside the river. She would awake soon, and everything would be as it had been.

The child kicked, and she knew she was awake. The dream was over, and she was alone. She couldn't give up. There was still her son. She must live for him. She took a deep breath, felt the rough ground beneath her bare feet and pressed down on a sharp stone until the pain brought her to her senses.

Behind her, someone apologised. "I'm sorry, someone mislaid the mead horn. What...?" Hild stopped. The brimming horn dropped from her hands, and she stepped forward. "Godric. What happened? Are you injured?" She noticed the silence, saw Saewynn. "Oh."

Saewynn watched the precious mead spread and disappear into the dusty ground. What a waste, she thought, before realising that there was no longer any need of it. There would be no more feasts or celebrations.

She remembered her duty. She lifted her head, straightened her back and rested her hand on the child. She felt Leola's welcoming warmth against her leg.

"Thank you, Godric. It must have taken courage to bring the news." She controlled her shaking voice. "You need refreshment. Hild!" The girl was staring at Godric. "Clear up that mess. You can speak to your husband later." Saewynn voice was sharper than normal. At least Hild still had a husband.

She addressed the stricken men. "I will leave you to wash, find food and drink. I must go and make myself tidy. We will meet later in the hall, and you can tell us how my... what has happened." She forced herself to move. The stone was still embedded in her foot. Every painful step distracted her from what had happened. Somewhere a woman screamed.

"Shut up, Edith. Aelf?"

"I'm here, my lady."

Saewynn walked slowly to the hall and into the cool darkness. She kept her head high and her pace measured. Aelf opened the door to the chamber for her and once inside, she stopped, her mind a total blank.

Aelf led her towards the bed. Saewynn saw the wolf skin and turned away. Aelf sat her on a stool and fetched a jug of wine. She poured some into a cup and pressed it into Saewynn's hand. She stared at it for a long, time then lifted it to her lips.

"I'll sort out your hair." Aelf removed the scarf and fetched a comb. "Have you been swimming? It's a good way to keep cool." Saewynn shivered. "Drink it all down. It will make you feel better." Saewynn disagreed but sipped obediently.

As the comb ran through her hair, she remembered Byrhtnoth doing it for her, before they went to bed. He would be pleased how long it had become. No. He would never see it, never run his fingers through it. Tears filled her eyes and she bit her lip. She mustn't lose control yet. She must attend the meeting, listen to what had happened. Perhaps it was a mistake. She rose to search for him. Aelf's hand on her shoulder held her in her seat.

"You can't go anywhere until you're dressed. Have you got anything?"

"There's something in the chest. I made it to wear when... when he came back. It will do."

"I'll finish your hair, then I'll look for it. If it doesn't fit, Edith might have something."

Saewynn gripped her hand. "I don't want to see her. I can't, not yet."

"You don't have to. I'll keep you safe."

"Did he get my letter? I hope so. I must ask Edward."

"Later," said Aelf firmly. "Do you want to wear your gloves?"

"What does it matter?"

"It matters a great deal." Aelf crouched before her, forcing Saewynn to look at her. "With Byrhtnoth gone," Saewynn flinched, "you are in charge. These people depend on you. Your child needs you. You can cry, but not in front of them. You must be strong, for all of us."

Aelf had confirmed what she already knew. Much as she wanted to lie down and never get up, she must carry on.

"The hall is filling. Fetch my dress and a cloak as well, with my best brooch. There should be a clean head cloth in the chest."

She had to summon all her courage to leave the chamber. Byrhtnoth had told her about the time he had arrived to attend the death of Lord Toli, when he became the lord. She had laughed, unable to imagine him afraid of anything. Now she knew how it felt.

She paused at her usual stool, then called for someone to pull forward Byrhtnoth's chair. It had been pushed back out of the way since Lord Athelstan's visit. Now she took her place in it. She had decided not to wear her gloves. She wore them often, and the bones of her hand had adjusted. Her fingers were bent, no longer tight and twisted, although she couldn't grasp anything without the help of the metal frame. She slid her hand along the arm of the chair, it was smooth, and she almost felt his hand on hers.

There had been whispers when she took the chair. Did they not think it was her right? Where was Wulfstan? Was he still in the fields? Should she wait? No, she would have to face him later.

"You all know why we are here. Thank you for coming. I hope Godric has recovered from the journey and can report everything that happened." He had more colour in his face. Like her, he must have taken shelter in the wine jug, or perhaps ale. "You are injured, there is no need to get up."

"I will stand," he said, as if she had accused him of cowardice. He struggled to his feet. He told of the events of the journey north. She had already heard most of this from Edward, but she allowed him to explain at his own pace.

"I was angry when my lord sent Edward away with the horses. I am glad of it now. We would have lost more men than we did." He described the retreat, the sudden storm and the panic. "Lord Byrhtnoth helped many to cross the river. He carried women and children to safety on his horse. He sent away the horse when Erik's army appeared"

"Thunor didn't protest?"

"Not that I saw, my lady. The family he rescued cared for him and refused to give him up until we found them. Byrhtnoth had promised them a reward. We paid it.

"I am glad. Do you want some ale?"

He nodded gratefully, and Hild filled his cup. As he drank, the door opened and Wulfstan entered.

"Why is everyone in here? What's happened?"

"Wulfstan. I'm glad you were able to join us. Godric is telling us about the battle at...?"

"Castleford, my lady."

Wulfstan's face paled as he searched the room and understood what must have happened. He sunk onto the nearest bench and put his head in his hands.

"Why did the Northumbrians attack?" she asked. "You said our forces were leaving."

"They were. No one understands why Erik did it or why he didn't attack the king. Why us?" He shook his head in despair. "Perhaps they wanted to retrieve the spoils we had looted. The speed with which they attacked the fleeing people after..."

"After what?" She didn't want to hear, but she had to know.

Godric took another gulp of ale. "We formed a shield wall. There were so few of us, the enemy was many. We knew we were doomed. Byrhtnoth was determined to delay them, give time for innocent people to escape."

266

"Then there was a battle?"

"Not really. Erik demanded to know who he was fighting. There was no proper leader and your husband stepped forward." It was typical, why she loved him, but why did it have to be him to make the sacrifice? "Go on."

"Are you sure?"

"Yes." She almost shouted the word. She wanted it to be over.

"He spoke to Erik. He insulted him, called him a coward. At the time, I didn't understand why he provoked him. Afterwards, I realised it was to delay the battle. Erik challenged your husband. Byrhtnoth accepted, to save us and everyone else. I still don't know if their army would have kept Erik's word and left if he had lost."

"He didn't lose," Saewynn said quietly.

"No. They fought with axe and shield. They were evenly matched. Although old, Erik fought like a younger man, he knew all the tricks. He cheated." A hiss ran around the hall. Saewynn called for quiet.

"How did he die?"

Godric knew she required the truth. "It was raining. Thunder rumbled, and lightning flashed from the sky. The ground turned to mud, thick mud, impossible to keep to your feet. Before the fight Bloodaxe dropped his cloak, I wondered why. At the height of the battle, he took refuge on that one small patch of dry ground." Godric looked away, reliving the events. "My lord never stood a chance. I should have intervened. He slipped, strained to get to his feet, Erik's axe fell. Byrhtnoth must have died instantly. I'm sure he didn't suffer.

Chapter 39

The pain in her chest was overwhelming. It was true. Godric had witnessed it. The motion of the child brought her back to her senses. She forced herself to breathe. In. Out.

"You buried him there? You didn't bring his body home?" She would never see him again. She must visit the grave. "Tell me where he is buried."

Godric shifted uncomfortably. He glanced towards another of the men, Thurstan, she remembered. Had there been no body? Had they...? She couldn't imagine what the enemy might have done to him. The room span around her.

"Are you all right, my lady?" Aelf's voice, quiet at her back. She would never be all right but nodded to show that she was not about to faint. She laid her hands on the mound of her belly.

"You have more to tell?"

"Yes, my lady." Godric cleared his throat. Hild lifted the jug, but he shook his head. "After... it happened, Erik attacked. I was injured." He indicated his leg. "We were overwhelmed, and they did not stop. That is why some of us survived. They were eager to recover the plunder, although much had been swept away. It was a massacre." He paused remembering the horror of it. "The injured escaped. We had to leave the dead. I'm sorry my lady, I..."

"I understand," said Saewynn. "And after?"

"It was a long time before we saw the site of the battle again. Erik left. King Eadred turned back, there were discussions; I don't know the details. They were still talking when we left. When we buried the bodies, we were unable to find him. We searched, asked witnesses. Someone said a cart had come to take him away. There was no trail, not by then. We searched the area and found a hut, little more than a rough shelter in the forest. Something had been buried there."

"What?" she asked, afraid of the reply.

Thurstan dragged forward a bundle, wrapped in a muddy cloak. Saewynn recognised it. She had sheltered beneath it, safe against his warm body. She gulped to hold back the tears. Thurstan lifted a fold and brought out a round object. For a moment she thought it was his head. Gasps around the room suggested others thought the same. She recognised the dull shine of metal. His helmet. She knew it well. She had repaired the lining when the worn stitching had split. Thurstan glanced at Godric, who nodded. He placed it on the table in front of her.

It was coated in mud, a few crumbs falling to the table, but she could not take her eyes off the damage. A blade had bitten deep into the metal. She picked it up. The blow had been powerful, breaching the metal. The impact would have been just above the right eye. She turned it over and gagged at the smell. The lining was soaked in dried blood, padding ripped by the blade. It was impossible for anyone to have survived such a blow. She bent closer. Was that escaped stuffing, or...? She pulled it out. Between her fingers was a lock of hair. Soaked in blood as it was, she knew it was his. She placed it carefully to one side. There was a clink of metal. More?

It was heavy. Thurstan held it up with difficulty. Everyone recognised his byrnie. It was streaked with mud and blood, sheets of blood. A few weeks in damp earth, and it was already rusting into a solid lump. Saewynn waved it away. Thurstan bent again to the cloak and produced a sword.

270

"That's not..." Saewynn frowned. She had been expecting Wolf Claw, the sword she had given him on their wedding day. This sword was old, its edge marred by the marks of battle. "Give it to me."

Saewynn held the sword. It was not covered in blood, only a few smears. She wiped the blade clean.

"I recognise this sword." She remembered where she had seen it. Egbert had shown it to her. Then she understood. This was a message. She raised her head, and her eyes met Wulfstan's. She saw that he knew it too.

The crowd stood back as he walked to the front of the hall. "That is Byrhtnoth's father's sword. I saw it last in the hand of Egbert." He had told her what had happened. How Byrhtnoth had been forced to choose between her life and the sword that he had always wanted. Byrhtnoth had never talked to her about it.

She understood the message immediately. Last time, Egbert was saying, Byrhtnoth had chosen her above the sword. This time he had made the choice. She could have the sword because he had Byrhtnoth.

Was he still alive? She glanced at the bloody helmet. Had he survived that? If so, what did Egbert plan to do to him? Had done. She felt sick. She would rather Byrhtnoth dead than suffer the things that evil man might do to him.

"He's alive. I know it." Saewynn stood up, "I must go, I must find him."

"You can't, not yet." Aelf's voice held her back. "Think of the child. Would he want you to endanger his son?" Saewynn slumped back into the chair. Her heart pounded as she tried to control her frantic thoughts.

"You can't go," said Wulfstan. "Where would you search? You don't know where he is. The men are tired and there are wounds to mend. Perhaps later, when the harvest is done, and you are... recovered."

271

"Thank you, Wulfstan," Saewynns voice was icy cold, "for reminding us, that the crops are more important than the life of our lord."

"You would rather starve? Food will be tight enough this winter."

"If I had to. You wanted him to die," Saewynn screamed. "You've always been jealous of him." The words fell like stones into the hushed hall.

Wulfstan shook his head. "No." His anguish was clear. It sounded too much like her own and Saewynn turned away.

"Take me back to the chamber." Her voice shook as Aelf helped her to her feet. "I must rest, then I will make plans."

*

She huddled under the thick fur of the wolf. Although it wasn't cold in the chamber, she sought comfort for her numb body. She had wanted to be strong and only made a fool of herself. They were right: Byrhtnoth was dead. What was the point in searching for him? Wulfstan was being practical, it was better to care for the living than search for the dead.

Aelf had given her more wine and held her until she stopped shaking. Saewynn had refused any food then dismissed her.

"I need to sleep," she said. "I can't talk to anyone."

Saewynn turned her face to the wall. She craved peace. The baby was quiet. Had she damaged it with her fit of anger? He must have fallen asleep after all the excitement; she wished she was able to do the same. How could she forget the images Godric had conjured up? He must be dead. Erik Bloodaxe would not have stopped the fight if his opponent had still been alive. Why had Egbert removed the body? Was it to torment her, make her believe Byrhtnoth was still alive? She remembered what he had done to her and shivered, pulling the fur over her head. If Byrhtnoth was alive, injured, he was in Egbert's power.

Saewynn threw back the fur and rushed to the bucket in the corner. She threw up the contents of her stomach, the sour taste of wine. She continued to retch until there was nothing left. She crawled back to the bed and curled around her child. Whatever happened, she would protect him.

*

She woke to feel his arms around her.

"My love." The words were whispered, she recognised them instantly.

When she tried to face him, touch his face, his arms, like iron bands, held her immobile. She waited for him to say more, but there was silence, just the touch of his breath against her ear, fast and light like a butterfly's wings. She recognised the smell of his sweat, though strong and rank as if it had been a long time since he had washed. Was that the metallic scent of blood? She felt the beat of his heart. It was not strong and slow as normal. In anyone else, the shallow rapid beat would have revealed fear.

She was afraid. "What's wrong?" There was no reply, then he gave a deep sigh.

"Pain." It was almost a groan. Then, "Help me." The pressure on her body was released. She felt the baby kick, and she sat up, feet flat on the wooden floorboards. In the dim light from the window, only the dog moved.

Leola's claws clattered as she stretched and moved towards Saewynn, tail moving tentatively. She sniffed at the disordered bedding. There was a strong odour of fish. Leola whined and rested her head on Saewynn's knee.

"You heard him too?" Leola licked her hand and looked towards the window. Hanging in the air like an echo was that final word, "Help me." Never had she heard such desolation.

She lay down and struggled to get comfortable. The memory of that desperate plea brought on the tears, long held back. She had heard no hope in his voice. She wasn't sure if any hope remained, but now she knew what to do. With the decision made she fell into a deeper sleep, her cheeks damp with grief.

Chapter 40

Aelf forced Saewynn from the bed. "You will feel better if you move about. And you must eat, keep strong for the baby." Saewynn ate obediently, without noticing what it was. "It can't be long now."

Saewynn struggled to think. "After harvest, they said."

"A few weeks yet. Plenty of time."

"Too long. I want to be rid of it, then I can leave."

"Don't say things like that." Aelf made a sign against the evil eye. "Are you sure about searching for Byrhtnoth? It wasn't your anger speaking?"

"I must go. If I find proof that he is dead, I will kill Erik and find Egbert. Death is too good for that man. I will have to think about what to do to him."

"With all these bloodthirsty thoughts, I hope the child is a boy," said Aelf.

"Perhaps better," said Saewynn, with a thoughtful expression, "if it is a girl. Aren't women better at revenge?"

"You might be right, but if you are to challenge Erik Bloodaxe, you need a lot more training. You began well, you can hold a weapon with your left hand and manage a small shield when you use the glove."

"How long after the birth can I leave?"

"It depends on how things go. Many women don't survive, you know."

"I don't mind if I die, so long as the baby lives. Someone will avenge Byrhtnoth's death." Who would do that? Any of the men - they all loved him. "How long if it all goes well?"

"You must allow time for your body to recover, or risk serious injury. I will ask the other women. A month perhaps."

"Not long. We'll start now. Where did I put my seax?

*

Saewynn refused to practice with the men, so Aelf found a place in the woods. Saewynn was shocked to discover how much her body had softened with pregnancy. She wanted to work harder, but Aelf limited the time spent on vigorous exercise. During breaks they would talk. Aelf told her about her life. How she had always wanted to fight. She described how she had met Byrhtnoth and Wulfstan when they first joined the training school.

"I did well until Oswald insisted that we all go in the bath at the end of the day. I remember Byrhtnoth, he was taller than the others, even then. Very serious, he didn't say a lot. In the end, when I had been found out, he was the only one who spoke up for me. He gave me his old tunic. It was threadbare but better than nothing. He gave me food. I think it was all he had. It kept me going for a while."

"What did you do then?" asked Saewynn.

"This and that, anything to survive. I remember Wulfstan that day."

"What was he like? That must have been before the accident."

"Yes, small, dark, rushing around asking questions about everything. He hero-worshipped Byrhtnoth, and his friend protected him. He would never have made a warrior, even if he hadn't been injured. Forgive me, my lady, you were unfair to him. He loves Byrhtnoth almost as much as you. He would never want him dead."

276

"I know." Saewynn stared down at the seax she was cleaning. "I must ask his forgiveness when he's not so busy."

"I must go," Aelf stood up and stretched. "I promised to help with the harvest."

"I did that once," said Saewynn. "I can't reach the ground now."

"It won't be long." Aelf patted her shoulder.

"Was Egbert there, that first day?"

Aelf frowned. "Elfhere was there, showing off, telling everyone else what to do. I don't remember Egbert until the horse fight, years later, when Wulfstan beat him. His finest hour."

"Is that what all this is about? Why he hates us so much? Byrhtnoth said he disappeared after the accident. They assumed he was to blame. He must have been with Elfhere when he attacked the village and fired the hall."

"No one says much about that," said Aelf.

"It was two years ago, almost exactly. I'll tell you about it sometime. I should be grooming the horses." Aelf helped her to her feet.

"Aren't they down on the meadows?"

"Only Thunor is left. I talk to him. I tell him we will soon go and find his master."

*

Saewynn was in the stables several days later. She had groomed the great horse and leaned against his shoulder, remembering their adventures together and with Byrhtnoth. The cuts that had marred the smooth black coat had healed, leaving the finest of lines. She stroked his neck.

"How did you get those? Rescuing children from the flood?" Godric had told her more about that day. She was glad Byrhtnoth had helped so many people. She knew he had killed men, and she knew how much he regretted it. Like Thunor, he scared many people, but she loved them both.

"I can't hang around here. I promised Hild I'd help lay out the food for the harvest meal." She rubbed her back, it had been aching lately, although the baby had been quiet. As she lifted the bar to leave the stall, she felt pain, a wrenching within her body. Liquid trickled down her leg.

"This must be it." She patted Thunor's nose. "I think the meal will be delayed. Wish me luck." The horse dropped his head and nuzzled her waist. Saewynn laughed, then flinched as pain grabbed her and squeezed. She felt a stab of fear.

"I'll see you later," she told the horse and walked laboriously from the stable.

*

They took her to the birthing hut. It had no windows, and it was dark when she entered. The floor was of beaten earth. She paused as she caught the sickening smell of blood and sweat.

"Don't worry," said one of the women, Freya, Saewynn thought, she was Inga's mother, or perhaps her grandmother. "It will be better when the fire has been lit."

"The fire?" Saewynn was already sweating.

"We need it to burn herbs, heat water and to give light." Someone lit the rushlights that waited high on the walls. They were feeble and added the odour of burning fat. She hoped she would not have to spend much time here.

She removed her clothes, except for her shift. Someone helped to loosen her hair. "There must be no knots, nothing tied, in the birthing room." The others did the same and in the dim light, women that she recognised from the village, were transformed into strangers.

When Aelf arrived, breathless from the fields, Saewynn clung to her.

"I'm frightened. What's going to happen?"

"Don't worry. Sit on the stool. Freya must find out how close the birth is." The stool was old; Saewynn wondered how many babies had been delivered on it. It was low, and the seat was narrow with a tall sloping back.

"Spread your legs," said the old woman and lifted the hem of her shift. Saewynn felt the woman's hands on her leg. She tensed.

"Relax," Aelf whispered to her. "She knows what she's doing."

"It will be a long time yet." Freya dropped the linen and leaned back. The women sighed.

"Has someone brought the birthing drink?" There was an argument, and someone left the hut. "You can walk around if you want," Freya said over her shoulder, "sometimes it speeds things up."

Aelf helped her to her feet. "She's right, keep to your feet as long as you can."

For hours, it seemed, she walked back and forth, stopping to lean on the back of the stool whenever a pain hit. Sometimes Aelf rubbed her back.

Hild arrived with honey, milk and a jug of wine. She said she would come later, after the meal. Saewynn managed to ask about the harvest.

"Coming along. We might finish tomorrow, then there will be the feast. It will be a celebration of the birth of your son, as well as the harvest." Saewynn groaned as another pain hit her.

The women had caught up with all the village gossip and started to tell stories of past births. Saewynn tried not to listen, and Aelf told them to be quiet. She took the rapidly shrinking jug of wine away from them. Although Freya sniffed, she lowered her voice. Saewynn found it was worse as she caught only the odd word, and every story ended with, "and then, of course, she died."

It was dark before the pain became almost continuous. Freya made another inspection and declared that it would not be long. She gave a signal, and another woman flung something onto the fire. A noxious smell filled the room.

"What's that?" said Saewynn, choking.

"Open the door," shouted Aelf.

"It helps with the birth, we always use it," said one of the women. She gave her a reassuring pat before returning to the fire.

Saewynn dozed, slumped on the stool. She heard a male voice. The women rushed to bar the door.

"It's Wulfstan," said Aelf. "I'll find out what he wants." Saewynn turned away her weary face, she didn't care who it was.

"He brought you this." Aelf held out a piece of parchment.

"A letter?" What was so important it couldn't wait until later?

"It's a spell. He went to Ely and studied their writings. He copied the best."

"What am I supposed to do with it?"

The women knew. They snatched it away and passed it from hand to hand, admiring the writing. It was written in Latin they said, which was even better, although no one was able to tell what it said.

"It must be wrapped around your leg," said Freya. This caused more argument, although the majority decided that the right leg was correct.

Saewynn thought perhaps it was a curse to kill her baby. In that case, would it matter which leg? She permitted the parchment to be wrapped around her lower leg, out of the way.

"It's working already." The pain got worse, and Saewynn no longer cared what happened, she just wanted everything to end. When the old woman pushed the shift up to expose the rest of her body, she didn't object. Firm hands moved over her skin, sketching the shape of the child's body. It ended with a gentle pat. "I can find no problem. All is well."

After that, everything was a blur. Saewynn screamed at the pain. She dug her nails into the wood of the stool. Aelf wrapped her arms around her upper body and Saewynn swore she would never allow a man near her again, then cried when she realised, none would.

"Shout as much as you like," Aelf whispered, "it will all be forgotten after."

"Not long now!" Saewynn had an overwhelming urge to push. She screamed at the voice that told her not to push.

The voice in her ear told her to pant, "like this," Aelf demonstrated, and Saewynn followed her lead. It went on forever, push, don't push.

"The head's out!" Women crowded around. "Who has the knife? Is the cloth warm?"

Saewynn thrashed her head right and left. "What's wrong?" The talk of knives terrified her.

"Not long now," said Aelf. She joined in the chorus of "Push".

Saewynn screamed as she fought the greatest pain yet. Then it stopped. What had happened? Were her guts all over the floor? Aelf's hand took hers. Was she dying?

"It's a boy, a healthy boy."

Then Saewynn heard a thin cry, a louder one. Soon loud screams filled the hut.

"A strong pair of lungs." Saewynn leaned forward to look, but Aelf pulled her back.

"He's beautiful, you'll see him in a moment." Saewynn relaxed. Freya handed her a bundle. It was smaller than she had expected. How was she supposed to hold it? It fitted into the crook of her arm as if she had done it a hundred times before. She gazed down at the angry red face. She touched it with the tip of a finger, and the crying stopped.

For the second time in her life, she fell in love.

*

"I can manage. Why don't you go to the feast?" Saewynn's son was two days old, and she had no time for visitors, least of all Byrhtnoth's sister, Edith.

"It has too many memories. Aelf said you shouldn't be left alone, so I told her to enjoy herself. How do you feel?"

"A bit sore, Freya said everything is as it should be. Of course. The harvest feast was when..."

"The attack. I still wake up, remembering. Less than I did, but it still scares me."

"I know, and as a mother, there are even more fears in the world." Saewynn checked the cradle where her son slept. There was silence while Edith concentrated on her needle. "What are you making?"

"A shift for the baby." She held it up. "It is similar to the one I made for...Inga's child."

"He is growing well. Isn't he walking now? To think that my son will soon be that big, he is so small."

"They grow quickly." Edith kept her eyes on her fast-moving fingers. Have you given him a name?" She tied off the thread and reached for another. "Or are you waiting? He will need to be baptised." There was no reply, and she looked up to find Saewynn staring into the distance, tears welling from her eyes.

"I'm sorry," Edith leaned forward and touched her hand, "I didn't mean to..."

"For a moment I forgot," Saewynn rubbed her face. "How could I do that?"

"You have someone else to worry about now. Have you accepted it, that Byrhtnoth is dead?" Tears appeared in her own eyes.

"No!" Saewynn's response was louder than she intended. "There is no proof of his death. How can I face his son when he grows up, if I didn't try to learn the truth?"

"You sound just like him. He was unable to find any peace until he could discover what happened to his father. Do you want the same for him?" Edith nodded towards the sleeping child. "Will he waste his life searching for something that is not there? Remember what happened to Byrhtnoth."

"He was prevented from going, he never had a chance." Saewynn realised she was to blame for him giving up. "Byrhthelm."

"What do you mean?"

"That was his name, his father's name. Now it will be his son's. He made a vow to find Byrhthelm. If his son has the same name, perhaps it means he will come back to us." Saewynn swung her legs off the side of the bed. "Call Aelf, I must go."

"Not yet. You must heal before you can leave. You don't want to leave your son with no parents at all."

"Yes," Saewynn lay back against the pillow, "I must start training again."

"Gentle exercise is good." Edith gave her a serious look." You know you will have to leave your son? You cannot take a child on such a journey."

"I know. I have spoken to Inga. She is willing to care for him." She glanced at Edith. "If you agree."

"What have I to do with it?" She returned her eyes firmly to the linen in her lap.

"Inga might not have enough milk for both children, my son and Wulfmaer."

"He eats other foods now; he does not need her milk. But that is no concern of mine."

"You are his Godmother, are you not? You are allowed to have an opinion."

"And that is all." Edith stuck her needle into the cloth. "You must be hungry. I will go and fetch some food, if there is anything left." She rose abruptly and headed for the door.

"I am sorry," said Saewynn, quietly.

Chapter 41

"Where did it happen?" Saewynn climbed from the small boat. Leola jumped after her and sniffed at the thin grass along the riverbank. Saewynn waited for Thurstan to stow the oars and secure the boat.

He pointed. "Somewhere up there."

They waited for the others to arrive. Lord Athelstan had given them a ship and Leif to sail it. No one acknowledged that it was to save Saewynn from having to ride. It would save time they said, although the winds had been against them, and once into the Humber, the rowing was slow.

Few noticed that two of the crew were women. Aelf was indistinguishable from the men, and Saewynn had returned to her boy's clothing. The tunic had been tight, but with exercise, the extra weight had dropped off her. Hild had given her herbs to stop the milk, and her breasts ached. She bound them and consigned the discomfort to the same place as the longing for her child.

They had reached the bridge. Saewynn remembered it. She had searched for the remains of the ships that Byrhtnoth had burned there. There was nothing left. Byrhtnoth had been upset at having to destroy his own ship. She had wiped away her tears by the time small boats were found to continue upstream. It had not been far to the battlefield.

"It was somewhere around here." Thurstan searched the rough ground, where little grass grew.

She looked back at the others. Wulfstan was at the back. He had overcome his seasickness to accompany them. Edward was telling him about the river, how shallow it had been when he crossed with the horses. They marvelled at the scars on the banks that showed how it had swollen during the storm.

"This is where we lined up to fight." Thurstan paced out the length. "It must have been here."

There was a circle, completely devoid of grass. It was clear something had happened here; blurred prints studded the earth. Saewynn walked to the centre. Did that footprint belong to him? It was large enough. She squatted and placed her hand on it. Leola approached and sniffed the ground, then wandered off. It was probably the foot of Erik Bloodaxe. Saewynn grimaced. She studied the spot, imagining the fight. As she walked back to the others, she stumbled on something buried in the ground.

"What's this?" Leola ran to her and began to dig.

"It's the remains of a shield," said Thurstan. He helped the dog to dig. "Just a boss and a few splinters of wood."

"Give it to me," said Saewynn. She brushed off the mud, rubbed at the remaining wood to expose flakes of blue and green paint. "It's his." She turned it over and slipped her hand through the remains of the grip. It dwarfed her fingers. "This is his shield." She smiled.

"I remember," said Thurstan. "It was smashed. He threw it away, injured one of the watching men."

"One of Erik's?"

"I think it was, my lady," he replied.

"Were you close, when it happened?"

Thurstan shook his head. "We were told to maintain the shield wall."

"You didn't witness his death?"

"There were too many people. Godric was close. Erik struck him next. He is lucky to be alive."

"Erik did that? Godric didn't say." He had wanted to accompany them, but the wound to his leg had not yet healed. Saewynn had told him he was needed to guard her son. "What happened... after?"

"We had to deal with the injuries, then get away before Erik returned to finish us off. I saw the body, the blood. Erik had trampled him into the mud. He must have been dead. I'm sorry we didn't do more, my lady."

"You did what you could." She touched his arm. "Where did you find the sword?"

"Over there." He pointed to a wood in the distance, close to the river. "It's a long walk, my lady. Shall we return to the boats?"

"I need to walk. It's very rough," Saewynn told Wulfstan. "Go back to the boat if you want."

"I can manage. Is that his?" Saewynn passed him the remains of the shield.

Edward peered over his shoulder. "It's definitely his. See that loose piece of binding, he kept meaning to repair it."

"Come on, or it will be dark before we get there." Saewynn wrapped her cloak tighter around her. "Show it to Leola."

The dog took one sniff and whined, her tail dropped between her legs, and she crouched close to the ground. She howled a long mournful note.

"She's been like that since you returned," said Saewynn. Does she know something, or just sense our sorrow?" She stroked the long narrow head. "If anyone can find him, you can." Leola rose to follow close at Saewynn's heels.

"It's very rough, can you help me?" Aelf took Wulfstan's arm. "Don't mind her, she's trying to keep cheerful."

"Aren't we all?" replied Wulfstan.

*

"How did you find it?" Saewynn poked at the shelter. Now, it was easy to spot amongst the leafless trees; in summer it must have been invisible.

"We sheltered in the woods after we escaped; others must have done the same," said Thurstan. "There were strange noises in the night. When we came back afterwards, a witness said a cart had headed in this direction. We searched and found this."

There was a door of sorts. Saewynn opened it and ducked inside. "There's not much room." Standing upright was impossible.

"We found the weapons in the corner, a scratch in the ground and a thin covering of dirt."

"They weren't hidden very well," said Saewynn. "Perhaps someone intended to come back to collect them."

"Why didn't they?" said Wulfstan. "Let the dog in."

Saewynn backed out. "Room for two people to sleep. In you go, girl." The dog disappeared. There was a bark, and a wagging tail was visible through the door.

"He was here," said Saewynn.

"Him or his body?" She ignored Wulfstan's comment and pushed the dog further in. The slim body stiffened, and a menacing growl shook the flimsy construction.

"What is it?" Saewynn pushed after the dog

"Be careful, it might be an animal," said Wulfstan.

"I've only heard her make that noise once before," said Edward "Last year, in the forest, when you... She growled like that at Egbert."

"Leola, out of the way." When Saewynn backed out, her face was white. "Two people were in there: Byrhtnoth and Egbert. There is blood too, on the roof as well as the walls. He must have been alive. What was going on?"

"Come." Aelf put her arm round Saewynn and led her away. "It's nearly dark. We must make camp. We need food and rest."

"Things will seem better by daylight," said Edward.

"Will they?" Saewynn glanced back at the shelter with horror.

"There might have been a small cart here," Thurstan studied the ground, "the ground is too soft to tell."

"Which way did it go?" asked Saewynn. Her face was pale and drawn from a sleepless night.

"Anyone might have taken it," said Wulfstan. "There must have been many bodies to bury. Thurstan nodded grimly.

"We asked everyone we met. No one saw a body buried resembling Lord Byrhtnoth."

"Could he have walked," asked Saewynn, "with an injury like that?"

"Perhaps. We all know how strong he was," said Wulfstan.

"The river?" Edward pointed. "It's not far, and it would have been even closer with the floods. If they had a boat."

"They must have gone downstream," said Wulfstan. "From what you've said, no one could have rowed against that current."

"The cart might have gone a different way, inland," Saewynn pointed towards the western hills, "or north. If Egbert was with Erik?"

"Not likely," said Thurstan "We searched for miles, on foot and on horseback. We found nothing. Erik has disappeared; the Archbishop and the Witan rejected him. He might be in Ireland by now, or Norway, anywhere."

"Where would a boat stop, heading down the river?" asked Wulfstan.

"The bridge is the first place," said Edward.

"We return there, to search for evidence," said Wulfstan. "Agreed?"

Chapter 42

Darkness. Pain and the overwhelming smell of blood. Where am I?

Someone pulls at my head, my helmet? I shout to stop myself sinking into the waiting blackness. Dull light filters through my lashes. I cannot open my eyes. I claw to clear them of the dried blood that plasters them.

I focus on a face, inches from my own. Blue eyes, like sapphires, stare into mine. Light hair, fair or white, frames the face. It is damp, disordered. Rain beats on a roof. It is a beautiful face, a woman, or is it a man, difficult to tell in the gloom. Perhaps I'm dead.

"Are you an angel?" My throat is sore, dry. Have I been ill?

"Don't you recognise me?" A man. I study the face. The frown is transformed into a smile; his teeth are white and even. "What do you remember?"

I think. The hammering in my head makes it difficult. What was I doing before this moment? Where was I? I remember nothing. I search for a memory, any memory. Everything is blank. I panic, desperate to recover something, a face, a place, a name, any name. My name. What is my name? Who am I? I scream and fall back into the darkness.

*

"Keep still. You'll feel better when I've cleaned off this blood."

Gentle fingers wipe a damp cloth across my face, clears the corners of my eyes and the crevices of my nose. When it reaches my lips, I turn away, to lick away the debris, but my mouth is dry. Strong fingers grip my chin. The man dips the cloth in a small bowl and slowly wipes my mouth. I suck at the water. The hand moves to my head, deft fingers run through my hair, separating the matted strands. I flinch when he touches my temple.

"I'll leave that for now, we don't want more bleeding."

He explores the wound, and I clench my jaw. It makes the pain worse.

He sits back and cocks his head. "You don't remember anything? Not even your name?" I shake my head then close my eyes until the dizziness stops. I reach for the bowl of water. He picks it up and holds it to my lips. I drink.

"It's lucky I found you. I don't like to think of you wandering round out there, not knowing who was friend or foe."

"There's been a battle?"

"Yes, we lost. That's why we're hiding. The rain's over now" The pounding on the roof has stopped. "We'll wait until dark to make our escape. Better get you out of that mail. It marks you as a fighter."

I hadn't noticed what I wore. I unbuckle my sword belt and lay it to one side. My companion helps me pull off the byrnie. We struggle in the small space, and the wound on my head bleeds.

"So many times I've done that," said the man.

"I know you?" I don't feel comfortable with him. It must be the blow on the head.

"We met years ago when we were boys. We've been friends ever since. Wherever Byrhtnoth goes, Wulfstan is never far away, closer than brothers."

The names are familiar, but there are no faces connected to them. "So, I am...?"

"You really have forgotten everything, haven't you? You're Wulfstan, and I," he sits straighter, "am Byrhtnoth, advisor to kings."

"Wulfstan?" It is a good name. I must get used to it. "How long until dark? I need to sleep."

"There's plenty of time. Lie down, you're quite safe with me."

*

I am trapped, unable to move. A red glow suffuses everything. I must escape. Strong arms hold me down. I remember. My friend Byrhtnoth? Warm breath on the back of my neck. He is asleep. He said he would keep watch. Is it too late? For what?

Panic makes the pain in my head worse. I push him away and sit up. His eyes open.

"Did you sleep well?" He stretches.

"The sun sets, we must go." I reach for the discarded sword belt.

"Leave it." He lays his hand on mine, I pull away. "It will be recognised. We will hide it, come back later when it is quiet."

He moves a pile of rubbish at the back of our shelter, moss-encrusted stones and rotting wood. The smell of damp soil and decay fills the small space. When he is happy with the hole, he bundles up the mail shirt and thrusts it deep into the ground together with the helmet.

"The sword," he says, glancing back over his shoulder.

I hesitate and draw the blade.

"It is the wrong scabbard."

"What do you mean?" He is nervous. What is he afraid of?

"It doesn't fit as it should. The blade is too long." I hold up the sword. It catches the last of the dying light, and we both stare at it, at the patterns that glimmer in the metal. I have seen them before, by the flicker of firelight. I reach out to touch the blade.

"Careful, there's enough blood on there already."

"Yes." The crimson light has disguised the smears. "It should be cleaned." Whose blood? Who had I killed? Why can't I remember?

"There's no time. I... we will come back." He takes the sword, slams it into the ill-fitting sheath. He wraps the belt around it, and it joins the mail. He looks around our hiding place. His eyes alight on my seax.

"Not that." His eyes meet mine, considering.

"All right, it might be useful."

I help to cover my treasure. Will I find it again? What if someone else discovers it?

"Come on." He waits, silhouetted against the fading light. I am reluctant to leave, to abandon what remains of my past. He holds out a hand. "You can't survive without me." He is right. I take his hand and follow him into the darkness.

There is enough light to show where we step, but we are hidden in the shadows of a wood. In the distance fires burn and figures move. There is shouting and the clang of weapons. Someone screams, over and over, then, abruptly, stops. The smell of roasting meat reaches us. When was the last time I ate? I turn towards the fires, realise human bodies burn in the darkness, not some succulent joint of pork.

"This way." The whisper draws me away, deep into the undergrowth, away from the light. I glance back, the shelter has disappeared. How will I find it again?

We stumble through the trees. It is wet underfoot, the ground soft and boggy. The rain must have fallen for a long time. I stumble, dropping to one knee before pulling myself upright. I lean against a tree, the bark damp and spongy. Why am I so tired? We have only come a few yards yet my muscles ache.

"Come." The insistent whisper calls. I abandon my tree and stagger on. Am I injured, other than the blow to my head? Does blood drip from my body into the sodden ground?

I remember my companion searching my body for wounds. Superficial cuts, nothing serious. I am used to it. How do I know? As we walk, I try to recall my previous life. Nothing. I concentrate on pushing through the thick foliage, damp leaves slap my face, and thorns catch at my clothes. I follow the dark shape ahead. It stops.

"Quiet!" I freeze. Someone else moves through the trees, several people, friend or foe? How can I tell? Every man is an enemy. I duck down to hide from searching eyes. A few words are exchanged: they agree to give up their search, they are tired, hungry, tomorrow will be better. I crouch, as their blundering steps fade away. Did I know them? Did I kill one of their friends? How can I live like this, knowing nothing?

"Are you there?" I want to ignore the voice; hide alone in the darkness.

"I'm here." I move towards him. "Is it much further?"

"Not far."

The trees change to willow and alder. There is a path, more solid than the quaking uncertain land surrounding it. We follow it with relief. My companion moves faster, he knows this place. The roar of water breaks the silence. It gets louder. Above, a multitude of stars lights our way. More trees.

"It has flooded. I hope it hasn't been washed away." He is worried. Does he have another plan is this one fails? "It's here." I join his sigh of relief.

Under the protecting boughs of a willow a small boat bobs in shallow water.

"Find the oars. They must be somewhere." I discover them hidden in the reeds under a fallen log.

"Get in." I sit down quickly on a small bench. He hands me the oars. They are familiar in my hands, I have been in a boat like this before. Where? The boat tips as he climbs in. He settles opposite me. He doesn't like boats, I can tell. I steady the boat with the oars as he pulls out a knife and cuts the rope that anchors us to the tree. Released, the boat is swept away. I manoeuvre away from the bank.

"Where are we going?"

"Downstream. The current runs fast after the rain. You won't even have to row."

"Good." I bend my back. The river is wide. The banks on either side move faster, and I lift the oars. The river has us. I draw in the oars and lay them away tidily.

"I have the steering. You can sleep." I check the condition of the boat and bale out a few handfuls of water. I curl up in the space between the benches. The sound of water flowing past the hull is familiar. It makes me happy.

*

"Wake up." I'm still in the boat, on the river. It is early, enough light to make out the man sitting, watching me.

"What now?" I sit up, and my aching head shatters the peace. I hold it in my hands before opening my eyes. The current still runs fast, but we are stationary. A lattice of wood, a bridge? We are tied against one of the uprights. "Are we there?"

"In a manner of speaking. We must go our separate ways. I am wounded myself." For the first time, I notice that his arm is bandaged.

"The battle?" I ask.

"No, before that. Someone stuck a seax in me."

"Why?"

"A disagreement. It's not important, not now. I have to get away. I was working for the king. Someone told lies, poisoned the king's mind against me. I was dismissed."

"That's terrible, what will you do?"

"I will have my revenge." His eyes bore into mine, and I shiver. He laughs. "Meanwhile, I must find another powerful man to serve. For now, Erik is that man."

"Can't I come with you?"

He seems amused by my words. "It's getting light. I've wasted enough time."

"What will happen to me?" I am scared. I accept that I have no past, but where am I? Where am I to go?

"You should be dead. I saved you, now your life belongs to me. Perhaps I will kill you." His expression tells me he is serious. I reach for my seax.

The sheath is empty. It is in his hand, and it points towards my heart. The boat is small. He only has to lean forward, and I am dead. My eyes flash to the water streaming past. The current is still fast, but the bridge breaks its flow. Dangerous eddies swirl, white water froths.

"Can you swim?" I don't know. Can I swim well enough to escape the river without injury? I jump. Not into the water, I catch hold of one of the bridge struts, try to claw my way upwards. I spy the sky through the gaps in the bridge surface. Such a beautiful pale blue. His hand grabs my foot, I resist, the pull is too great. The wood is smooth, wet from the flooded river. It slips through my fingers. I search for another. Nothing. Another tug and I am forced to let go. Pain shoots through my leg. I land on my back in the boat. It rocks violently. I stare at the hilt of my seax. The blade is buried deep in my thigh. Blood stains my muddied trousers.

"Not quite what I intended, but an apt exchange for what your whore did to me." What is he talking about? "She lived, and no doubt regrets it. Now you will do the same. I hope we meet again. Remember me." He heaves my legs over the side. I struggle. He grabs the hilt of the seax and twists the blade. I scream. Water fills my mouth. I sink. The chill revives me, and I reach for the boat. The oar swings towards me. It hits my head, and the world explodes.

Chapter 43

"I have news." Leif held the boat against the bank as Saewynn stepped out.

"You were right, Wulfstan," Saewynn shouted at the other boat. Aelf shipped her oar and grasped the edge of the small jetty. She held it steady while Wulfstan pulled himself back onto dry land. She handed him his stick, and he hurried to where Saewynn waited with Leif.

"Someone heard something, a few days after the battle," she said in excitement. "Tell him, Leif."

"We spoke to many people without success. It was the man who takes the tolls at the bridge who told us something useful. We were waiting for you to return, and he has some excellent ale."

"Isn't this where Byrhtnoth set up his toll gate?" asked Edward.

"Someone must have noticed how lucrative it was and continued the tax," said Saewynn, "probably under Erik's control. What did the man say?"

"Come and have some ale. He can tell you himself."

"I remember the tall warrior and that vicious black stallion of his."

"He's not vicious," said Saewynn.

299

"As you say," the man frowned and studied her, "my lady. It was a good idea to charge people to cross the bridge. They say he refused King Erik himself passage across."

"It's true," said Leif. "I stood at his side when he did it, nearly shat myself with fear."

"I saw the money he was making. When everyone packed up, I slipped in quick and took over. Not done badly until this latest trouble. I saw that English king and his men gallop south, all in a hurry, then back again when they'd heard King Erik had attacked the remains of his army. It was a bad time." The man shook his head and raised a jug of foaming ale to his lips.

"Did you see Byrhtnoth, the tall warrior, again?" asked Saewynn, eagerly.

"No, don't think I did."

"You said he had information." Saewynn turned to Leif. "All this is about last year." She remembered galloping Thunor over the bridge, so happy to meet Byrhtnoth again. That was just before they argued, and she had caused so much heartbreak.

"Let him tell his story," said Leif, turning to the man. "You said it was the morning after the battle?"

"Or the day after. It's months ago, why didn't you come and ask me about it then?"

"Yes, why didn't you?" Saewynn stared angrily at Thurstan.

"I'm sorry, we had men wounded. We didn't know he was here."

She took a deep breath, "I apologise."

"As I was saying," the man glared at the strangers who had intruded into his hut, "it was early morning. I had spent the previous day clearing everything that came down the river. It was still raining, everything was soaked. Debris had built up against the bridge supports. The pressure could have destroyed the bridge, then where would we be? All I wanted was to get the obstructions out of the way. Then King Erik's men arrived to take the loot. There was fighting, arguments, more death." He

300

took another drink, wiping the froth from his beard with the back of his hand. "The river was cleared, the bridge was safe."

"Next morning?" prompted Saewynn.

"I was tired, although you have to be a light sleeper in this job, people want to cross at all hours. It was early, first light. I heard voices. I tried to ignore it, I was stiff from the previous day, but it sounded as if they were beneath the bridge. My job is to protect the bridge. People have tried to set fire to it, to destroy it."

"Was that what they intended?"

"Whatever it was, they didn't agree about it. There was an argument."

"Did you know who they were?" Saewynn leaned forward across the table.

"No, they were beneath the bridge, in a boat, I heard splashing; the river had calmed a bit by then. There was a shout, then a louder splash, then it went quiet. I thought they had gone when I heard the splash of an oar and a laugh, an evil laugh, it made my hair stand on end. I found the boat caught in the willows later, there was blood."

"Which way did the man go?" asked Wulfstan.

"He didn't cross the bridge, he must have stayed on the north side. I think he headed upstream."

"Did you see his face? Can you describe him?" whispered Saewynn.

"The mist was thick on the river that morning. I saw nothing."

*

"It must have been them." Saewynn paced beside the river. "It couldn't have been anyone else. He's alive!" She turned and hugged Wulfstan.

"He might have been alive when he went into the river," he said, pushing her away. "It doesn't mean he is now."

"We have somewhere to start. All we have to do is follow the river downstream. Someone might have rescued him, or if he

301

escaped on his own, someone would have noticed him." She gazed along the river as if he was waiting around the next corner.

"Or he might be rotting on some deserted beach."

"Don't be so gloomy." Aelf frowned at Wulfstan. "Anyone would think you wanted him dead."

"I don't!" he shouted. "I just don't want Saewynn to get her hopes up."

"At least she has hope. Byrhtnoth didn't die on the battlefield. Come on, she'll have the ship off down the river before we can catch up."

"At least I can rest my leg on board."

"Does it hurt?" asked Aelf. "Do you want me to rub it for you? It helps."

"Thank you."

Chapter 44

I stare into the darkness. I am in a cave or a barn. It is peaceful, silent. Sometimes I hear voices, far away. Perhaps the pain in my head has made me deaf. I lie on a dirty floor, chained, like an animal. Like the animals whose home this is. Where have they gone? No one has cleaned this space since they left. The acrid air catches in my throat and makes me cough. I wait until the pain subsides. My leg aches, I don't know why; I cannot move to find out. I have no strength.

Why am I here? Am I a prisoner? What have I done? My mind is blank. Is this death? A never-ending nothingness.

Do they have doors in hell? There is a creak as one opens. A beam of dusty light leaps through the still air and lights up a wall of rough boards. I study it for clues. Ropes and harness hang from hooks, a shelf stacked with pots. The shapes of what might be baskets, or buckets, invisible in the gloom.

"You're awake." A female voice, young, not old.

"Am I? I thought I was dreaming." I crane my neck to catch sight of her, the light hurts my eyes. She is a dark shape against the brightness. "Where am I?"

"Who are you?" She is nervous. She moves closer, but not too close. Does she fear I will attack her?

"I don't know." Perhaps she will let me go, or at least tell me why I am here.

She stands, uncertain. Her dress is ragged, and her feet are bare. They shuffle in the dirty straw, stirring the dust. I sneeze, and she leaps away. I groan and turn my head into the soothing darkness.

"You don't remember anything?" Her accent is strange, she must be a servant, a slave from across the sea. Which sea? Perhaps I am the slave. That can't be right. "What's your name?"

I think about it. What is my name? A voice in the darkness tells me, "You are Wulfstan."

"Wulfstan?" I repeat the name, trying it for size.

"Where are you from?" I shrug as best I can beneath the chains. It is less painful than nodding.

"I don't know, I can't remember." She stands there for a long time. I am helpless beneath her searching gaze. She stoops to look into my face. I can see her now. She is thin, half starved. Strands of greasy hair hang from a dirty rag wrapped around her head. Her features are uneven, not ugly, but unfinished like badly risen dough.

"How do you feel?" She smells of fish.

"How do you think I feel? My head aches and my leg hurts." Fear makes me angry. "The ground is hard, and the chains are heavy. What have you done to me?"

"I haven't done anything. I..."

Someone shouts. Why is the girl afraid? Darting eyes search for somewhere to hide. She pauses and then smiles. Without another word, she walks away. The door slams, and I am left alone.

The door must be thick. I hear voices, no words. The girl and, I think, a man. Arguing. About me? About my future? Do I have a future?

The sounds fade. Everything is quiet. I have nothing to do except wait.

*

A man stands over me. The door is open. No shaft of sunlight, just enough brightness to lighten the dark space. I am cold and stiff; it must be morning. The man has not brought food, or drink, just a large stick, thick with menace. Is this what injured my head? Has he come to finish the job?

He doesn't appear angry, but the weapon taps against his leg. A threat? A habit? Perhaps both. I tear my eyes from it and look up at him, as defiant as a helpless man can be.

"You have no memory?"

"I told the girl. I remember nothing before I woke up here. Yesterday?"

"Don't you know me?"

"Should I? I don't even know who I am, why should I be expected to know anybody else?" I struggle against the chains. Pain stabs my leg. I can't lie here, helpless. If he plans to kill me, I refuse to submit.

"You should know me." He smiles. I don't think he does it often. "I'm your father."

My father? He can't be. I have no sense of recognition. How can he be my father? My father was... I stop. No image lights my mind. No name comes to my tongue. Perhaps this old worn man is my father. I lie still, close my eyes. I try to remember our life together. Nothing, although I have no other memories to replace them.

"If I am your son, why am I chained like a prisoner?"

"You have been ill. That blow to your head sent your senses flying. You were angry, violent, you attacked us. Not just me, your mother, your wife."

I had a family, parents, a wife. Did I have children? Had I hurt a child?

"I'm sorry. I didn't know."

"No permanent damage. Let's get those chains off. You don't mind keeping the rope around your hands? It will make the others happier, until you get to know them, again."

My legs shake like a new-born lamb's. There is a bandage on my thigh, stained with blotches of long-dried blood. What lies beneath is something that I must explore, later. My father supports me as we walk out into the light. It is not bright, the sun is invisible, but my head swims. I close my eyes against the stabbing. I wait, head low until I venture a glimpse through the smallest slit. The ground shifts, and then steadies. I raise my head. Everything is grey. A vast sky, interrupted by neither tree nor hill, merges into a land of tufted grass. There is nothing to stop the eye travelling forever, to the end of the world. A handful of low humps surrounds us. Behind is the dark doorway from which I emerged. A building covered by turf. The other humps are buildings too. A woman stands in the doorway of the largest, observing me. She disappears.

"Stand a while, until you feel stronger. You lost a lot of blood."

"What happened?"

"You were down by the shore." He points towards a sheet of glittering water. I flinch as reflections send a rain of needles into my brain.

"The sea?"

"River. The sea is further out." As he mentions it, I recognise the constant whisper of waves in the distance. I know that sound, the only familiar thing about this place. "Someone attacked you, I don't know who. Perhaps from a ship, English returning home." He spits onto the churned mud of the yard. "You didn't return from the fish traps. We found you floating in the river. We thought you dead, but you recovered. Come on, the meal is ready."

I follow him towards the house, placing my feet carefully. Did I learn to walk here, long ago? How long? I expect they will tell me. First I must fill my empty stomach.

*

I am still hungry. We eat thin gruel tasting vaguely of fish. It is cold. A loaf, several days old, is produced. It is carefully divided, half for my father, Gunnar, the rest between the three of us. My mother's name is Sigrun. She is scared of me. A cauldron hangs over a pile of ashes. She is careful to keep it between us. What have I done to make her fear me? There is a half-healed bruise on the side of her face. Did I do that? After an initial greeting, I keep my head lowered. Beside me on the hard bench sits the girl. Her name is Siv. She is my wife. I try smiling at her, she edges away.

The only light comes from the open door. The floor is lower than the ground outside; I feel like an animal peering from a burrow. The room is long and narrow, the hearth offset from the door. Benches on either side, built against the walls. There are blankets, folded neatly, ready for the night.

Above the hearth, shapes hang from the blackened ceiling. Joints of meat, most flesh carved away. It must be late in the year. Soon fresh meat will hang there, to be smoked for the winter. I look forward to the killing time.

Shadows linger in the ends of the room. There is a table at one end. More provisions gathered and stored. A pile of shrivelled blocks, dried peat for the fire. I wonder how far it is to the nearest tree.

At the other end, beyond a surprisingly ornate chair, a hurdle divides the building. It is empty; no doubt animals will fill it later. They will provide warmth in the coldest time. Something is missing, and for some time I cannot identify what it is. I stare at the blank walls. There are no hangings. I take another look around the room. There is no colour, no decoration apart from the carved chair. Even the cushion that waits there, plump and comforting, is grey.

My father stands. There is work to be done. What work do I do? He mentioned fish traps. Where are the animals? Who cares for them? I rise, ready to help and find my head touches the ceiling.

"Rest today. You are weak. Tomorrow you will be stronger." His attention moves to the girl. "Check his wounds, make sure he is well." He raises a foot to the threshold and pauses. "The water is low, fetch more." He disappears.

My mother hurries to pick up the buckets that stand beside the entrance. She gives me a tight smile as she leaves. She is still tense, though not as scared. Is it me who scares her? Or my father?

Then the two of us are alone. What do I say to her, this woman who is my wife?

I feel her hand on my leg. I try not to pull away.

"I think it has healed. Do you have any pain?" I have forgotten about it.

"Not much, my head hurts."

"I'll deal with that later." She unwraps the bandages.

"I'd help, but..." I hold up my tied hands.

"Why did he do that?" She takes out a small knife and cuts the rope. I rub my freed wrists. The rope was tight, and I stretch my fingers as the blood flows back. She coils the piece of rope and puts it to one side. I remove the wrapping, stopping to separate layers that have stuck together. Together we stare at the wound. Caused by a knife, I think, a long knife. I reach for my belt. There's nothing there. Should I have a knife?

"It was a clean cut, then twisted. See the jagged edges?" She gave a shy smile. "Someone didn't like you much."

"No." I wonder who it was.

"It's healing well, but you must be careful not to overdo things. You're lucky it wasn't any higher, you would have bled to death."

I am aware of her hand stroking my leg.

"Do I have any clothes? Apart from this." I pluck at the rough tunic.

"Of course. You must be cold." She goes to the end of the room and rummages through a pile of rags. "Here, I washed and mended them." She holds up some trousers, rather the worse for wear. I feel more comfortable with them on.

"When Mother comes back with the water, I will clean the wound on your head."

"Mother?" I frown; I shouldn't do it. "Surely she's my mother, not yours."

"Well, yes." Her face glows pink, she is almost attractive. "I've been here so long, I think of her as my mother as well."

"I understand. You're going to have to tell me all about our family."

Chapter 45

The journey downstream was even slower than when they had come. Saewynn insisted that they let the ship follow the currents. Every person they met was questioned. Every settlement was visited. Whenever the ship pulled in to the bank, she leapt onto dry land, Leola close behind her.

Thurstan or Edward went with her, and a couple of other men. She fretted at the imposition.

"I'm asking a simple question: has anyone seen a tall man, with a head wound, above the right eye? I'm not causing any trouble."

"No," said Wulfstan, "it's just that people are wary. This area has been at war, and don't forget, it was months ago. What if the wound has healed? Why would anyone notice him?"

"I would," said Saewynn, "any of us would recognise him."

"Because we know him," said Edward. "What if we offer money, a reward?"

"Can we afford it?"

"We can," replied Wulfstan, "although I'm not sure it's a good idea."

"Why not?" said Saewynn. "I should have thought of that. Take my brooch." She unpinned it from her cloak and handed it to Wulfstan.

"Keep it. I'll find something suitable."

Once word spread, everyone was eager to help. Men and boys were brought at every stop. One rumour sounded hopeful. A man had been pulled from the river, soon after the battle. He was wounded. Someone had taken him to a healer, up in the hills.

"It must be him." Saewynn shouted for Leola, "Let's go. The dog wagged her tail and stood ready at the edge of the ship.

"Not so fast," said Wulfstan. "Where is this healer?"

"It's a long way, you'll need horses, I can show you the path." The man stood on a broken-down jetty, a greasy leather helmet clutched in his hands. "I saw him myself, a tall man, taller than him," he pointed at Thurstan, who nodded. "Blonde hair, all bloody."

"That's him, it must be. How was he? Was he well?" Saewynn asked the man.

"He was alive when I saw him, ill, feverish. Calling a name."

"Saewynn?"

"That's it."

"It is him! We must hurry. Did you hear what he said? Byrhtnoth is ill. Perhaps it's already too late. If he dies, it's your fault," she told Wulfstan.

"The reward?" the man held out a hand.

"When we find him," said Wulfstan.

"Of course, my lord. If you want horses, I can find some for you."

*

"I told you it was a waste of time." Wulfstan climbed wearily from his horse. "Two days and that boy looked nothing like him."

"They'd cut him on purpose, that wound was fresh," said Edward.

"No success?" asked Leif as they crossed the plank onto the ship.

"No, how were things here?"

"A few dodgy men hanging around. They soon disappeared when they saw we were well armed. And there was a ship. I've seen it several times. Must be on regular business or some local lord keeping an eye on what's going on."

"Did you get a look at the crew?" asked Wulfstan. He scanned the busy river.

"Never gets close enough to see who's on board, which is strange. We might have more luck further on." Leif cast off the ropes, and the ship floated slowly downstream.

"I'm sorry, Saewynn." Wulfstan sat down beside the despondent girl. "It might have been him."

"No, it wouldn't. You knew the story was false, and you were right. I've been a fool, but I so wanted it to be true." She sniffed, trying to hold back the tears.

"You're not a fool." He put an arm around her shoulders. "Anyone else would have given up long ago."

"What do I do now? You think he's dead, don't you?"

"I just don't know." Wulfstan shook his head. "If you still believe, then he's alive. We're tired, get some sleep, we'll continue the search tomorrow.

Chapter 46

Wounds heal, swelling subsides, the pain remains. I wrap a cloth around my head, to cover my eyes when the light is bright. I cannot think, so I obey instructions without complaint. I eat what I am given. I am always hungry but dare not ask for more. I go down to the river when the tide turns, to collect the fish caught in the traps. The women praise my strength when I carry the heavy basket back. I watch as they gut the fish and learn to pack the small ones in barrels. I cover them in salt. I must use enough, but not too much. The season for harvesting salt is over. The sun shone hot in summer, I am told. We have plenty of salt, but it must not be wasted. I hang the larger fish on the drying frame. They turn hard as boards in the ever-blowing wind.

When it grows colder, we kill some of the beasts, and strips of their flesh join the fish on the frames. It is a constant job to ward off the birds that try to steal our meat. Their cries tear through my head. Shouting is painful, so I walk up and down the rows, waving my arms. Sometimes my wife stops her work to watch me. When I catch her eye, she looks away and returns to slitting the pale white bellies.

The discarded scraps, the heads, the pieces too small to be of use are boiled for our meals. Sometimes there is seaweed, collected from the sea shore. I enjoy collecting it. I walk for miles, basket on my back, bent almost double, searching for the choicest varieties. I collect wood from the shore as well. Where does it come from? How long has it floated the ocean, all roughness washed away to smooth greyness?

There are not many ships, the weather is stormy. Where do they go? There is no shelter here, from the wind and rain. It must be endured. If I spy a ship, I run, hide in the dunes that fringe the beach. Father says it was men from a ship that injured me. What will they do if they catch me again?

*

When the evening meal is over, we wait. Father sits in his chair, legs stretched out, feet resting on the hearthstones. Sometimes he criticises us for something we have done wrong that day. He tells us our jobs for the next day. Mostly we sit in silence, as close to the fire as we can get. I do not stretch out my legs. They take up too much room. I hug my knees close to my chest, my head resting on them, desperate to hold on to the warmth.

I feel the wound in my leg. When it cramps, I dare not stretch. My legs are too long, my feet too big. I sit and wonder at them. How did I grow so tall? Why am I different?

I stare into the embers of the fire, watch the pictures there. Where do they come from? What do they tell me? Like my dreams, I remember things, then when I try to grasp them, my mind blurs, and the image collapses into grey ash.

It doesn't take long for the fire to die, the darkness to descend. We lie down to sleep, pull the covers over us. My mother shares my father's cushion. My wife and I share our warmth. The first time she touches me, I turn away, unwilling to react, with my parents lying so close. We listen to them, the grunting, the creaking of the boards, his final exhalation of satisfaction, the snores that follow.

It is difficult to avoid her searching fingers. She feels my body's response. We wait until the darkest dead of night when they are asleep. There are no words, no caresses. It is quickly done.

316

"About time." A sleepy voice murmurs in the dark.

I do it whenever she asks. I regret it. This is not the woman I want. She feels wrong, she smells wrong. Although we rarely speak, her voice is wrong. But I crave contact with another human body. I drown in her heat for a few moments, then lay awake for hours, searching the dark caverns of my shattered brain for someone else, another life.

*

Father is late. We are hungry, we cannot eat until he arrives. I sit, head bowed. The door is open, the dusk light falls onto a patch of floor in front of me. I watch. Someone has dropped a crust of bread. It lies there, not even a mouthful, filling my whole world. I have only to lean forward and pick it up. Dare I do it? I look to the right. Mother huddled close to the heath, stares at the cauldron. She stirs the contents. I found a wild onion today. The smell torments me. My stomach growls. I look down. The crust is still there. I glance sideways at my wife. She has noticed it too. I catch her eye. She gives the briefest shake of her head.

I reach out a foot, scuffle in the pieces of crushed reed and the dust, draw the piece of bread closer. I bend down as if to scratch my foot. I have it. It is soft, fresh, not as old as I thought. How did it drop from today's baking? My mouth waters, but I must share it with my wife.

"Ulf? What are you doing?" The room darkens. A shape fills the doorway. I freeze. I hold out my hand. The crust is so small. He takes it, shows it to my mother. She denies all knowledge, shakes her head, terrified. He rests a hand on her shoulder and nods patiently.

I am on the floor. He drags me to the door. Dazed, I stumble up the step and fall to the ground. He beats me with the stick, kicks me. I curl in a ball, protecting my head with my hands. Anger fills me. I want to fight back. He is smaller than me, older. Something, deep inside, tells me I could kill him with no trouble. I don't. I accept it. He is my father. It is his right to chastise me. I broke his rules. I must be punished.

He stops. He is panting, it was hard work. I keep still, not moving a muscle. He gives a final kick and returns inside without a word. The door slams. I am alone. I assess my injuries. Nothing broken. I crawl away.

They will be eating now. Will my wife, get my share? I doubt it. I make myself as comfortable as I am able. It is cold, but I will survive.

What can I do? I will decide when the pain stops, and I can think.

*

It is better when the beasts are brought in. The heat of their bodies warms the space. The sound of their movement fills the silence. I get used to the smell, sometimes it drives out the stink of fish.

It is part of my duties to care for them. The waste must be cleared. I shovel it into a barrow and push it across the yard to the muck heap. All the waste goes onto it, animal and human. Even the remains of the fish processing, although the savage dogs that returned from the fields with the beasts consume most of that. They are chained in the yard. I recognise the chains. I give them a wide berth.

Several loads and the floor is clear. I collect buckets of water and clean the building, dodging the moving animals. I fetch fresh hay. It is stored in the building where I woke in chains. It was a lifetime ago; I suppose it is. I still remember nothing from before. Perhaps there is nothing to remember, this has always been my life.

I climb up the stack of hay, to drag more from the back. I duck beneath the roof, and as I turn, my shoulder knocks something resting on the beams. I pull it out. A soft package wrapped tight. I take it to the door, where the light is better. I check no one is about. I should put it back, but I am curious. It is blue cloth, wool, better quality than I am used to. I unwrap it. The rope is the same as that used to tie my wrists. I glance towards the rings on the floor where I had been confined.

My heart beats faster, the pain in my head increases. I shouldn't be doing this. My hands unfold a tunic. There is something else, long and hard, a knife. It is heavily stained with blood? My blood? Is this the knife that injured my leg? It is rusty, no one has cleaned it. I hear voices. The women are returning. I wrap the knife. I must put it back. As I retreat, I notice a pattern. I turn back to catch the light. A dog embroidered on the cloth, another. Threads are missing, then I see them clearly. Running dogs, black and white. The voices get closer, then fade. They have gone indoors. Hurriedly, I rewrap the knife, retie the rope. I find the place it had been hidden, pushing it back until it is invisible. The dogs in the yard bark. I bundle more hay into the barrow and rush to the door.

"Haven't you finished yet?"

"I'm sorry, Father. My head is bad today." It is. Jagged pains have joined the throbbing. "Excuse me." I rush to the muck heap. The smell is the final straw. I am sick, from the pain, the stink, and fear. What will happen if he discovers what I have found?

*

I cannot bear the taste of the rancid broth. My wife brings me water. As I drink, I watch the flames. Dogs appear, disappear, curl up or stand and watch me, mostly they run, legs stretched, heads low, ears streaming in an unknown wind. They make me dizzy. I lie down, face to the wall. I pretend to sleep. When my wife joins me, I push her away. I can't give her what she wants. I want nothing except to watch the dogs, racing through my head. Where have they come from? Where are they going? I try to run with them, I stumble. They leave me behind, and I mourn. I press my face into the filthy rags and cry.

Next day, my wife fusses over me. I am pale, she says. She prepares a poultice for my head. It will reduce the swelling. She has tried before, without success. I pretend it helps. I return to my work, and the dogs fade away, into the bottomless pit of my memory.

Chapter 47

Saewynn stared across the wide expanse of reeds. It was marshy here, and settlements were sparse. They had been reduced to searching the muddy banks for anything, although if he were there, he would be long past life. Leola stood with her front legs up on the ship's side, nose damp from scenting the wind. She looked back at Saewynn and gave a sharp bark.

"Is he there?" The dog's tail swung. "Stop the ship. Leola's found something."

Leif pulled on the steering oar, and the ship nosed its way into the bank. As soon as it touched, Leola was over the side, swiftly followed by Saewynn.

"Come back," shouted Wulfstan.

Aelf was sitting beside him. "I'll go." She climbed over and lowered herself to the ground. Wulfstan signalled Thurstan and Edward to go with her.

Saewynn ran hard to catch up with Leola. The land was half water, and thick stands of reeds blocked the way. The river must flood this area, perhaps they should search further from the river. She almost tripped over Leola. The dog sat, head lowered, ears flat against her head. She gave a thin whine.

Saewynn realised it was a body. It resembled a bundle of sticks, wrapped in cloth. It had been in the water for a long time, before being deposited here. Some bones had been stripped clean. Something scuttled from the clothing and into the reeds.

"Don't look." Aelf caught up with her and held her tightly, hiding Saewynn's face against her chest.

Thurstan arrived, then Edward, who must have fallen; his clothes were covered in mud.

"It's a body," Aelf told them.

"Is it...?" Saewynn's voice shook.

"I don't think so." Thurstan picked up a piece of wood and prodded the bundle. "It's too small and I don't recognise the clothing." He pushed hard, and the body turned over. He jumped back, then gave a nervous laugh. The skull grinned back at him. "That's not Byrhtnoth. This man doesn't have any teeth."

Saewynn ventured a quick glance. "You're right, that's not him. Is that the remains of a spear in his chest?"

Thurstan bent closer. "I think it is. He must have been killed in the battle. At least it proves that some bodies floated this far."

"Do we bury him?" asked Saewynn.

"It's not worth it," said Thurstan. "It's so wet he'd just float up again. Wulfstan can say a prayer for him."

"I wonder what side he was on?" said Aelf.

"Does it matter?" Thurstan poked the body again.

"I suppose not." Saewynn turned to go back to the ship.

"Hold on." Edward was studying the body. "That bag. Could it be Byrhtnoth's?"

Saewynn pushed him out the way and bent down to look. "You're right. It is similar." She reached out to touch it.

"Let me do it, my lady." Thurstan took out a knife and cut the belt. It was all that was keeping the body together. He opened the bag and peered inside.

"There's not much: a knife, comb, nothing valuable." He pulled out the comb. Saewynn stared at it. She gave a cry of recognition.

"That's it. That's Byrhtnoth's comb. I'd know it anywhere." She reached for it.

"We can't stand around here," said Aelf. "Wulfstan's calling. We can investigate this better back on the ship. Edward, bring the bag. Thurstan, search the body. There might be something else." She took Saewynn's arm and led her back through the reeds.

Wulfstan inspected the bag. "It's wet, but there's not much smell after all this time. Do you want me to search it?"

"I'll do it, I don't want anyone else to." Saewynn snatched it from him and went to her seat in the bow.

"I think we've finished here, Leif. Carry on. We'll stop for the night soon," said Wulfstan.

Saewynn sat and stared at the bag for a while before opening it. Thurstan had been right, there was not much left. The comb had dark hairs caught in the teeth. Had the corpse had dark hair? It had been difficult to tell.

There was Byrhtnoth's knife, still in its case. She slid it out; the blade was sharp. His fire steel was there and a few rags. She pulled them out, old pieces of linen. That was all. Anything valuable had gone. She sat clutching the bag. What else was missing? Caught in the linen, there was something else, wrapped by a small piece of silk. Where had he found that? She opened it. It was her letter. Inside she found the strands of her own hair, carefully coiled and knotted. She sat and held it, oblivious to the tears that flooded down her face.

*

Saewynn's hope had been renewed, but soon faded. They reached the estuary, not far from the sea. So much empty sky and water. They visited settlements along the shore. Everyone had heard of their search, and no one had news.

"We are going to have to leave soon." Leif stood next to her in the bow, searching the water ahead for obstacles. The sail was up, there was no current to follow, just the regular battle of tide and river. "It's late in the season. We've been lucky so far. The winter storms would normally have started by now."

"Lucky?" Saewynn gave a gloomy sigh.

"I know you hoped to find him, but if his body made it this far, and we have found no trace, the sea will have taken him long ago. It's your decision, although I think it is time to give up."

Was it? She was torn. She didn't want to give up; she couldn't give up. Byrhtnoth must be out there somewhere, and it was her duty to find him. But she was so tired; she wanted to go home to her son. Did he miss her? He must have grown. Would she recognise him when she returned?

She stared across the water. It was tinged pink from the setting sun. The sea must be close; she heard the surf crash against a beach. It was empty, then she spotted movement. An old man disappeared into the dunes. How did he survive out there?

"We must find somewhere to stop for the night."

"There was a settlement." Leif pointed back the way they had come. "We can find shelter there."

"And warmth as well, I hope." Saewynn gave a wan smile and pulled her cloak closer around her. The nights were getting colder. "Then tomorrow we will go home."

Leif nodded and gave the signal to change direction. The ship heeled, and Saewynn held on to her seat. Leola gazed out across the water. She gave a sharp bark and without any warning jumped from the ship.

"Come back," shouted Saewynn. "Leif, she's fallen overboard. Turn the ship, we must find her."

"The waters are dangerous here, sandbanks constantly on the move. We have a channel. It would be dangerous to leave it, and it's getting dark."

"What's happening?" Wulfstan limped forward to join them.

"It's Leola, she's in the water." Saewynn searched for the dog. She spotted the shape of her head, spearing through the water, making no attempt to return to the ship.

"She's close to land," said Wulfstan. "We'll pick her up in the morning. She might even return to us tonight. We're heading back to that village?" Leif confirmed the destination. Wulfstan put a hand on Saewynn's shoulder. "Don't worry, she'll probably be waiting for us."

"Yes," said Saewynn, dubiously. "But why did she jump?"

Chapter 48

Although the days are short, I go down to the river. The traps must be cleared, the fish must be preserved. Where do they go? To market they tell me, to pay for the flour to make our bread. However many I catch, we never have more bread. I must try harder. I stare out across the water.

It is a perfect day. All is grey; the sky is soft like feathers plucked from a goose's breast, and the river matches its greyness, only flat, like beaten metal. Like me, it has no past, only an endless present. As I watch, the metal melts; all is motion. The wind ruffles the surface where the current runs fast and dark. It soothes my mind, but I cannot stay and dream. There is work to do.

I walk down to the shore and follow the departing tide. Already the black stakes of the trap rise above the water, and fish flounder in its jaws. Carefully I avoid the patches of mud. I am unwilling to disturb the smooth, slick surface, and it can be dangerous. The crunch of my feet on freshly washed stones disturbs the birds that have collected for the feast.

I take the first fish from the water and smash its head on the rock that stands ready. I toss it into the basket that I have hauled across the abandoned riverbed and reach for the next. I judge the blow carefully, to stun or kill, and not draw blood. I do not want the violent scarlet to mar the day's peaceful grey.

A breeze disturbs the surface of the water. In the west, the grey clouds are tinged with pink. I must hurry. A few small fish remain. I will award them life if the birds don't take them before the tide returns.

I struggle through the mud, back to the bank. A distant movement catches my eye. I squint. Is that a sail silhouetted against the rosy clouds? I hurry, hunched to hide my presence. Nearly there. I look back. The ship is closer. The sail, black against the bright sky, drives it towards me. An arm points in my direction. I abandon the basket and run. The dead fish spill across the mud, perhaps the enemy will be content with them. I crawl on hands and knees up the slope and over the top, landing in a ditch of brackish water.

I climb out, search for the path that will lead me back. I find it. I stop. What if they are not content with the fish? What if they follow me? They will kill my family. What will I do without them? I leave the path, head away from home, out into the marsh. I run until it is too dark to see. I throw myself into a dip in the ground, sheltered by a patch of reeds. Soft sand. I must be close to the sea. I burrow into it, covering my head with my hands. No one will find me. I wait in the darkness.

Although I am sheltered from the bitter wind, my legs are cold. I removed my trousers, before wading into the water. I always do. They must be still there. I remember the mended tear. It matches the scar on my thigh. If I was attacked in the water, why the hole? There must be another explanation. Perhaps my father hit me. Why stab me?

It is quiet. Any late birds have found their way home. Soon the creatures of the night will emerge. Am I safe, lying here defenceless? I find my eating knife. It is small but sharp. I hold it in my hand. Should I turn over, onto my back? I am too comfortable. This ground is softer than the bed at home. A pity

I have no covering. I burrow deeper into the sand, perhaps I will sleep. I close my eyes.

A sound. Something moves with stealth through the stiff grasses. Snuffling. Has it followed my trail? A fox? I can fight that off. I have a vision of a wolf, glaring out of the darkness. There are no wolves here. Are there? How do I know? I grip the knife tighter.

Something touches my leg. I resist the urge to pull away. Perhaps it will ignore me. Hot breath, panting. Has it been running? Is it excited to have found a meal? Before it can sink its teeth into me, I twist. I grab something, a leg? I pull the animal close to locate a target for my knife. Sharp claws scratch me, but there is no growl, no snapping of teeth. I hesitate. Have I scared it? Will it run if I release it? I let go. It does not run. It sits, lies down. A plaintive whine breaks the silence. A dog? I reach out. Something licks my fingers. I move my hand, a long muzzle, the dome of a head and soft pricked ears. I locate its throat, my knife ready to strike. Something around the neck, a collar? It must be a dog.

A sudden thought. Dogs have owners. A dog can be used to track an animal, a man. I listen. No sound breaks the night. No voices call. Only the sound of my gasping breath and soft whimpers from the dog. My hand is around its throat, squeezing. I let go, and the animal moves forward. It licks my face. It is comforting. Dark eyes gaze into mine. I run my hand down its back. A long tail beats the ground.

"Are you the dog from my dreams?" I whisper. The licking increases. Where did it come from, if not my dreams? I lie down, content. I will wake up soon, and it will be light. The dog lies beside me, warming my chilled body. I sleep.

Chapter 49

In the faint light of dawn, something watches me. It is the dog.
It is real, not a dream. It is the dog from the stitching that haunts
me. I reach out to touch it, solid, warm. It is a bitch.

"Hello, girl." The tail beats, disturbing the sand. I remember
hiding from the ship. I sit up, there is no ship. Did the dog come
from it, or is she hiding too? I stand up. My leg aches from the
cold, but my head has felt worse. I scan the horizon, no ships,
no people. No plume of black smoke to signal a burning house.
What has made me think of that?

I pat the dog. One ear hangs forward, how did that happen?
Well healed, long ago. The collar is red leather, embossed with
twisting patterns, expensive. This is the dog of a rich man. She
pushes her nose into my hand.

"You're hungry?" She waits, expectant. "I don't have anything,
I'm afraid."

If I go home, my father will not waste food on a useless dog
like this. Despite my own hunger, I linger. It is peaceful here.
Waves sigh against the beach. I clamber up the bank, still no one
in sight. The sea is calm and empty. There is no cloud, the day
will be bright once the sun breaches the horizon. Driftwood has
collected along the high tide mark. I walk the line of dry and

stinking seaweed until my arms are full of fuel. At least I will not arrive home empty-handed. I remember the fish I had collected. Is it worth returning to find it? It will be gone, let the birds enjoy their feast.

The dog watches me from the top of the dunes. I return to her. We must get back. Perhaps there will be some bread left, and fish soup to take the edge off my hunger. We walk away from the sea. I am grateful the sun does not shine in my eyes. It is warm on my back. I am almost content.

As my home appears in the distance, my leg begins to pain me. The limp makes my headache worse. I plod along the familiar path, head low, eyes half closed. Perhaps I should leave the wood, come back for it later. No, I cannot risk my father's wrath. Raised voices reach my ears, he is already angry. I hope he doesn't blame the women for my disappearance. Usually, I can divert his anger onto myself, this time I am too late. There are no screams. I listen, more voices, male voices.

I raise my head. A group of men, some mailed, with helmets and weapons. From the ship? Did I lead them to my family? Should I run? I cannot, I must protect my wife, my family. Too late, they have seen me. They point. I drop the armful of wood, retaining only the largest, thickest stick. I walk forward.

One figure, smaller than the others, turns from an argument with my father. He walks to meet me. He wears a helmet, and I cannot see his eyes. He must be young, a beardless boy. He waves the others back. Mail glitters in the sunlight. I narrow my eyes. Beneath the byrnie, I glimpse a bright blue tunic. It reminds me of the one I found, the one with dogs. I glance towards the barn. What does it mean? The dog barks. I had forgotten she was there. She leaps forward. I want to warn her about the sharp seax in the warrior's left hand. He stoops to pat the dog.

"The dog belongs to you?" I am sorry to lose her but glad she has been found. I would not have been allowed to keep her.

"No. She is yours."

"I don't understand." Everyone is watching, waiting, for what?

"It is you, isn't it?" The voice sounds very young, uncertain. He glances back. One of the men, leaning on a stick, the only one without armour, gives a nod of reassurance. The young man takes a step forward, another. He sheaths the weapon and removes his helmet. "Don't you recognise me?"

Dark hair falls to the figure's shoulders. A woman? She pushes back the hair to reveal worried brown eyes. The echo of a scar runs down the side of her face. Why do I want to touch it?

"Do I know you? I'm sorry, I..." The pounding of my head drowns all thought. I feel sick from the sunlight reflected from the mail. She raises a hand towards me

"Leave my son alone. He's not well."

She steps back as my father approaches. She gives me a smile. "When you told me, you were searching for your father, I wasn't expecting someone like this."

The women follow him, casting anxious glances towards the watching men.

"I suppose this is your mother and sister." I shake my head, confused.

"Of course not. I'm his wife." Siv takes my arm to lead me away. "Come inside. You must be hungry. There is still some broth left."

"And bread?" I ask.

"A little." She meets my eyes with an apologetic glance.

"May I ask how long you have been married?" the warrior woman's voice is cold as an icicle in midwinter. "Do you have children?"

"No children, not yet." Siv glances at my father then faces the other woman. "We have been together for years, many years." I am proud of her. I put an arm around her shoulders.

"You prefer this," the mailed arm swings to encompass the yard, the crouching buildings, the colourless land that stretches into the distance, "to me, to our son?"

333

"Our son?" I had a son? I cannot think. "Where?" I look around, there is no child.

"I left him, abandoned him." There are tears in her eyes, and she swallows to hold them back. "They told me you were dead. I didn't believe them. I have searched for you, for months. All that time you were here, fucking this slut."

"Don't talk about my daughter like that, she's a good girl." The words faded into a stunned silence.

"Daughter?" I stare at him. He tries to bluster.

"I didn't mean it in that way. Get inside, Ulf. I'll explain." Used to obedience, I turn towards the door.

"He's coming with me." The woman's eyes glitter in the bright light, I want to go with her, but my father reaches her first. He holds a knife to her throat. It is the blade we use to gut the fish; scales dust the sharp edge. I clutch my head, what can I do? I have no weapon.

"You will not have him," says my father. "I pulled him from the water. I saved his life. He belongs to me." The woman struggles, the man with the stick limps closer. "Get back." A drop of blood blooms on her neck. I watch in horror.

The dog growls, worrying at my father's legs. He grips the woman tighter, kicks out, the dog yelps. It moves in, barking. So much noise, men shout, women scream. I want to run, to hide, the woman's eyes meet mine. I know them. They are the eyes I see in the dark of night. The eyes I long for. I ignore everything else: the noise, the flashing light, the pain. I concentrate on the knife. The dog sinks her teeth into my father's leg, he shouts, the knife jerks, away from the woman's throat. Before I think the thought, I have struck. I grab his wrist and twist. The crunch of breaking bone drowns everything. The knife falls. My other hand encircles his throat. I pull him away from the woman, drag him to the centre of the yard. Both hands are around his neck. I squeeze. His eyes bulge, he fights for breath. So often I have wanted to do this. How many times have I submitted because he was my father?

334

"You are not my father!" I shout it louder, for all the world to hear.

I notice my mother and wife, no, sister. No. Nothing to me, but they have been kind. Should I take their husband, their father from them? Silently I ask the question. The older woman puts an arm around the younger. Why had I never noticed they were mother and daughter? Together they give the same short nod. My fingers tighten. I watch his face as he dies, then drop him to the ground.

Everyone is safe. Pain and confusion roll in like a winter storm. I cannot withstand it. I drop to my knees. Someone touches my face. The woman? It is too much. I fall into swirling darkness.

Part VI: Winter

Chapter 50

"What happened? Is he injured?" Byrhtnoth's face was white. A thick worm of blood crawled from his matted hair. "He's so cold." Saewynn took his hand, rubbing it to bring warmth to it.

"Let me." Wulfstan listened for breath. "He's alive, just." He searched Byrhtnoth quickly. "There's a nasty wound in his leg and minor injuries from the battle, all healed. It's his head that worries me. Remember the helmet?"

"So much blood, you said he could not have survived."

"Obviously he did, although he's not far from death now."

He turned to the young woman staring down at her father's body. "I'm sorry, I need to know, what has happened to my friend?"

"Ulf? We haven't seen him since yesterday. He went to collect the fish. It was late. He didn't have to go. He could have left it until morning."

"I saw him from the ship," admitted Saewynn. "He ran away. It must have been him. Leola knew." She was devastated that she hadn't recognised her husband.

"Our father made him fear the ships," said the woman. "He told him raiders had attacked him, caused his injuries."

"And they hadn't?" asked Wulfstan.

"I don't know. Father found him, unconscious in the water. There was a knife..." She stopped then ran to the barn, returning with a bundle of cloth. "Father hid it. I think Ulf found it. He didn't say anything. He had dreams. He wouldn't..." She blushed and gave Saewynn a quick glance.

"They're his clothes." Wulfstan inspected the dirty blue tunic.

"I'd know his seax anywhere," said Saewynn. "It's covered in blood."

"It was stuck in his leg. It pained him for a while, his head was worse."

"He was like that when he arrived?" asked Wulfstan. The woman nodded. "When was that?"

"Months ago. There were many bodies in the river after the flood. Was there a battle?"

"There was," confirmed Thurstan.

"He was the only one living that we found. I kept him alive."

"Not for much longer, unless we get him warm. Thurstan, help me get him inside. Leif, go back and collect some food, there's little here. Then move the ship closer. I think we'll be staying here some time."

They laid Byrhtnoth on the bench.

"It's not much warmer in here." Saewynn shivered. "Clear the ashes from the hearth and light it quickly. Is there fuel?"

"Plenty, but one of your men will have to light it." The old woman lifted the cauldron and headed for the door. "We aren't allowed. My husband lights, lit, the fire."

"Where are you taking that? We need food."

"I'm throwing this away. I'm sick of it. Siv, make yourself useful; fetch the beef father was saving for yule. Chop it up with some of those onions we hid behind the barn."

"Aelf, go with her," said Saewynn. She didn't know if she could trust these women.

"Can your men fetch some water? It's not far."

"Thurstan, organise the water, Edward, light the fire, then find someone to bury the man outside. I'm sorry Byrhtnoth killed your husband," she told the old woman, "we'll discuss the weregild later."

"Don't worry. We would have done it ourselves if we'd had the courage. Gunnar was a nasty, vicious man. We're better off without him. Sling him on the dung heap."

Saewynn recoiled from the woman's outburst. "As you wish. Do you have blankets?"

"I'll fetch them."

"How is he?" Saewynn kneeled on the floor beside Byrhtnoth's lifeless body.

"He's in a bad way." Wulfstan shook his head. "He's half starved. His body is covered with bruises. He's been beaten, several times. How could he submit to that, without protest?"

"He was a good son." Siv stood in the doorway with an armful of plump onions. "He obeyed his father. He took the beatings earned by us. We were grateful." She laid the onions on the table. "I'll fetch the meat." As she reached the door, she looked back. "Don't let him die. I'm sorry for what we did."

"What happened here?" Saewynn stared after her.

"It doesn't matter. We've got to help Byrhtnoth. Hold him still, I have to inspect his head."

Byrhtnoth didn't move at all while Wulfstan explored the wound. He pulled up an eyelid; the eye stared unresponsive up into the dark roof.

"It's difficult to tell, but I think he's been hit twice. The first blow happened in the battle when his helmet was struck. The second is different. It came later, caused more bruising."

"That man beat him when he was already injured. Who would do such a thing?" demanded Saewynn.

"It might not have been him. Someone removed the helmet and hid it. Why would they have done that?"

"Egbert," whispered Saewynn. "He needs no reason. What better than to abandon someone helpless, to live without hope, without even a name. He even sent us the sword to tell us what he had done."

"Nobody could be that..."

"No? Didn't you tell me, Wulfstan, that when he attacked you all those years ago? He might have killed you. He didn't, just made sure you would never walk straight again." Wulfstan nodded slowly. "Last year he tried to destroy me, as a woman." She held her injured hand close against her chest.

"Why?" Wulfstan asked her. She shook her head.

"My lord humiliated him before the king this summer, just before..." said Thurstan.

"More than enough reason," said Wulfstan, returning his attention to the wound. "The bruising has subsided. I can feel a depression where the bone has sunk."

"Will he recover?" asked Saewynn.

"I don't know. It might heal itself, although it has been a long time. We must find out how long. If it doesn't..."

"Are you saying he might not recover?" Saewynn's eyes widened. "He might stay like this? He can't." Her voice rose.

"Calm down. It's possible, or he might die."

"No, not now," Leola whined and licked the tears from her face. Saewynn hugged her, hard.

"I might be able to do something."

"What?" Saewynn grasped at this small straw.

"Nothing for now. Warmth, a decent meal, and he might wake up."

"Yes." Saewynn wiped her eyes. "No point in worrying for nothing. Thurstan, pour some of that water in a bowl before you fill the cauldron. I don't think Lord Byrhtnoth has had a bath since he left home in the spring. He'll feel better once he's clean."

Chapter 51

Leif arrived with the rest of the crew as the sky was lightening. They had collected the fish that had gathered in the trap, and the older woman, Sigrun, cleaned them quickly.

"We've enough dried fish. I'm not doing any more." She glared at the men, challenging them to argue. She threaded the smaller fish onto a skewer over the fire. They cooked quickly, and she piled them on a platter, before cooking more.

"How is he?" Leif asked Wulfstan.

"Not good. I need to talk to you, outside. Where's Thurstan?"

"In the barn." Leif took some of the cooked fish and followed him out.

"There'll be fresh bread soon," Siv shouted after them. She measured out flour, added water and kneaded them together. She broke off a piece, flattened it and placed it on the stones at the edge of the hearth.

"Can you watch it?" she asked Saewynn. "I need more flour."

"There's flour in the ship. Not much, but you're welcome to it. We'll find more if we need it. We passed a town along the coast."

"I know it. You can get anything there, for a price." Siv hurried out.

Saewynn moved the bread back from the flames, rolled the next piece and added it to the flat stone. Byrhtnoth lay still, eyes closed. Was he able to smell the cooked fish? Sigrun had added herbs to the fire to add flavour. Saewynn picked up the first loaf. She held it close to Byrhtnoth's face, wafting the smell towards him. There was no reaction. Once he would have been first to the kitchen when that smell reached him. She dropped the bread into the waiting basket and added another lump of dough to the heat. Siv returned, nodding her thanks. Saewynn picked up one of the hot fish and nibbled at the soft flesh. She sat back and watched the still face beside her. Perhaps he needed help. She took a few flakes of fish and pushed them between his lips. They lay there, not eaten, not rejected.

"He needs liquid," said Siv. "That's more important than food." She handed her a cup of water."

"Can you help me support him? Otherwise, he'll choke."

They got him upright. Saewynn lifted his head and poured some water into his mouth. It trickled down his chin.

"You've got to drink. When was the last time you drank something? Or ate?" She watched Siv knead more dough. "You have plenty of food. Why is Byrhtnoth so thin? Did you starve him?"

"Byrhtnoth? Is that his name? Father said it was Ulf, and he answered to that. We didn't starve him, we all starved." She looked up at her mother, who nodded sadly.

"My husband wouldn't admit it, but he was scared. His grandfather travelled across the sea to this country. At first, times were good, then there was fighting, years of hunger. Afterwards, the family never trusted their good fortune. Nothing was wasted; every morsel of food must be hoarded, hidden away for when the bad times came." She sat up, stretched her back. "You won't believe this, but we are rich. We have sheds full of dried fish. When he decided we had enough, he would sell some to the town, to passing ships. We never drank milk from the animals. It all went to make butter and cheese, hidden away in

344

the bog. That reminds me. Siv, when you've finished the bread, find some cheese. Remember the one he let us try last yule?"

"How could I forget?" She licked her lips.

"Life has been hard," said Saewynn, "for all of you."

"Not anymore." Sigrun removed the last fish from the skewer. "Thanks to your man, we can enjoy life. Why not soak a rag and squeeze it into his mouth? There's some beef stew left. It's still warm, it will do him good."

"That's a good idea." Saewynn offered the remains of her fish to Leola, whose head was resting heavy on her lap. It disappeared in seconds, and when no more was forthcoming; the dog sat close to the hearth and fixed her imploring eyes on the plate of fish. Sigrun grinned and moved it out of her way.

"Later," she promised. She tipped some of the beef juices into a bowl and handed it to Saewynn. "Take it slowly, not too much. Siv, put that cushion behind his back, and tip his head back for the lady."

Saewynn dipped the corner of the cloth into the meaty broth. His lips opened slightly. Was he waking? No, just the angle of his head. She forced them apart with a finger. She remembered other times she had touched them. Now they were dry, unresponsive. She ran her finger down his neck, noticing his hair, untrimmed for weeks, months? His throat was clear.

"Mind his head, the wound," she warned the other woman.

"I know it better than you."

Saewynn gave Siv a sharp look, and she dropped her eyes. "Sorry, I didn't mean..."

Saewynn shook her head. "You cared for him the best you were able. He'd be... worse if it weren't for you." She lifted the cloth, allowed the excess liquid to drip back in the bowl and then pushed it between his lips. She stroked his neck, encouraging him to swallow, then gave him more, repeating the actions until the bowl was empty.

"Enough for now. We'll try again later." She lowered his head and watched. There was no reaction at all. "Is there more colour in his face?" she asked anxiously.

"Perhaps," said the older woman. "Lay him down, or he'll fall." Saewynn lowered him back onto the bench, replacing the covers. "I think he's warmer. He was so cold yesterday."

"He was out all night, the coldest night so far this year. He was lucky to survive."

"Why didn't he come back?" said Siv.

"He was frightened." Her mother patted her shoulder. "The dog scared him,"

"It was the ship," said Saewynn. "Your husband had made him fear them. Leola saved him."

"Why are you arguing?" Wulfstan ducked through the door. "We must concentrate on getting him better. Come, we must talk about it."

Saewynn glanced at the other women. "Sorry." She stood up, noticing her legs were stiff. She followed Wulfstan out into the fresh air.

"He's had some food. We got a little broth down him."

"Did he react?"

"No." She hung her head. "Will he recover?"

"I don't know, but I don't think he's got much chance if we leave him as he is. I've spoken to Leif and Thurstan. They agree. Leif has seen such injuries before; ships are dangerous places. Thurstan has met other warriors, discussed injuries. The blow on the helmet cracked the bones. Another blow, or just the passage of time, has caused the bone to press on his brain. The pressure must be relieved. If not, he will die, or remain in this state of half-life."

"Can you do that?"

"Perhaps. It will mean cutting open his head, and that might kill him outright."

Saewynn's legs buckled. Thurstan rushed to support her. She waved him away and took a deep breath. "What do you need?"

346

Chapter 52

They gathered everything that might be useful. Linen was ripped into strips. Siv was sent into the marsh with one of the men to collect moss, to soak up blood and act as a dressing. Sigrun offered a knife used to skin fish, it was long, narrow and very sharp.

They carried the table outside and placed it on firm ground in the lee of the building. Wulfstan said it was too dark inside, even with the light of the fire. It was a cold day, frost had settled on the grass overnight, but the sun was bright. When Wulfstan was ready, Thurstan and Leif carried Byrhtnoth out and laid him carefully on the table. Saewynn arranged him in a comfortable position before ropes anchored him firmly.

"It's important that he mustn't move, especially his head. Fasten one across his chin, another around his forehead. Tilt his head so I can see what I'm doing."

"Shall I cover his eyes?" asked Saewynn. "Siv told me the bright light causes him pain."

"No. I might need to check them. If we're successful, it will solve that problem."

"Why don't you give him something to make him sleep? You have some poppy juice."

"I thought about it." Wulfstan stared straight into Saewynn's eyes. "I would have used it if he was conscious. It is dangerous, the dose difficult to calculate. Too little, and it doesn't work, too much, and the patient never wakes." He looked down at the pale face. "He is already asleep, or something close to it. He may stay like that. If not, the straps should keep him still." He glanced up. "That is your job."

"How? I don't have the strength to hold him down," said Saewynn.

"You don't need to. Thurstan and Leif will do that. Talk to him. Keep him calm. I don't know if he can hear you. I am told," he glanced at Leif, who nodded, "people in this state, when recovered, report conversations that took place when they were asleep. Even if he doesn't understand, the sound of your voice may calm him. Just don't panic."

"I'll try not to." Saewynn grimaced. She bent down and whispered into Byrhtnoth's ear. "Did you hear that? We mustn't panic." She moved out of Wulfstan's way. She took one of Byrhtnoth's hands and squeezed it, then nodded to Wulfstan. "We're ready."

What to say? She imagined herself in the same situation. She had been last year. Wulfstan had mended her broken body. What had she wanted? To know what was going on. She leaned towards her husband.

"There's nothing to be afraid of. You're safe. All your friends are here. Although you may not remember them now, you will. Wulfstan will heal you; he's your best friend. Leif is beside him, he is a sailor, he guides your ship and will guide you back to life. Beside him is Thurstan; he is here to defend you. I know you can protect yourself, but for the moment he is on guard while you are asleep. Edward is here too, and Leola." The dog put her paws up on the table and licked his cheek. "I expect that feels cold." She stroked his face, bent and added a kiss. "I love you," she whispered.

"We're outside, in the yard of the farm where you have been living. It is a beautiful day. The sun is shining, and the sky is a deep blue. Can you hear the gulls screaming? If you listen carefully, you will hear the sound of the sea. There is a strong smell of onions. It must be the last thing they cut up on this table." She glanced up. "Wulfstan is cutting your hair. I know you don't like it, but it is to stop it getting in the way. Oh, he is going to shave some as well. Perhaps you can become a monk to disguise it." She bent close to his ear and added in a whisper, "Or not. I don't want a monk in my bed." She watched the locks of hair fall. She wanted to catch one, hide it away to remember him, if... No, he was going to live; she refused to imagine his death.

"Do you remember the first time we met? I was caught under a thorn bush. You had to cut my hair to release me. It would soon grow back, you said, and it did. I had seen you before that day. You didn't notice me, only my mistress, Lady Elfflaed. Did you meet her when you went to the Witan, earlier this year? You'll have to tell me all about it when your memory returns."

Wulfstan touched her shoulder and held up the knife.

"You may feel some pain, Wulfstan is cutting the skin. He is making a flap to inspect the bones." She brushed the spray of blood from her face. "It shouldn't worry you. You've had lots of injuries, although none, I think, from a fish-gutting knife. Do you remember, when we married, I was ashamed of the scars I had from my injuries? You said we should compare them, and then..." She noticed Edward staring at her and blushed. "Think about that while Wulfstan tells me what he's going to do next."

She straightened and watched as the blood was cleaned away. The flap of skin was raised, and she saw the bones of his skull. The damage was obvious.

"I was right," said Wulfstan, "there were two blows. You can see where the helmet was hit, a clean break. Then afterwards, something else pushed down the fragments of bone. To relieve the pressure, we need to raise them."

349

"Did you hear all that? Wulfstan is going to use the tip of a knife to raise one piece of bone. There shouldn't be any pain, just pushing and pulling. He's doing it slowly. Keep very still, whatever happens, you mustn't move." Saewynn held her breath, squeezing Byrhtnoth's hand as she watched the knife move. It slipped. She stifled a gasp and calmed her voice.

"He's removed a piece of bone. It's quite thick, I always knew you had a hard head. He's given it to Leif to hold. I expect Wulfstan will put it back when he's finished. I'll have a peek."

Through the small triangular window everything was black. Weren't brains grey? She looked at Wulfstan with concern.

"There was bleeding, it could not escape. We need to get rid of it. Where's the spoon?" He picked it up and probed the hole. Saewynn swallowed and returned to her one-sided conversation.

"There was blood beneath the bone. Wulfstan is removing it with a spoon." She suppressed a nervous giggle. "He's using my horn eating spoon. It's softer than metal. Do you remember our wedding feast last Christmas? All that wonderful food that Hild produced, you remember Hild. You must remember the boars head. She cooked the brains separately. You didn't like them although you ate some because I asked you to. Please come back to me, and I'll never ask you for anything again." She swallowed and regained her composure.

"Then the Christmas before. Remember the heat in Lord Athelstan's Hall? Are you warm enough? Your hand feels cold, shall I put it under the covers? So many people. You gave me a shield, to go with the seax the Ealdorman gave me. You must have known what he intended, why didn't you warn me? I got them out recently, I've been practising with my left hand as you told me to. My right hand is better than it was, straighter although still not strong. I can thank Wulfstan for that. What would we do without him? Are you feeling better? He's got rid of the blood clot. He's cleaning it with mead. Will it make you drunk? The broken pieces of bone are level, just the last piece to go in. It fits. I can see the relief on his face. He is tired. He wants me to sew up the skin. Shall I?" She stood up and took the needle.

"Try not to press down. I don't want to go through that again," groaned Wulfstan.

"Will he be all right?" She drew together the lips of the wound, bent and whispered, "A few stitches and it's over." The needle entered his flesh.

Wulfstan sank onto a stool. His face was as white as Byrhtnoth's, and he was shaking. "I've done the best I can. He's in God's hands now."

Saewynn watched as Leif spread honey on the wound then covered it with a layer of moss and a clean piece of linen. He wrapped strips of cloth round Byrhtnoth's head to keep everything in place.

"Get him inside, before he gets cold," said Wulfstan. "Support his head."

"We've built a nest of blankets to rest his head on," Saewynn told him. "Why don't you get some food? You haven't eaten at all this morning."

"Later. I'm going for a walk. I need to clear my mind." Wulfstan gave a wry smile at his words. He wrapped himself in his cloak and headed towards the river.

Saewynn disappeared into the building. She continued to tell Byrhtnoth what was happening.

*

Was she repeating herself? Saewynn inspected the pale face. Was there more colour in his cheeks? Had his lashes fluttered? The door opened, and the flames on the hearth flared. There was no change, she realised.

"Shut the door, there's a draught."

"Sorry, Sigrun. I wanted a word with Saewynn." Wulfstan beckoned

"Outside? I can't leave him. Something might happen."

351

"Edward can watch him. It won't take long." Edward raised his eyes from the piece of wood he was whittling and nodded. He moved closer to Byrhtnoth.

"All right. Leola needs some exercise." The dog glanced up before returning her eyes to the meat that Sigrun was preparing. Saewynn followed Wulfstan and closed the door behind them. The sky had clouded over, the sun had disappeared, and darkness was falling. Already? The days were so short, it must be close to mid-winter. She had lost count.

"How is he?" asked Wulfstan.

"There's no change. I've been talking to him, without any response. Should there be?"

"I don't know." Wulfstan leaned on the fence, gazing out over the expanse of grass and reeds. "Let him rest a while. He doesn't need someone chattering in his ear all the time. He needs to sleep. He's been through a lot."

"I'm sorry, I didn't think." Tears formed in her tired eyes.

"You did well, very well, earlier. I'm not sure I could have kept calm for so long." He put an arm around her shoulders. "I don't know if it made any difference to him, but it helped me."

"I'm glad. I thought he was listening at one point, that he knew we were trying to help him. Will he recover? How long will it take?"

"Only God knows that. I prayed out there, but there was no reply," said Wulfstan. I sometimes wonder if He exists."

"Of course He does, otherwise what's the point of everything?"

"I don't know, we just have to hope. Byrhtnoth might open his eyes at any moment." Saewynn glanced back at the closed door. "If so, there is still a long way to go. You have to accept he may never recover. Do you want to spend the rest of your life caring for an invalid?"

"He is my husband. It is my duty. And I love him, I will never abandon him."

"Let's hope you never have to make that decision." He patted her hand. "It's getting cold. We must get back. Did you get any sleep last night?"

"No, I was awake, watching."

"Make sure you get some tonight."

"I don't need to sleep."

"Yes, you do. You're no use to anyone without sleep. We'll have something to eat. Then I'll watch over him while you rest.

"You must be tired as well."

"There's always Siv. She is his wife after all."

"No! she's not! She's not going anywhere near him," announced Saewynn. "When can we go home? Is it safe for him to travel?"

"Give it a few days, and we'll see what happens."

Chapter 53

"We've got to leave." Leif shook his cloak spraying everyone with water. It had been raining for days, and the floor was a morass of wet mud. "The ship attracts too much attention. That vessel we saw earlier has come back. We discouraged them this time. The crew are getting restless."

"We all want to go home," said Wulfstan, "and I'm sure Sigrun and Siv want us out of their house."

"Of course not. Stay as long as you want." The words belied the harassed expression on the older woman's face.

"The wind is on the change. The rain should clear soon. I think we should risk it." Leif held his hands to the fire and looked towards Byrhtnoth. "Any change?"

Saewynn shook her head. "Wulfstan's just checked. The wound is healing, but..."

Byrhtnoth was propped beside her, as inactive as a sack of vegetables. "Is it safe to move him?"

"We don't have any option," said Wulfstan. "We could send the ship back and care for him between us. By spring the bone will have mended, and it will be safe to move him, whatever his condition.

"He wants to go home," said Saewynn.

"You don't know that."

"No, but I know him. He wouldn't want to lie here, in a stranger's house," she gave Sigrun an apologetic smile, "however hospitable. He would want to go home, sleep in his own bed. You've known him longer than I have, don't you agree?"

"I suppose so. Edith needs to know what's going on. There are monks at Ely, they must have a healer. They might know of a different treatment. Perhaps I made a mistake. Without me he might have recovered. I'm sorry."

"Don't be, I'm certain you did the right thing. It's decided. We take him home."

"I'll prepare." Leif stood up. "We found room for him last year when he was wounded at Bebbanburg We can strap him in," he glanced at the table, "we'll find something. It must be well padded. Are there any sheep skins?"

"In the barn," said Siv. "I'll show you."

"We'll need shelter as well, to protect him from the weather, and the spray." He hurried out, and Siv followed.

Saewynn smiled at the thought of Byrhtnoth needing shelter from the spray, he had loved it, and the wind. "It might be what you need. What do you feel about a sea trip?" If the worst happened, it would be a final voyage together. "Not long, and we'll be home, and you can meet your son."

*

By the time the rain stopped, they were ready. Byrhtnoth was laid on a padded bed, built from a couple of rowing benches. Sheepskins were piled around and secured with ropes. They covered him with a cloak. The bier was lifted onto the shoulders of his men.

Like a funeral procession, they moved down the path to the shore, where the ship was pulled up on the beach. The cold north wind caught a corner of the cloak and Saewynn grabbed it, tucking it beneath his body.

"He's not as heavy, as I expected." Thurstan moved the load into a more comfortable position."

"Mind your footing, there's a muddy patch here."

"I've seen it. I promise we won't drop him."

"I know. I can't stop worrying. He was starving when we arrived, and he hasn't improved. It's difficult to feed him, without his co-operation."

"Who would have thought it? He was always hungry, always first to the table at meal times," said Thurstan.

"Does he feel hunger? Perhaps, inside, he's shouting for roast pork and ale." She imagined his frustration. "Hild will kill a pig as soon as we are sighted. It won't be the same, mashing it up and forcing it into his mouth."

"All the more for us."

"You should be eating less." Saewynn eyed his expanding waistline.

"All muscle."

"Of course. How are you going to get him onto the ship?"

"Leif has set something up. Here we are. Put him down, we only need two to get him on board."

"It's all right," she told Byrhtnoth, his face as pale as the surrounding sheep's fleece, "they're taking you onto the ship." She watched them negotiate the narrow plank. It bent under the weight, and she prepared to catch him if it broke. With relief, she followed them on board. Her legs ached after the short walk, and she realised how little exercise she had taken since she arrived.

She glanced back. Aelf was helping Wulfstan along the rough path. Behind them, the house she had sat in for so long was almost invisible, just a thin smudge of smoke marked the spot.

"I hope the women will be all right on their own," said Aelf as they reached the ship.

"Better off than with that bully of a husband," said Leif. "We've left them plenty of food, they'll survive."

"But two women on their own, with no man to defend them?" said Wulfstan.

"You still think a woman needs a man?" asked Aelf.

"No." He smiled at her.

Saewynn watched Thurstan lower Byrhtnoth into the space. She went to check he was comfortable.

"Loosen the ropes," said Leif. "The sea is calm, at least for now, but keep them in place. That ship's back."

Saewynn looked out across the smooth silver water. The tide was close to full, lapping around the hull. The other ship was far away, watching, the occasional dip of an oar holding it in position.

"Who is it?"

"I don't know, they haven't made contact."

"They must know we are leaving. They saw the procession. They will think we take our dead lord for burial."

"So long as they don't set fire to our ship, like in the old days."

"To your oar, Thurstan. We need to leave." Leif showed Saewynn where to sit, close to Byrhtnoth. "There's enough space beside him if you need to hold him still, although Leola's claimed it for now." The dog lifted her head at the sound of her name, then settled down, stretched beside her master.

"I'll manage." She checked her seax, in case the other ship attacked. She noticed the rowers kept axes and other weapons close at hand. They were well trained. Leif gave the command. The ship caught a rising wave and slid into the water with barely a splash. The bow turned towards the sea.

She looked back. Already the gap was wide. Sigrun stood at the top of the bank, her arm round Siv. Saewynn had had a long conversation with the younger woman. They had talked about Byrhtnoth, and what had happened. They would never be friends, but they had made their peace. She waved.

The other ship followed them slowly, maintaining its distance until they got close to the mouth of the estuary.

"They're getting closer," Leif warned from the steering bench.

"Prepare for an attack," shouted Thurstan.

"Why would they attack?" Saewynn asked Wulfstan. "They've been watching us all morning, it's obvious we have nothing that they would want."

"I don't know. Can we outrun them?" Wulfstan looked towards Leif.

"They're bigger than us, with more rowers. There's not enough wind yet to set the sail, and they are too close."

"We'll just have to talk our way out of it," said Wulfstan.

"Yes." Saewynn glanced down at Byrhtnoth's pale still face. It was as if he was already dead. The seed of an idea came to her. She folded the corner of the blanket across his face. "If they think he is dead…"

"Yes," whispered Wulfstan, "whoever they are, they'll be wary of disturbing a corpse."

"Anyone but him," hissed Saewynn.

"What do you mean?" Wulfstan looked over to the approaching ship and gasped "It can't be." Leola raised her head, caught the breeze and leapt to her feet. She revealed her sharp white teeth and a threatening growl caused her lean frame to quiver.

"Egbert!" Saewynn drew her seax. The rowers abandoned their oars and seized their own weapons. The ship slowed, and the enemy approached.

"Don't come any closer," shouted Saewynn as she stood up. "You're not wanted here."

"Saewynn, I thought it was you. I only came to offer my respects."

"Respects," Saewynn spat with anger, "You don't know the meaning of the word. My lord is dead, and you killed him."

"Me?" Egbert spread his hands. "I haven't seen Lord Byrhtnoth for months. We were passing and recognised some of your men. Is it you Wulfstan? I thought I recognised the limp. How's that ugly horse of yours?"

Saewynn sensed Wulfstan about to reply. "Don't rise to his taunts." She gripped her seax tighter. "Yes, you killed him. Your friend Erik Haraldsson struck him down, but it was you who threw him into the river to drown. You didn't even have the guts to kill him yourself." She was close enough to see that she had angered him. "Since you are here, I would like to know. Why do you, did you, hate him so much?"

"Now, there's a question. Did I hate Byrhtnoth? I could say I was jealous, but I wasn't, why should I be jealous of a great oaf like him." He grinned. "Perhaps I envied him having you. How was he in bed? I doubt he was as good as me."

"We both know that you never touched me, and I have a ship full of witnesses there." She scanned Egbert's crew, recognising the faces of the men who had stripped and debased her. For a moment, the memory threatened to overwhelm her. She swallowed and struck back. "I remember you, Orm. You wanted me." The big man made an obscene gesture, and she pointed her seax at Egbert. "That man wouldn't let you, any of you. He wanted me first, and he knew he would fail." She saw some of the men consider her words, one even started to nod, before thinking better of it. "Get out of our way, I have a husband to bury."

"Yes, you have no husband now," blustered Egbert. "Why not come with me? I think we would do well together. Remember those days we had together in that tent in the forest."

"I think you mistake me for my husband. What did you do to him when he was injured and in your power?" She realised she must be careful what she said. "Or rather, what did you want to do?" As the blood rushed into his face, she knew she had struck upon the truth. "Think about that," she said as her eyes moved from one face to the next. One man sniggered, then with a fearful glance at Egbert, ducked his head.

"Isn't that the truth? You tried to destroy me, not because you wanted me, but because you wanted my husband. Well, now he's dead. We have both lost him. At least I had him for a while." she didn't attempt to stop the tears pouring down her face. "You never had him. Never."

There was silence, only the lapping of water against the motionless ships. Saewynn stared straight at Egbert. There was a curious expression on his face, regret? Before she could decide, it was gone, like a door slamming, and his usual bland mask returned. He gave instructions to his men, and they returned to their oars.

"We head north. Should you decide to join me, you will find me with King Erik."

"One day I will seek you out, and I will kill you," swore Saewynn.

The oars dipped in a ragged stroke that soon developed into a smooth rhythm. Egbert's ship moved away. He grinned and gave a dismissive wave.

"Take care of your son," he shouted.

She gripped the ship's side tightly, to still her shaking hands. Although she knew it was a threat, she refused to let Egbert upset her. She nodded and turned her back on him, returning to her seat.

"Are you all right?" asked Wulfstan. His face was white and strained.

"I am now. Let's go home."

She sat in silence until their ship was free of the estuary and turned south. In the distance, the full sail of the other ship merged with the sea and the sky. She gave a shuddering sigh and brushed her sleeve across her face to get rid of the last of the tears. She patted Leola's head, and the dog lay down, close to the shrouded shape. Saewynn gave a final check that Egbert had really gone and lifted the blanket she had laid across Byrhtnoth's face.

"I'm sorry about the shouting. You're safe now." She studied his face. Indoors, in the gloom and shadows, it had been easy to imagine him as he had been. She knew he was thin but as thin as this? In the bright, revealing sunlight, his nose was sharp as a blade between sunken cheeks, the dark shadows like bruises beneath his eyes. His slack lips held no colour. Was he still breathing? Had he drifted away without her noticing? She laid a hand against his mouth, felt the warm breath, so slow. Would she ever get used to that sharp stab of worry, then the relief of finding him still alive? His lips were dry, flaking. Where had she put the cloth to moisten them? It was dry. She looked for the flask of water.

"What was all that about?" asked Aelf as she handed her the water. "What you said to Egbert," she added in a voice quiet enough to be heard only by her friend.

Saewynn was aware of the silence that hung over the ship. Leif watched her from his place at the steering oar. She exchanged a glance with Wulfstan and pushed back her hair.

"I don't know what I said," she said in a clear voice. "I was angry, upset, I just wanted that man to go away. It must have worked; he left." She forced a shaky laugh and felt the tension on the ship relax. She poured some water onto the cloth and dabbed it against Byrhtnoth's mouth.

"You weren't upset by what he said. The threat to the child?" asked Aelf.

"Of course I was worried, but not as I once was. I discovered that Egbert no longer frightened me. For far too long, I let him control my every thought. Everything I tried to do was contaminated by what he did. I thought that our marriage had saved me," Saewynn laid a hand on Byrhtnoth's shoulder, "but still the evil lingered, like something dirty brushed to the corner of the hall, forgotten until the light from the hearth exposes it. Today my anger forced me to see Egbert as he is. Not some all-powerful force that threatened to destroy me. Just a pitiful, vindictive man.

"Yes, I worry that he might return to hurt my son, but only as I might fear accidents, or illness, or lightning striking the roof. Things happen, and I will deal with them." Wulfstan nodded in agreement. "Egbert might return, but he knows I will kill him if he does, and that might make him pause. At present, I have other

362

worries. Aelf, can you find that broth Siv made before we left? Byrhtnoth needs nourishment if he is to recover."

*

"We're stopping for the night," said Wulfstan, "Leif says we're not far from The Wash. It'll be dark soon, and we need light to continue from here on. The water isn't deep. We'll drop the anchor and eat. We can organise a fire if you're cold."

"I'm fine. I'll give Byrhtnoth some more broth while it's light." Saewynn clung to the bow post. "I've been sitting too long; my legs are stiff."

"Go and help with the anchor, then find some food for yourself. I'll give him his meal. Aelf will help."

"Are you sure? I won't be long."

"Take as long as you like. We haven't anything else to do."

"If you're sure." She waited until the sail was lowered and packed away, then helped some of the rowers to stow their oars. Wulfstan hadn't even asked how Byrhtnoth was, she thought. Had he given up all hope? She sat down next to Edward.

"We don't seem to have moved at all." He pointed to the flat heathland protected by the low line of sand dunes. "It all looks the same."

"We'll be home tomorrow."

"Good, some decent food again. It must be getting close to Christmas. That will cheer everyone up."

"Yes." She pretended to be happy for him. "Perhaps we can catch some geese, or ducks, for Hild to cook."

"I could eat one now."

"Sorry, we've only got," she searched the bag, "bread, it was fresh this morning and smoked fish. There might be some cheese. There's not much ale left."

"The fish will do. What do you want?"

"Just a piece of bread. I'm not hungry." She glanced back to where Wulfstan was spooning mush into Byrhtnoth's mouth. "Perhaps a piece of cheese."

*

363

Saewynn slept uneasily, wrapped in her cloak, while Wulfstan watched. After he woke her, she sat and listened to the sound of the sea and the seals gathered on the beach. Their calls carried across the water. There were no lights, no sign of habitation. She watched the sky lighten and the sun rise with a hectic display of competing colours, before inspecting Byrhtnoth. He remained impassive. The others stirred, and the boat rocked gently. There was an underlying sense of excitement. Men were talking about home and who would be waiting for them. The anchor was hauled up, causing more violent motion. Saewynn checked that Byrhtnoth was comfortable. She squeezed water between his lips and wiped his face with the damp cloth, then dried it with the corner of her cloak. The oars splashed as they entered the water, and some of the crew complained. The ship swung, and the steering oar took control.

"Not long now," she whispered. "What was I talking about?" She no longer thought he was listening, but it helped to pass the time.

Chapter 54

It was a long slow journey through the fens, through the vast expanse of reeds. They needed to take care they kept to the river, there were so many channels that could lead them astray. When they passed Ely, Saewynn knew they were nearly home. She had hoped that the familiar sounds, and particularly the smell, of mud and rotting vegetation, would awaken Byrhtnoth's memory. A slow drizzle had started and she rigged a cover to keep the rain from his face. Perhaps she should have let it fall on him, but the spray from occasional waves had not had any effect, and it would only chill his body. He needed warmth and hot food.

She recognised familiar landmarks. A boy was trudging along the riverside path. He stopped and stared at the ship, and then before she could shout a greeting, he took to his heels. The village would know that they were close. Everyone would be out to welcome them. What could she say when they arrived? Why had she thought that they would be able to creep back without anyone noticing?

The new dock appeared ahead. Saewynn had been so proud of it. Only a few posts and a wooden deck, it had been her idea, and she had looked forward to showing it off to her husband. At least it would make it easier to carry him from the ship.

The people were gathering. Godric was at the front of the crowd, beside Hild who held the mead horn. She had put on weight, was she expecting a child? She hadn't mentioned it before they left. Perhaps she hadn't thought it right with Saewynn having to leave her own baby. Saewynn scanned the crowd for Inga. No, she wouldn't bring the child out into the cold damp air. Edith pushed through the villagers to stand beside Godric and Hild. Hands clasped, her lips moved in prayer.

The ship hit the dock with a gentle bump and the ropes were thrown to a waiting boy. Saewynn took a final look at her husband; nothing had changed. What could she say? She stood up and scanned the hopeful faces.

"Our search was long, but we found Lord Byrhtnoth. He is alive but sick. I will explain more when we have brought him ashore and into the warm." The oars had been shipped, and a couple of the strongest crewmen were waiting beside her. She forced a smile. "Hild, can you arrange a fire in the chamber and organise some food for everyone, some broth for... Save the mead for later. We all need to get dry." The rain fell faster.

Hild nodded and hurried away. A plank had been placed between the ship and the dock. Saewynn stepped across. Godric offered her a hand onto the slippery wood.

"He was alive? I should have searched harder," he said.

"You did the best you could. We found him a long way downstream. He lost his memory, and it has not yet returned. He sleeps and cannot be woken." Saewynn turned to Edith. "He will need a lot of nursing and your prayers." She pushed back the crowd to make room for the sailors to carry their burden onto the dock.

Saewynn walked slowly up the path towards the hall. She hadn't really thought about the return home, expecting it to be either sad or joyful, not this halfway state, neither one thing nor the other.

The yard was thick with mud and Saewynn was relieved when the procession reached the hall without mishap.

"Reminds me of the battle with Bloodaxe," muttered Godric.

"It was like this?" asked Saewynn.

"Worse, the rain came down in sheets, although," he glanced up to the sky, "I think we're in for a lot more now."

"You're over your injury?" She noticed he was walking with a slight limp. He straightened up to disguise it.

"Completely, I've been back in training a few weeks now. Everything else is going well. It's not long until Christmas. Do you think he'll be recovered by then?"

"I don't know." She lowered her voice. "I don't think Wulfstan believes he will wake at all. He thinks that we've brought him home to die."

"As bad as that?" Godric looked around the village. "What will we do without him?"

"I don't know," snapped Saewynn, "we'll deal with that when we have to." She hurried towards the hall, following the others into the gloomy space. She directed Leif and the men towards the chamber at the end of the room. She hadn't realised how narrow the doorway was and was forced to watch as they tilted the bier to get it through. Thank goodness they had tied Byrhtnoth tightly to the boards.

It was brighter inside, Hild was still lighting candles, and flames flickered in the hearth.

"I brought logs from the central hearth to warm the room quickly."

"That's a good idea. I expect the hall will manage without for a while."

"We've plenty of firewood," said Hild, "one of the few things we have got enough of, this winter."

Saewynn gave her a curious glance and then forgot her words as the sailors lowered Byrhtnoth to the floor. The wolf fur had been removed from the bed and hung close to the fire. She nodded with approval and knelt beside her husband, placing a hand on his cheek. It was cold and damp from the rain, otherwise, there was no change. She struggled with the knots of the ropes that held him immobile until one of the sailors handed her a knife. Soon the bonds were free, and she told them to lift him onto the bed, still wrapped in blankets and surrounded by the sheepskins.

"I can manage now. Thank you for your help. I am sure there will be food and ale in the hall."

"Follow me," said Hild. "The bread might be a bit dry. I'll set the kitchen to making more. We usually kill a pig when the lord returns." She glanced towards the bed. "Perhaps another time. I'm sure I can find something."

"We've got some fish on the ship," said Leif. He followed the others out and closed the door behind him. Silence descended on the room.

"What happened to him?" asked Edith finally.

Saewynn stood, unable to decide what to do next. She looked at Wulfstan for help.

"The head wound is the main problem. The bindings need changing, these are wet." He lifted Byrhtnoth's head and unwound the cloth, exposing the wound. "It's healing nicely."

"Is that the wound from King Erik's axe?" said Edith.

"He's not king," said Saewynn.

"Yes, it's the wound from the battle. It took away his wits, and somehow, he ended up in the river." Wulfstan gave Saewynn a warning glance not to mention Egbert's involvement.

"We don't know what happened, perhaps he wandered and fell in," she said.

"He was swept a long way downstream, nearly to the sea," added Wulfstan. "He was taken in by a family. They didn't know who he was. They looked after him, although they had little themselves." He ran his fingers gently through Byrhtnoth's hair, and Saewynn handed him a cloth to dry it. "He suffered from headaches. They got worse. If we hadn't reached him in time, he could have died. I removed the pressure. Saewynn sewed up the wound, very tidily, I don't think anyone will notice the scar when he is recovered." He gave Saewynn an encouraging smile.

"He will recover then?" asked Edith with relief.

"We hope so. It is in God's hands now. Pass me my bag; I'll put more salve on this. Can you find me some strips of cloth to bind it?"

"I'll fetch some," said Edith. "Is there anything else you need?"

"Ask Hild if she has any warm broth. He needs something hot inside him, once we get him out of these wet clothes." Wulfstan watched her leave.

"Are you all right?" he asked Saewynn.

"Yes, of course. Get rid of those blankets. If you prop him up, we can get his clothes off.

Saewynn was rummaging in one of the chests looking for a clean shirt when Edith returned. She heard her gasp and squared her shoulders.

"What did they do to him?" Edith stretched a hand towards her brother and then raised it to her shocked mouth. Saewynn had to admit he looked worse than she remembered. Most of the injuries from the beatings were half healed or scabbed over. Bruises were every colour of the rainbow, black, yellow, even a fading green. Almost as bad was the parchment coloured skin, stretched over his bones like the image of death she had seen painted on the wall of a church. She flung a sheet over the sickening sight.

"He was not treated very well," she said tight lipped.

"Was he enslaved? What did he do to be beaten like that?"

"The man who did it is dead. It is over. We will not speak of this, to anyone." She shot Edith a warning glance. "He would not want anyone to see him in this state."

"I understand. I will help you with nursing him."

"I can manage."

"No, you can't. Look at yourself, you are exhausted, you need sleep." Edith studied Saewynn carefully. "And food, you have lost weight."

"I can't ask you to..."

"Don't forget, I first met him when he arrived at my monastery in a fever, from that wound to his shoulder. I nursed him then. I expect I know more about these things than you."

Saewynn nodded. It was a relief to hand the burden to someone else, if only for a short time. "I must speak to the villagers, tell them what has happened."

"Yes, eat with them, answer their questions. Wulfstan and I will sort out my brother," Wulfstan nodded, "then sleep. You can take up the load again tomorrow."

"Thank you." Saewynn headed for the door.

*

"Come on, one more spoonful." Saewynn pushed the spoon between Byrhtnoth's lips and tipped it so that the semi liquid mush ran into his mouth. She returned the spoon to the bowl and stroked his neck until she was sure it had been swallowed. She estimated how much had been consumed. It would do for now. It had taken so long to get that small amount into him that it was now cold. She wiped away the excess that had dribbled down his chin with a damp cloth, then altered her position to ease her aching back. His head fell onto her shoulder, and she held it upright until she was sure all the food had been swallowed.

"Why don't you bring the child to see him?" Edith didn't look up from her weaving. "It might help him to wake."

"The child?"

"Your child, his son. Sometimes his screaming is enough to wake the dead." She realised what she had said. "Sorry I didn't mean it like that."

Saewynn laid Byrhtnoth's head back on the pillow and smoothed his hair.

"How is he getting on? Are you pleased with his progress?" Saewynn's eyes were drawn towards the figure on the bed. "Not him, the baby," snapped Edith.

Saewynn shrugged and ran the spoon around the rim of the bowl before placing it close to the fire. "We'll need some more fuel soon."

"You have been to see the child?" Edith's fingers stopped twisting the colourful strands of wool. "You haven't, have you? Why not? I would have thought you would be eager to see your son after all this time. You must have missed him."

"I did, to begin with." Saewynn sat down on the stool next to the bed. "Then... I've been busy. I'm sure someone would have told me if there were any problems."

"That's enough. I'll have him brought. No, I will fetch him myself." She pushed the tablet frame to one side and stood up. "Make him tidy, I won't be long."

Make myself tidy, she means, thought Saewynn. Byrhtnoth did nothing to become untidy. She pushed her hair back from her face and looked around for a cloth to cover it. There was no point in changing her dress, it was only Inga and the child. She straightened the fur over this body.

The baby was quiet when they arrived. Saewynn hardly recognised him, he had grown so much. Inga handed him to her, and she fumbled the awkward bundle. How was she supposed to hold him?

"He has just been fed," said Inga. "He should be asleep, but the lady Edith said he should be brought immediately."

"I didn't say..." stammered Edith.

"Don't shake him or he'll be sick."

Saewynn found a comfortable position and looked down into his face. Wide blue eyes started back at her, Byrhtnoth's eyes, full of life and curiosity. Why was he so alive when his father lay oblivious to what was happening? She suppressed a stab of jealousy and moved the child closer to the bed.

"Byrhtnoth? This is your son. His name is Byrhthelm. We named him after your father because you were not here. We thought... I hope you are happy with the decision. He looks just like you."

"One of the older women said he takes after his father. She was here when Byrhtnoth's mother gave birth," said Inga.

Saewynn leaned closer, the baby wriggled, and she nearly dropped him. He started to scream. Tears sprang from his eyes, and his face turned red. Saewynn panicked. "What shall I do?"

Inga stepped forward and took the squirming child, patting him gently and murmuring calming words. She shot Saewynn a look of triumph, quickly hidden. "It's quite easy when you know how. Do you want to try again?" She offered the damp, hiccupping baby to Saewynn.

"No, it's all right. The child seems healthy, you have cared for him well. I will come and see him later when things are more settled."

"I am sure you have more important things to do." Inga stared down at the bed. "He doesn't look very well. Do you expect him to survive?"

Edith gasped, and Saewynn put a calming hand on her arm. "Yes, I do," she said, meeting Inga's eyes with a challenge. "You may go. We must discuss the child's weaning. I'm sure it is overdue.

"Yes, my lady," said Inga. "Of course, you know all about such things." She headed to the door with a smirk.

"What's all this noise?" Wulfstan closed the door behind Inga and gave Saewynn a questioning look.

"Edith thought the presence of his son might cause Byrhtnoth to wake. It wasn't successful." Edith hurried from the room and Saewynn covered her face with her hands to stem the threatening tears. She felt Wulfstan's comforting hand on her shoulder. She took a deep breath and attempted a smile. "How are things in the village?"

"Not good. I already knew the harvest was bad because of the lack of rain. It continued dry, so the beasts did not put on much weight, and the milk yields dropped off."

"Will there be enough food for the winter?" asked Saewynn anxiously. She had been so wrapped up with her own concerns that she had paid little attention to anything else.

"There's nothing to worry about, we're not going to starve. Things will be a little short, that's all. I sent Leif and the ship back to Lord Athelstan, we can't afford to feed the extra mouths."

"You didn't tell me. Leif must think me rude, not saying goodbye. And I didn't even have a chance to thank him for all his help."

"He understands. He'll come back in the spring, to take you and Byrhtnoth north again, when you go to seek his father."

"Do you think that will ever happen?" asked Saewynn.

"We must have hope." He leaned forward and raised one of Byrhtnoth's eyelids. "I need to deliver our tribute of eels to Ely. I will speak to the monk who looks after the sick there. He might be able to suggest something to help Byrhtnoth that we haven't thought of. The screaming baby didn't make much of an impression."

"No, it didn't," Saewynn attempted a smile. "When will you go?"

"In a few days. Any longer and it will be Christmas, and the monks will be occupied."

"It's that close?" She hadn't realised. What was there to celebrate anyway?

Chapter 55

"This is Father Albrecht. He is visiting Ely from across the sea."

Saewynn looked up from the pile of damp clothes she was hanging around the fire to dry. She had washed the clothes in a bowl of water in the corner of the chamber. It was a never-ending chore and she was sweating from the heat of the hearth. She could have asked the other women to help, but it was her duty to protect the dignity of her husband. She brushed the damp hair back from her face as the tall figure followed Wulfstan into the room. She wished he had given her some warning, a chance to tidy the room.

"We are lucky, he is an expert in medicine and has agreed to take a look at Lord Byrhtnoth. Is there any change?" asked Wulfstan.

The visitor pushed back the hood of his robe. It was wet, it must be raining again, she thought. His head was completely bald. Saewynn wondered how people recognised him as a monk, but his look of disdain as he surveyed the room made it obvious.

"The woman can go." His accent was thick but recognisable.

"This is the man's wife, the lady Saewynn," said Wulfstan.

The man's hooded eyes raked her body, and he gave a sniff. "She may stay, but keep her out of the way." He added something in a foreign tongue. Saewynn didn't think it was a compliment. She frowned angrily at Wulfstan, and he shrugged an apology.

"This is the patient?" In his loose black habit, he stood over the bed like a raven over a fallen warrior and Saewynn shivered. He aimed a storm of questions towards Wulfstan. He spoke Latin now, but it still sounded harsh and alien, unlike the language spoken by the priests in church. She tried to follow the conversation. He was asking about what had happened to Byrhtnoth, how long he had been in this state. Would he want to inspect the body? She was glad that she had washed him not long before when she had changed his clothes, although the smell of urine still lingered in the room. She wanted to open the window, but it was difficult enough to keep the room warm. She realised the monk had addressed her, Wulfstan looked embarrassed.

"He is asking does his member swell and make emission, as happens with some men without their control."

For a moment, Saewynn didn't know what he meant, then she understood. Her cheeks flamed, and she avoided the men's gaze, shaking her head. The monk nodded and resumed his questioning. He inspected the wound on Byrhtnoth's head. It was healing well and had been left uncovered. The hair was starting to grow back. The monk seemed pleased, but when he started to question Wulfstan on what he had done, his expression changed, and he spoke sharply. Wulfstan protested, reverting to English.

"He would have died if I hadn't done it."

"You have killed him with your clumsiness," proclaimed the monk.

"No!"

Saewynn stepped forward. "He did what he could, I agreed with everything that was done."

Father Albrecht looked from one of them to the other and shook his head in what might have been disgust. "I will do more tests. Perhaps he only sleeps, but for so long? Bring my bag." He beckoned to the boy who had followed him into the room. He lifted the strap from around his neck and set the bag on the ground beside the bed and backed away, avoiding Saewynn's eye.

The monk pursed his lips, studying the form before him, then clapped his hands loudly close to Byrhtnoth's head. Both Saewynn and Wulfstan jumped. Even the boy, who must have expected it, looked up. There was no movement from the bed. Father Albrecht rummaged in the bag and brought out a feather. It was a goose feather with its end sharpened, like those used for writing. He smoothed the filaments then brushed it beneath Byrhtnoth's nose. Saewynn stifled an urge to sneeze herself, and Wulfstan smiled.

The monk moved to the other end of the bed, lifting the fur to expose Byrhtnoth's feet. He ran the feather across the sole, without response.

"When we found him, he was not wearing shoes, had not for several months. His feet feel little."

Albrecht raised his head and stared into her eyes. "Sometimes a fire applied to the feet produces a response. Do you think he will feel that?"

"Don't you dare," she said, angry at the suggestion. The monk held her gaze for a few seconds longer and then released her.

"Not today." He walked back to the head of the bed and reached under the cover for Byrhtnoth's hand. He brought it out, inspecting it as if it could tell him something. He pressed fingers to the inside of his wrist and stood in silence, his lips moving silently, as if counting, then he ran the feather up the smooth pale skin of the forearm. He glanced up at Saewynn with what might have been a smile and plunged the quill of the feather into the tender flesh. Saewynn leapt forward to stop him, and he withdrew it. She watched in horror as blood welled from the wound. Albrecht took a small piece of clean cloth from his bag and pressed it against the wound.

"It will soon stop, and as you see, he feels nothing." He let go of the arm, and it dropped to the bed. Saewynn pushed the monk out of the way and held Byrhtnoth's hand, tightly. "He cannot feel that either." He straightened, looming over her.

"Is that really necessary?" said Wulfstan, with a frown.

"She has to know the truth," said Albrecht, walking towards the hearth. He held the feather against a glowing ember until it caught fire. Quickly, he moved back to the bed and held the flame close to Byrhtnoth's nostrils. Saewynn was forced to back away as the fierce smell filled the room, but her husband remained still. The monk pulled back an eyelid and moved the dying flame close to Byrhtnoth's eye, then back and forth. He repeated the action with the other eye. He tossed the remains of the feather into the fire.

"It is as I thought. The man is dead. All senses are gone, touch, smell, sight and hearing, I could test for taste, but judging by the contents of that bowl waiting by the fire, that is also absent."

"But he can't be. He breathes." Saewynn lifted the piece of cloth and watched the blood trickle slowly from the wound. "He bleeds."

"Yes, the body still works, for now. You told me," the monk looked towards Wulfstan, "that he did not improve, was gradually getting worse. A body cannot survive long without a soul. That is what you did to him with your meddling. When you opened his head with your knife, you released his soul and so he died." He closed his bag and stood. "I will arrange for prayers to be said for him at Ely. If you would like, I will take his body back with me and arrange his burial when the final breath comes."

"No! You will not take him." Saewynn sprang up, looking desperately at Wulfstan.

"Saewynn is right. He will remain here. If I am to blame, it is my responsibility to care for him, as long as any part of him remains."

"As you will. Shall we pray for his soul together? I have a little time before I return to Ely."

"I would appreciate that," said Wulfstan. His face was nearly as pale as Byrhtnoth's, and Saewynn touched his arm in consolation. He shook it off. "You had better go, we'll speak later."

Saewynn lowered her head in agreement and with a final fierce look at Father Albrecht opened the door and closed it firmly behind her.

Chapter 56

"It's Christmastide," Saewynn sat down in her familiar place beside the bed, "not that you'd think it by the lack of noise from the hall." She couldn't tell him that his lingering illness was the main reason for the muted celebrations. "It's a difficult winter and likely to get worse. We dare not broach the meat that was salted at Blotmonath, it must last a long time yet. Did Wulfstan tell you that the harvest was poor? He has been rationing how much is available for bread. Today at least, everyone has enough and more.

"You must be hungry. That foreign monk left medicine for you." He had said it would do no good, but Wulfstan had insisted he do something. "It must be administered after fasting for a night. As the rest of us were forced to fast yesterday, we thought you should join us." It was difficult enough to get enough nourishment into Byrhtnoth, he was becoming more emaciated by the day, and she had not been in favour of the plan. "It is to be taken dissolved in warm wine. You'll enjoy that. I'll check the wine isn't too hot." She went to the fire and tipped a few drops onto her wrist. "Just right. I hope I can remember the correct amount." She poured a little wine into a cup then took three pinches of the powder left by the monk and dropped them into the liquid. She stirred it until it had dissolved.

"Up you get." With a practiced move, she raised his head and tipped the mixture carefully between his lips. She wiped away the excess that dribbled from the corner of his mouth. "Mustn't give you too much, or you'll be getting drunk. Let's sit you up properly. Once that's gone down, I've got some food for you. She picked up the board that leant against the wall nearby, placed it at the correct angle and covered it with a thick feather pillow, before lowering Byrhtnoth's head onto it. As she made him comfortable, she checked the head wound. The scar was disappearing beneath the stubble of hair that had grown over it. Soon no one would even know it was there.

"There's no venison. Some of the men went out but found nothing. The weather has driven away most of the deer. We killed a sheep that had broken a leg. Hild made a tasty broth from the bones and roasted some of the meat for the feast. Godric took out a boat and brought back some ducks and a plump goose. Which would you prefer, goose or mutton?" She paused as if waiting for an answer. "I thought so, goose it is. Edith has chopped the meat very small so you can swallow it." She picked up the bowl and dipped in the spoon. This was going to take a long time.

*

"The feast has finished already. People are pushing back the benches and preparing to sleep." Saewynn finished her own plate of meat, it was cold, and the fat had congealed, but she mopped up the juices with a piece of bread. She mustn't waste anything.

She took a sip of wine. "This is very good. Do you want some more?" She dipped a finger into the cup and wiped it across his lips, they were greasy from the goose meat. It would do them good, there was always a danger of them becoming dry and cracked. She remembered doing the same the previous Christmas. Then it had been a game, as they lay together in this same room, on that same mattress that was now a sickbed.

She took the empty plate and the remains of the goose and placed them on the table. She stared at the flask of wine for a long time, then topped up her cup and returned to her seat. "I'll never forget last Christmas, so different from this one. It was our wedding day, do you remember? Everyone was so cheerful, we were happy. Ale and mead flowed like water. Was there wine? I don't know, things got a bit hazy at times. I remember the boar's head that Lord Athelstan sent. Hild had cooked it perfectly. You ripped off the cheeks, stuffing them into your mouth. She had cooked the brains separately, with exotic spices, because I said I liked that. You didn't, but you ate some because I asked you to. I remember offering them to you with..." With the same spoon that Wulfstan had used to remove the clotted blood from his friend's brain. She took a gulp of wine and coughed.

"Sorry, where was I? The wedding feast: so much food, and the dancing. Do you remember the scop who arrived unexpectedly and the stories he told? They lasted long into the night. I remember now, that was the first time I noticed there was something between Godric and Hild, and now they are married themselves. Did they tell you that I organised it all myself? They are expecting a child, I wonder when? I've hardly had a chance to talk to her, perhaps after..." She looked down at the pale face beside her. No, she would not think about that.

"You got me drunk that night so that I wouldn't think about what was to happen later. If only I'd known. I'm sorry I was so nervous. I loved you, and yet I was still afraid. You were so patient and gentle, and when it happened, it was so wonderful." Saewynn wiped the dampness from her eyes. "I thought we would spend the rest of our lives together. Perhaps we were too happy and deserved punishment. Just those few months and then you went, and now I am alone."

Her throat tightened. She walked back to the table and refilled her cup, how had it emptied so quickly? She swallowed most of the contents. It slipped down so easily. She turned back towards the bed, and a burst of anger hit her. She slammed down the cup

383

and the flask shook. The dregs from the cup splattered the table. She stalked back to the bed.

"Why did you go? Why did you leave me alone?" She dug her fingers into his shoulders and shook the unresisting body. "What will I do without you? I can't stay here; it's not my home and never will be. I did what I could. I thought I coped, but all along, they blamed me. It wasn't my fault. You brought me here, married me, and then you left.

"It's not only me, everyone depends on you, not just the men who swore to serve you, although what will they do without you? What about Edith? How will your sister manage without your protection? Then there's Wulfstan. Between us we have destroyed him. You managed to patch up your quarrel, which would never have happened if it hadn't been for me, and then, when we found you, he tried to help, he didn't have to. He failed, and now that monk has blamed him for what happened.

"You think I will stay to look after your son? There are enough women in the village to care for him. He doesn't need me, he doesn't even recognise me. No, I will leave. I will find Erik Haraldsson, and I will tell him what he has done. I will challenge him, and I will die. Don't you know that I cannot live without you? Death is the only solution. Is that what you want?" She collapsed onto the stool. "Oh, my love, what did we do to deserve this?" She grasped his hand and held it to her face, desperately holding back her tears, then she placed it gently back on the bed. So thin now, she could count every bone in it. His nails were long and yellow, like claws.

"I'm sorry." She took a long deep breath and waited as her pounding heart returned to normal. "I shouldn't have said that. It doesn't really matter, you can't hear me." She looked around the room. So much remained the same, but they had both changed so much.

"I nearly forgot, I have a gift for you." She got to her feet, and the room spun. She clung to the table and poured more wine into her cup. It was nearly empty. Had she drunk it all herself? She

384

took a sip, then carried the flask back to the bed and placed it carefully on the floor, with two cups. "For a toast," she told him, "I won't be long."

She walked slowly to the corner of the chamber and pulled one of the chests to one side. She scrabbled at the floor until she found the hidden ring and pulled up the lid to the secret space. When the hall had been rebuilt after the fire, it had replaced the original hiding place below the great chair. Only she and Byrhtnoth, and, she supposed, Wulfstan knew of its existence. She ignored the other contents and pulled out the richly decorated scabbard.

The other objects that Godric had brought back after the battle were stored in one of the chests. Edward had spent hours cleaning and polishing the byrnie, and it was rolled in protective oiled cloth for his son, Saewynn thought. The helmet was with it. She had refused to allow that to be cleaned and it remained as a memorial.

The sword was another matter. It had been hidden once, and Saewynn had known it must be returned to this secret place for whoever claimed it in the future. It had been no surprise to find that it had fitted the empty, waiting scabbard exactly. She drew it out slowly and admired the shifting patterns of the blade, cleaned and kept sharp by her alone. It was Byrhtnoth's sword, but he had never held it properly, never fought with it. Now he would hold it, one last time.

She carried it back to the bed and laid it on the thick black pelt of the wolf that he had killed, the hilt close to his hand. She sat beside him and took his right hand in hers and wrapped his fingers around the hilt, holding them there as she spoke to him.

"This is your sword, your father's sword for which you searched so long. Don't ask me how it has returned to you, I do not know, not really. I hope that wherever you are, you know that it is yours, that you hold it at last, and forever. Keep hold of it, and one day we will be together again, you, me and the sword." She leaned forward and kissed him on the forehead. She lowered his hand, and his fingers released the sword. It threatened to slide off the bed, so she bunched up the fur to keep it in place.

Suddenly tiredness overwhelmed her. There was no sound from the hall, everyone must be asleep. She knew Aelf would be sleeping outside the door of the chamber in case she was needed. She hoped Aelf was asleep and not listening to what had occurred inside. Saewynn stood and stretched. In a daze, she found her mattress and laid it beside the hearth. There was enough warmth remaining, although at some point more fuel would be required to keep it burning through the night. She removed her shoes then pulled off her over tunic, folded it carefully and laid it on her chest. She found her comb, released her hair and combed it through. The rhythmic strokes calmed her.

She was reaching for her blanket when she remembered that she had left Byrhtnoth propped up and the sword on his bed. What if he fell? She jumped up and fetched the scabbard from where she had dropped it. She took hold of the sword, careful to avoid the sharp edge. It didn't move. It must have got caught in the covers; she pulled harder.

"No."

"Yes, I can't leave it here, someone might get hurt." She was so tired she was hearing voices. It must have been some animal rustling in the thatch, perhaps a bird. She noticed Byrhtnoth's fingers were clasped firmly around the hilt. She glanced up, his eyes were closed, his face unchanged. She pulled at his fingers to loosen the grip.

"My sword." It was no bird. The voice was as dry and rough as a rusty blade stuck in a sheath, but it was a voice. She watched as his eyes slowly opened. They were glazed, staring sightlessly into the distance, then they focused on her face, and his lips moved. "Saewynn?"

"Yes." Her voice was nearly as hoarse as his. "How do you feel?"

"Cold." He tried to raise his hand, and the sword dropped from his grasp and clattered to the floor. He flinched at the noise. "Weak. What happened?"

Saewynn sat down on the edge of the bed. "What do you remember?" His eyes closed, and a frown wrinkled his brow. She held her breath until they opened again.

"A fight, Bloodaxe, he... I was dead."

"Not quite, but close to it."

"Thirsty, so thirsty."

"Of course." Saewynn bent and picked up the flask and poured wine into one of the cups. She placed it in his hand and raised it to his mouth, then watched as he took several greedy gulps. "Not too much at once." She took the cup away from him and took a sip herself.

"Wine?"

"Yes, it is Christmas."

"Christmas? But it's still summer." His voice was clearer now. He looked around the chamber. "I'm home."

"Yes, we brought you home. You survived the battle, I'm not sure how, but then you were lost. You forgot who you were. You were injured and nearly died. It took a long time to find you and then Wulfstan healed your wound." She gestured towards his head then stopped him raising his own hand to it. "Not too hard, you might damage yourself. Wulfstan! I must tell him you are awake." She rushed to the door. "Don't move," she said, looking back with a smile.

As she opened the door, Aelf rolled over and stared up at her. "Do you want something?"

"Go and fetch Wulfstan, tell him..."

"Has something happened?" Aelf disentangled herself from her blanket and leapt to her feet.

"Yes. Tell him Byrhtnoth is awake, go quickly."

Aelf studied her carefully and then grinned. "Good news." She gave Saewynn a brief hug and set off across the hall, leaping sleeping bundles. Someone stirred and she whispered an

387

explanation before continuing. Saewynn closed the door and looked towards the bed. Byrhtnoth was lying still, eyes closed. Had it all been a dream? As she reached his side, he looked up and smiled.

"I'm hungry, is there anything to eat?"

Saewynn dropped to her knees beside the bed. "Anything. What do you want?"

He shrugged, then grimaced. His muscles must be stiff. "I can taste something, duck?"

"Goose." Saewynn found the bowl she had been feeding him from earlier and handed it to him. He took one look and frowned.

"Is this what you've been feeding me? No wonder I'm weak."

"You try feeding someone when they're asleep. Finish that first."

"Sounds like things are back to normal," said Wulfstan from the door. "Saewynn is right, finish that and we'll find something else. You must take it easy, though. You won't be able to eat very much for a while. Wake Hild and ask her to warm up some of that mutton broth," he told Aelf who was peering over his shoulder. She nodded and disappeared. Outside in the hall, the noise was increasing as people woke and the news spread. "Better latch the door, or we'll have the whole village in here." He touched Saewynn's shoulder as he headed for the bed. "What did you do?" he whispered.

"I don't know, but it might have been the sword."

"The sword?" Wulfstan bent and picked up the discarded blade.

"Give that back, it's mine," said Byrhtnoth, "and bring me some ale."

"No need to ask if you've recovered," replied Wulfstan.

Chapter 57

Much later, when the excitement had died down, and the villagers had returned to their beds, Aelf closed the door leaving the two of them alone. Saewynn sat on the edge of the bed, clinging to Byrhtnoth's hand. For the first time, after weeks of talking to his silent figure, she didn't know what to say.

He looked tired. It was better than no expression at all, she thought. "I don't suppose there's much of the night left. We'd better get some sleep." She noticed the sword was still lying on the bed. "I'll put this away."

"The sword." Byrhtnoth frowned. "Egbert had the sword. I remember that. Is he dead?" He paused. "Did I kill him?"

"No, you didn't kill him, but there is no need to worry, he is far away. If he attempts to come anywhere near us again…" Saewynn looked down at the blade; its patterns seemed to ripple in the firelight. "…I will kill him."

"You?"

She heard the scepticism in his voice, and for a moment, it irritated her. She walked across the room and slid the sword back into the scabbard. She stared at for a moment, before placing it carefully on the chest.

"Anyway, it doesn't matter anymore."

"Doesn't matter? I swore to kill him for what he did to you. Once I've recovered, I will seek him out, wherever he is, and kill him. I know you try to hide it, but you will have peace with him gone."

"But that's the point. I'm not afraid anymore. I lost that when... Never mind, I'll tell you about it another time. It's late, I need to sleep."

"The baby. Where's my son?" Byrhtnoth struggled to sit up. "Did something happen? Is he...?"

"In all the excitement I forgot. You have a son, a beautiful son."

"You forgot? Where is he?" He looked around the room. "Why isn't he here?"

"He is with Inga, in the women's hall. He will be asleep." She was surprised Inga hadn't been disturbed by the commotion. She would have expected her to be the first to arrive with Byrhtnoth's son clutched to her chest.

"Shouldn't he be here with you? Fetch him immediately."

"There's plenty of time. In fact, he has already met you, weeks ago. His name is Byrhthelm, after your father, I hope that was the right thing to do. Your sister insisted on having him baptised." She returned to his side, smoothing down the wolf skin. "For the last few weeks your care has been more important."

"Of course, you have had to look after me. How long? What happened after the battle?"

"Tomorrow. You can meet your son then. He looks just like you." She stroked his cheek, yawned and returned to her own bed.

"What are you doing?"

"That's where I sleep." She pointed to the mattress.

"Please, I need you." She looked at him. All the bravado had slipped from his face. How confused he must feel. There was a gaping hole in his life of which he knew nothing. It would take a long time for him to recover, not just physically.

"I'm sorry, I didn't think." She looked around the chamber, checking all was in order. She realised she was wearing only her shift and her hair was loose. What had people thought? They hadn't been looking at her. She shivered.

Come here, we'll keep each other warm." Byrhtnoth had moved away from the edge, giving her room to slip under the wolf skin.

It had been so long, and he had changed so much. When she put her head on his shoulder, it was like resting on a pile of sticks, no solid muscle to support her. She was afraid to move, afraid she would hurt him, but when he wrapped his arm around her, she knew she was safe. She relaxed as he buried his face in her hair.

"I hope you're not expecting too much. I don't think I can manage anything for a few days."

She raised her head and stared into his eyes. They were still the same, holding the same expression of love that she remembered.

"It's all right, I've waited all this time, a bit longer won't make much difference."

"Thank goodness for that," he said. "I've missed you."

"I've missed you too." She smiled and then realised tears were running down her face. She tried to apologise.

"Don't worry, I'm here now, I'll look after you." As he drifted into sleep, he murmured, "and our son."

As she lay there, listening to the beating of his heart, she thought that perhaps this Christmas hadn't been so bad after all. It was a new year and everything was going to be all right.

Historical Notes

A.D. 948. This year King Edred overran all Northumberland; because they had taken Eric for their king; and in the pursuit of plunder was that large minster at Rippon set on fire, which St. Wilferth built. As the king returned homeward, he overtook the enemy at York; but his main army was behind at Chesterford. There was great slaughter made; and the king was so wroth, that he would fain return with his force, and lay waste the land withal, but when the council of the Northumbrians understood that, they then abandoned Eric, and compromised the deed with King Edred.

The Anglo-Saxon Chronicle gives a detailed account of what happened in Northumbria in A. D. 948, although the motives behind the events is another matter.

The fight by Eadred, King of England, to maintain control on what had been the Kingdom of Northumbria was part of a continuing attempt to uphold the victories of his father, Edward and elder brother Athelstan in the area. Ten years after the decisive Battle of Brunanburh, the short reign of Edmund (939-946 and only 18 on his accession) and now Eadred, still in his early twenties and in bad health, had encouraged anyone with a claim to Northumbria, and some without any claim at all, to take a chance. It was not helped by the meddling of Archbishop Wulfstan of York, Northumbrian patriot or thorn in the flesh of England, depending on your point of view.

The previous year (947, see Bright Sword, Book Two of the Byrhtnoth Chronicles) Northumbria had pledged allegiance to King Eadred, but broke it shortly afterwards, naming Erik of Norway as King. Understandably, King Eadred was angry and travelled north for revenge.

The famous "Harrowing of the North" by William the Conqueror in 1069 was only one in a series, both before and after, of a British King's final solution to rebellion in the north. This instance in 948 was one of many.

I have no idea if this occurrence was planned in the way I have portrayed in the book. I just imagined how I would do it if I were in charge. It also enabled me to separate Byrhtnoth from his wife at a vital point in their relationship.

Several people have asked why I sent ships from Exeter to the west coast of Northumbria, surely the Humber Estuary would have been the obvious choice? I could say that King Eadred needed troops on the North Western Coast to encircle Erik. Or Lord Elfgar was Ealdorman in Devon, and I wanted to bring him into the story. The honest answer is, it made the story more interesting. Byrhtnoth had already sailed up the Humber the year before.

Who burned Ripon? It seems certain that King Eadred was responsible for the burning of the town and Minster at Ripon as part of the general destruction, but whether it was accidental or a deliberate act is not known. It is certainly convenient for Canterbury, as St Wilfrid's relics were removed there after the fire. It is difficult to discover if these were the saint's bones or objects associated with him. What is certain that when the crypt at Ripon was excavated in 1900, traces of a medieval altar were found "having behind it a small rectangular enclosure bounded by other wrought stones... moreover, the enclosure was found to be a pit containing bones, some of which had belonged to a man, others to an ox, others to a bird."

Brother Elfrid and his History of St Wilfrid is a complete invention.

Byrhtnoth is, of course, a real person, but his adventures during this period are a product of my imagination. All characters in his village, including Saewynn and Wulfstan are invented. Byrhtnoth did have a sister although her name is unknown. All other minor characters are fictitious, especially Egbert!

Elfhere and his father, Elfgar and his daughter and Ealdorman Athelstan of East Anglia and his family were all real people, as is King Eadred and other members of the royal family.

Finally, Abbot Dunstan (later Saint Dunstan) did not, as far as I know, construct mechanical hands, but as a metalworker who became the patron saint of blacksmiths, goldsmiths, locksmiths, musicians, silversmiths and bell ringers, I am sure he would be capable of it and would be happy to take the credit.

*

I have spent a lot of time devising events to delay Byrhtnoth's search for his father. Will he ever find him?

The fourth and (probably) final book in this series will be published sometime in 2020.

Read Bright Helm to discover the answer.

Acknowledgments

I would like to thank everyone who has helped in the production of this, my third book – it doesn't get any easier!

First, thanks go to my structural editor Andrew Noakes. Apparently, this was not quite as bad as the last book. I did not have to delete large chunks of it – I managed that myself before sending it to him. He has taught me a lot.

Writing about the tenth century, it is unusual to find places that have remained comparatively unchanged. When I visited Ripon Cathedral to view the crypt, the first person I met was Helen Logan, Cathedral guide and fellow Anglo-Saxon fan. We had an interesting discussion about the Anglo-Saxon church, and she showed me objects I might have missed. She also checked my manuscript for any mistakes in the description of this wonderful space. Thank you.

Thank you too, Beta Readers, especially M J Porter, who is currently writing about the same period – it is interesting to read another person's view of Byrhtnoth.

Many thanks to Fran Neatherway, who polished my prose so beautifully – and so cheaply!

I would also like to thank my fellow writers who have helped and supported me in my efforts to bring Byrhtnoth's life into print. Those whom I have met at Gill Vickery's inspiring course at the Percival Guildhouse and the members of Rugby Café Writers. In particular, David Boulton, who gave advice on medical matters - any mistakes are my own.

Thanks also to those writers (and bloggers) I have only met online, who have encouraged me to greater efforts with advice and reviews:

The members of the Historic Writers Forum on Facebook,

Helen Hollick, and her team of reviewers on the Discovering Diamonds blog,

and Mary Ann Yarde and The Coffee Pot Book Club.

Not to mention all those writers out there, especially those writing about the Anglo-Saxon period, who inspire me to keep going in the hope of emulating their success.

Thank you to everyone who has posted reviews on Amazon or elsewhere. It is greatly appreciated, and it makes such a difference to know that you enjoy my books. And to those who have not, yet, left a review, please do – you will earn my undying gratitude.

Special thanks to Cathy Helms of Avalon Graphics for the beautiful cover – they get better and better.

Finally, thanks to my family, especially my husband, without whose efforts the garden would be overrun with weeds – and the house with dust.

Printed in Great Britain
by Amazon